"I've decided to offer you a bargain," the sorcerer said.

Harmon had heard many stories about the kinds of "bargains" magicians offered. The mortal usually ended up dead or suffering on some alien Plane.

"You want with all your heart to be an adventurer. You shall have that adventure."

Harmon had planned to ease gently into the sea of adventure, not try to swim across it on the first try. But an adventure—a real adventure!—with real blood and magic! Suddenly there were more stars in his eyes than the reflections of all the Thousand Stars above.

BARROW

BARROW

John Deakins

A ROC BOOK

ROC

Published by the Penguin Group

Penguin Books USA Inc., 375 Hudson Street, New York, New York 10014, U.S.A.
Penguin Books Ltd, 27 Wrights Lane, London W8 5TZ, England
Penguin Books Australia Ltd, Ringwood, Victoria, Australia
Penguin Books Canada Ltd, 2801 John Street, Markham, Ontario, Canada L3R 1B4
Penguin Books (N.Z.) Ltd, 182–190 Wairau Road, Auckland 10, New Zealand

Penguin Books Ltd, Registered Offices:
Harmondsworth, Middlesex, England

First published by Roc, an imprint of Penguin Books USA Inc.

First Printing, April, 1990

10 9 8 7 6 5 4 3 2 1

Prologue

I am a meddlesome old man. Though I promised once that I would not meddle in some specific lives, I have been forced to fall back on the exceptions even to those vows recently. I am not sure why I begin writing this, though it is easier for me to pen my thoughts than for most. (I have but to think them, and the pen that I conjured forms the letters on the scroll.)

Perhaps this immortal has learned that there is no immortality in any body formed of matter, even for a Master of the Mysteries. I have just witnessed the passing of another Master, who was more than merely a fellow magician to me. I can leave this record for one who might come after me, though I do not know who that could be among the tangled infinities of the Planes. I must meditate deeply, to delve into those parts of the mind that even the Masters have not conquered. Perhaps some part of me has foreseen my death and seeks immortality in the written word.

Ah, foolish man! What mortal or what mage would believe that a Master used the word "perhaps" about himself!

Perhaps (there it is again!) I am lonely. What castle is there in the meanest kingdom of all the primitive Plane (that I call "home" at times) that has but one human inhabitant? Yet, mine does. My minions comfort me; they were chosen for that, the toys and fantasies of children come alive. But they are not human. The humanity within these stones is my own, and the empty bodies of two I loved in their coffins. Those are not enough, not after what I have just experienced. I would chide a mortal child who suggested that such a life could be normal for a man; yet I live it. The pain I feel in my spirit rings the message over and over to me—I *am* human.

I have lived behind the shield of my powers and my intellect. The Great God help me, I had to learn to *feel* again! I did not need again to *reason* my way to feeling love or hate or pain or rightness. Now, I can perceive them again, as I did long ago—directly!

I must never forget the events that led me to this point. At first, I most regretted that mortals had been drawn innocently into a battle of immortals, but that has passed. I made no promises that I would not interfere in any other than two specific lives. In fact, I have already done so, and the feeling was . . . good. It is seconded by the *telling* of the tale of that interference. I begin to see the power of the pen.

Poor Jessup! He cannot ever write the story he wished to tell; so, I will do so for him. Along the way, I will write of Jessup's telling into the tale as well. I am not ashamed to say that I nudged his mind—ever so slightly—toward the notion of taking a walk to the fishing district. Then . . .

BOOK I

Secrets of the Teaching Master

JESSUP-THE-YARN, master storyteller of the city of Barrow, was intent on getting royally drunk. Not uproariously drunk, mind: that was not his style. A storyteller was given two ears by the Great God, but only one mouth. If that orifice flapped too freely, even when oiled, it cut the throat of its owner's living (and possibly the owner's as well).

He had really had no pressing business down at the docks, other than a tale spinner's unending search for new material. Nothing worth a story had turned up on his swing, but since he was in the area, he had an excuse to drop in on his friend Fishin' Jed at the Jumping Salmon.

Jed was always happy to see him; they had grown up together in Upcruster Town. Over the years, their paths had run side by side many times. Besides, time hung heavily at this hour of day, with the fishing fleet down the River Wat and not due until sunset. The taverner, a good judge of others' behavior when they drank, noticed that the storyteller was unnaturally quiet.

"Why so down in the gills, mate?"

The tavern keeper's homey speech always emerged more strongly when he had been drinking himself. Jessup, usually tighter with a coin than a fish's skin, was buying. Since the accident years before that had gimped his leg, Jed had had few chances to be unsober himself. As a businessman now, instead of a fisherman, he needed a clear head to keep track of a roomful of drinkers, or he gambled with his life and property. At the moment, one napping drunk made up all his clientele besides Jessup.

Not only was Jessup buying for his friend, he was

drinking long and deeply himself. He hesitated before answering Jed.

"It was K'tiri," he said finally. "And Brieze and Krovik were in it, too. She's gone now. Ah, my queen!" A drop of liquid trickled into a crevice on his cheek as he resumed drinking.

"Aye, mate. Remember, Jess: I'm one of the few in Barrow that knew what the two of you were to each other. Didn't I hold the horses when you and her rode out to the plains, to take them vows under the moon? Who but you an' me know why she took the wheels off her wagon and settled permanent in the bazaar? Wasn't it me that helped you cut the trapdoor in her wagon bed—in the dark, too—so you could come and go without her losing face before her people? No Townsman ever bespoke K'tiri bad, an' ye know it, but few it is knows who the daddy of them five kids is. The Upcrusters don't care, and the Tellarani are too proud to mention it, but *I* know."

"I'm sorry, Jed. I forgot. My feet must be smarter than my head; they carried me down here today. My own children don't even know me! By the Thousand Stars, how I miss her!"

"Aye, we all do. Everybody loved K'tiri. Only some stranger could have hurt her, probably thinkin' she kept cash in her wagon. May have been some wild-eyed freak from over in the Slews, lookin' for a way to get more Mugambu Black to stop his bones from shakin'. Any Upcruster would have known she stowed all her coin with Ibraim the money changer. Say, didn't they find a likely stranger dead not long after, in an alley? Wire of some kind knotted about his neck, wasn't it?"

"Yes. That's what I heard."

"Jess, as one 'Cruster to another, best get the missing string replaced on that musical gismo of yours, that I stowed behind the bar." The faces of the two Townsmen became unreadable masks for a moment.

"A good idea, Jed." Jessup drank again. "There was more to her tale, you know, at the last, than was ever told."

The yarn spinner's voice could be profitably heard over the hubbub of a busy tavern, but now it was barely audible. Still, the smell of a story was in the air. Jessup had never tried to sell his services at the Jumping Salmon. The folk who patronized it were generally poor, and fishermen were such liars by nature that a professional yarner could starve among them.

Jed was surprised. "What—what? A tale that Jessup never told? Now, that's one I'd like to hear. Unless"—his voice dropped to a whisper—"it involves stepping on some toes that might be a wee bit sensitive, like that drug-running Onion Gang west of the river. Or some high mucky-mucks in the north end. I don't want to hear anything more, if it'd be worth your life to tell it."

"No. Nothing like that . . . Well, this once, then . . . for K'tiri.

"Remember back not long after the Mugambese came upriver, before the Prince threw the Big Party last year? K'tiri was still alive then, when . . ."

• 2 •

Fraximon was spitting dirt and itching. A bloodletting or any kind of violence to others would let him scratch that itch nicely. He didn't care where he found relief for his anger, or what form that relief took. The very sweat slung from his beard turned dust balls in the street into scuttling scorpions. How long, he seethed, how long had he been left to snuffle dirt and gobble garbage like a street dog? The fools, the offal of the Planes, had robbed him—him! Fraximon, the Terrible Stump, an adept of the highest. Everything that he had been carrying had disappeared during the months that he had rotted mindlessly. The part of his beard that hadn't fallen out from mange and mistreatment was streaked with the essence of Barrow streets, and it was far too long to have grown in only a few days.

The diaper of rags that he had picked up in the Slews was deserting him fragment by fragment as he stalked on. (A postulate of Upcruster Town said, "If it's thrown away west of the river, let it lie!") The few Townsmen abroad in daylight asked no questions of the ugly, maimed figure that was stamping its way north down the center of Straight Street. They might have been curious about how he had gotten across the Old Wat Bridge to the Town in that getup, though the answer was probably something as simple as the watchmen on the west side being drunk again. However, asking unnecessary questions of dangerous strangers was an item ruled out by those wise in street survival.

Fraximon was not interested in the name of the street he was traveling and would have found no humor in the misnomer of that serpentine alley. His path led to madness; to anywhere anger could be expended. Sparks leaped from his ragged toenails, turning grass to maggots and fruit rinds to jagged glass. Where once a steel prosthetic ring, with a piercing point, had encircled the stump where his left hand should have shown, a ball of bluish lightning swirled, ready to leap from that blunt end onto anyone who hindered him. Blood flicked from his right fingertips, drawn without cut from any living thing that approached him too closely. The paling victims skittered away from that favorite spell of Fraximon's, narrowly missing the death he would have been glad to dispense. Only two dogs and a comatose drunkard failed to escape. The dogs would be put to use, but even the broadminded Townsmen frowned on devouring the other human residents. In hard times, you only looked close enough at the meat in the stew to make sure it wasn't Cousin Elmo, who disappeared last week.

The door of the Gryphon and Goblet was blown from its hinges by the hot/cold wind running before Fraximon like the song of death. It had been knocked down so many times before, in its years of lively service, that a rehinging was an expected weekly operating expense. Even Barrelgut, the owner, had developed the habit of opening it with the head of anyone who was too boisterous in his taproom. That chubby bartender froze, with his hand wiping a dirty mug with a dirtier rag. The face that came bristling through his door reached for his soul like an ice-water enema. It was obvious that the hatch of sanity over this man's mind was flapping in a breeze blowing off the Nether Pits.

"Drink!" crackled the face.

Barrelgut might have appeared to a casual observer to be a hundred kilos of quivering blubber, but only strangers were ignorant of his ability to lift an equal-sized, troublesome drunk and punt him ten paces. No matter his strength, however, he was pinned in place by the gaze of the weird figure lurching toward the bar. He decided to bypass the tavern's ironclad policy of asking for cash in advance. There was no way he was about to refuse *this* customer anything. On the other hand, if this was going to be free service, it need not be painful to the bartender's pocket. The man before him had the frightening demeanor of some mad hedge wizard, but the smell of him said "scum." He probably wouldn't know Swamp River Red from honey water. Barrelgut automatically groped out the net-covered jug of cheap wine that he used when some far-gone drunk ordered a round for the house.

The wild-eyed face tasted the glass of Swamp River Red and then whispered, "The best!" as sweet as cyanide.

What Fraximon then did to the wine jug made Barrelgut hastily remember a bottle of Maldavian White that he had squirreled away. The small flask of clear liquid had been freeze-strengthened and rebottled during a particularly cold Maldavian winter, and it was worth the price of a keg of beer. Barrelgut's mother had raised no fools. It was better that the purse suffer than that the life that filled it be discontinued.

The tavern's regulars sometimes thought of Barrelgut as a paunchy, poor substitute for the former owner, Dirty Kevin. In that, they did not give him proper credit. Barrelgut had had the gusto to drop directly into Dirty Kevin's shoes, before anyone else could claim the Gryphon as abandoned property. The day man, Gorgio, had had as good a claim, but Barrelgut was now sixty-percent owner (and Gorgio had had to work his shift for a long time with one arm in a sling). Barrelgut and his inn had survived more riots and disasters than any other standing institution in that part of the Town. His bulk concealed both a tough core and a sizable chunk of gray matter.

The grisly magician had been momentarily satisfied by the wine. "Food!" he growled, a few minutes later.

Barrelgut gestured hurriedly for the pot boy to bring a plateful. He continued to blot at his fingertips, that the bursting, red-hot mass of the wine jug had seared. The bar top was a smoky mess, but destructive magic was no newcomer to Barrow or the Gryphon. The patrons of the tavern, for example, had disappeared (as if by magic) out the back exit, within seconds after Fraximon's eye-catching demonstration. Only old Jessup remained, snoozing(?) under a table. Had he been aware then of the fate of a similar sleeper, whom Fraximon had lethally encountered only moments before, he would have immediately joined the emigration. Gathering material for a new story was not always a safe activity.

The pot boy returned with a plate of mystery meat and nameless legumes; the Gryphon had no better. He cringed as he placed it in front of Fraximon and hopped back.

"Food, I said!" The magician gestured at the lad. The small body sailed into one corner, unconscious, and the plate into another. The wizard's finger twitched across Barrelgut's ample front. Fiery letters spelled out "F—O—O—D," cutting through cloth and searing skin.

The bartender decided to get more food himself. As many fat men, he was surprisingly agile when speed meant the same thing as life. Fraximon fumed and drank, drank and fumed, until the food arrived: begged, bought, stolen, or forced from someone else's decent meal. The source was immaterial to Fraximon. He ate.

"A room," he grunted.

Barrelgut was trembling as he showed the mage up the stairs to the best he had, noting in passing that Jessup now seemed to be snoozing under another table, considerably closer to the exit.

"Bah!" The fetid magician charged into the room.

A load of verminous bedding struck Barrelgut in the face. The room's other fixtures sailed out, to scatter on the landing and across the taproom below. The door slammed. Barrelgut went down the stairs three at a time and across the common room as a snake would go over hot coals.

Fraximon was alone with his power. For vanished months, possibly years, he had not worked so much as a parlor trick, Master though he was. He had reawakened, and with him, his power. The dark caldrons of his soul were full, boiling over. Though he was filthy, he felt energies flowing within him. Magic had never before come to him so easily. Though darkness would have been better for the work he had in mind, he would begin now.

He could have conjured better food and drink and a finer room, but even the smallest item cost power to pull

from other Planes. That energy would be better spent
finding the one being in all the Planes whose discovery
(and death) held any significance. That being was on *this*
Plane. Fraximon had forced the minor services from the
mortal innkeeper because they involved degrading some
other human. Other! Ha! None of the vermin in this
backwater could hope to stand at his level—save one.

A wave of his hand brought a clean robe and a soft
chair to the room. Washing away the street filth would
wait, lest its removal take the edge and power from his
anger. He deftly stirred the alternate Planes with his
mind as he summoned the first of his familiars.

A watcher (in Upcruster Town, there were always
watchers) would have seen a puff of cloud slip from the
sky and dip under the eaves of the inn. It remained
behind the slightly parted shutters of Fraximon's room
for only a few minutes before flying away, against the
wind. It would have been much harder to see when it
returned by starlight, reduced and tattered, to report to
its demanding new master. It was the first of many.

In the shadows of twilight, a collection of strange messengers crept or flew into the narrow upper window. All
returned later, but the information they brought did not
please their summoner. Fraximon scorched the room with
sorcerer's curses. He would have let the showering sparks
burn the inn down entirely except for the inconvenience
and energy expenditure of moving elsewhere. The inn
did no business but his that night, however. Townsmen
gathered in gossipy clusters at what they considered safe
distances. From concealment, they lay bets on whether
the Gryphon would be standing at daylight. It was said
that an Upcruster would bet on the number of nails in his
grandmother's coffin, and that his grandmother would fix
the outcome before she went, for the right price.

The night waned. Fraximon felt cheated—cheated! For
all his effort, his quarry had not been found. He had long
planned a different outcome. He had followed the man,
his former mentor, to Barrow, after searching for decades for the one Plane where the old magician had been
hiding. With that discovery, Fraximon had come striding
dramatically toward the city's gate, on the last few hundred meters of his quest. Disdaining a magical entry, he
had been unprepared when his enemy had appeared be-

fore him without warning. With his own mental forces
barely moved toward muster, Fraximon had no memory
beyond the moment when he had seen the dust of the
street rushing toward his face. The foul, old cheat had
ambushed him! The time that had passed since might as
well not have existed, for all that Fraximon remembered
it.

He had sent a sea wraith to investigate every departed
ship for hundreds of kilometers. That familiar had looked
into the face of every passenger, to the undoubted terror
of many. Creatures whose forms were most like giant
desert scorpions had trailed every caravan, both east and
northwest. Aerial servants had questioned every flying
creature.

There was no trace of any traveling sorcerer fleeing
Fraximon's retribution. No paths of magic had been left
in the air or across land or water. Fraximon himself
verified that there was no sign of a hasty wizardly flight
across Elsewhen to any other Plane, although it was
impossible to check all the near-infinite number of cross-
ings that immortals had made there. A torrent of tiny
cockroach demons had sought his enemy everywhere in
the darkness of the city, but in vain. There were magicians in Barrow, but not the one their summoner sought.

Cold-eyed and frustrated, Fraximon pondered in the
predawn hours: no trail could be *that* cold. If his enemy
was yet in Barrow, the man must have equipped himself
with some new concealment spell that made him invisible
to magical spying. In that case, there were other ways!
Let him try to lie in ambush again, intending to humiliate
his better; it was hardly worth a sneer. Now was the time
for caution, however, before the hidden fox turned on
the hound. Hate could be stored and tempered until the
quarry had been flushed.

With a wave of his hand, he dismissed his servants.
Those which had not already been disincorporated by his
curses fled the tavern like rays from a dark nova. The
huddles of watchers were scattered by gaggles of things
with red eyes and white fangs, not realizing that the
fiends they were fleeing from were themselves flying
from their own fear. The familiars' freedom was momentary only; they would be called again and again at the
whim of their master. Fraximon, however, had become

uneasy about his careless, overly public debut. During the confusion, he slunk away through the tavern's gaping door, seeking to be as unseen as other nocturnal slinkers in Barrow.

He helped himself to the clothes of the blood-drained sot, whom he had left in the gutter before the inn. As an afterthought, he helped himself to the man's face as well. The body had still been undisturbed because of its unnatural method of passing, despite the intervening hours. Inspired, Fraximon used another minor spell to locate the residence of his victim. Calling up some of his insectoid minions, he sent them ahead to confirm that the man had lived alone. He hurried in that direction, leaving the body to disappear, as nameless corpses often did in this hard part of the city.

Ig-the-Shiv remained as he lay—naked, faceless, and blanched—in the mud, never again to practice his true talents: drug running, assassination, and drinking to excess. He had emptied his pockets by boozing it up on the unexpected bonus he had received from the customer he had met at the Gryphon with a packet of Mugambu White. He had passed out (and, thus, passed away) before he could reach the small room he had rented this side of the river. Ig's landlord would look favorably on a pseudo-Ig bearing the silver of rent overdue and more rent in advance. Ig had reduced his life to so near zero by alcohol and bad living that he would be only mildly missed by some business associates across the river.

Fraximon's plan worked well. Landlords seldom intruded on silver-paying renters, but the mage remained cautious about major sorcerous changes he worked within the crude apartment. He was becoming more and more certain that his prey was still somewhere in Barrow. The faint traces that had first led Fraximon to the city were yet present, and he could find no real evidence that the man had fled. Tapping the arm of his chair with his pink stump as he reasoned, Fraximon decided that if his quarry had created a new kind of concealment spell, it must be effective not only against spells but also against detection by magical familiars. A spell that major might have required so much power that the energies formerly channeled into minor spells, such as the one maintaining Fraximon's mental vacuum, would have to be diverted into it. If that had been the case, then the old meddler had foolishly released an unrelenting enemy and drained his power reserves in the process. The man had signed his death warrant. Fraximon smiled in anticipation.

In the alley below, a healthy weed died.

There was one fleck of spoilage in Fraximon's stew of revenge, however: his enemy was still not to be found. Wait! He had not been found *by magical means*. Eyes needed no magic to see, and description of every event that had ever been seen in Barrow was for sale by someone.

Gold, whose method of gathering was better unknown even to money-grubbing information brokers, disappeared into many sashes over many days. Fraximon accumulated a sizable biography on each of the few major sorcerers who used Barrow as a base. Two of them, Brandelvar and Threebortin, might have (together) presented a challenge, had they been foolish enough to withstand him.

He was able to identify and snuff out all of those who had robbed him while he had been helpless; he even recovered his prized armband stabber. It had been meant to extend from a man's wrist, across the back of his hand, making a punch doubly deadly. In Fraximon's case, the exposure of the point was even greater. He could have hardly become more dangerous, but the weapon had always fit his personality so well. On the other hand, its felicitous return had brought him no closer to finding his enemy. It was almost as if a magician, a major adept of his own level, were sitting around some sunny alley in Upcruster Town, not practicing the art at all. That was unthinkable!

The man had assuredly found a way to conceal himself from mortal eyes as well as from magical ones. Barrow was full of eyes, before and behind, and none had seen a sorcerer of the kind that gold had sought. Gold had spoken loudly, but no one had answered. Magic had failed; a thousand spies had failed. Nothing remained . . . almost.

There were those who revealed things without using true magic and without spies—the Tellarani. To anyone else, their services would have been the logical solution, but they would be no help to Fraximon. None of the bronze-skinned People-of-the-Grass would have so much as shooed away a rat that was gnawing out Fraximon's eyes, had he lain paralyzed on their doorstep.

Decades before, as he had been wandering the Planes in his unrelenting quest for his mentor, Fraximon had proposed a magical exchange with the Tellarani shamen. At the time, they had been beleaguered by the Bloody Onion Cult that had later annihilated them. Through uncaring sloth and indifference to mortals' troubles, Fraximon had taken what they offered, returned nothing to them, and gone blithely on his way, leaving the greatest part of the people to be slaughtered. The scattered survivors might now be encountered anywhere on the continent, with their hawk noses and dark eyes peering out of the wagons they called home, but they had not forgotten Fraximon.

A Tellarani curse was as permanent as the last member of the race. It would be carried to the ends of the world, wherever their wagons rolled, and remembered for ten unhappy generations of mortal descent. Nor was it without real power of its own. Fraximon, an expert in such matters, could feel the probing of the Tellarani magic-that-wasn't-magic against his protective spells. It hadn't eased in more than thirty years, though, to his conscious knowledge, the curse had never penetrated his shields.

Their dispersal among other cultures after the massacre seemed to have made the other-than-mortal powers of the wagon people stronger instead of diluting them. The cards that were now commonly called "Tellarani cards" had been introduced among them about the same time as the disaster that scattered them. The cards had come from somewhere beyond the eastern limits of the Saikhandian Empire; Fraximon had never bothered to investigate the source. It had been almost as if the cards and the People-of-the-Grass had been seeking each other. The surviving shamen and seers could focus their substantial powers through the reading of the cards, but none of them was about to turn a single card for Fraximon.

Being a Tellarani didn't necessarily make anyone a seer, any more than being from Sai-khand made a person a sharp trader, despite popular beliefs to the contrary. Fraximon had no use for the trickery that was the best that most Tellarani "seers" could accomplish. On the other hand, any one of them with true ability would know him at the first turn of the cards. Most of them were women of no great stature, but they could block him from his objective by merely refusing him a service only they could accomplish. Any thought of forcing an experienced seeress to perform for him likewise had to be abandoned. He had not been able to seduce all their magic from the Tellarani; one very dangerous portion remained.

Although no single one of them could have withstood a Master of his level, seers did not draw their power solely from personal ability. The part of the People's art that made it so different from his own lay its foundation in the gene pool of the entire race. Wielders of real power among them drew from their "blood." An individual seer, in desperation, could call on the race's entire energy pool. When that rising wave of power was focused through one seer, that person died, but the being toward whom the power had been directed—mortal, magician, Dragon, or god—died also.

Fraximon had never grown so desperate as to test that particular defense of the People. In fact, he would have been happier if none of the Tellarani even knew he was in Barrow. An arrow fired from far enough away could kill even the highest adept; it was impossible to maintain extended, in-depth defenses in all directions simultaneously.

He felt as if he had been boxed into a corner, stymied by every circumstance. Yet he remained certain that he would triumph. There had to be a way!

• **3** •

The Old Man sat on a tall, battered stool and spoke to the ring of children around him. Here, in the Scoop, he knew that he and his students were safe from the rush of traffic. The beer merchant who had built this semicircular blind alley, the better to turn his wagons, had gone out of business long ago. There was room here for the harmless and the children, since they had nothing desired by the intent, hurrying adults that passed them. Few grown ones paused here, and those ignored the gathering.

The old teacher drew letters on the whitewashed wall with charcoal or mud, or made figures in the dust with a stick. Brieze Wagonhawk, daughter of the seeress K'tiri, crouched entranced among the children. The lines and wiggles on the wall, that the little ones didn't understand yet, made words to her now. Some of the wiggles were numbers; when they were stacked in certain ways, they added up to other numbers. She remembered what a miracle that had once seemed, as she had worked the sums on her fingers and toes in the abacuslike style of the People, only to have the Old Man beat her to the total each time. It was a delightful magic that she had come to understand, unlike the blood magic that she could feel surging within her at times.

She never grew tired of hearing the Old Man speak. He was unique. Even the youngest urchin, gnawing on an almost bare bone, listened bright-eyed as he expounded. Today, he was speaking about the history of Barrow and the Saikhandian Empire; tomorrow, he might talk about how stones were formed or about plants or sea creatures. The children came when they could, never the same group twice. There were no rolls, no books, no written lessons: only the white-haired man, the ring of children, and the clean wall. Youngsters were always so full of questions that he followed no set lecture, except every day to give a lesson on letters and numbers. The young knew that he would fill up any cup that they held out to him for knowledge. They loved him: he had time for them when the mothers (that some didn't have) and the fathers (that some didn't know) could spare them none.

Women of the Town didn't mind their broods hanging about the Scoop. It was rumored that none of the Old Man's students ever came to harm as long as they kept coming back to him for learning. Naturally, such an idea brought a snicker and a knowing nod if spoken aloud. After all, the Town was not some pampered neighborhood for the nobles north of Caravan Way. Death, injury, and privation were permanent residents. Besides, no one knew of the rumor ever being tested. When children grew to that age just beyond childhood, they became certain that they already knew everything important that there was to know. They stopped visiting the Scoop on their own.

Brieze was the oldest student present. She loved to listen, although it might be a week before she could pass

that way again. Few other teens would find the Old
Man's words still as fresh as they had always been. The
afternoon sun glinted from the bare, wrinkled forehead
of the old teacher, highlighting a few blue veins in skin
spotted by uncounted years of sun. His hair was white
and thick above his forehead. It gave the impression of
having been white from the day it first grew. Children of
the streets, now grown, remembered him from their youth
the same way that he was now. He had always been
there, telling the secrets of the universe to those most
interested, just because he wanted to. When you came to
the Scoop to learn, you paid no fee, although the Old
Man never offended the pride of the poor by refusing a
gift.

"Learning a lot?" asked a quiet voice next to Brieze's
ear.

She started. She'd heard no footsteps, and the voice's
owner had been unexpected. He was seldom seen in
daylight outside the room he was using as base that
particular week.

"Krovik!" she cried happily. Then, "Shhh. Listen."

The teacher was finishing the lecture, explaining how
Barrow's Young Prince, Bartello Bancartin, was a full
Val-trak of the Saikhandian Empire, as his father and
grandfather had been. Small groans from the children
indicated that they had already absorbed the local consensus about the Prince's ineptitude. Too many had been
heard to say, "This wouldn't be happening if the Old
Prince were still alive."

In many of the cities of the Empire, bandying about
negative opinions of rulers would have meant the loose-
tongued culprit's neck would be stretched by a rope
before sundown. In the Town, a man's opinion was his
own. It didn't matter two figs which Prince ruled, Young
or Old, as long as the Town was left to profit in peace.
All the gold of Caravan Way couldn't have swayed them
from an opinion, nor could it have purchased loyalty to
any cause. Monetary gain, legal or illegal, was the arm of
the Town, but where its heart lay was its own business.

The Old Man touched briefly on the Mugambese. They,
or at least their leader, seemed altogether too dear to the
Prince. Some unstable elements had suggested that their
colored skin pushed the immigrants from Mugambu a

trifle beyond the definition of humanity, but most of the Town withheld judgment. Mugambese gold was a lot better for business than were a pack of mouthy trouble-makers. Black skin and strange customs were something to be tolerated in customers who paid cash. Later, if they couldn't be dealt with . . .

A small boy brought the teacher back to the usual lesson with a question about some easy letters already on the wall. Brieze could give Krovik the longer moment that she had been wanting to. She was not a child any longer; other priorities had risen in her life. The Town's citizens did not find Krovik's dumpy figure particularly exciting, but he was magnificent to her.

Krovik seemed anything but awe-inspiring. His normal armament was one ordinary dagger, though he had ac-quired a new sword somewhere that glinted in the eve-ning light. Although Brieze was not especially tall, she topped his height by half a hand. He had a shock of dirty-blond hair above a forgettable face, and a body that was barrel-shaped rather than herculean. He looked too clumsy to pick a pocket or climb anything more challeng-ing than stairs. For all that, he was probably the best second-story man in Barrow. He could clamber through openings that others knew to be too small to fit him and climb flimsy structures that couldn't possibly have held his weight. Krovik's other, acquired name was "Quick-hand"; lack of tangible parents also meant lack of a family name. Still, many a stranger was now poorer for confusing Krovik Quickhand with his appearance.

Brieze's heart oozed a little at the sight of him. She had managed to become acquainted with the basically fine young man behind the bland exterior of the success-ful thief. (When young people would get together, they *would* get together.) It was too bad that Mother refused to get to know him as well as Brieze did. The daylight was making him nervous, not just because of his noctur-nal profession. He was probably worried that someone would report to Mother that he had been seen talking to her wayward daughter again. Mother had been clear about her feelings toward courtship of her daughter by the stocky young man. She had implied that she would remove certain of his body parts with a dull knife if she caught him hanging around the wagon again. A thief

(emphatically) was not an acceptable husband for a
Tellarani girl.

Krovik had been watching the Old Man playing with,
what were to him, unintelligible scribbles on the wall,
explaining them to the child. Perhaps someday he would—

"I'm here a lot of the time. How is it that I haven't
seen you here before?" She brought him back to the
moment by taking his arm. "Where were you coming
from, and where did you get the sword?" She looked at
him wistfully.

"Well . . . that's a long story . . . er . . . I can't talk
about it right now." He glanced nervously over his shoulder toward the north, where a column of smoke yet rose
from the Ba-La-Nar Temple disaster. He wasn't hostile
about it, not to her, but the answer obviously came from
his professional life. If it was Krovik's business, then it
was better no one else's business. The young man didn't
carry his weapons for decoration.

"Oh," she said. She could have inquired further, and
he would have tolerated it, but something in her blood
said no. The Tellarani listened when the blood spoke.

She glanced past Krovok, noticing the shadow on the
wall. It was getting late. She must hurry off, leaving
learning and, perhaps, love. Mother would be wanting
the needles that she had sent Brieze for hours ago; she
liked to sew in the evening, between customers. She had
always been generous with the time she allowed her
daughter to dally in the Scoop, but the sun was almost
down. If Brieze were too late, K'tiri might become suspicious and ask the wrong people questions about Brieze's
meeting Krovik on the sly. The fat would indeed be in
the fire then. Even this chance encounter would bring on
another row if Mother heard about it.

"Oh, I must run! Mother is waiting for these." She
waved the package of needles. Casting him a last look,
flushed with the wonderously mixed emotions of the young,
she hurried away down the street.

Krovik had been seriously considering walking her
partway home, dull knife or no, when a last question
caught his attention. A ragged little girl had called out,
"Tell us about the gods, Master!"

"Hoo, ha, I am 'Master' to few, little one." He smiled
at the child. "As for the gods, there is but one that

counts in the great scheme of things, though one or two godlings are important in this city.''

Street-wise Krovik had thought that it would have been impossible to shock him. "What's this, old man? There's a dozen temples in Barrow alone!" The all-knowing sage had turned out to be an aged windbag after all. Having given up any idea now of ever becoming his student, Krovik decided to take the man down a peg or two. "I—"

"Not so, young sir," the teacher said, with a piercing smile. "All the 'gods' of our Planes did was to reshape some flaked-off pieces of the true creation and rough out a partial copy of the actual universe. Who ever carved a perfect statue that didn't throw away the chips? That universe is the masterwork, and we're a chip!

"If you want to know the names of all the Thousand Stars, come by sometime for a week, and I will teach them to you from a book that I have. They may seem impressive in the here-and-now, but one glance at the night sky in the true universe would show you more stars than all the fine little ones in Barrow have freckles. It cannot be helped that men build buildings to worship beings whose need for worship is questionable. Gods! Hah!" He laughed fully, accompanied by the giggles of his class.

Krovik felt the forerunners of a blush creeping up his neck. "But, I've seen—"

"Of course you have! Who hasn't? I didn't say that the 'gods' weren't real enough here, but within the true creation, they're just a bunch of sulky, rebellious beings called 'angels.' Look at the way this Plane is made, and I'll show you a hundred pieces of sloppy work. Why, magic itself wouldn't work here if the lazy 'gods' had bothered to finish out a complete set of natural laws!"

Krovik was quickly finding himself in a place no individualistic nineteen-year-old could tolerate: cornered and outargued in broad daylight by a decrepit old man, in front of a pack of giggling street urchins. Both his self-concept and his external reputation were suffering. People just didn't talk this way! A vein of prudish conservatism in defense of a familiar worship system was surfacing in him. (A few hours before, he would have sneered at it

himself.) Surely there was a thunderbolt gathering somewhere with this old man's name on it.

The whole thing needed thinking out, somewhere safely
away from the divine vengeance that must be closing in
on this bigmouthed old fool. Krovik simply walked away
toward his lodgings, perhaps hurrying a little faster than
was absolutely necessary. He would rest until night stirred
him and spend a great deal of time *not* thinking about
what the teacher had said.

The Old Man led the class in a happy laugh, trying to
leave no echo of hurt for the confused youngster: at that
age their feelings were as soft and easily damaged as a
flower. He hurried on to the next question; night was
coming on.

• 4 •

Fraximon was seething. That triply cursed spoiler of his
life had so robbed him of peace of mind that he hadn't
even taken a woman since his awakening. It seemed as if
an age of the world had passed since his last pleasuring
with a female. His quarry's face needed to be replaced in
Fraximon's mind for a time. He needed it now. One
nicely young would do: virginal; innocent; defenseless
against him. Yes and yes again! After many days of good
feeding and magical manipulation, he had redeveloped
his former hulking, powerful body. Its hungers for more
than food demanded feeding. If he were careful, he need
not even draw attention to himself by using magic. He
would simply take what he wanted.

From his cramped window, he saw her then, her brown
cloak of wisent skin flapping as she hurried. Within a
minute, she would pass the dark entry at the bottom of
his own rickety stairs. A Tellarani girl . . .

The pieces fell in place. He would have them all: the
woman he craved; the Tellarani seeress he required; and,
through her, the man he sought. A minor spell, the
concoction of a moment, would fool the eyes of any
casual observers, for the fraction of a second as the girl
was passing the alcove. He would stun her for the few
heartbeats that it would require to drag her up the stairs.
The rest needed nothing except efficient brute force. He

rubbed his palms and cackled in glee. "All! All! All!" his
spirit sang.

The heart of a carrion crow, on the building opposite,
stopped, and it plunged to the ground, already half-decayed.

As it was planned, so it went.

One unimaginative, brutal rape was the same as any
other, even by a mage, even in Barrow. Brieze lay naked
and bruised in a corner, her clothing shredded and her
cloak slung away somewhere. The rent package of needles lay scattered about the floor like the plucked whiskers of some silver cat. An otherwise harmless geas held
the room in total silence and blocked her from any attempt to leave it. Fraximon had left his den to celebrate
elsewhere. Five livid bruises—four fingers and a thumb—
were already darkening around each young breast, mirror images of degradation, with the thumb prints dug in
hard over her breastbone. She bled; she hurt. In the glass
of her life, she could find no reflection. She was empty,
but filled with abomination. Gouts of tears rolled silently
out of her eyes into the magic air. Night was falling.

• 5 •

K'tiri was uneasy. The sun was still above the horizon;
Brieze was often this late. There was no reason to worry,
but K'tiri was Tellarani: sometimes she *knew*. Was that a
whisper in the blood, like tiny, blowing crystals that
couldn't make up their minds whether to be ice or cinders? But, no: nonsense! No one, not even a stranger,
would touch a Tellarani girl in Upcruster Town without
her permission. The Tellarani men carried sharp knives,
and no one would protect a rapist from them. The Tellarani
women were even more feared, especially those with the
power. No mortal could stand against the curse of the
gathered People. Such a curse would fall not only on
the attacker but on those who helped him. It could no more
be escaped than breathing. In the long run, it might even
overthrow an immortal, though it had been tried against
few such in history. (Now, that was odd: she hadn't
thought about using that curse in years.)

With the cards, a woman with the power could find
any hidden thing or person. No, it just wasn't possible.

Still . . . K'tiri bustled through the afternoon's end, and worried. She primped her thin form into slightly improved appearance, and worried. She prepared for the coming of the night's customers, and worried. Night seemed to come on with unseemly haste, without her daughter's return. In her stead came a certainty: something was dreadfully wrong with Brieze.

When Fleetfox, her oldest son, parted the curtains at the back of the wagon to warn her of that night's first to come seeking a scrying, she waved him away with a thrust of her gaunt hand. Those wanting a reading would have to go elsewhere tonight. The silver rings on her fingers flashed over her black-covered board. K'tiri, one of the elite among the People's seers, able to trace a true seeing from the possessions of strangers, found herself almost too jittery to concentrate. Instead of the simple purity of the seeking trance, she would have to use the cards as some novice would.

She laid out the stirred cards in the ancient pattern, careful to modify it by the calculated placing of a card whose symbol stood for the key figure in her question. For the Significator she chose the Page of Pentacles, almost the personification of her dark-eyed daughter.

"This covers her," she intoned, turning the Six of Cups. Strange: that card usually meant an end or a beginning, especially the end of childhood. It set an indecipherable atmosphere for the rest of the reading.

"This crosses her." It was the Magician, reversed. Whoever opposed her and her daughter would not hesitate to use power toward destructive ends. Possibly magic was involved. A sneering face flashed for an instant before her eyes.

"This is beneath her." The Seven of Swords: someone is trying to steal from the one seeking. That was the foundation of the matter. It was neither good news nor a surprise. The same hard face flashed before her again.

"This is behind her." The Two of Cups hinted that Brieze had just left some friend or lover. A more familiar face glowed momentarily in her mind, but she lost it again. The rest of the reading would reveal more. The blood energy had begun to flow through the framework of the cards now.

"This crowns her." The Six of Wands, reversed, in the

near future meant delay and a possible victory for the
enemy. She could almost smell the rottenness of the soul
of the aggressor. K'tiri was sweating now, despite her
thin frame. The "crown" card was only a possible future,
not a certainty.

"This is before her." The near-future card was the
Page of Swords. This time she knew him at once. "Krovik,"
she hissed, through clenched teeth. With difficulty, she
purified her thoughts. The jumble of her blood music
cleared momentarily. Krovik was revealed as the future,
but not the enemy. She reached quickly for the last four
cards.

"Her fears." The Devil himself: someone of evil and
power had loosed himself on the family. "Her family."
The card called Strength was the first hopeful sign. Yes,
Brieze could depend on the strength of her family.

"Her hopes." The Lovers: that card was no help. All
young women struggled with the choice between sacred
and profane love. Krovik had better not be involved in
that!

"The Capstone." The one card that would determine
the whole picture was the . . . King of Swords? No amount
of concentration could make Krovik mesh with that powerful figure of judgment and law. What person was so
potent as to put his mark in this entire reading, yet not
be revealed by it? She found herself shaking.

"Fleetfox!" she shrieked, overturning the board in her
haste.

The cry brought the boy in, but he was quickly reversed and launched into the Barrow night to find Krovik
Quickhand. He was no less Tellarani than his mother. His
legs were running almost before he ordered them to, and
his blood had begun to sing of magic and danger afoot.

The cards had spoken to K'tiri in ebon murmurs, boom-
ing with distant threats and fears. They had been awakened, but their echoed messages were unspecific. In the
heart of this dark moment, she feared to consult them
again too soon. Instead, she drew and hoarded her powers, waiting for the return of her son and a young man
whom she didn't trust. Yet the Tellarani blood had shouted
it plainly: Krovik was to be a major actor in the drama
that would soon unfold around her daughter.

• 6 •

Fraximon sat at the board of his feasting hall and raised a toast to himself. He held the place of honor, with the glow of a fine wine on his tongue. Its pleasure was bested only by the warmth of his sticky loins and the red glow of his charcoal heart. He had them all! "All! All! All!" seemed to sing down his veins. His smile extinguished a creeping fungus that had spread down the room's walls.

"To me, my fine companions! To me!" He saluted the gathering.

The sea wraith burbled softly in its tub of water and offal. A multitude of his cockroach demons skittered a dance on the boards. The thing something like a lizard, but more like a toad, licked a dope stick with a gray tongue and whistled its agreement. The thing all red eyes and needle points crackled something by discharging static against the ground. A Dirak flapped its vertical lips and uttered several "Yesssss, Massssters." Other strange servant/guests whined or woofed or telepathically cried their approval.

Upcruster Town contained many empty, reportedly haunted houses. Some had been tainted by plagues too ugly for the bravest thief to dare, the bones of their occupants gnawed by rats. Some were safe houses for men more desperately murderous than any plague, seldom used by their owners, but never visited by the locals. Let his quarry smell out magic in one of them! By dawn, Fraximon would be gone, *walking* as sweetly as somebody's nanny, leaving no trail of magic at all. And, oh, the goodies that waited for him in his own domicile! He clapped his hands in joy.

An assassin in the next street became a mossy skeleton, gathered by the Death Angel in a clatter of bones, his knife just poised over his victim's throat.

"Let's have a story, my friends! A story . . . Let's see . . . of how I became Fraximon the Terrible Stump! Yes!" He glanced around the board.

"Yesss, do tell usss, Massster," the Dirak huffed, balefully watching its summoner with the eyes in the palms of its hands.

All would proclaim astonishment when Fraximon related the story of how he had lost his left hand in a dragon's mouth. Let no astonishment be forthcoming at his hundredth telling of the same, stale tale, and the unastonished familiar would find itself disintegrated. It was the only story Fraximon was interested in telling. He had bored his last (murdered) concubine more than once by recounting how he had been drawing the powerful blood of a dormant dragon from its lolling tongue when the monster's jaws had snapped shut in its sleep. (That woundless blood-drawing spell had always been one of Fraximon's favorites.)

He had returned with the dragon's blood, with a tiny amulet he had pilfered from the dragon's horde, and with the solution to the problem of where to hide his soul power. That vital essence was concealed where he could easily keep an eye on it, protecting it from seizure by other greedy Masters who might wish to add his power to their own. However, he had also returned with a pink stump, showing where his left hand should have been, to stand for elevation in the Mysteries, before the man he had then counted as his mentor. That same man was now the enemy whose life he sought.

Fraximon's talents might not have run to storytelling, but his servants shrieked, hissed, and clicked their applause nonetheless, as he once again declared his coming vengeance. They were happy at any telling that involved violence, but they were especially glad to have survived another telling whole. Sometimes their master's brain was too much like an overripe, poisonous fruit, ready to spray seeds of death on whoever touched it carelessly or happened to be nearby when it ruptured. Their cacophony fell silent when they noticed that Fraximon's eyes had gone out of focus, remembering.

Fraximon had never been overburdened with human friends. He had chosen to tell only a few mortals, such as the concubine, the rest of the tale. Like her, they had all had to die once they had heard. In his mind, he once again stood before the seat of mastery of his teacher. He had looked up into the face of the Master of the Mysteries, expecting the approval that he knew he deserved.

"Master, have I not now earned the right to elevation to the Upper Mysteries?" He smiled, assured of the answer.

The pause was far too long. There was more than

enough time for the older magician to have inserted a dozen yes's. Instead, the master mage looked sorrowful, thoughtful.

"Well?" Spidery cracks fragmented the surface of Fraximon's self-confidence.

The second pause was even longer. "Fraximon," his mentor said at last. "Fraximon, you are strong in the art, almost as strong as I am. You could grow stronger still, but you are not ready for the Higher Mysteries. You may never be ready."

"What do you mean?" The younger wizard's face flushed with disappointment at the assessment.

"Fraximon, it is so subtle, so ingrained in your very being, that I don't believe that you will ever be able to see it. Fraximon, how did you gain entrance to the dragon's lair? That was admittedly no mean feat; that, and covering your trail across Elsewhen so that he will never find you."

"Why, I bribed the guardian spirits with blood, as the midlevel books had hinted. 'Blood is life.' They had shriveled so badly from lack of character that they were willing to accept anything that smacked of life, even mortal life."

"Whose blood, Fraximon?"

"Oh, that. Some useless mortal. A snot-nosed street kid I snatched from a pest hole of a port on the Saikhandian Plane."

"I knew you had been there, but I had no idea . . . Do you really not see what you did? I am pledged to fight Chaos wherever I encounter it. You could have overcome those guardian spirits with knowledge patiently gained; without murder. Instead, you created another disruption in the spirit world, another splash of Chaos, for your own convenience. You ripped a life from the fabric of its Plane, making the whole a tiny part less stable, that much sooner to fall into Chaos forever! You destroyed where I had sworn to protect. How could you think that I would elevate you?"

Fraximon released his anger. "You and your Lawful prudery! A mage, an immortal should go his own way without being strangled by some goody-goody philosophy. Why should I have your blue-nosed morals tied around my neck like a dead turkey? There are many of the Masters of the Mysteries who think exactly as I do. What is one lousy mortal, more or less?" He had been roused to a hot bitterness by his rejection, but his teacher looked back at him in pity rather than anger.

"I repudiated those 'Masters' long ago, as you well know, Fraximon. At their beginnings, they took the same oaths as I did: to fight against the Chaos that had been left in all the Planes by the careless 'gods.' How do they perform that oath? They'll all meet 'at the end of Time,' they say, to fight against Chaos when it tries to overwhelm the last of Order and Law. Meanwhile, they ignore it; they wallow in it! Day by day, the Planes are eaten from under us! Have you any idea how few thousand years we actually have left? It is aesthetically pleasing to them to promise to keep their oath in some far time, because it allows them to flee any responsibility for the misery they condone in the here and now! And since those immortals cannot sin (in their own minds), they can embrace any black magician or demon-kissing sorcerer who will make the same 'someday' promise! I plan to be there, even at the last. I wonder how many of the bloody-handed wizards that you have held up to me as examples will be able to say the same? Each could retreat into his own pocket Plane, declaring it the last bastion of Order, trying vainly to hide from the face of the Great God, when He calls all this gargantuan experiment to account. Fraximon, do you not remember that *you* were once a mortal, with mortal hopes and dreams? Those Masters were as well. I regret letting them have so much sway over you before I made you my journeyman. You are young; have you so soon forgotten?

"I wanted better for myself, and better for you. That is why I have no part with them."

"What *you* want for me is obviously no longer of any importance! From this day, I will make my own way. I'll take what I want!" Fraximon threw up his hands and began a gesture, never afterward able to understand why the tears were rolling from his eyes.

"No, Fraximon—"

It didn't matter what might have been said if they had talked further. The older mage had no choice but to throw up his own wards. In the test that followed, Fraximon quickly realized that he was being bested. It was then that he had remembered the amulet that he had taken from the dragon's cave. It dangled from his gesturing right hand; he had planned to present it to his mentor as a gift. There had been no time to test it, other than to know that it was powerfully filled with magic. With nowhere to gather more energy for the contest, with his forces being slowly overwhelmed, Fraximon began to intone the chant etched into the back of the amulet.

His teacher's eyes widened in surprise. Then the older man uttered a word of power that Fraximon had believed unable to exist in the mouth of an individual mage. The concussion tore Fraximon's prize from his fingers, flinging it into the wilderness of the infinity of Planes, and threw his own drained body into a distant, barren dimension.

After decades, Fraximon had scraped together enough energy to recross Elsewhen to Planes where he could collect power to return him to full practice of the art. The tiny Plane where he had battled his teacher was entirely empty. The palace of blue-veined stone, where his mentor had trained him, night after night for a human lifetime, was missing. Any trace or trail to another dimension had been erased or blurred. Fraximon was alone with his growing hate.

The obsession to destroy the teacher who had turned on him carried Fraximon through the years and Planes. He had been driven away; so, he learned on his own now, building strength, paying his way with bits of his soul. The wild-eyed wizard with one gesturing hand became feared as the Terrible Stump in cities that were not even a whispered name to Barrow's furtherest traveler and on Planes where no other human foot had touched. His search had led him at last to Barrow, and to the reunion that had again left his hunger for revenge unsatisfied. (By then, Fraximon was quite insane, for all his powers.)

In a haunted house in the back streets of the city, the glaze of remembrance slowly left Fraximon's eyes, but the kiln of black emotions in his heart had again been fanned to a white heat. He came back with a snarl, among his cowering, silent minions. They didn't know what to expect from him. Too often, past introspective withdrawals by their master had meant distribution of pain and dismemberment upon his return to consciousness.

This time they were luckier; Fraximon merely dismissed them with the right combination of phrases and gestures, leaving the hall to its true haunts. It was long before daylight, but he had business to do toward his mission—and soon.

• 7 •

In the tawdry room that was Fraximon's retreat, Brieze screamed silently and ran, but there was nowhere to hide from his gloating face. The magician waved his hands, and the englobing silence pulled back to the walls. She could hear herself moan again. In the absence of other sound, the sobbing only made the fear worse. She stopped, fearful eyes following his approach.

"I have use for you, girl." The sorcerer leered. Brieze shrank away from him, curling herself into a fetal ball of dread. Her breath began moaning in and out, despite all attempts to control it.

"Enough! Enough!" Fraximon said, licking his lips. His strong hands lifted her to her feet. "Clothe yourself." He forced the wisent cape into her hands. "I have need of your powers."

She had dropped the rags of her dress and had been knotting the cape into a crude shift. Her eyes flew wide.

"I have no powers!" Had she been brutalized by this pig for the sake of some kind of talent that he only imagined she had?

"You are Tellarani, of the right blood. You have the power. I know your People."

"I . . . I've never trained—"

"Enough! What I need from you requires little training for one of your heredity, only awakening. It needed the inserting of a key, so to speak." He grinned with an icy lechery. "I merely want you to read the cards for me. You will use them to focus on the simple task I have in mind."

"I have no cards. I—"

"They will be provided." He decided to switch from imperious to businesslike. He simply brushed aside his earlier violation of her as a matter beneath a worldly trader's consideration.

"And . . . and if I do this for you?"

Brieze was no wilting lily from some noble's drawing room. The Wagonhawks had never flinched from blood, even their own.

"You will go from here with gold and never see my face again." He smiled a hypocritical smile, that spoke only of fairness in business dealings.

"And if . . . I don't?" Fear crept back in a soul-shivering wave.

He seemed to swell like a poisonous lizard. "Then we will repeat the hour we had together until I tire of you and find better sport for which to use you." His smile held infinite, evil promise. "No doors will open to your friends. No rescuer can reach you here with me."

She shook, and her bladder loosened momentarily, but she caught herself and straightened. "You will swear this—by all the gods?"

"I swear it by all the gods." He chuckled jovially.

Brieze was too inexperienced to know about the special kind of honor that magicians gave the gods; that is, none at all. "Done!" she said, spitting into the floor between them to bind it. In Barrow, a child learned before it was weaned that going back on a deal was the foulest form of obscenity. She had yet to realize that she was dealing with a man who lived beyond that boundary.

"Now, the cards . . ." Somewhere, from a distance, an unfamiliar power was calling her.

He gestured: a black, velveted board sprang into existence before her. In the center lay a pack of the Tellarani cards and a bit of cloth. "Take them," he commanded.

She touched them. The blood spirit confirmed: they were genuine and untainted by evil use. "Whose—"

"Never mind. I obtained these cards thirty years ago, but I have never tried to use them. The cloth is from the hem of the robe of the man I want you to locate. I found it in my hand after—never mind. Now, find him for me! Find him!" He leaned forward, eyes blazing with hate.

Brieze could feel the unnatural need burning within him, but she did not understand how the knowledge came to her. Mother had showed her the right form for reading the cards; she had even practiced on a few easy customers, who could be put off using the cards as props and applying verbal sleight-of-hand. Vague oracles would not be enough for this wielder of magic, but somehow she *knew* more than she had ever known before.

"You must choose a card to be the Significator. Choose one that matches the man you seek. If you are anything but honest in the selection, the entire reading will be wasted." Patiently, for Fraximon was a seething pot of madness, Brieze explained each card to him that might fit the man he sought.

Fraximon at last selected the Hermit. Though he was surly, his choice seemed honest. Brieze concentrated: a silent counselor, one who guided a seeker, a journey. Yes, the Hermit already seemed familiar to her somehow. She lay the deck on the cloth fragment and allowed Fraximon to divide it, in any way he was moved to do.

She turned the first revealing card. "This covers him." It was the Ten of Wands; the power was beginning to expand within her.

"Magician, you are carrying a heavy load. You have not always used your powers wisely, but your burden will soon be lifted."

"Keep your—never mind. That is good news." Fraximon had almost interfered in a reading-in-power by the seeress whom he had gone to trouble to possess.

"This crosses him." The Magician card opposed the Hermit. That was no surprise, but as she reached to place the card, it seemed to turn in her hand of its own accord. Mother had said that the "crosses" card could not be played reversed, but this card *wanted* to be reversed. Will, mastery, and occult wisdom had been changed to power used for destructive ends. "This is your card also," she told him. "It says that you oppose the man you seek."

Fraximon grunted a generally positive sound and waved for her to continue.

"This is beneath him. This is the card of the two of you—what you were together in the beginning." It was the Heirophant. "You were bonded to this man in some kind of organized ritual." In her mind's eye, she could see a younger Fraximon standing before the chair of a teacher, a man whose face was becoming more and more plain to her. "He was your teacher." The statement was bald truth.

"This is behind him. This is your recent life." The

King of Cups usually meant a man noted for business, kindness, and generosity. She had explained that to Fraximon; so that he didn't notice that the card was played reversed—violent, double-dealing, unjust. Hope for her own bargain with the magician vanished into the card before her.

"This crowns him. This may come." The Knight of Swords didn't belong in this reading at all! He was neither the Significator nor another image of Fraximon. "Someone else is to be involved. A young, reckless man will charge into the middle of your plan." Did she know the Knight? Yes! Her heart began to hammer in hope.

"A mortal?"

"Yes."

He waved away the importance of such a person with a negligent hand. She resumed the reading, relieved at not having to reveal more. A Tellarani seer must honor a reading-in-power, or be swallowed by it.

"This is before." The near future revealed the . . . Eight of Swords. She sighed. "Remember: You brought me into this. This is my card." She was wavering slightly, sitting before the board. The strain of drawing on internal energy was beginning to tell.

Fraximon lunged forward to examine the bound woman, pictured on a field of eight swords. Even he could see a clear image of the bondage, uncertainty, and censure it portrayed. "Go on anyway. Your freedom depends on it."

"I will, but for all the last cards, your reading will be entangled with my own.

"His fears," she said, turning the Tower. She shivered as fright met power. "Everything is about to be upset. Catastrophe and overthrow are certain." The burning, lightning-struck Tower loomed over her own soul.

"Good! It will go as I plan, then." Fraximon rubbed his palms together in anticipation.

"Wait! I can't see if the overthrow is for you or me or for the man you seek."

The sorcerer's glazed eyes showed that he was not listening. Brieze was growing very tired; she did not have the endurance to turn around a psychotic of Fraximon's mental strength. She would have to go ahead without him.

"The family." It was the Fool, stepping into the abyss of choice upon which turned all the rest of her life. She had no doubt that that personage was herself. Two more heavy tears trickled silently down her cheeks. What she did would affect not only her own life, but the lives of everyone she loved.

"The hopes." The Sun shone at her: attainment, pleasures, achievement, simple joys. They were her hopes, but they were also the hopes of the man she sought. She saw his face clearly now and almost cried out his name. Fraximon, still retreated into his tiny, warped cosmos of anticipation, did not notice her agitation.

"The Outcome." It was last of all, and it was . . . Death. She felt Fraximon stir and advance to peer over her shoulder. "Sometimes it only means a great change. This time it means death. One of us—you, me, or the man you seek—will die." Perhaps the blood power had shown her the Sun to ease the certainty of her passing. Every thought now floated in a growing cloud of fatigue, ready to slip from consciousness.

"It will be him!" Fraximon said, with the assuredness of the great or the insane. "Now, where *is* he?"

It had not come to her from the cards. They were merely focusing agents, not sources of power. The real message had come from her blood, and she feared it. Tiny drops of sweat beaded her whole body. She brushed wet, black hair out of her eyes. She must speak or forever let go of the power. Her own life might well be forfeit, no matter what her decision. But if she revealed everything to this bloody perverter, it could mean the death of a man of greatness.

"You will not find him tonight. Look for a man in the sunlight, surrounded by others who look up to him." She eased the incomplete message out through a constricting throat. "A sedentary man, of ordinary dress."

"So! He disguises himself in fear of me! Little good it will do him. But where, where is he?" He clenched his hands on her shoulders and pulled her up to face him.

Brieze would rather have bathed in slime than have him touch her again, but her feelings were a thin fog before the blazing light of his hate. "He is not in this city tonight, nor in any direction toward which I can point a finger." She could see a palace of blue stone and the Old

Man's face. She knew that what she was saying was as true as the pain from Fraximon's fingers clawing into her arms. "He was there." She waved a vague finger toward Pimpgut Way. "And he will return there. Not far. A few minutes' walk." No force in the universe could have wrung more from her without breaking the strand of her life. She collapsed when he released his hold.

"May I go now?"

It was a formality, to release the last bonds of the coerced contract between them. The message of the reading had removed all hope.

"Not so soon, my dear." His mood had taken another swing. He was again the towering conqueror, speaking downward to a degraded, pitifully funny, sexual tool. He had the work of a conqueror to do.

"I must first see if what you've told me is correct." He laughed brightly, and swinging a self-indulgent finger in the air, he was gone.

In the alley below, a street dog stiffened and fell to the ground in midsnarl.

Brieze was left alone in the ensorcelled silence as the dawn came up.

• **8** •

A hammering at the door to his room fully roused Krovik. He had heard the hurrying footsteps, certain that they were bound for another of the Gryphon's rooms. No long-surviving thief would have missed them, but a thief was seldom fetched in haste in the night, as a healer might be.

"Open, Krovik!" called a strained voice.

He opened. The unexpected caller almost rushed onto the point of Krovik's dagger. It was withdrawn so quickly that Fleetfox had no time to focus on it.

"You must come! You must—ugh! Phew! How do you stand the scorched smell of this place?"

"What are you—the building inspector? You get used to it, and it's all I can afford right now. Say, I'm supposed to be asking *you*. What, in the name of the Thousand Stars, do you mean getting me out of bed this way? And what do you mean I 'must come'?" Krovik got on better with Brieze's brown-skinned brother than he did with her mother, but this was pushing it.

"Something is really wrong. Brieze didn't come home, and Mother is . . . more than upset. Come on! She did a reading with the cards, knocked over the board, and began yelling for me to fetch you. Come on!"

"Just a second. Is this some kind of trick? Your mother wasn't messing with a knife, was she? She hasn't taken up chewing grabit weed, or anything?" Krovik was a young man, but he planned to be an old man. If it had been Brieze's mother at the door instead of Fleetfox, he would still have had his knife out.

"No! No! No tricks. Come on!"

The sincerity in the young Tellarani's voice was reaching Krovik. Fleetfox couldn't have made him understand about the fire chorusing in his own veins, but he had been tugging mightily on Krovik's arm. So far, he hadn't budged him. Although he had only a few years on Fleetfox, Krovik's ten extra kilos made him as shiftable as an anvil.

"All right." Krovik reached for his sword, letting the spring of curiosity tapped by Fleetfox flow only beneath the surface.

They were quickly at the exit of the Gryphon, ignoring the stares of the crowd. No need to stop to settle for the room: all the Gryphon's rooms were cash-in-advance. (Some past renters had wanted to stiff Barrelgut by turning up "robbed" in the morning or dead overnight from their own carelessness.)

Krovik contained his questions. Fleetfox had made it obvious that he had no answers. It might be better to maintain a little distance until the situation became clear. He was low on funds. The only profit he had shown from a couple of weeks of hard legwork was the sword that he carried. Anything strange enough to stir up Brieze's skinny shrew of a mother, enough to get *her* to call for *him*, might also mean a little gain. It was bound to be something that would break the monotonous path of his life. Besides, Fleetfox had said that Brieze was missing. On that thought, he hurried his steps.

The two men cut through the darkness of the Town like war craft on patrol, a ram and a sloop. Their drive could not take them into K'tiri's presence, however. They were stopped at the wagon door as if by a wall of glass.

Krovik, who had never been sensitive to the nonmaterial, could feel the pent-up force radiating through the curtains. Fleetfox was almost knocked to his knees by the surges of energy. With the hairs on his arms standing up of their own accord, Krovik quickly upgraded his estimate of the seriousness of the situation. Something far from normal was going on. Bracing himself, he stepped inside.

"Krovik! You've come!" She whipped across the space between them and seized his biceps in her talonlike hands.

It was all he could do to keep from groping for his dagger. His hand twitched to reach for it, but this woman was unarmed and in trouble. It was not like this tough, old crow to collapse into vapors at the slightest upset, like some rich, foolish matron from north of Caravan Way. Death was in the air.

"Krovik, you must find her."

("Why, she's been crying!") he thought. He would have been as likely to expect a saddle to cry. Maybe there was more to the old bag than he'd given her credit for.

There was little to tell, beyond the fact that Brieze hadn't come home. Krovik even admitted to seeing her at the street tutor's before sundown. He protested that the meeting had been accidental and innocent, and K'tiri *believed* him. Things were serious indeed. Emotions were so intense in the wagon that they had become more tangible than the facts. Krovik had begun to understand the deep attachment that Brieze's mother had for her missing child. To his great surprise, he discovered that his own feelings for Brieze ran deeper than he had previously admitted to himself.

Yes, he would find her. In Barrow, in the darkness, if it could be found with a dagger at the right throat or a coin in the right hand, he could find it. If it took stealth and guts, and some of his blood, he would find her. The scales of his life would be forever out of balance if he didn't. He rose to go, still uncertain why this woman, who had always scorned him, had chosen him as her champion. His heart was stammering, "Begin! Begin! Begin!"

"Wait," she called. "We search in all ways tonight!" She gestured toward the cards on the black-cloth board.

"The cards . . . They will tell us . . . perhaps, where to search, or . . . or who has taken her!" Her back stooped and a heavy sob rattled her frame.

Krovik almost went over to lift her, but when she straightened, K'tiri had regained the toughness that he had always known in her. The power that radiated from her face was hard even to look upon. A queen of the People-of-the-Grass stood before him. The Tellarani had lived as refugees among the hardened Upcrusters for so long that it had been easy to forget the noble lineage of some of the dark-haired nomads.

She swept to the board; Krovik merely sat down. He was not able to refuse her, no matter how much he wanted to begin his quest. He didn't believe in what she was about to do; he had made it a point *not* to believe. There were fake fortune-tellers in every other booth in the bazaar. He didn't want to be like some fat merchant's wife, trying to spy on her husband's extramarital dalliances through the cards, or some superstitious caravaneer, twitching to be told the safest day to begin his journey. Such kind shaped their own true prophecies. Krovik wouldn't believe—no, not exactly. But he had heard from previously skeptical sources about the things that K'tiri had done for them, without even using the cards.

The gaunt woman called him to awareness when she took his hand. He was ashamed that he had almost pulled it back in fear. Feelings with razors' edges were carving at the very air of the room.

"You must separate the cards." She urged his hands to touch the stacked counters.

The deck seemed to cleave apart like a neck before the headsman's ax. The only correct position for them to be divided was *there*. K'tiri's flying hands spread them in a crosslike pattern. The card she called the Significator lay in the center. She had chosen the Star, she explained, because it best mirrored the emotions that the two readers had for Brieze: love, hope, courage, inspiration.

"This covers . . . Ah, the Moon. We will meet peril, deception, bad luck, enemies. Krovik, it is not a good card to begin this." She went on immediately.

"This crosses . . . The—it cannot do so! The King of Cups turned in my hand! We face a man of incredible power: a violent, dishonest artist. I can almost . . . No.

"This is beneath . . . The High Priestess. It is my own card, but there is much yet hidden." She was immersed in the reading.

Krovik felt some of the bathing of power as well. Something like tingling, invisible water was flowing around him, the cards, and K'tiri. K'tiri was drawing more from the pictures than any picture could possibly tell.

"Behind . . . The Page of Swords. It is you Krovik: you are our spying eyes. Ah." She leaned back and closed her eyes. "There is more. I have been a foolish mother. I have read the future a thousand times and never once thought to reveal the two of you together. I didn't want it, but you two will be joined, in a way I cannot see. I have kept her for a Tellarani husband. I have lived as a hypocrite, and now my daughter must pay! For what awful being have I kept her?" She wrung her fingers, and tears streaked her cheeks, but she reached for the next card.

"This crowns . . . The Five of Cups, reversed. An old friend; a new ally? Hmmm." She concentrated again.

Though Krovik could see nothing on the card but a cloaked, hidden figure, K'tiri spoke with certainty. "It is the Old Man. He seems such a minor person to play a part in a reading of the power, but I can unravel it no further." She noticed that Krovik was fidgeting. "Stay. One more card. I will view the rest alone.

"This is before . . ."

Even Krovik could recognize his Brieze as the blind-folded woman, bound to the blade on the Eight of Swords. "I . . . I *must* go!" He rose.

"Wait." She dropped a small bag on the cloth, that clinked. "To smooth the way. It is all I have in the wagon."

At last Krovik went, following his heart, deeply ashamed that he had ever considered taking a profit from the woman behind him. Many an information broker awoke that night to find a sharp blade against his throat and a coin pressed into his palm. A voice whispered the same questions in many ears: Can you find someone who has seen Brieze Wagonhawk, K'tiri's daughter, since she left the Scoop just before sundown? Where can the Old Man be found tonight? The copper coin would become silver, the voice hissed, if the right answer were delivered to the Gryphon and Goblet before midmorning tomorrow. The sharp blade then went away, to trouble the sleep of some other paid informer.

The Thousand Stars rose and set.

By daybreak, a bone-weary Krovik had his answers, or lack of answers. Brieze had last been seen leaving the Old Man and his students, walking down Pimpgut Way toward the bazaar. Somewhere along its snaky length, she had vanished. The same thing might have happened to other women, or children, or strangers caught in the wrong street at the wrong hour of the night. It didn't happen to Tellarani girls—ever.

As for the Old Man, many eager informants would have taken cash to tell Krovik more of what he already knew. The Old Man would be in the Scoop when the sun was high. No informant knew where he lodged at night; no one had ever seen him abroad after sunset. No one in Barrow lacked a lodging for long, if only a doorway. No mortal existed that could not be followed. Equally, the Old Man, one of the Town's most tenured residents, had no lodging and could not be followed. It had been tried. "Odd" was the only right word.

Krovik limped back to the wagon in the bazaar to report nothing gained. Although he had purposely cre- ated a public image that was as bland as possible, Krovik had never doubted his own abilities. He had become used to secret victories; certain of success every time he had pushed himself this hard. Many hands and many chances would have seen him dead before this, had he been any less than he was.

K'tiri parted the curtains at the back of the wagon before he could enter. "I returned to the other cards after you left. Krovik, I cannot tell them to you. My interference could turn all against us!" She clutched him suddenly in a hug with her thin, brown arms that made his ribs ache. "You must try for all of us!" she cried, and darted back inside the curtained recess, shaking with sobs.

He did not follow. Krovik stood still. The edge of the day had been blunted beyond use. The sun, just breaking the horizon, made his night-loving eyes water strangely, but it filled him with new strength. His feet began walking toward Pimpgut Way on their own.

K'tiri sat and wept as she stared at the final four cards. "She fears." The Nine of Swords lay, filled with doubt, shame, fear, desolation, and possible death. The blood magic could not separate her own fears from that of her daughter. "Her family" was the Queen of Swords. K'tiri saw her own face in the stately, seated figure. Subtlety and keenness were overlaid with sterility, privation, and separation. They were mingled beyond hope of dissection. "Her hopes" were with the Knight of Swords. Ah, Krovik: he would be the last hope of mother and daughter alike. She could tell no more. Out of the tangled song in her blood had come the meaning of the last card; sharp as the Two of Swords. The card called the Conclusion shouted at her, "Meddle no more! The forces are in balance!"

She had pushed her calling too far tonight, as she had feared she might. Neither cards nor blood would help now. As impotent as the blindfolded woman on the final card, she laid her head down on the black board and washed it with her tears. The battle for her child's life would be joined by others. She had sent Fleetfox to find Jessup, without explanation, but K'tiri, the self-proclaimed best of the People's seers, could not lift a finger!

The sun rose into the day.

· 9 ·

Fraximon hated walking, but it was the mode of travel least likely to leave a trail of magic that could be backtracked to his lair. Perhaps his quarry had reasoned similarly and was even now planning to walk away from Barrow and Fraximon's just revenge. Half an hour of slogging, ranging over the area that the Tellarani girl had pointed out, revealed nothing overt. Occasionally he stopped and drew some shining dust from the air, rolling it in the scrap of cloth taken from his mentor's robe long ago. The powder was unique and hard to prepare. He had labored long over its design so that it could not be turned on its maker's own tracks.

For hours he paced and sprinkled, conjured and mum-bled. The few abroad so early thought him to be a mad beggar. None were desperate enough to try to rob him. With the coming of daylight, the city's most dangerous footpads had gone to their beds. Besides, a madman could be unpredictably dangerous himself. At last, a few glimmers appeared in the dust of the street. The glowing powder would only adhere to the tracks of the man he sought. Hundreds of other feet had almost erased the spoor. It was impossible to tell whether the fragments of a trail that he was now following led toward or away from the man he sought.

Sweating and muttering, with downturned face, the magician threaded his way through the narrow streets of the central Town. Every few paces, he cast more dust into the street. If he were jostled by someone in the increasing crowds, one glance at the contorted, magical glow of his face sent the jostlers elsewhere in a hurry. With the scent of his enemy hot in his nose, he was no longer worried about discovery of his presence by the locals.

The faint trace turned at last into a tiny alley and ended there—to the eye. Fraximon detected within it a nexus of magic, a slight puckering in the fabric of the real, that indicated that a door had been created there into Elsewhen. A road no mortal could walk had been opened. Having dispensed with mortality even before abandoning morality, Fraximon opened the sorcerous door and stepped through.

The timeless, formless wilderness of Elsewhen lay before him. It was time to call a better tracker than himself. He raised his arms and sent out the summoning. The answer was reluctant and power consuming, but the creature came. Created by a mad god in a fit of humor, the beast's body was all tiny legs and clinging claws. Its eyes were like great, clotted goose eggs, set behind nostrils like down-turned teacups. It hated the timelessness and the glowing nothingness of the space between the Planes, but it could run the paths there as few creatures could. Its master had called; there could be no refusal. It sniffed at the scrap of cloth, able to scent both the prey and the magic clinging to the fragment.

It would follow that scent now, its legs a blur. With the magical enhancement added by its master, the thing could outrun the wind. Fraximon would trek behind it, letting his hound spring any traps in the path. The trail was convoluted, as he had expected it to be, twisting through many layers of the Planes of Forever. The tracker was often lost from immediate contact with its summoner. Somewhere, through many distortions of time, late afternoon came to Barrow.

Fraximon's tracker returned to its master far too soon. "Well?" He moved to tower over the spindly monstrosity.

It whined its words in a voice as shrill as torn metal. "Master, Master, I could go no further. A small, blue man in a nightcap stopped me and told me to turn away!" A hundred of the creature's legs spasmed in fear.

"And you did, fool?"

"No, Master, nooooooo! A bear—a great, brown bear with funny little buttony eyes and strange, round paws— appeared and held me down. I struggled, Master, but a swarm of little blue men in baggy white pants came and danced on me! They sang a silly 'La, la, la-la, la, la' song. Finally, the one with the white beard told me again to go no further. *Their* master forbids it, he said."

"And you came back then, worm?" Fraximon's face was the color of polished brick.

"*Noooo,* no, Master! I circled away from them to cut the trail further on. I knew you would be displeased if I didn't." The thing shook as a stick puppet would in the wind, rolling its eyes independently.

"And . . . ?"

"Master, O Master, there was a wall. It had no person scent, but it smelled a little like the magic in the bit of cloth. It made no sound when I bounded against it. I saw nothing, but I could not pass it! Don't be displeased with me, Master! Doonnn't!"

Fraximon carefully questioned the beast, to establish the exact location of the magical shield. He always chose his minions for low, but adequate, intelligence. It gave them the abilities to use their special talents exactly as he directed. It also gave them anticipation and appreciation of pain. Fraximon satisfied himself by tearing off only three of the creature's small legs—slowly, of course— before he dismissed it to howl off into the distanceless dimensions.

He now knew the location of the boundary around the

stronghold of his foe, and none of that stronghold's odd guardians had detected his presence. With a spell prepared in advance, he could breach its wall and lay it waste—blue men, brown bears, and all. He would return to Barrow and destroy his mentor, and if the man fled, Fraximon could be at his hideout before him. Its security had been nullified; Fraximon would finish his quest there. There would be no mercy. Mercy! He almost strangled on the word/thought. The concept died in a shower of wizardly curses.

A lesser, evil member of the Planes, which had the misfortune to be nearby, disintegrated with all its inhabitants.

Home again, then, to build his power further and prepare for the coming victory. Home he would go, to the Tellarani girl who had thought she would escape him by riffling a few colored cards (as if he could ever let her go to bring the rest of the People down on him). There was much pleasure yet to squeezed from that skimpy morsel, perhaps even some of the secrets of the Tellarani magic that he had not yet obtained. If the right experiment could be devised . . . Perhaps a hybrid child of himself and a full-blooded woman of the People . . . He simply couldn't wait. With a skip of glee, a wave, and a joyfully wasteful expenditure of energy, he flung himself back to his small room in Barrow.

In the alley that contained the nexus that he had used to exit the Town, a clump of poisonous brambles crumbled to a fine, brown dust and settled into the mire.

· 10 ·

Krovik Quickhand had spent many of the hours in his short life observing and waiting, usually for that right moment of relaxed watchfulness that meant that someone else would be poorer in the morning. However, the patience of the successful thief had not prepared him to lounge in open sunlight for hours, waiting for a big-mouthed old man, while . . . while . . . Imagination of the unseen was worse than a demon face-to-face. He paced, flipping and catching his dagger nervously: point to hilt; hilt to point. The third hour was almost gone, and still no Old Man. He glanced down the street, and then up at the sun, wincing.

"May I help you?" a voice asked, from where no voice could possibly be.

No one slipped up on Krovik! Still, there sat the Old Man on his stool, calmly brushing dried mud from the wall. The dagger went point to hilt again as Krovik advanced on the white-haired teacher. Something smelled bad, stank of magic, didn't fit—and it all centered on this decrepit old fogey. The Old Man looked Krovik in the eye as the edge of the blade met his withered throat. It stopped there, slicing just beneath the skin.

"Well, young man, back again? What may I help you with? A lesson in letters, perhaps?"

"Where is she?"

"Whom do you seek, young man?"

"Brieze!" Krovik almost shrieked it. He mentally cursed at his loss of control. The Old Man's unnatural calm was peeling the scabs off Krovik's raw nerves.

"Oh," the Old Man said. He looked at Krovik.

The stocky thief felt as if a great, cool hand had spun the scroll book of his life and read all that was written there, in a blink.

"I see," said the Old Man. "Yes, I see."

"Well?"

Krovik dared not be short of bravado; Brieze's life was at stake. He would not be diverted from his search by spinning scrolls or strange old men.

"Brieze is in the loft that used to belong to Ig-the-Shiv, the first stairway past where Sow's Purse cuts across Pimpgut Way," the Old Man said.

"Thank you very much!" Krovik snarled as he whipped the dagger dramatically back from the teacher's throat. In the back of his mind, the doubt lingered that all the force of his young body could have pushed the blade even a millimeter further. He turned to go, but swung back. "*Old* man, how did you know that answer? Am I being played with by one of the gods?"

"No . . . hardly." The ancient figure chuckled. "I thought we talked about that once before."

Krovik brushed aside the reply. "Whatever was said, it means your life, whoever you are, if you had any part in harming her. Understand?"

"Of course. Now, shouldn't you wait . . . ?" The Old

Man's wry smile was wasted on the air: Krovik Quickhand was gone.

It was as if all the training that he had subjected himself to, to better steal from others, had been aimed at this moment. This matter was of life, not of petty property. Even in daylight, those he passed were never afterward sure whether a body had skirted them. He stalked: first, the dark stairway mouth; then the rickety stairs themselves, tread by fractured tread. A man's weight could be placed just so, there would be no creaking from even the most wobbly steps. Krovik was that man.

With his kick, the door splintered and shot open. Immediately, there was the thrust of a sword through it, followed by the lightning-strike spring of the short, bulky man who held the sword. The room seemed empty and quiet—too quiet. An odd figure rose in the dimness of the far corner, threw up its arms, and rushed him. Up came the sword with a (soundless?) shout, only to flinch safely aside as Brieze flew into his arms.

He cried her name, and she his, but their cries fell into a cottony, dead abyss, beyond human hearing. He held her in the silence, and her tears wet his chest. Her soft arms squeezed him so hard that his eyes watered, too. His arms about her shoulders were as right there as the foundation stones of the world.

Coming to himself, Krovik broke his hold and pulled them both toward the door. There would be time to hold and console later, just as there would be time for him to return to carve out the liver of the slug who had imprisoned her. That could come only after he had delivered her safely to K'tiri. At the door, he stopped. What made him hesitate now, when another heartbeat could mean danger for Brieze in this ensorcelled room? Starting forward again, he found himself stopped flush with the doorsill. He stepped back, moving Brieze aside for a moment, and lunged. His own hand seized the door's edge and held him. A second lunge: his other hand flipped his sword's scabbard between his legs, causing him to trip and fall, his head just short of the doorway. His arm reached for the open landing, only to turn aside on its own and push him back.

Rising, he moved toward the room's one window. He could not bring himself even to touch the closed shutter.

He was a rat trapped, and well trapped, it seemed. Brieze shook her head sadly at him in the empty, magic air. Two silent rivulets trailed down her cheeks, where other streams had flowed before. She moved to hold him again, the song of a mute mother in her blood. Would that her life had been forfeit, she thought, before Krovik had fallen into this madman's pit with her! He closed his arms about her in the stillness.

The sun climbed to the height of the sky and sailed down the day. In the small, upstairs room, Krovik repeatedly cursed himself for not asking the Old Man more. Magic's varied nasty forms had crossed his path before. He should have known: those who called uninvited at a mage's house might stay longer than they planned. He had rushed in as a blind fool, perhaps causing the loss of the person he valued the most and his own life as well. Sundown found him on Ig's narrow bunk, facing the door, a sharp-toothed rat: the girl on his left; a bright sword on his right. Waiting.

· 11 ·

With an audible *snap*, Fraximon returned to find company come calling. A husky figure with a sword lunged straight at his heart . . . and froze like a gladiatorial statue in midstrike. Although he could not defend against every distant bowman, no assassin dared try to strike from so close at Fraximon the Terrible Stump. The protective spell had been recently retrieved from his tomes, but it was quite effective. A chunky, young mortal had been left with his mouth open in a killing shout and his eyes bulging—an unbecoming icon in stony flesh. Fraximon walked around him twice, curiously. He gestured; sound returned to the room in an avalanche.

"Well, well: a rescuer! A rescuer who needs rescuing, it seems! Hah!" He laughed happily.

A circling vulture, high in the fading light, became a falling ball of flame.

This must be the interfering mortal the cards had hinted at. This "Knight" was only bereft of movement. Fraximon knew that the intruder's senses functioned as always. He meant to enjoy the moment fully. The magician seized Brieze and dragged her before Krovik's staring eyes.

"Notice the decorations this little dear has?" He ripped the make-do shift from her. Ten purplish-green bruises around her breasts matched others on her belly, arms, and legs. Blood was streaked down her thighs. "I'm going to decorate her some more, just for you, rescuer. Now, watch closely!" He turned toward the whimpering girl.

"Fraximon, Fraximon," said a voice, "up to your same old nastiness." The Old Man in his plain robe came in the doorway as Fraximon turned to face him.

"Well, well," Fraximon replied with gritty welcome, "still interested in your goody-goody meddling after all these years." His tone could as well have been used as a greeting for an old friend or as words said just before daggers were drawn.

"You really shouldn't have hurt the child."

"Oh, her." With a careless gesture, the younger wizard flicked Krovik and Brieze from sight, as a child might stuff a favorite toy in his pocket when some other child arrived uninvited.

· 12 ·

In Elsewhen, there is plenty of time. As all the rivers run to the sea, all the time streams run there to collect. After millennia, Krovik would have drifted close enough to Brieze to reach her hand. For countless centuries, they would have wept and held each other. I know now that they talked and planned, and ages passed. They fell more deeply in love, declared their love, consummated their love, matured their love. They grew to a plateau of high devotion and beyond. The pair explored the strangeness of Elsewhen together.

They fought. They grew to hate each other. They physically and verbally abused each other. They became pathologically vicious and went ages without speaking a word. However, no place or time exists that can compare to the loneliness of Elsewhen. The love and mutual need of the two lost mortals always returned.

Elsewhen is a function of Mind, but only a Mind great

enough to contain it can survive its eternity. Each of the pair discovered the possibilities of control over their own body. With eons to practice, each mastered everything that could be done by a mind within its private microcosm. Brieze healed all her hurts; Krovik tricked his body into growing taller, but reversed the process. A mortal in Elsewhen either comes to terms with what he is or dies insane within it. Each was sustained by the love of the other through internal crises that would have destroyed a solitary mortal.

Each became everything to the other that a person can become. She came to know every secret of slinking in darkness and stealing from those burdened with more than their share of treasure. He came to be as much a Tellarani as any not of their blood could be. He understood the reality of the sight-without-eyes, but neither that nor any informal magic worked at all in Elsewhen.

In the end, each could chronicle the life of the other, second by second. Krovik became Brieze; Brieze became Krovik. They were every tangible thing to the other that remained of their lost world. They matured to a single entity, far greater than they could ever have been alone.

Elsewhen is a strange place, being no place at all. In Elsewhen, no time passes. As all the rivers run to the sea, all the time streams run to Elsewhen—and there they stop. My heart might have beaten once by the time the lost duo had matured to all they could be. In the eternal present tense of Elsewhen, they could only go on existing.

· **13** ·

"Fraximon, I'm disappointed in you. So much power; yet for all the years that have passed—still so rotten." There was more sadness than hate in his voice.

"Ah, Master, I think you're right about the power. You won't be able to discard me again so readily; at least, not without a certain Secret, which I will (of course) not tell you."

"I had hoped that your mind would straighten itself out after being reduced to, let us say, the lowest common denominator of humanity. I left you bound in unreasoning mortality for only a few years. Ah, the workings of the mind are so poorly understood, even by those of us who use them most! It was my final experiment with you."

"Did it work, *old* man?" Fraximon smiled a false smile. Behind his eyes, the wordless summonings of power began.

It was met by an equal defense from the mind of the ancient mage. Somewhere on a Plane of Fire, two opposed spirits rose and began fencing with rapiers of ice.

"Sorrowfully, no. I cannot trace your warping to anything in your upbringing. Your adoptive parents were good, solid people. I would hate to blame your flaws on heredity, knowing your real parents as I did." The master magician stood as motionless as his former student, but both had advanced in the art to the point that spoken words or gestures could generally be dispensed with.

"No need to taunt me, old fool. One more example of your righteous meddling—you erased all record of my origin so thoroughly that I will never know it! Unless, of course, I can force the information from you. You make a worthy opponent. Age doesn't seemed to have dulled you entirely!"

On Planes no mortal could ever visit, armies of indescribable beings drew up their battle lines and hammered at each other in the names of the gigantic, soundless voices that had summoned them.

"Fraximon, I fear that you may have grown a bit *too* strong."

"I can't tell you how pleased I am to hear that!"

On towering mountains somewhere, wraithlike giants flung lightning bolts at each other across a bottomless gulf, deflecting their opponents' attack with rainbow shields.

"Go back to your blue palace, *old* man. I promise to visit you once more, and not at some nebulous end time to play games at holding off Chaos from this worthless mudball of a Plane. We will wrestle once more—when *I* choose!"

The two bodies in the small room had hardly moved as the armored spirits had taken the measure of each other across the expanses of the Planes. Now they drew back. For the moment, neither could destroy the other by force alone, without himself also being destroyed. For Fraximon, however, a stalemate now was the same as a victory later.

"Are you ready to go along home quietly now, *old* man?"

"No, not quite. There are secrets to be opened and heard here. I had hoped just now more to weaken you back to your former measure of power than to destroy you. So, you have renounced even your first oath to fight against Chaos? Your life has always been more its friend than that of Law. Whatever happens at the End of all is not as important as my work here. I want to continue it, without having to battle you. In the long run, the rest and strength I mistakenly gave you would undoubtedly let you win that battle. I would much rather that you left this city now and went your own way. I would promise never to interfere in your affairs on other Planes. However, you have made it clear: only one of us is to live to see the End come."

"Was that a hint that I should retreat from your precious city? When I finally take your powers from you, my new total strength will be the greatest of any Master of the Mysteries who ever lived! I'll level this dung heap, just because it was important to you! Look for a quiet spot to spend your last days, old fool! You'll soon have no more chance to choose anything, even the spot for your grave. Why don't you just *command* me out of your city, using my birth name! Hah! You are as dead as the last Dragon, from this moment!"

"Fraximon, Fraximon, more the fool I, then. Since you so heatedly wish my death that you will make it your only goal, you might as well have my Secret as well." Thus, in a shabby Barrow room, the sorcerer told his former student how he had hidden the heart of his power.

The younger adept stood still, stunned, mulling over how best to wring personal gain from this gem of freely gifted knowledge—how best to destroy the giver with the gift. He had no doubt that the Old Man had indeed revealed his Secret. With proper manipulation, no later battles would be necessary. Victory could be his within the next few minutes. Perhaps he would send his mentor to Elsewhen when all was over, powerless but not dead, chained to a small, hungry demon. It would have eternity to hunger and forever to feed. Perhaps—

"Good-bye, Fraximon." The Old Man waved his hand, as if in sad farewell. The wave became a sparkle; the sparkle became a knife with a winged blade. As he spoke, the master wizard sent it flying at Fraximon's heart. "There is one more Secret to be revealed yet—yours!"

Fraximon threw up warding arms to gesture, confident of blocking such a simple attack. The flying blade had flickered in midair to become a flying cobra. It struck, not at Fraximon's visible body, but at the empty air where Fraximon's left hand should have been. The venom-dripping fangs sank into . . . something.

The place where a wizard kept his Secret could not be protected with layer upon layer of precision spells. To another adept, their presence would make the "Secret" glow like a beacon. The ages had shown that the only way to hide the heart power of a mage, a Secret worth more than his birth name, was out in the open. All that had ever concealed Fraximon's left hand was a first-year apprentice's invisibility spell, the kind a major adept could strew about like dust: not worth detecting or probing by any worthy opponent.

Green ichor injected into veins that suddenly appeared as gray cords strung from the stump of Fraximon's arm. Veins went to the heart. Cobra venom gave the victim about a hundred heartbeats to remember the life fading from him. Magicians, once established in the external spell of immortality that sustained them, no longer bothered to examine their internal funtions. Once the body of such a wizard was pierced, the sorcerer lost all control of the damage. Their perfect defense was a perfect wall, but there were no magical guards patrolling it within.

Fraximon had lied so often about the incident with the dragon's mouth that he had almost forgotten the truth himself. He had indeed returned to his mentor with the dragon's blood, but the snap of its dreaming jaws had missed. All ten of Fraximon's fingers were now grayly visible as his powers bled away into the Old Man's hand through the elongated cobra.

"How? How?" the dying sorcerer gasped, sinking to his knees.

"If only once, you could have kept your sick emotions in check . . . I have long known that you killed every woman you afflicted with a sexual act. Until a moment

ago, I didn't know why. Your hands—whole hands—on
the breasts of the Tellarani girl gave you your death.
And, Fraximon . . . I have always known your birth
name."

The younger man continued his slide to the floor, the
contortion leaving his face as the life departed. As the
Master bent to close the clouding eyes, his tears fell on
the gray cheek of his failed apprentice.

In the alley below, a single flower pushed its way
between the tiles and opened its face to the sky.

• 14 •

In Elsewhen, there is plenty of time. As all the rivers run
to the sea, all the time streams end there. Like the sea, it
is never full. Yet mortals that must exist there fill up with
time until they bloat, until they have thought all that can
be thought. Their skins might not burst with an obesity of
time, but their spirit can dust the dark corners of memory
only so many times before it must lie down to sleep in its
swept and garnished room. In Elsewhen, there is plenty
of time. It is the final test of the apprentice magician to
be sent there and to escape by his own powers, but
mortals are not all born to be magicians. As all the rivers
run to the sea, all the time streams empty there, and the
souls of mortals sleep there, drifting in its ever-tangling
currents—always.

Krovik/Brieze rested quietly in each other's arms, when
called back to Fraximon's room by the Old Man. Even
their dreams had already all been dreamed. The ancient
magician hovered over the pair with an infinite sadness,
for theirs was an infinite greatness and a universal hurt.
He meditated long on what to do with them.

"Children, even with all my knowledge, I am not sure.
Perhaps I am about to take from you something of wonderful worth. Perhaps I will be lifting from you a burden
too great to bear. Would the Oneness that you are now,
thank me or curse me if I woke it?" He sprinkled their
eyelids with a green powder and spoke a spell in the
throat-twisting language of mages. "Awake now, two
again, and know nothing of Elsewhen! I have not erased
what you were, but I have hidden it where it can only be

reached to save your very souls. Awake, fledglings! Awake, most ancient of all this city!"

As babes, they opened their eyes. As infants, they rose to greet a new world. Their dewy consciousnesses looked about in a great, echoing vault where memory should have been. As babies, they toddled to the stairs, skirting Jessup, who was crouched on the landing, dagger in hand. He rose to follow them.

"Don't be off too quickly, old friend," the magician called. "Your daughter is safe now, and I have a story that you might be interested in."

In Upcruster Town, taking candy from babies was not necessarily considered criminal. Somehow, however, the worst of Barrow's candy-stealing cutthroats decided to turn away from the pair of grown babes who strolled, hand in hand, toward the bazaar. Perhaps a protective spell still lingered on them; perhaps the unearthly innocence of the duo brought an unease to potential attackers; perhaps Upcrusters were simply not as gut-busting mean as they wanted the softies north of Caravan Way to believe. As predators, they should have been irresistibly drawn to the helplessness and odd behavior of Krovik and Brieze, but as human beings, they were drawn to them by other forces.

A lumpy mob had formed a protective wedge around the two young people as they strolled across the bazaar. When it was plain that they were headed toward K'tiri's wagon, a handful ran ahead to warn her. She had cried until her face was wet, red leather. Now, she swept the two up in her arms and nursed them, oh, so tenderly, for the days it took their minds to return.

The uncrowded memories of their former lives were resurrected, but Krovik's ended at the moment of his lunge into the wizard's room. Brieze could find no trace of any memory of the time after she had left the Old Man in the Scoop. Her body was as unmarked as her mind, except for some dried blood from an unknown source. Krovik refused to talk about his meeting with the Old Man, but he assured K'tiri that the teacher was innocent of any harm to Brieze.

Jessup-the-Yarn reported seeing a corpse in the upper room from which the pair had first come wandering, but it was gone when Fleetfox checked later. Krovik's new

sword was also missing. Neither the disappearance of a
body nor of a loose weapon in the Town was out of the
ordinary. Some speculated that the sword had had some
magical property that had saved Brieze and its owner,
before departing for places unknown. Krovik was so closemouthed about where he had gotten it that the possibility
could not be dismissed. Had the participants consulted a
magician, such a one might have told them that things
(such as swords) were sometimes left adrift in Elsewhen.
However, all the survivors were leery of magic for a long
time after.

The powerful attachment of Krovik and Brieze for
each other did not diminish. Though K'tiri was no longer
struggling against the idea, she convinced Krovik that
their joining should be postponed "for a while." She had
made arrangements for horses to take them on a nuptial
journey to the Grasslands in the Tellarani manner, when
next the moon was full. Krovik had gone back to the
Gryphon the night her killer came. Perhaps, if he'd been
there . . .

* 15 *

The telling of the tale had been long and had called for
the emptying of many cups. Jed would have to let his
wife and daughters do most of the management of the
Jumping Salmon that night. He had even forgotten his
one other customer, slumped down out of sight in a
nearby booth.

"A fine stroppin' tale, an' sad, too." Jed dabbed at an
eye. "But there's a thing or two bothers me about it.
Why are ye keepin' a fine money-maker like this in the
bank, so to speak? It should've turned you many a coin.
Why, everybody knows Krovik and Brieze, an' we all
loved K'tiri. She was a fine woman. She wouldn't ha'
minded."

"Na, she'd have been glad of the telling. Her children
won, don't you see? How I wish—"

"Here, now, none of that! The story itself, now—say,
what was the great secret, the one the Old Man told
Fraximon? Ye never said."

Jessup became agitated, more so than could be explained by the load of alcohol he had imbibed. "There! I knew you'd spot it, drunk or not! Everybody would! I'd tell this tale as a perfectly formed saga, and there wouldn't be a dry eye in the house. And then some clod (no offense) would call out the same question! And when they all heard the answer, the silver that was headed toward my cup would become copper, and the coppers would stay in the purses. In a week, it wouldn't be worth the telling anywhere!" The bard cursed enthusiastically and creatively, at length.

"There, there now, friend." The taverner gave the despondent storyteller a brotherly hug about the shoulders. "At least tell *me*. I'll not laugh at ye. May'ap it's not as bad as ye think."

"You'll see. If I tell it, I'll be known all over the region for *making up* the stories I tell." The wine was not having a calming effect on Jessup. "I had it straight from *him. He* told *me* a tale, and slipped me a little bag of gold—out of pity, you know.

"This is Barrow. I have a reputation for reporting the truth, but making it interesting. Not only will folk think that this is fiction, but they will complain that it's not even *believable* fiction. No knave, no matter how stewed, is going to believe *that* secret. That will mean that the rest of the story is also a pack of lies. It's spoiled—spoiled, I tell you!—and butter wouldn't melt in his mouth!

"That old rascal is still up there, sharing with a pack of rug rats knowledge that can overturn empires, and who will ever believe me if I tell who he is?

" 'Jessup,' he says, 'I am a Master of the Mysteries because long ago I found the one Secret that makes me stronger each time I use it. . . . Jessup,' he says, 'I *always* tell the truth!' "

"That's his secret? Oh. Aye, mate, 'tis best this one stay in the bank. The next round is on me."

Interchapter

Poor Jessup: he thinks I won. I committed a murder of the foulest sort, no matter that it was in self-defense. My inattention allowed an innocent girl to be raped, no matter that she has neither mark nor memory of it. My lack of watchfulness left that girl an orphan later, no matter that she and young Krovik are now husband and wife, in every way but legally. All came out for the best, many would say, no matter that death sank his claws into a second victim of the Wagonhawk family after missing the first.

I remember.

I am not omniscient: I couldn't have been expected to have watched Brieze and K'tiri for every second of their lives; yet the guilt I feel is as deep as if I could have. Perhaps it is because I have not stopped meddling since. If I (partially) included Brieze and Krovik's lives in my experiment, then I should have guarded the lives I toyed with a little more closely.

I must ponder it, but this pen has taken me in thrall. I begin to see why the gods, though they were imitators rather than creators, are so possessive of their "creations" and took such joy in forming their Planes. I merely place ink on paper, yet the thrill of creation, if only of words, is increasingly seductive. I need not have written down this second set of events: I am no storyteller of Jessup's class, but to be both participant and secret recorder of a human history . . . Ah, it thrills me!

It is my human nature, a nature I had held to in purity (I thought). Fraximon died as much for denying his humanity as for any action of mine. But being close to the youth of Krovik and Brieze has reminded me of feelings I have not experienced since my own adolescence. That was so long ago that I do not easily recall the events, as if those times happened to another youngster. Still, I begin to remember the feelings. . . .

However, the hunger to set this tale onto the page calls me. I will mine my ancient memory for those remembrances some other night. Jessup, you see, was not the only Townsman whose path I nudged toward the Jumping Salmon. . . .

BOOK II

Loose Ends

HARMON YORN was slumped down a booth of the tavern, mostly drunk—mostly, but not entirely. He was unlikely to get any drunker, with his purse as flat as a dried apple. The landlord of the Jumping Salmon had taken enough coin off Harmon that morning to keep him off Harmon's back during the slack midday hours before the fishing fleet came in, but Harmon was bored. He didn't mind the smell of the place; he couldn't smell much of anything after the second drink anyway.

He was nursing a large, cheap mug of ale, brooding on Fate's cruelty to himself: one deserving of so much better. Being an adopted only child had been load enough, by his thinking. Lately, however, too many rounds for the house, too many cheap women, too many bad sessions with the dice had leaned his birthright to the edge of extinction. He was nearly broke, and not one step closer to achieving the ambition he had embraced as his reason for leaving home.

His ale-softened gaze barely cleared the back of the booth, fixing hazily on the pair at a central table. Fishin' Jed was in close conversation with another man of his own age, who looked vaguely familiar to Harmon. The two were probably talking business. Business! Bah! Father had forever been nattering at Harmon to take a place in the family grain business. Papers; invoices; reports on the corn harvest in Mugambu—to blazes with the lot! Harmon knew that he was a man of soul and destiny, not to be shackled forever to the workaday world of (ugh!) business.

Adventure! Love! Magic! Pleasure! Those were Harmon's future. With a soggy sneer at the milksop lives of others, he raised himself a deserved toast. It was beneath him to consider the depression of his fortunes at the moment. Just now, he was . . . between adventures; that's all.

The voices of the other men rose briefly, and Harmon caught a name: Jessup. Ah, yes, the storyteller: Harmon had seen him once at the Gryphon and Goblet and once at another gathering weeks before, where Jessup had been entertaining. Harmon had formerly often attended such gatherings. Mothers of marriageable daughters had particularly sought him out—once. Lately, there had been a drought of such invitations. His disdain for making any more money in his family's traditional endeavors and his increasingly patchwork appearance had chilled their matchmaking. Father, Harmon was sure, had wanted his son married and settled down, just as he had wanted Harmon chained to a mountain of paperwork and sweating over grain inventories. Again, bah.

Jessup and Jed had been talking sorrowfully while Harmon's mind had been elsewhere. After a long silence, however, Jessup launched into a tale. There was no mistaking his professional manner, even though he kept his voice muted at first. The story was something about a sorcerer named Fraximon; a thief that Harmon had met named Krovik Quickhand; and the card-reading Tellarani.

Harmon didn't want to miss a performance by the man who was probably the best bard in Barrow. He hunched all the way down in his booth to reap some quality entertainment and to keep it free for himself. He listened as closely as his lubricated auditory facilities could manage. By keeping quiet, he would not be obligated to part with a single copper when the telling was done.

Jessup and Jed were as intent on serious drinking as they were on the tale. They failed to recall Harmon's presence, just as he had hoped. It was a fine tale, too: full of magic and adventure; secrets and bloodshed; and a strange place called Elsewhen. Harmon loved it, even the part after the tale telling when Jessup became so agitated. As he mulled it over in his mind, however, Harmon fell into a deep, ale-induced sleep.

Rousing was unpleasant. Hard innkeeper's hands dragged him from the booth; he had felt their like before. Being dragged semiconscious toward an exit had become too regular an experience over the past few weeks.

"Out ye go, lad! Time to be on the way now!" Jed's voice strained next to his ear.

The taverner wasn't unkind about it, as other bartenders had been. He was simply overwhelmingly physically insistent. One strong hand on Harmon's arm and another on his rear propelled him toward the street. Off balance, he stumbled at the door and fell into the dust of the wharfside road. His head was buzzing like a swarm of bees as he crawled over to an empty keg near the door and propped himself up on it. Bright twilight filtered through his hangover, signaling the arrival soon of the thirsty fishermen who were the tavern's steady trade.

Jed had probably done Harmon a favor: the fisherfolk might resent Harmon's presence in a tavern that they considered their home territory. If Harmon brushed himself off and went back inside, Jed would still accept his coppers, but he would have to drink anything he bought in isolation. If he were insulted or mistreated, Jed might send him outside to protect the furniture in case of a fight, but as the interloper, Harmon would find no allies. Any heckler or bully would be on his home ground. It would be better to go to some heterogeneous water hole, such as the Gryphon and Goblet. Everyone there was as sharp and individualized as handmade razors, and sometimes as dangerous. Harmon couldn't remember why he'd come down to the docks in the first place.

He hated to think about the long walk involved in switching to another tavern, but better to think about anything than the ache in his head. He needed something to calm him. Now, what was that tale of Jessup's again? Like a broken string of beads, the memory of it lay scattered about the floor of his mind. Some of its units were forever lost. There had been . . . umm, something about an evil wizard and a Tellarani girl, and about a thief/hero who went to her rescue. The rest was useless fragments, except . . . One shiny piece of the story still reflected up at him, waiting to be picked up and examined. The old street teacher, the one Harmon had seen off Pimpgut Way, was secretly a great magician, one of the Masters of the Mysteries! His Secret, the one by which the Masters hid part of their powers, had also been part of the story: the Old Man had to tell the truth—always! There had to be some kind of power just in knowing that much!

Harmon forgetfully leaped to his feet. The surge, to his toxified brain, was like leaping straight up into a large, brass bell and using his head for the clapper. He sat down again with a moan. Nevertheless, he rose more cautiously again in a few minutes and, holding his head in his hands, hurried toward the Gryphon and Goblet across town. Tonight he would plan, plan, plan. This was the door to adventure that he had always been sure would open for him. Tomorrow he would no longer be the shabby, sometimes drunken son of a grain merchant: he would be an *adventurer*! He would be a man who held power over a wizard, by knowing his Secret. Harmon could hardly wait.

• 2 •

Droxdromixalangdang the Dirak didn't mind the swamp, even if it wasn't exactly like the sloughs of his home Plane. As long as there was enough to eat, it was close enough. When that power-mad, one-handed wizard had dragged Drox to this Plane, he had placed the Dirak in great danger. (He dared not even *think* the name of his summoner, lest he attract the man's attention.) The mage had been too much like a bore-bird that had flown head-first into one too many iron-wood trees. Humans normally could cause Drox no problems, but the magician could easily have disincorporated the Dirak during one of his flights of fancy or fits of psychotic anger. Drox had watched that happen to other familiars before his eyes. As a result, he had been a *very* faithful servant.

The same lack of equilibrium that had fed the mage's anger had also made him careless. He had sloppily everted two of the telepathic syllables in the Dirak's dismissal spell. Instead of being flung back to his home Plane, Drox had found himself cut loose inside Barrow. Drox would dearly have loved to crunch the wizard the instant he had felt the dismissal, but the protection spells around the sorcerer had not been rescinded. However, the next time a summons was sent for Drox on his home Plane, he wouldn't be there. The Dirak had scampered away on his stubby legs, among the crowd of familiars, happy to have been released alive anywhere. Because of his habit of dismissing his minions in wholesale lots, the spellcaster hadn't noticed the Dirak's unplanned direction of departure.

It had been dark at the time, because such things were better done in the dark. No one had seen Droxdromixalangdang as he fled across the Old Wat Bridge, past the sleeping gate guards in the slum called the Slews, and into the swamps beyond. In a deep bog, with only his belly slit above water, he had needed many days of sucking in the stagnant air to ease the fear of his sorcerous tormentor.

He had finally run up one of the eyes in the palms of his hands like a periscope: all clear. After many days, Drox had crept fearfully from the water, hungry—awesomely hungry. The bulky points on his skin were still partially curled under, showing that the nervous Dirak was not himself yet. Normally, he resembled a cross between a truncated cactus and a giant, purple avocado, with a fanged slit splitting one side vertically. When in full array, his bright pink nostrils flowered on each side of his mouth. His eyes could peer two directions flexibly from behind their reinforced lids, protected by clawed digits. He was a hunter to be feared, but he yet lacked the backbone to do anything but slink gutlessly from tree to tree, showing a mere edge of a hand as he peered balefully about.

He contacted human dwellings in only a few minutes. The perimeter shacks of Slews-Outside-the-Walls blended so gradually into the swamp that it was difficult to recognize a boundary, other than one more especially deep, muddy ditch. The last few hovels were so rotted down that their inhabitants entered them by crawling through denlike openings. Drox hadn't realized that he had reentered the city until he came face-to-face with a bony child playing in a nasty puddle, to the surprise and dismay of both. In desperation, as much to stifle any outcry as to satiate the ache in his middle, Drox leaped to cover the child. The Dirak's mouth opened in midleap into a toothlined bag. The effect was like capping a purple, carnivorous teacup over a squirming mouse.

Babies born in the Slews either cried until they died, or

until they were cried out forever. The wiry slum child fought back against the Dirak, as he had always fought against fear and privation, but he made no outcry. Drox bounded back into the swamp, shredding and digesting.

Again, days passed. Drox's summoner failed to call for him. Perhaps his insane master was busy elsewhere. The Dirak had an innate "taste" for magic. He peered cautiously with an inner sight at the planar pathway down which he had initially been drawn into Barrow. Though its memory had been burned into his mind, he could not return that way alone.

There was no sign of the mage. In fact, the magical "signature" of the magician seemed to be fading, almost as if the wizard were dead. That thought brought a surge of hope to Drox, but it seemed to renew his hunger.

He stalked the pathetic game of the swamp. Edible animals had been thinned out by the proximity of the hungry slum. The remaining warm-bloods were mostly too small or too agile for him to catch. Turtles, snakes, and small crocodiles were slower, but they were low in the metals he craved. Drox had soon shrunk their numbers to where he had trouble finding even those.

There was no choice: he would have to begin hunting the massive, slow, organic humans. Not only were they easier to catch and higher in food value, but most carried bits of metal such as coins, buckles, or weapons. He felt no moral restraints against eating fellow sentients, but missing people might arouse the population. Human hunters would fail, and provide several meals while doing so, but they would bring unwanted attention on him.

A Dirak's hide could turn the finest weapons. Its purple points only seemed fleshy: they were mostly gold, alloyed with the thirteenth element (for which the metal workers of Barrow had not so much as a name). That alloy accounted for the lavender color, but not the hardness. The living cells of his skin had laid down atoms of the (also unknown) twenty-fourth element among the others. Only the base of each overlapping, hand-sized scale was organic. Arrows and swords might nick him a little as they bounced off, but their steel would dull quickly. Drox would gain a few shiny scratches, and the weapons' wielder would lose his life.

The humans would learn to avoid his territory, forcing

him to hunt closer to the city. When they called home the useless hunters, the worst would happen: they would call for a magician. They might even call . . . him. (Drox shuddered at the thought.) A magician need waste no time untangling the mess of spells that had called the Dirak to Barrow and stranded him there. Mages knew Diraks well.

The Plane of Drox's origin had been assembled long ago from metal scrap abandoned by some careless god. A great Master of the Mysteries had manufactured a Plane of his own, in imitation of the gods, who themselves had constructed the dimensions (that they pompously called the Planes of Forever or the Houses of Infinity) in imitation of a greater reality. Cosmology and the history of magic meant nothing to the Dirak. All that mattered was that because magic was an integral part of his makeup, Drox could no more be immune to it than a fish could reject water.

If he were very fast and lucky, he might crush a mage sent against him before that one could cast any spell. Succeeding once would only mean that the humans would employ another magician of higher level. A strong enough sorcerer could afford continuous protective spells. Drox would be unable to come close to him, though it meant his death.

Drox feared death. In the millennia since he had been hatched, he had eaten many creatures. He had often seen fear and death at close range, but for others. He had no desire to be their victim; he planned to live millennia more by contacting death only as an instigator.

A Dirak's prominent features were teeth and claws and maw. It was for those that the wizard had summoned him, to devour some people who had crossed the mage while (the other familiars had whispered) that one had been helpless. Drox had difficulty imagining his former master as helpless—ever. The sorcerer had always located the victims for him. He would whisk Drox magically to the ambush and caper with glee as the Dirak leaped out of the darkness, completely covering the target of the wizard's revenge and digesting the muffled screams. The mage had always been fastidious about leaving no traces, as if he were afraid to leave a trail for some enemy. He had conjured Drox away, to hide in an empty building or return to his home Plane, ready to be summoned again at his master's need.

Drox had been in no personal danger during the escapades, except from his summoner. He had been such a useful tool that he was sure that his master would not lightly discard him. He almost wished that the wizard would call for him again—almost. At least he hadn't been hungry. As he sought vainly for more game, he recognized that he would have to catch another human.

A smuggler, heavily laden, straggling behind the rest, set his pack down to rest beside a boggy pool. The shadowy line of bearers didn't miss their compatriot until they rendezvoused in their safe house in Slews-Inside-the-Walls. To their great relief, they found his pack of contraband, but not the man. Men were replaceable.

Drox hid for days, fearing the search that was sure to be made for the missing man. None was made. Inevitably, the Dirak grew hungry again.

A slatternly broad slipped into the brush on the outskirts of the Slews to relieve herself. She never returned. Her drunk of a husband kissed off the whole matter, after extensive cursing, and moved in with her slut of a sister. He assumed that his former spouse had taken up with his thieving brother over in Upcruster Town.

Drox assimilated her, half underwater, and mulled over the matter. Diraks had never been intellectual giants, but Drox had an adequate brain. Eons of disuse, its owner being faster with fangs than mentation, had left that brain rather slow. It almost seemed that humans didn't *care* that he had eaten three of their kind. More careful watching was called for.

Wheezer, a nasty little creep if there ever was one, had planned to sneak across the swamp and be forever free, spending his time and his friends' money in a warmer clime. Though the bag of gold he was carrying had been hoarded by a whole syndicate of hardworking smugglers, he intended to put it to more direct, personal use. However, the merchant captain who had agreed to meet him downriver waited for him in vain.

Drox found little nourishment on the bony slinker he had devoured, but the bag of gold lent the meal a rare bit of spice. This time there *was* quite a search, but the searchers made it obscenely obvious to Drox's eaves-

dropping ears that they wanted the gold back far more
than they were interested in the man. They had planned
to do Wheezer severe bodily harm anyway. Drox had
done them a service. The men's reactions to the loss
confirmed the theory of human behavior that the Dirak
was forming.

He waited two days before engulfing two smelly lovers,
copulating fiercely in a weed patch behind their shack.
He peered from behind a tree, waiting for the outcry that
was sure to come when they were missed. There was
none.

After the sun was well up, a shabby neighbor ambled
by. Spotting the obvious signs of a struggle, the man
investigated inside. He picked over the abandoned fur-
nishings of the shack, robbed his deceased neighbors of
all their portable possessions, and left. Before two more
days had passed, the creaking pile of a shack had not
only been picked clean but it had been reoccupied by
another family of desperate slum dwellers. The new occupants were a family of over a dozen who bickered
constantly, probably to pass the time while starving.

Well.

The group of humans who inhabited the Slews seemed
to have little concern for human life. Admittedly, there
was little enough to respect about their lives in the slums.
Proceeding cautiously, Drox reduced the brood of new
tenants by three, choosing middle-sized young that were
at an obnoxious age—most likely to run away or wander
and least likely to be missed. His choices proved correct:
there was no visible mourning or search.

The Dirak was joyous. The magical signature of his
mage mentor was fading day by day. The man must
be—must be!—dead, or ensorcelled and helpless. Drox
had established a new hunting territory, almost like the
one at home. He would only be hungry enough now to
make pursuit interesting. Though there was still some
danger, he began to enjoy the stalk-and-pounce again.

Feeling the urge to add some spice to his activity,
Drox planted himself in the path of a well-armed smuggler. He allowed the rogue four useless swings before
munching him. He played peek-a-boo with some slum
children across the boundary ditch, flashing his staring
hands in and out from behind trees. He enjoyed the

game so much that he left that group uneaten (for that day) and instead caught an easy old man who had been sunning himself in front of his hovel.

That particular victim proved to be a mistake. In a moment of playfulness, Drox simply seized the man in his maw without biting down. He quickly bounded into the swamps and ejected the oldster in a clearing surrounded by bogs. He had every intention of eating the human, but he had found that letting fear build up in the body gave the meat a different flavor. Besides, he also had a growing hunger for intelligent contact, however brief, to go with his food. Drox spoke the human language well enough; his summoner had seen to that through some cruel, intense lessons. Drox had grown used to communication among the other familiars.

He had decided to dull his small loneliness with a little cat-and-mouse, a little conversation, and a shared meal—all provided at the expense of the human. Surprisingly, the target of his communication cum feeding, just sat itself down and brushed off the dirt picked up when Drox had spat it out. It made no attempt at the running or praying or begging that were to have been a part of the Dirak's predinner entertainment. Perhaps some sentients developed the same kind of morbid fatalism that Drox had seen in trapped animals, or perhaps the Slews made such a good hunting ground because its residents were too spiritually lethargic to resist death, in Dirak form or any other.

The man spoke first. "Well, creature, I reckon you're the one who's been thinnin' out the gentry round here."

"(Ah, so I am known!) Yesss, and pressently I will eliminate you asss well!" Drox's too-long vertical lips made him hiss in his speech, but his words should have stepped up the terror in the prey.

"I figured as much. That weren't no hayride you took me on! So, I'm to be supper, eh?" The toothless old man laughed and slapped a knee.

This human was anything but lethargic! The conversation had already taken a turn that the predator hadn't expected. Drox suspected his own lack of experience had misled him, since he had not actually conversed with any other human than his master. On the other hand, simple, instinctive self-preservation should have had this bony hulk gibbering in fear and running by now. Since he had meant to learn more about humans from the encounter, Drox decided to ask a few questions.

"Why, human? Why do you not fear me?"

"Oh, come to that, I suppose I do fear you, ye great, purple cabbage. By the Thousand Stars, what a mouthful of teeth! But my system is so pumped up right now that I'm somewhere on the other side of fear. I'm from the Slews, ye see, and old, too."

"Ssso?"

"Wellsir, you don't get old in the Slews, ye see. Not only that, but I've been everywhere and done everything. I've caught all the right boats just to last this long. I've bumped up against the Death Angel so many times that he's pretty near an old friend! Being near death kind of makes me numb now, but not scared much. By the way, that old friend of mine is hanging about us right now. I've never rightly seen him before, but I ain't scared to go off with him."

Drox had been concentrating on the conversation too closely, or he would have felt his magic sensors tingling. He had heard of the shadowy agent of the true Life Giver who haunted all the Planes, but he had never looked for him. Until recently, Drox had not killed enough sentients to have had many chances to see that being in action. His master had always hustled him away from the arranged death scenes, and the Dirak had made it a policy to vacate the site of his own kills immediately. Now, a peek with an inner eye did show an ethereal figure hovering near the clearing: sometimes swooping near; sometimes pulling back into distant shadows. The death of a sentient was soon to take place (but Drox knew that). Still, he had never heard of that being, who carried souls back across Elsewhen, as having stayed more than a fraction of a second in one place.

The shadow shape paused for a moment over the old man, an unearthly hand draped in comradely fashion about the human's shoulders. Drox heard an almost-sound of whispering. The human giggled with glee.

"My old friend says he's going to reveal a bit to you about your own death. He says it's been a long time since he got to pick up a Dirak, and he's looking forward to it! Lookee here, all-teeth-and-no-brains: puzzle this out, if you can. He says, 'The Dirak can only be killed by a human's metal weapon older than himself.' He seems doggone certain that that will happen soon enough!'' The ancient human cackled again.

That last dig was more than Drox could stand. With a lunge, he covered the man and crunched him, but the dry laughter seemed to go on and on in his gut. Worse, a splintery shinbone slipped past his crushing teeth and reached Drox's soft, organic interior. Its jagged end rammed into the duct of his parapharangeal glands and stuck there. Drox wasn't able to chew without pain for days. On top of it all, the bony beast gave him indigestion! Mother thing had warned him against playing with his food before he ate it. He so wished he had heeded her advice, this once, that it made him almost sorry he had eaten her.

". . . a human's metal weapon older than himself." Hah! Drox decided that he had been on the receiving end of an unfunny practical joke by some supernatural clown, who had gotten tired of the monotony of his job and decided to interfere in someone else's business. No, there was no cause to worry. Drox had been an adult for many centuries before a human smith on this Plane had worked his first, raw lump of copper into a knife. There was surely nothing to fear. Yet . . .

· 3 ·

Harmon Yorn, the newly hatched adventurer, was badly hung over. Only last night, he had been a down-and-out grain merchant's son, just as last night, instead of plan-plan-planning, he had drunk-drunk-drunk up every last copper in his shrunken purse to celebrate that newness. He stalked on, in anticipation of treasures to come, wincing as he turned across the bazaar. There was a shorter route to Pimpgut Way through the Town's twisting streets, but he hadn't been able to remember it this morning. He was still headed toward a magical old man and his own destiny.

If the sun hadn't been at his back, his eyes would have bulged their painful, reddened selves out of his skull. Sadistic imps had taken residence behind them and were pushing, pushing, pushing. His walk wasn't his steadiest, and his hand clutched at his mistreated middle, but the discomforts did not distract from his goal. He was an adventurer—now!—today! Dragons beware! With the illogic of those whose blood had been too thinned by alcohol, he meant that entirely. He was quite ready to dismember a Dragon, if one of those extinct, semimythical beings crossed his path—especially if it made any loud noises. The few Townsmen crying their wares at this early hour were making an enemy of him with their racket.

He trudged across the bazaar, among the fruit rinds and splintered crates, stepping heedlessly among the undesirable by-products on the ground with the practiced tread of the Upcruster. He could recognize visitors, newcomers, and the inexperienced elite from the city's north end by their unique gait. They always stopped every few meters to clean their shoes and look disgusted—exactly as the party ahead of him was doing at that moment. Too late he realized that he knew them, and worse, one of them had recognized him.

Melinda, the daughter of Aragon the wine-merchant, and Gargina, her fat crab of a mother, had been nimble-footing across the bazaar. Gargina was as tight as a priest's purse with her coin. She had probably dragged Melinda down to the roaring, stinking bazaar in the early morning to buy lace or something. The old crow wouldn't trust her servants to haggle for her, though she did have the horse sense to have brought along two burly housemen with cudgels to clear the ladies' way.

Melinda wasn't at all like her. In fact, Melinda was different from the other girls that various matchmakers had tried to set him up with. In the past, when Harmon had still been receiving invitations to polite social gatherings, he had grown more than fond of her. There had been talk of marriage between them, as well as negotiations of dowries between their two families. However, Harmon's self-inflicted decline in social status and Gargina's objections had frosted the romance—that and Harmon's being thrown bodily off the wine merchant's property: twice. He might have persisted if he had not already been turning more and more to . . . adventuring.

Until today, that adventuring had been entirely in the form of wetting down his brain with drink and listening to heroic tales in the taverns. Jolted back to his mission, he started quickly on his way again.

Melinda intercepted him. Like a dinghy slipping away from a barge, Melinda (and her professionally invisible bodyguard) had peeled away from Gargina under the cover of the crowd. She stepped squarely in front of Harmon with her little feet planted (never mind in what). With her fists on her hips, she came just up to his shoulder. Her red lips were pouted, just right to bend down and—no! Feelings swam in the backs of her eyes. He recognized "pity," with a bit of "disgust," but there were other emotions there for him that should have faded months ago.

"Harmon," she said. "Oh, Harmon." She reached out without thinking to tug the threadbare drapes of his cloak together. Of the pair, she had always been the neat one.

"How have you been keeping yourself, Melinda?" he asked, croaking, trying for a tone that hid what he was feeling.

"I have been well. And you?"

It was almost as if she were looking past the three-day beard stubble, past the soured-wine smell, past the stains and wear. Harmon felt that she was looking directly into his heart, as only someone in lov—no!

"I've been doing fine." He squared his shoulders. "Uh . . . I'm on my way to kick off a new quest right now, as a matter of fact." He lifted his chin and tried to look heroic instead of hollow, but it didn't come off, not for her.

"Oh, Harmon, aren't you ever—"

"No! Not until I've made my way as a real man: a hero; an adventurer!" No one was going to divert him from his rightful path. He squared his jaw until the molars hurt. "You should find some else. Marry. (Oh, how I don't mean it! But what would a hero say?)"

"Mother wants me to marry Elgo, the son of Muringo the clothier." She turned her eyes downward.

A vision of Elgo's moonlike face—round, yellow, and cratered—rose in Harmon's memory as the bile rose in the back of his throat. He couldn't let—

"Harmon Yorn! I might have known! Come, Melinda!" Gargina's meat-hook hand whipped around Melinda's arm and flicked her away before Harmon could voice another word. He was left staring up into the eyes of the two cudgel bearers. Their faces said, "We threw you out before. . . ." He understood. He turned north. They turned south.

Although it was only a few minutes' walk to the Scoop off Pimpgut Way, Harmon was already later than he had planned to be. A ring of children had already gathered around the old teacher he had come to confront. The man was drawing letters on the whitewashed wall as Harmon came up behind the group. Harmon was struck by the fact that no one had seemed to notice that that piece of wall stayed perpetually clean, despite continuous use.

He had counted on meeting the magician alone. He stopped outside the sprawled pack of street urchins, unsure how to proceed with a crowd present. The teacher/sorcerer turned and looked Harmon in the eyes. That gaze rolled through Harmon's soul like a bucket of ice water. His hangover disappeared, struck by cold lightning.

"Well, young man, it seems that Jessup finally told his tale." The old eyes twinkled brightly, and he clapped his hands. "Children! Children! This young man came here today to tell us a comic tale, but he must depart sooner than planned. I will quickly have to tell you the gist of his story, before some other clever tale spinner steals his idea." He chuckled in anticipation.

Harmon's jaw sagged idiotically. It wasn't supposed to go like this at all!

"It seems," the Old Man said behind a smirk, "that in this tale *I* am a sorcerer." He tapped his chest. "And . . . and I am even a *master* magician." His face reddened, as if he were barely able to contain his mirth.

The children began to giggle. Harmon's mouth worked, but no sound came out.

"And . . . and I am even one of the Masters of the Mysteries, with a great magical secret to guard." He puffed, choking on a belly laugh.

The children were laughing fully now. The Old Man waved a limp, laughter-washed hand, and Harmon found himself laughing with them. Sweat popped out on his forehead; he simply couldn't stop laughing. The magician paused to wipe his streaming eyes before continuing.

"And my magical secret is . . . is *I always tell the truth*!" The old mage slumped back on his stool and guffawed until he had to hold on to the wall.

The children were leaning against each other, roaring in their tiny voices and slapping the ground. None of them seemed to notice that no tale told so indirectly could be *that* funny. Harmon couldn't enlighten them because he was in the throes of a belly laugh that threatened to knock him to his knees. Within him, his heart was pounding, and he was scared white.

Everyone winded themselves, and the mass of mirth subsided, but the damage had already been done to Harmon's plans. The "comic tale" (that had never actually been told) would reach every corner of the Town by nightfall as surely as if Harmon had shouted it from the center of the bazaar. No one would find it nearly as funny as the children had, but everyone would remember its oddity. Remembering, they would dismiss it, if they ever heard the tale again. Only a fool would always tell the truth, in Barrow or anywhere else.

"I'm sorry you have to leave so soon," the teacher said, bringing his group back to reality. "We might have had some more good times."

Harmon found that, indeed, he *had* to leave. His legs were taking care of the matter for him, without his volition.

"You'll need your rest, young man!" The ancient's voice called.

Harmon realized that just as the Old Man had suggested, he needed rest so badly that he could barely hold his eyes open. Something waved his hand for him in a weak farewell. He toddled groggily for a couple of blocks and fell sloppily asleep in a patch of weeds. The residents of the house whose yard had become his bed had died months before in a cross fire between two drug-running gangs; however, it was generally believed that they had been the victims of some nameless plague. Harmon's body among the weeds was left quite alone.

• 4 •

The sun rolled across the top of the day as I taught the ring of youngsters. As evening came on, they scattered to their homes. I brushed the remnants of letters of mud and charcoal from the white wall, tidying up the loose ends of the day. Walking the short distance to a particular blind alley, I opened the nexus to Elsewhen that I had created there. To anyone but a user of magic, there would have been no trace of the road I stepped onto, and even a mage would have had to look closely to detect the puckering in three-dimensional space that marked my exit.

I needed to meditate before facing Harmon Yorn. The Plane that housed my possessions and my laboratories was tiny, one of the myriads of "empty rooms" left by godlings long past. Most of such beings had tired immediately of assembling and manipulating their pocket universes, preferring instead to return across Elsewhen, either to humble themselves and align with the Great God or to join the rebellion against Him. They had abandoned Planes half-formed, without either shape or natural laws. One such had become my new base, after fleeing another with all my possessions. I had wanted to avoid a confrontation with Fraximon. Poor Fraximon!

Seated on a throne of blue-veined stone, I mused: I could have stopped then and let Harmon Yorn go back to his life. Perhaps I had meddled enough. I sighed as I remembered the promises I had made to a woman long ago.

She had first been a child, another face among my gatherings of children. She had come and gone, as they all did, and I had cared for her, as I cared for them all. She had come back, year after year, as others dropped away and were replaced. She never tired of learning; she loved me as a child does her teacher. After her parents died, she still found ways to come to listen, but she was growing taller and older. I shielded her, as I had promised to shield all my children until they left learning on their own.

Except that . . . she didn't leave. The eyes of a child became the eyes of a woman, and she loved learning yet. And she loved me. She saw through the adult mystery that the other children overlooked, and still she loved me! I found, in the surprise of the ages, that I loved her as well—no longer as a teacher loves a student, but as a man loves a woman. I never before or since knew anyone who loved wisdom and knowledge the way she did.

Because of the Secret that held my power, I could not deny her the protection I had promised my students as long as she chose to learn. And she never tired of learning! When she asked me if I loved her, I tried to deny it, to myself and to her, but that Secret wouldn't let me!

Oh, how I wish I had her touch of humanity beside me again! What poor substitute it is to meditate beside a coffin of blue stone in a palace that no mortal eye but hers has ever seen.

· 5 ·

As the last orange edge of the sun slid below the horizon, Harmon Yorn woke, thoroughly rested. For the first time in weeks, he had almost no hangover. He *had* needed sleep, no matter the unnatural way he had obtained it. If he had taken less time in waking, he might sooner have remembered the deep fear hidden in his bones, ready to harry him as he ran away. All the stories he had heard about encounters with magicians had not prepared him for the reality. However, as he sat up, he looked straight into the face of the old magician.

The sorcerer was standing at the edge of the weedy lot, eyeing Harmon thoughtfully. "Well, young man, you did hear Jessup's tale, then? Do you think the telling of it will make him more famous?"

"No," Harmon answered. "I doubt he tells it even once more."

Harmon's head was unusually clear. From his experience earlier, he was certain that the Old Man could go further than asking quiet, innocent questions. The mage could squeeze answers from Harmon as easily as he could mash pulp from ripe fruit. Harmon answered truthfully: he had no desire to play another round as human puppet or to have his brain reamed out for answers the wizard thought he was holding back. Perhaps he really was a kindly, old soul, who wouldn't go that far, but there was no doubt that he could press Harmon in any way he desired.

"Sooo . . . Whatever am I to do with you, young man?"

The fear left Harmon's bones and tried to take refuge in the deepest recesses of his soul. The mage's question was like the riddle "Where does a thousand-kilo bear sleep? Anywhere he wants to!" A Master of the Mysteries need have no more care for Harmon than Harmon had for a mouse. Harmon wondered briefly who had made up all those stupid stories about adventurers overcoming magicians. So far, adventure was fear, danger, and a sour taste in the throat.

"You could make a bit of trouble for me," the Old Man said grimly.

"(Oh?) But I would never—"

"The children will kill the story, true, but not altogether. If you insisted, really insisted, enough to make nosy people ask the wrong questions or look for witnesses . . ." He paused as if in thought. "It's difficult to tell exactly how much you remember of Jessup's story, and how much you will remember later. It is just possible that you could be a nuisance to me."

Icy little birds began to sing a song along Harmon's nerves, about his spending the rest of his existence as a tree toad.

"You could, for example, keep on loudly—and probably drunkenly—proclaiming the truth of your tale. Sooner or later, someone would believe you enough to bother me about it." He looked *very* displeased.

Continued life as a tree toad or anything else was beginning to seem good to Harmon.

The Old Man continued. "I am satisfied with my present situation. It has taken me many years to establish it, here in Barrow. Harmon—oh, do stop shaking so! I haven't decided to disincorporate you—just yet." He chuckled.

Harmon relaxed slightly, but he wasn't sure he should be relieved "just yet."

"I've decided to offer you a bargain," the sorcerer said.

Harmon had heard many stories about the kinds of "bargains" magicians offered. The mortal bargainer usually ended up dead or suffering eternally on some alien Plane. On the other hand, he was in no position to refuse to listen.

"Harmon, I have decided to offer you what you need the most. In exchange, you will never, never repeat the story you heard about me."

Harmon's brain told his mouth to say, "Sounds good to me!" but the words that came out were, "And if I (gulp!) refuse?"

It felt as if someone else were moving his lips. He opened his mouth to retract the words, but the Old Man's rheumy eyes met his and seemed to grow until they filled the universe. Dark pupils opened into a cold, empty nonexistence, a place where frail humanity could not venture and remain whole, sane, or human.

"You know my Secret, Harmon. I wasn't entirely joking about your disincorporation!" The eyes receded, and the void was replaced by the harmless, ancient face of the mage.

"Oh, I agree! I agree! It was just a theoretical question!" Harmon was almost babbling, with a cold sweat soaking his body.

"Good. Now, as to what you will receive: you want with all your heart to be an adventurer. You shall have that adventure. Jessup's tale included the fate of Fraximon the Terrible Stump, whether you remember that part of it or not. He is gone now, and all his minions are returned to their proper Planes—save one. That one remains in the swamps beyond the Slews. It has killed many already. It will kill again soon. You will kill *it*!"

"But—but—but—but—"

Harmon had planned to ease gently into the sea of adventure, not try to swim across it on the first try. But an adventure—a real adventure!—with real blood and magic: suddenly there were more stars in his eyes than the reflections of all the Thousand Stars above. He wasn't afraid anymore. He was making a deal with a sorcerer as an adventurer should! When that was done, he would be off to fight a . . . a monster, surely, but as a *hero*! He found himself on his toes, leaning forward.

Whoa, here! He had been about to omit an important part of such transactions: the magician wasn't supposed to send the adventurer off unequipped. "Say, just a second! How am I supposed to kill this thing—bare-handed?" This time he was sure: he had moved those lips himself. His bravery was as much a surprise to him as his earlier speech.

"No, son, I'll give you enough gold to buy a good sword, but be warned: it had better buy metal, *not* wine!"

"Oh, sure! Sure, it will!" For an instant, Harmon had felt the touch of a spell that could have polymorphed him into a tree toad. "But what about the . . . er . . . reward?" If Harmon knew the rules of adventure, surely the Old Man did.

"Your life isn't enough?" The magician began a threatening gesture.

(Gulp!) "I . . . I guess so." Bravery had retreated from the field, leaving Harmon looking up from his shoe tops at the frowning sorcerer.

The Old Man's face softened. "You're right, son. What's an adventure without treasure? You'll find that creature's hide will be worth quite a lot to a smith or a weapons maker. Catching comes before skinning, though!"

"Am I supposed to do in your monster with only a sword? Won't a magician's familiar be tougher than that?" Something in Harmon's mind had said, "Why not up the ante one more time?" Another part of that mind was running about with a net trying to catch more such crazy impulses before they escaped through his mouth.

"Very well," the mage agreed. "I suppose that you do need a little more protection, knowing the beast as I do. Here."

His palm uncurled to show a tiny, silvery cylinder with a button at one end. Harmon handled it gingerly. He looked up with a question, but the magician anticipated it.

"What is a hero without some magical help? When you are in the greatest danger, press the button. You will be instantly transported safely off this Plane. Press it again to return to the locus you left. It will work as many times as you press the button." He held up a hand to restrain Harmon's questions. "It will take you to an interesting . . . place called Elsewhen. You will be in no danger from Fraximon's monster there. Now, young man, 'but' me no more but's, if you value your life." His hands made a whirling gesture.

Harmon cringed back, but the gesture had had another purpose. The Old Man was gone—just gone. Like a breaking harp string, Harmon dropped into the mashed weeds and shook. Darkness had fully come by the time his sweat had dried and the goose pimples had stopped playing tag on his spine. Looking around, he discovered that he had nowhere to go. He couldn't go home, not yet, nor to a tavern to ease his thirst. All the coin he had was the magician's gold, in a small bag he had found dropped by his feet. He dared not wet his throat as it cried to be wetted, not and be sure of continued existence. Promises to that wizard were meant to be kept! Besides, he didn't want to jeopardize what might be the one chance at an adventure in his entire life. He would find no weapons maker to sell him a sword after dark, not with the human predators of Upcruster Town beginning to emerge from their lairs. Even the abandoned house behind him looked none too safe. This miserable weed patch would have to do until after sunrise tomorrow.

As the here-and-now gradually crowded out the after-effects of his shock at awakening, Harmon realized that the great adventure was off to anything but a rousing start. Why did adventure feel so much like misery? That hadn't been in the sagas at all. He was already sick of being terrified, of sweating like a pig, of urinating on himself when his life was threatened, of *having* his life threatened. His next test, instead of some properly heroic deed, was to hold this cold, hard piece of ground against the terrors of nighttime Barrow. Tonight would be a toss-up between the two-legged sharks who nosed everywhere, seeking those moneyed and unarmed, and pneumonia.

As he huddled by the ruined house and shivered through the damp of the night, he began to worry about where he had heard the name Elsewhen before. As alcohol continued to leave his unretoxified brain, his teeth rattled like a prostitute's bracelets. As the dew formed on his nose, he cursed himself for drinking up his own money—money that might have bought him a warm room, had he been brave enough to creep through the lightless streets to an inn. It was a miserable, desperate Harmon who set out in the dawn light for the bazaar, marching to the pace of his shivering knees.

First, the sword. First—first—first, the sword. He strode up and down, down and up the bazaar, chanting the thought over and over, waiting for something to open. He had let his discomforts drive him there too early. Mama Threechin's cooks let him warm himself by their chimney, but he looked too much like a beggar to be let inside before opening time. He could have wakened Bargo, sleeping behind the counter of his beer stand, but Bargo sold beer only. Harmon was still too frightened by the mage's threats to risk a drink before he had a sword in hand.

The first swords maker to open his heavily shuttered booth threw Harmon out at sword's point. He had almost overwhelmed the man in his eagerness to enter and strike a deal. After he had retreated and given the matter some thought, Harmon couldn't blame the weapons maker. Thieves had often played first-customer-of-the-day to rob unwary merchants.

Forced restraint made Harmon enter the next swords maker's shop peacefully. He actually drove a pretty fair bargain for the weapon he chose. Father had long ago paid to have Harmon trained in swordsmanship. Though there hadn't been a war in Barrow in three decades, there had never been more robbers. Harmon's conglomerate appearance—gold in the hand, a mass of crusted clothing, and eyes red enough to cut metal—had thrown the weapon smith off his haggling style.

Harmon left the booth with one remaining gold piece and a handful of copper, though he had trouble counting it with trembling fingers. Had he been thinking clearly, he would have gone back to Mama Threechin's for breakfast. Sustained misery had unmoored him enough that before he knew it, his feet were carrying him toward his favorite tavern. Committed, he headed north to the Gryphon and Goblet with his new sword flopping in its scabbard like a dark phallus.

He burst rudely into the common room, but he caused no stir. Those who had slept the night there were far past being awakened by a door opening suddenly. Yesterday morning, Harmon had been sleeping there himself. Barrelgut looked up from trimming flakes of silver from a coin that he planned to pass off to some drunk as full weight. After one disdainful look, the bartender ignored Harmon entirely.

Barrelgut was a vault of indifference for anyone who lacked money. For any services, if you wanted something, you could ask. Harmon had paid Barrelgut his last copper to sleep in a booth night-before-last. He was therefore as likely to get attention from the chubby tavern owner as were the snoring inebriates behind the back tables.

Harmon wavered forward and dropped onto a rickety stool at the bar. "Fooood!" he croaked, with a throat that wanted to scream for wine. He clinked a copper on the bar top.

Barrelgut was immediately alert. "Lad, don't you usually have, say, a bit of something to wash the dust down first?" All of Barrelgut's beverages had a higher markup than his meals, and they were presently closer at hand.

"Nooo . . . Just some food." Harmon's knuckles were white on the edge of the bar. "'Aannd . . . a *small* glass of Canary Red to wash it down."

"Canary Red! Lad, that stuff has no more kick than a dead grasshopper." It also was a low-profit item; where there was one copper, there might be another.

"Just the Canary Red!" Harmon rasped through teeth clenched in the pain of withdrawal.

"Whatever," Barrelgut said.

The tall bartender ambled back toward his seldom-visited kitchen and returned with a plate of . . . something. "Something" was the food specialty of the tavern. Harmon had had no past experience with it, except to know that the Gryphon served some kind of food.

Its quality made it obvious why the tavern served many drinks and few meals. It was organic, and for the most part, it had stopped moving. Some of its components had once been cereals, and others resembled vegetables. The meat—you didn't ask. The whole had been heated and reheated, topped off with more questionable ingredients, and generally mistreated into a gray, amorphous sludge. You had to be hungry.

Harmon was hungry. It was all he could do to keep from bolting the mess in three bites, a tribute to the anesthetic effect that repeated applications of alcohol had on taste buds. The wine did go in three gulps. Though the best adjective that had ever been applied to that vintage was "awful," it contained alcohol—life-giving alcohol! In an event of cosmic rarity, Harmon ordered seconds of "something"; it gave him an excuse to have a second glass of Canary Red. His shaking hands spilled some of it.

Through the haze in his mind, Harmon clung single-mindedly to beginning his adventure. In an act of incredible bravery, he stopped drinking with money still in his pocket. That one gold piece might end up as his sole treasure from this jaunt. He thrust two coppers across the bar at Barrelgut and suggested that he invest them in hiring a cook. That was such a standard comment at the Gryphon that Barrelgut considered it a private joke between him and his regulars. The burly bartender went back to shaving the coin and practicing his sneer as Harmon lunged out the door.

He had been fed and watered, if inadequately. Now, if Harmon was to kill some bloody monster, then he would go kill the thing, and no son of a pig had better get in his way! He started toward the Old Wat Bridge as rapidly as his quivering legs and acrobatic stomach would let him, trying to ignore the microscopic voice in the back of his mind that kept screaming for him to wake up to the madness he was afloat in. Two muggers, dry from a night of unsuccessful thievery, moved to intercept him, until they saw the way his hand gripped his sword's hilt. Harmon marched on intently, without noticing them.

The Slews emerged before him from its early-morning cloud. Its noxious vapors, which could not charitably be called "fog," were beginning to clear as he crossed the high arch of the bridge. Skirting the beggars sleeping near the bridge footing, he rolled on through the bizarre architecture that characterized the Slews in its years of decline. Unkempt business houses, mostly of marginally legal nature, gave way to the sturdy shacks and leaning tenements of Slews-Inside-the-Walls. The dozing gate guards ignored him. Few residents saw him; fewer cared.

If one ignored the barely habitable piles of the citizens of Slews-Outside-the-Walls, the swamp beyond was almost lovely. It would have taken an exceptional aesthete to have ignored the stink. Even Harmon's numbed nostrils were offended. He plunged ahead, eager to find the creature and spike its black, little heart with his sword. Too much of Harmon's intellect was also numbed, or he might have noticed how minimally his desire meshed with reality.

His entire system was hurting. The blood was buzzing in the veins in his legs as their sensations reawakened, but the incredible breakfast that was entering those vessels threatened to halt circulation. It was surprising that his muscles worked at all. His eyes felt like cinders. If a killing would let him rest and drink, let him wet his throat properly as a true hero, let him soothe his fears in wine once more, then a killing was to be done and soon. His brain, the most sensitive of organs, was overmatched by exhaustion, alcohol withdrawal, and bad food, and it had been driven into a hopeless muddle.

Now, all he had to do was find the god-awful *thing*! This was no time for subtlety: Harmon marched directly to the boundary ditch of the swamp and started across. He went immediately hock-deep in slime: no go. He backed out and tried a hundred paces to the right: more slime. This time, he slipped and covered his whole right side in mire. After two more muddy misadventures, Harmon looked like a chocolate dessert with two red eyes for cherries. The mud finally prevailed over desperation and anger. Harmon was forced to stop and ooze, confronted by a mindless barrier that threatened to end his career as an adventurer at the bottom of some sludge pit.

He *must* prevail! Something inside kept pushing, pushing, though another tiny, shrill voice kept begging him to quit and run away. There had to be a way in! The rusty gears of his mind began to turn. As the mud coalesced into flakes on his skin, he noticed the narrow trails that had been worn between the shacks. All he had to do was follow them until he found one that crossed the sewage ditch to the swamp.

Smugglers had trails that entered the swamp; it was common knowledge. The midnight merchants had been so long established that no prince or empire had ever done more than scratch the surface of their organizations. Enough feet treading the scanty firm ground in the swamp would have packed it into trails. The smuggler paths would be many, branched, and winding, but anyone should be able to find them in daylight.

By midmorning, Harmon, proud of his deduction, had found a trail crossing into the bogs. It was next to a shack occupied by a gaggle of slum dwellers, mostly children of stairstep ages. The residents decided that he was some rich tourist when he purchased a drink of questionable water and a loaf of hard, black bread from them for a copper. Their eyes implied that they would have swarmed him with teeth and nails in the hope of finding another copper if he hadn't kept his hand on his sword. He was the alien among them, though his appearance would have made him alienated almost anywhere. The whole thing was crazy, his inner voice insisted, part of a day assembled by an insane puzzle maker.

Off into the swamps: hi-ho! The trail did indeed branch, but smugglers liked wading no better than Harmon did. They had long ago found every ridge of solid footing through the morass. Luckily, they had gotten out of the habit of building traps on specially faked trails to discourage uninvited explorers. Too many gangs had rapidly succeeded others in the chaos of the Slews. Abandoned pitfalls couldn't tell honest smugglers from revenue men. The tax men had generally given up on the swamps anyway, unable to watch all the nocturnal routes, no matter how obvious the trails were in daylight. Thus, Harmon walked safely, saved by a discontinued practice of which he had never been aware.

On dry ground, Harmon could have walked the fifteen or twenty kilometers to the seacoast in a few hours. Fast travel in the swamps for even short distances was difficult, but the mage had implied that the monster would be found in the part of bogs fairly close to the city. Even so, Harmon soon realized that penetrating the swamp was not the same as finding the monster. Even this small end of the sloughs could easily hide a company of monsters. By the Thousand Stars, he might have to search for days! Why hadn't this come up before, such as last night, when he had had plenty of thinking time? One part of his mind kept crowing I-told-you-so's as another part shushed it.

Harmon was not about to admit to himself how little thinking he had been doing lately. If he had only insisted on getting the answers to a few more questions! On the other hand, if he *had* insisted, he might now be entering this swamp hopping and croaking amphibiously. Standing in the center of a soggy trail, he reviewed the Old Man's words. The killer thing was due to feed again soon. Reasonably, if Harmon were supposed to stop it, finding it should have presented no problem. Yet before him lay kilometers of gooey green, looking bigger by the minute. The flakes of mud dribbling off him were a reminder of how little this swamp cared for a direct human attack.

He sat down on a stump barely within the swamp's boundary. His mind groaned into action like a rusty crank forced twice in one day. He pursued flocks of head-hurting ideas through the thickets of his mind, but they all went to ground at the same place: he needed more information. He was not about to face the Old Man again to get it, but maybe the locals knew something. They couldn't have lived near a man-killer without seeing at least a little. He rose in resignation and began to trudge back toward the shacks.

Loosening the sword in its scabbard, he dug out his last copper coin and hid the gold piece deep in his garments. He was resolved not to die by being mugged by a pack of slum children for pocket change. A hero deserved better than that. The fearsome, red-eyed, mud-covered hero, ignoring the dregs of his d.t.'s, slogged down a muddy path toward the outskirts of a slum. Ho, for the life of adventure! Ho.

· 6 ·

Droxdromixalangdang the Dirak wasn't exactly worried, but he was uneasy. Curse that bony old man! Drox had been off his feed for days while the damage healed in his pharynx. Nothing normally passed his metal-sheathed teeth unshredded to damage his softer organic interior. That one splintered bone had been just a fluke. The old human's prophecy had been pure twaddle, no matter which immortal had thought it up! Time to put all this silliness behind him.

He flared his rose-petal nostrils and sifted the wet air. Ahhh! The game was afoot once again. With a vertical rictus of a smile on his maw, the Dirak eased from his resting pool and began the stalk toward the smugglers' path.

· 7 ·

Harmon waved the copper piece back and forth, back and forth. Seven pairs of eyes followed it.

"Now, one more time: tell me about the monster in the swamp."

They seemed to be an unusually obtuse group. Harmon failed to recognize the peasants' I-don't-know-nuthin' routine, predating all the forms of authority that it was meant to frustrate. Some Stone Age chieftain had first seen it when he had come to confiscate Ugg's bearskin.

Ugg's relatives had suddenly become incredibly stupid: they just couldn't remember where either Ugg or the bearskin was. This gathering of the unwashed, however, was held in thrall by a single copper piece. One finally broke.

A little girl spoke up. "Mister, mightn't you be talkin' 'bout the thing that carried off Chester and Snot-nose?"

"Maybe."

It was appalling to Harmon to imagine this unsanitary brood as having once been even larger, but the door had been opened. He would give the copper piece to the one that helped him the most, dangerous stranger that he was in their eyes.

"I has seen it," said the same little girl, followed by a tardy chorus of "me, too's."

They all moved in one step on Harmon. Perhaps their action was only harmless anticipation, but he withdrew his sword another few centimeters. They retreated the step.

"What's your name, small stuff? Say on, and the coin is yours." The girl had the inside track for now.

"I is Ollie. Well, mister, I seed his hands, kind of." Under his stare, she looked down at her bare toes drawing lines in the dirt.

"Go on."

"Well, it weren't 'xactly a hand. It had fingers and all, and some claws, but it had a big eye right in the middle."

"It had an eye in its hand?"

"Yes. We uns played a kind of game wif it."

The girl's dumpy, aging mother looked even more grim at that surprise news, if that were possible.

"What does the rest of it look like, besides the hand?"

The child fell silent. The group fidgeted, seeing their coin slipping away. The oldest girl stepped forward. She might have been pretty if she had been better fed and clean. Her eyes peered at him through a shock of hair as straggling as an abandoned field.

"I seen it," she said. "I seen it too well, when it got Gramper Jarvis! It looks like a great purple cabbage, with arms and legs. I seen it jump over Gramper Jarvis and carry him off. It had a great, huge mouth and ever-so-many teeth! Swallowed him whole, it did, and hopped off with him!" The pain of the memory showed in her face.

Her mother's frown lines deepened another notch; she must have just gotten another surprise. Harmon picked up the girl's hand and quickly folded the copper into it. He backed away from the unstable group, already muttering among themselves. The two pieces of disquieting news and the cash would be too much of a shock for him to get any more information out of them. He faded down the path, leaving the slum dwellers to work out what their shares of one copper should be. He now had plenty to think about.

His contemplation took him little farther than before. He was to watch out for a large, purple cabbage creature, with eyes in the palms of its hands and lots of teeth. The color was the best clue. The fog had burned away under the midday sun; everything was a bright green. Anything purple should show up well at a distance. Though he was already beyond tired and afraid, the pressure within to continue was relentless. So he was going into an unfamiliar bog to kill a predatory, purple cabbage: so what?

He turned again down the smugglers' trail.

· **8** ·

Drox was in position at his favorite ambush. Food would be along any minute now. Time for some fun!

Harmon was well away from the city when the flash of purple came—right in front of him! He had been walking with sword drawn for many minutes; the weapon had mindlessly crawled into his hand before he had gone a hundred paces. As if something within him was gradually letting his fear surface, his gut felt as tight as a bowstring.

The violet shape bounded into the path ahead. For one heartbeat, the antagonists faced each other eye to eye. A second later, Harmon realized that they were actually meeting eye to nostril. The claws surrounding the eyes themselves were poised to strike him from left and right. With all his force, he swung at the obscene cabbage shape. Surely, this was what being a hero was all about.

CLANG!

The sword bounced off! Harmon's hand felt as if he had slammed an anvil. There was only an obviously minor

dent to show where his sword had connected with the
monster. The creature bounced forward a step.

Fair was fair: The Dirak had agreed with himself to
give this warrior three free hits before he ate him. The
man had gone to a lot of trouble to find Drox, walking
through the swamp with his sword drawn. Why, that first
strike had almost tingled. As he advanced, the Dirak
smiled, a bloodcurdling spectacle in itself. Prey had been
known to collapse simply from the sight of the clustered
fangs protruding from top and bottom of his maw. Fear
in the game either made the meat taste better or made
for more interesting sport.

Harmon had wet himself during the first surge of adrenaline, but he hadn't had time to notice. He was, he knew,
dead meat. Running was useless. Somehow he managed
another goodly blow, horizontal this time. The sword
broke the monster's thumb coming around, so that it
dangled uselessly from the staring hand. The follow-through
also trimmed off an edge of one of the pink nostrils.
Great: at least he would go down properly. His racing
brain realized that the Old Man must have been pushing him, not to come here and kill this beast, but to
be killed by it. The book *Harmon the Hero* was about to
be closed out forever.
    WHING!
    The momentum of his last stroke had carried his blade
against the creature's body. The mistreated sword snapped
across the middle. Harmon was left with only a hilt and a
hand span of bent steel. A certain swords maker owed
Harmon a refund that he wasn't going to live to collect.
The monster roared in pain and flopped its damaged
hand. Its entire mouth opened wide; Harmon found that
it was just as well that he had already emptied his bladder.

Aaarrrrgh! That hurt! The hand would heal, but that
might have been an eye! His nostril was also tingling and
taking in driblets of his own purplish blood. Forget the
three free hits! No more Mr. Nice Thing! He whipped
open his maw and leaped.

His mind working at emergency speed, Harmon threw

the useless stump of his sword at the monster and leaped
to the right, off the trail. The open path was a death trap
where the bounding purple killer would finish him in
seconds. He began a crablike crawl as soon as he hit,
sprawling between two tree trunks. He had lucked into
one of the few patches of firm ground near the trail.
Harmon lunged to his feet and glanced back. A ring of
teeth larger than he was tall was flying directly at him!
He groped in his sash for the tiny, magic cylinder as he
threw up an arm across his eyes protectively. By not
viewing his death, he willed it to be negated.

Drox caught and swallowed the broken sword; it would
add spice to the meal. The warrior cum food had jumped
aside, much good it would do him. The Dirak turned left
toward his prey and leaped, opening his mouth fully.
WHAM!
His teeth slammed into the trees on either side of the
target. Only a few fangs in the upper and lower corners
of his mouth whipped forward to snag at the man. Drox
was jolted, but uninjured. Trees in this swamp were only
made of wood; one of the metal-organic trees of his
home Plane would have broken some teeth. He would
have to be more careful, advancing slowly to drive the
prey into water or the open. Even in close confines
between trees, he had only to get close enough to reach
the human with the claws of his undamaged hand.

Harmon felt the teeth ripping into his upthrown arm
and shins as padded blows. He knew distantly that he
was hurt, but he wasn't dead yet! His hand closed on the
mage's cylinder. Why hadn't he had it out all along? He
pushed the button.
POP!
The swamp, the sky, the monster—everything disappeared! A bleeding Harmon in his muddy rags remained,
drifting. It was not dark where he was, but no light
source stood in the bright grayness. He was floating or
falling or . . . something. This place wasn't uncomfort-
able, but lacked all tangible detail. At least he was out of
danger, as promised, but where, by the Thousand Stars,
was he?

*   *   *

POP!

The prey vanished right in front of the Dirak's reaching talons! His palms spasmed in the equivalent of a blink, but within a moment, his nostril caught the whiff of magic.

So.

That warrior had certainly been no magician himself, but he had fled across the Planar boundary into Elsewhen. Peering with his inner sight, Drox realized that the small item clutched in the human's hand was the source of the magic used in his escape. Drox couldn't follow him, but the situation presented no real problem. Elsewhen was familiar to the Dirak. Since no time passed there, the prey should be back very soon.

• 9 •

In Elsewhen all times passes, but no time passes. All time streams flow toward Elsewhen, and all Planes border it, just as all the rivers run to the sea, and all lands are lapped by one great ocean. All the paths, all the beings, all the forces that cross between the Planes of Forever must first cross it.

Human wizards go to Elsewhen to meditate or to sleep undisturbed—but only mages. Even the gods avoid it, spending only the briefest existence there, because it reminds them of something or Someone greater than themselves. Time is there: all of it and none of it. Its timeless realm is said to border another universe, one complete and infinite, and as like the Planes of Forever as the sky is like its reflection in a puddle. No one knows for certain, because no one goes beyond Elsewhen and returns, not even mages.

Harmon decided to rest where he was for a moment, although doing anything "for a moment" in this strange place seemed intrinsically wrong. He would go back to the swamp after a while, and if the monster were still there, he would simply *pop* back here again, wherever "here" was.

His wounds didn't feel quite natural. They hurt no more than when he had taken them, but they hurt no less. He was not bleeding now, but all the visible blood hadn't dried. He was neither hungrier nor thirstier than he had been the moment he had left the swamp, nor less so. Perhaps the strangeness of the place was beginning to get to him, or perhaps he was just feeling a delayed reaction to what he'd just been through. Speaking of which, it was time to see whether the cat still guarded the mouse hole.

POP!

Indeed it did: teeth, claws, and all!

POP!

He had better wait a good deal longer next time, but waiting presented the problem of counting time in this godforsaken place. Wait: he only had to be quiet enough to count off a thousand heartbeats. He listened to pick up the count.

There was no count! His heart was silent! Harmon screamed and clutched at his throat. No carotid pulsed there! He pawed at his wrist: no pulse! He beat at his chest and listened, but the errant pump had not been jolted back into action. He mentally begged his heart to beat.

Bump-BUMP! Bump-BUMP! Bump-BUMP!

He relaxed again; the beat stopped. He shrieked and thrashed: no beat! He commanded his heart to beat.

Bump-BUMP! Bump-BUMP!

He stopped struggling to concentrate on listening. No sound! No beat! He cried out. . . .

· 10 ·

In Elsewhen, all time passes but no time passes. Clocks won't run there, either mechanical or biological. Blood doesn't clot; tears don't fall when shed; hearts don't beat on their own. But minds and souls are higher functions than clocks or hearts or the repealed laws of matter and energy. They are even greater than time. A mind can order a breath to be drawn in Elsewhen, or a heart to beat or limbs to thrash or a voice to scream. Souls could command other, higher things, but most never do. No matter that souls are very like the beings that first placed the Planes; they usually follow the body as dependently as a loyal dog. The mortal mind cannot conceive of things for its soul to do that the body finds too alien.

Harmon shrieked and writhed, relaxed and listened, cycling into and out of terror, perhaps for millennia. Perhaps it was only seconds before he realized that he was taking no harm from his silenced heart, and stopped struggling. When he finally calmed enough to listen again, he heard . . . nothing, except some distant screaming borne back to him on a vagrant eddy of time. He could hear no beat, no breath, no life within him, but there was also no hunger, no pain . . . nothing. Nothing—unless he commanded it!

He wondered whether his wounds ached. They did, as long as he wondered, and they didn't, as soon as he turned his attention elsewhere. His mind swept through his body, gleefully switching organs and limbs on and off again. All of them were working! He simply had to tell them to. The child within the man began to play with the new toy that was his body.

After many circuits, the mind tired of the game. What was left then for the mind to explore, save the mind itself? Alone and safe, with only himself to face, he found that he did not want to look too closely at that part of Harmon. Better not to think at all than to slip and find yourself staring into some unpleasant inner mirror. He might have seen there that the true reason that he had chosen to escape first into fantasy and later into alcohol was to avoid a similar painful self-examination. That would have led to self-change, a process that he feared. Instead, he now saw in his new powers the portal to the ultimate escape.

On command, stop thinking!

After the undiluted successes at taming the other systems of his body, that command was, unexpectedly, a complete failure.

As all the rivers run to the sea, all times end at Elsewhen. Minds and souls can drift for an indefinable portion of eternity in its ever-tangling currents. All is possible to them within the microcosm of their body while there, save one thing: a mind cannot be a mind and stop thinking.

*   *   *

The more his mind blustered in its orders to itself, the tighter grew the spiral. To command the mind, thought was necessary, but thought was the thing to avoid. Harmon had trapped himself in an endless loop, an inner whirlpool that pulled him ever closer to himself. The laughing savage who formed one part of himself was eager to start digging to expose the whole self. Though the immature part (that had built a psychological cage around itself in order to *remain* immature) struggled, its maneuvers only drew it closer into the embrace of the other fragments of the self. With the eternity of Elsewhen as a tool, even a quickly averted glance at the nakedness of the rest would add up over the eons to an unfaceable totality.

Before he was overwhelmed by that unbearable sum, the superficial Harmon decided to try the mouse hole one more time. Surely—

POP!

Not only was the monster not gone, it seemed to be preparing for a killing leap toward the very spot where Harmon emerged.

POP!

Reminded forcibly of the terror without, the surface Harmon, the Harmon mask he had shown to the world, surrendered itself to the terror within. With his last image of the Dirak's all-too-tangible teeth before his eyes, Harmon allowed the whirlpool of fragmented Harmon personalities to drag him into it. The scrutiny was as painful as he had feared. It was as if he stood in a room with mirrors on every surface; yet, instead of an infinitely repeating set of images, each Harmon was an aspect of the whole rather than the image itself: some bodied, some bodiless.

Each would need an infinity to understand its complexity, but infinity was at hand. The dominant fragments within the multitude would not be satisfied until they had rolled over every stone that the conscious Harmon had wanted to leave unturned. They would insist on merging with the personality that had been directing the body but suppressing them.

He stood before a perfect mirror: naked. The wrinkles and obesity of his soul, that he had deceptively clothed to hide from others and from himself, were stripped by the mob. The many things that he was stood starkly revealed. One by one, he must take the dusty, sometimes ugly bric-a-brac from the shelves of his being and examine each piece. Some would be to keep forever; some, to discard in disgust.

· 11 ·

All the rivers run to the sea, but the sea is never full. All time runs to Elsewhen, but it doesn't spill over. Elsewhen is a function of Mind, bound by no temporal rules. Sorcerers go to Elsewhen to meditate or sleep. With that sleep come the dreams that are sleep's real function, dreams denied us by lives stretched in tension between mortality and godhood. When the dreams end or the meditation is full blown, we can return to our existence in the Planes. The graduation test of every apprentice magician is to be able to both enter Elsewhen and escape again.

To fail that test is madness and death.

Mortals trapped in Elsewhen must stay forever, without even a cosmic clock to mark their march toward a nebulous infinity of time. However, if a mortal were given a device that allowed him to come and go from Elsewhen (a device that only a mage of high level could prepare), then he, too, could leave when his meditations had been completed. Though he could escape Elsewhen, he could not escape that meditation. Elsewhen is a function of Mind: you must think as long as you are there.

Harmon drifted and thought, ran through his feelings as a mortal would play the strings of a lyre. Perhaps in the dimensionless distance he saw sorcerers or demons or gods flitting between an infinity of portals. He may have seen the streaks of color where some "scientific" magician shortcutted between Planes, but no one took notice of him. There were other mortals there, but most had gone insane after only brief mind-time exposure to the enormity of Elsewhen's sideless space.

There were eddies of time in Elsewhen, invisible to human senses, where time streams ran briefly parallel before mutually dissolving. Harmon rode one such, with time meandering like a sleepwalker. His heart beat intermittently on its own for a few minutes, and he was again aware of thirst and pain that could not be banished by mental command. He was swept near a pair of other mortals, asleep in each other's arms, adrift in eternity.

He recognized them, from Jessup's story, but he stopped short of wakening them. To what would he wake them? He knew that they would be rescued. That part of Jessup's tale was clear to him now, as were all his memories. Harmon, however, was part of another story, whose end he did not know, though he feared it. He only took away the sword of the young man. That action, also, was woven into Barrow's reality.

He now had a better blade, forged by some Saikhandian craftsman, to replace the one he had broken on the monster's hide. It lacked any touch of magic. With a charmed blade, he might have had a chance, but this sword had been ensorcelled only by the lives of the mortals who had formed it and carried it. That touch of mortality would be no better than a feather against the ravening purple beast that waited for him.

The Harmon who had entered the swamp was gone, though he yet bore the sword of an adventurer. The new Harmon had lived with himself, struggled with himself, faced himself for too many ages. Every memory from the former Harmon had been clearly etched, a book to be read and reread. The new Harmon was saddened that the book's title should have been *Portrait of a Self-deceiving Drunk*, but that sadness, along with his other emotions, had been smoothed by the erosion of eternity. He was uncertain how to title his new life. Ahead lay either death in the jaws of a beast, that had waited only moments now for one more human meal, or the eternal madness or sleep of a mortal stranded in Elsewhen.

He would probably be denied even madness. The presence of the escape device so near had held his mind together until it repaired itself. He was incurably sane now. He understood more than (he suspected) the Old Man had meant for him to know. Perhaps the magician had forgotten what Elsewhen did to certain mortals. Harmon had had more than enough time to think, more time than a magician would devote to meditation—all the time there was.

No more the hero: he wanted none of the empty misery of adventuring. He had rediscovered the things he deeply loved. He had shined a light into the destitute shell his life had become without them. The rawhide of his mind, with its childish, scribbled messages, had been cured into a supple leather scroll with its vital messages lettered clearly.

Now he was to die.

The hero-no-more, the retired adventurer must return to the Plane of his birth to fulfill the final function of all life. Perhaps he could wound the beast, making it easier for the next man who faced it to destroy the monster. Plainly, the Old Man could have done the job himself, but for no reason that logic had been able to grasp, he had sent Harmon to die between its teeth. Perhaps a swamp plant would be fertilized by his remains. That seemed a pitifully small accomplishment to be the total positive sum of his life, especially now that it had been hammered straight. He sighed and gripped the hilt of his sword. With his other hand, he pushed the silver button.

· 12 ·

Drox had been drawing himself back when he noticed that the food human had reappeared. The Dirak was just far enough away to pick up momentum for a terminal feeding lunge. The prey had a few seconds more for a final appreciation of life. Its lurching reemergence had brought it out upright, with its back against one of the trees that had saved it earlier—a perfect target. The little pest had gotten itself another sword from somewhere, much good it would do.

He leaped.

Memory, no matter how many times intensified, could not equal reality. All his meditation had not prepared Harmon for the avalanche of reactivated pain, the mud, the stink of his own body. He toppled, catching himself on his left knee and throwing his sword arm up for balance. He half fell backward, feeling the slam of a tree trunk against his right shoulder and against the knob at the base of his sword's hilt. He had meant to die fighting, to take at least one slice at the invulnerable enemy. Though the sword over his head was butted against the tree, it was pointed at a useless angle. It was impossible to pull it into position before the day was blotted out by a purple maw and its dagger teeth. His whole body, from sword point to toes, felt the impact.

He hurt.

Why didn't the monster finish it? Why did it pull back, after only wrenching the sword from his hand? He had come to die: must he be killed slowly? He steeled his mind.

Droxdromixalangdang thrust with his powerful hind limbs. His maw opened gracefully in midleap, and his teeth flared into killing position. He had felt the same surge of anticipation thousands of times before, but he never tired of it. Feeding was a Dirak's poetry. He sensed the solid impact of his mouth lining against the food and—

The pain! The awful *pain*! Something terrible had entered his nostril and driven a river of fire all the way to his brain! The whole world was *Pain*! PPAAIIIINNnnn! He convulsed! He was paralyzed! He con . . . vulsed. He was par . . . a . . . lyzed. He con . . .

• 13 •

Harmon leaned against the tree and wiped the blood from his eyes again. He hurt in too many places to count, but his mind had learned to give no place to pain unless he chose. The monster lay before him, in the center of a mat of crushed weeds and branches that it had churned up in its death throes. There was still an occasional twitch from the clawed limbs. In its agony, the creature had evacuated its maw, spitting out the stump of his first sword and a piece of splintered bone.

He idly picked up the hilt of the second sword that he had owned so briefly. The rest was broken off inside the mass of the beast. It was a pity to have lost it, though it had been worth it to save his life. The weapon had been unique for more than its workmanship: it had been the oldest sword in Barrow or anywhere else; infinitely old.

The Harmon of two days ago would have limped and whimpered until he reached the nearest tavern, blessing all the gods of luck. He could have used his last gold piece to drown the memory of his forced labor and near death. The tavern stories from his one adventure could have kept him in drinks for months to come, as it did other adventurers.

The new Harmon used the stump of his sword to hack one of the monster's purple skin leaves loose from its fleshy attachment. With his dulled, makeshift cutter, he patiently chopped two shiny teeth from their iron-hard roots. Wrapped in his cloak, they made all the load a wounded man could carry down a boggy trail. He covered the monster as best he could with brush. Animal scavengers would still find the body, but they wouldn't be interested in the metal. Human exploiters should be few in the area. Limping, Harmon started toward the city.

He staggered from the swamp: a muddied, bloodied scarecrow in red rags, carrying a makeshift bag that dripped purple, with eyes able to turn lesser men to shivery stone. He passed the shack of the slum family; only the oldest girl was outside. She was trying to sun the pain from the black eye and bruises that she had gotten trying to defend her only copper piece, ever. Though his face would have curdled milk from a white cow, she dared to stare back at him. She started in fear and bit reddened knuckles, but she did not flinch from his eyes.

Harmon had lived too many ages with the truth not to know: there was something better than the Slews about this girl. At the touch of her finite humanity, he could feel the unbearable weight of infinity leaving him. She was reality; he stopped in front of her. Reaching into his last surviving pocket, he extracted the gold piece remaining from the wizard's grant. He tossed it; she picked it out of the air like a sea gull striking a flying fish. He gimped on toward Barrow without a word.

Because it was the way of the Slews, the girl bit the coin. At the softness of gold on her teeth, wonder and unbelief spread across her dirty, tear-streaked face. The frown lines, that had been the forerunners of the crevices in her mother's face, turned outward in her first full smile since infancy. Harmon would have been pleased, had he ever looked back.

• 14 •

Jovorn the master smith had never seen such metal, but he prided himself in being open-minded about metallurgy. The wounded man who had brought him the sample watched him with eyes like molten iron as Jovorn tested it. One of the pieces, which this trader said were the teeth of some monster, was able to scratch cast iron easily. The chunk shaped like the leaf of some purple succulent left a telltale of gold on the smith's touchstone.

The stranger then drove a bargain in selling the metal to Jovorn that would have made Ibraim, the moneychanger, blush. The smith found it difficult to haggle without looking the other in the eye, but when he did, he found that hedging and double-dealing became impossible. In the end, he parted with more honest coin than he had intended, though he had not been cheated. Each tooth would become a unique dagger; Jovorn's mouth watered at the thought of the profit he was going to make selling the alien knives in sets and pairs. Once he figured out how to work the purplish metal, he would form it into pieces of armor affordable only by generals and higher nobility. He also sold the stranger six sturdy axes, to be delivered to the Gryphon and Goblet the next day.

Barrelgut had been ready to ask for cash in advance, until he had looked Harmon in the eye. The bartender knew that he would be paid, but he was not going through again what he had with the crazed wizard a few months before. Instead, he prepared the best room for Harmon, without being asked, and found him food that wasn't "something." He even procured a dented bathtub and had it filled with warm water.

After a bath, the healer that Barrelgut had sent for arrived, along with a clothier and boot maker. The healer bandaged Harmon's several wounds as the returned adventurer negotiated for two sets of clothing: one sturdy; one fine. He also needed new boots and a belt to replace others damaged beyond use.

The tavern began to fill with idlers who hoped to snap up some of the new trade (or to pick a pocket or two, or who were just nosy). Barrelgut's day-shift business was up. As flies will find a freshly dumped chamberpot,

Upcrusters smelled money, touched with that low taste of mystery that made it particularly interesting. In the midst of the bustle, Harmon hired an honest guard for his door, went upstairs, barred that door, and fell fast asleep.

With the main attraction retired to bed, Barrelgut noticed something strange: everyone in the room had been drinking—everyone except Harmon. Using water to bathe in wasn't too unusual in the Town, but *water* with food? What was this city coming to? My, how things did change, he thought, as he counted the day's unusually large receipts and pocketed a little more than his share. My, too, how they did stay the same!

• 15 •

A new dawning found Harmon sleeping as if he deserved his rest. Near noon, the young man with the ancient eyes emerged and paid off his watchman, with a small bonus for good service. When the food he had ordered from Mama Threechin's was delivered, along with some decent water, it brought with it another crowd to watch him lunch. It was a slow day in the Town, and he was developing into one of their favorite things—a moneyed oddity. Some had formerly known Harmon and offered to stand him to a drink. He stared them into silence.

A few called for the tale of what had happened to him, remembering that the Harmon of old loved a well-turned story. He curtly informed them that stories were for children and fools. The crowd took his blunt judgment to refer to themselves and were rather offended. This new Harmon had become a hard, one-sentence teetotaler overnight. His former acquaintances were put off, but like children, they were not off balance long. A few drinks of their own made Harmon's abstinence of no import, especially since he was hiring on the spot for cash.

Harmon bought by runner several large, tough grain sacks. He put out the word that he wanted good cudgel-and-ax men who weren't afraid of work. He wasn't taking just anyone: each applicant had to look him in the eye when promising faithful service and sealed lips. Some balked at this strangeness and remained unemployed. Some tried to lie and were sent away frightened, refusing to talk about the experience. Even the six who were finally chosen seemed relieved when the interview was over.

Harmon and his crew became a miniature parade as they crossed the Town toward the Old Wat Bridge, but followers dribbled off at every intersection. Seven men with axes and sacks were just not that interesting. The Slews ignored them, since they were neither rich nor unprotected nor seeking any of the slum's unique services. Neither were they agents of the law; so, they fell outside all categories of interest.

Harmon called a halt at the shack he had passed yesterday, in some earlier age of the world. He wordlessly folded a copper coin into the hand of each goggle-eyed child and gave a silver coin to their mother. They stood in an astonished line, as if they were trying to catch all the flies in the Wat River Swamp with their gaping mouths. Harmon noticed that the oldest girl was no longer among them.

Once his party was in the swamp, he took them directly to the carcass, remembering every centimeter of the muddy trail. He ordered the ax men to unship their equipment and move in on the purple remains. Until they had seen that body, his hirelings had been whispering "smuggler" behind his back. They were dismayed to learn that he expected them to hack up a reeking heap that couldn't make up its mind whether it was a decaying carcass or a pile of lavender, metallic scrap.

Harmon had chosen well. His crew went at the smelly task with a single, basic approach: copious sweat and hearty swearing. Through the heat of the day they cursed the bugs and the mud and company present and relatives distantly removed, but they kept on chopping until every distasteful chunk had been clunked into a sack. Harmon worked as hard as they did, injured or not, but he had become a man of few words, good _or_ bad.

Cursing and slipping under their loads, the bearers slogged out of the swamp. Back across the Slews and all the way into the city proper, their progress could be followed by anyone with an ear. By the time the tired procession reached the booth of the master smith, even their enthusiasm for the vocal side of their task had waned.

The smith was happy to see another load of the purple metal. It had proven to be almost as easy to melt as gold, but as hard as steel when set. The negotiations for the Plane's remaining supply of it began in earnest. A crowd gathered immediately, with Harmon's paid-off crew as the nucleus. Townsmen always harkened to their favorite music: coin clinking on coin, to the counterpoint of creative haggling.

The newcomer, a semisilent eccentric, was about to come up against a local champion in the fine art of negotiation. The smith had a number of fans in the crowd who admired him for his ability to acquire and keep other people's capital, but he had an equal number of enemies, for the same reason. Still, it was expected to be a mismatch, with the neophyte trader, Harmon, coming off badly skinned. Few people bothered to bet on the outcome, even in a crowd of Upcrusters. (Upcrusters had been known to bet on how many sparrows would fly over in the next ten minutes or the relative weights of rodents that would be first trapped by the rat catchers on a given day.)

The smith's experience did not help him. Harmon said less and got more than any haggler the bystanders had ever seen. Two of his porters, who had had all day to size up the dark-horse contender, walked away with a handful of copper from those who had backed the smith. Jovorn had to borrow ready cash from Ibraim the money changer even to complete the transaction.

Afterward, the pale metal worker stood in his door, watching Harmon carry much of his coin back to Ibraim for deposit. The entire transaction had been tinged with the unreal. Jovorn had tried every trick he had ever heard of, even the sick-mother-at-home routine, and nothing had worked. Again, he hadn't been cheated, but he would now grow nowhere nearly as rich from the transaction as he had planned.

Harmon made a purchase at another shop after only the briefest bargaining. His lack of flamboyance disappointed the crowd. He rehired the two bearers who had just added to their purses by wagering on him, from among a throng of applicants. The trio pushed their way back to the Gryphon, where Harmon changed into his better clothes.

Harmon and his two swaggering side men set out north. It was a long walk to the mansion of Aragon the wine merchant, well on the other side of Caravan Way. In the afternoon heat, the three shed their tail of unwanted followers.

The doormen looked at Harmon's clothes and his outriders, and finally at his face. They stepped aside, having decided to play "let's pretend"; that is, let's pretend that we don't remember him, and maybe the rich young gentleman will forget that we twice threw him out. Harmon's hirelings were basking in their new prestige. Even the house servants were happy to join the game, since the gentleman had a copper for each retainer and a present under his arm for their mistress. They hurried to summon Gargina. The stir also attracted a pale Melinda to the receiving room.

As the lady of the house entered the room, Harmon stepped forward with a smile. "Ah, our gracious hostess!"

Harmon bowed to the startled Gargina, who had never, in all her meetings with this young man, failed to get in both the first word and the last. All the servants were huddled just out of sight, but not out of hearing, of the receiving room.

"A token of my esteem, dear lady." He tugged the wrappings from his package and extended the contents toward his hostess. It was a beautiful bronze statuette, inlaid in gold.

Gargina lost another layer of composure. "Why, it's . . . it's . . . ." She stepped forward.

"Oops!"

The heavy statue had slipped from Harmon's fingers. It landed with a meaty *thunk* on Gargina's toe. The large woman dropped to the floor in an undignified heap.

"Ooooowwww!" Gargina followed her howl with some unladylike oaths, that her servants hadn't even suspected her of knowing.

Showering apologies, the new take-charge Harmon summoned the servants to take their moaning mistress to her chambers. In the thirty seconds he was left alone with Melinda, he swept her into his arms, gave her the most intense kiss of her life, told her how much she was loved, and informed her that she *would* wait for him.

The servants returned to find Harmon gone, but to

discover that they must now help Mistress Melinda to her chambers as well, before she fainted or floated around the room.

Harmon and his grinning servitors next visited the shop of Muringo the clothier. He spoke briefly and intensely with Elgo, the clothier's moon-faced son. Elgo would never afterward tell anyone what was said, but it was months before Elgo would approach to within a hundred pace of Aragon's house or speak Melinda's name above a whisper.

Near sunset, Harmon turned toward his father's warehouse. He expected to find the older man working late and alone again. He left his hired men outside. The warehouse workers were closing the building down for the night: stabling the horses, lifting the bar on the main door into place, and putting out the few lights. Only a couple of watchmen would spend the night, since few would want to steal grain in bulk and any money was stored elsewhere.

The man whom Harmon had always called his father was working by a lantern's light at a battered desk, scribbling on account sheets. Harmon stopped before him. The older man's skin seemed gray in the yellow light, and he seemed to have aged in the months since Harmon had left home. Since his wife, Harmon's mother, had died two years before, the seams of his father's body had begun to fray and loosen.

"Father," Harmon said.

The man looked up. Behind the deep lines around his eyes and mouth, a light seemed to come on when he saw Harmon. He hurried around the desk to embrace the prodigal.

"What has—?"

"Never mind, Father. I'll tell you about most of it someday. I've brought back my birthright, and then some. Now, tell me," he said, giving the older man a hug about the shoulders, "how was the corn harvest in Mugambu?"

• **16** •

Before a year was out, Harmon married Melinda and took over the grain business. He brought to it a spirit of adventure that made him a wolf among the lapdogs of his competition. He would be noted for being a loving family man, but also for being an eccentric whose waters ran deeper than most could fathom. What kind of man, they would ask, would refuse to carry a sword unless absolutely necessary, but keep a sword's *hilt* on his mantelpiece? Many would envy how well he got on with his mother-in-law, a strong-minded woman who shared with him a powerful love for the same person: his wife and her daughter.

He would forever afterward belittle the quest for adventure, but he would discover, as so many did in Barrow, that adventure sometimes came seeking the adventurer unbidden. It is possible to be a hero within the walls of one's home city.

· **17** ·

Through it all, I had only needed to be gone from the children for a few minutes at a time. They must have assumed that I had some intestinal disease. I forgot to remove the mud splatters from my robe when I returned from Harmon's confrontation with the Dirak in the swamp, and the little ones laughed at me. I was relieved to be able to laugh with them; it made me, their teacher, more human. I needed that. What I caused to happen to Harmon could have gone wrong easily. I am not the Great God.

Jessup told his tale for Harmon's ears. Harmon's drive toward adventure would never have been strong enough on its own to carry him right into the teeth of the Dirak. I pushed him, all the way to Elsewhen.

My palace seems lonelier tonight, because I have stirred up her memory. I was too old by centuries to marry, but we did. I was far too ancient to have children, but we had two: both boys, less than a year apart. Then she died. It is still hard even for me to write it.

She was taken by a disease so prosaic that somewhere a hard-eyed god must have been laughing at his joke—measles. I will never know that for sure, for I fear that I could not withhold my revenge. I am strong, but a contest with one of the creators of the Planes . . .

Magicians don't bother about disease, secure in our

own immortality. Once we fortify our own lives against any pestilence, we lose interest. There was no time for me to do the research required to defend the body of a mortal against a pathogen. I would have carried magic from the ends of a thousand Planes. I would have sold myself to some demonic power to stretch time or to bind her soul in an undead body. Even through her fever, she gently refused me those insanities. It was better, she said, to meet beyond Elsewhen, when Chaos swallows the last of the Planes. She only extracted two promises from me, a man who couldn't lie.

She made me swear it: I must never cease my struggle against that final night, though it postpones our reunion. I must never forsake my oath, nor the teaching of children, or the power of good would be weakened forever. Once she had that promise, she knew I could never violate it and retain my wizardry.

As the second promise, she made me agree never to interfere in the lives of our children, except to save those lives. They were not to grow up in my shadow. The woman in her, wiser than my magic, could see the trap that I might lead the three of us into.

Then she was gone. I remain: a Master of the Mysteries, clothed in enigma, wrapped in secret power—all of it is empty without her.

With the care of a father and the powers of Master, I separated my sons from me and from each other in time and space. They were still too young to remember me, but my son Fraximon inherited the blood of mages. He was drawn to magic as surely as the acorn will fall under the oak. I have always suspected that the blunderer to whom Fraximon was first apprenticed sent my son to Elsewhen before he was ready. Although Fraximon escaped it, as every wizard must, his mind was too immature to stand the stress. Something within him was permanently warped.

Before more harm could be done (I hoped), I took him as my own student. However, that flaw in him, that no wishes of a father or sorcery of a Master could erase, seduced him beyond white magic. In the end, I sent his soul to the Great God, before it could be further tainted by the blood he would have shed. Instead of a son, I have a second, blue coffin beside that of my wife and a heart that will never forgive itself.

I placed my other son under a stasis spell so that he would be "born" long after his brother. He arrived at the door of a grain merchant in Barrow in the arms of an old street teacher. The merchant and his wife were good people, ground down by sorrowing for children they couldn't have. They were happy to take in the healthy "orphan." I don't know what went wrong, though I suspect that I was the death of Harmon's adopted mother that dislocated his life. Perhaps in my seed is a spirit of exploration, twice misdirected now.

Harmon was headed toward alcoholic ruin. I lived up to my promise to save his life, though he may now believe I tried to kill him. I discovered Fraximon's escaped familiar when it killed my friend Jarvis, and I used it. I could have killed it at any second during its encounters with my son. The purpose of all—the overheard tale, the meeting with the secretive magician (me), the unshakable drive to hunt for the monster, and the Dirak's attack—was to isolate my son in Elsewhen and make him face himself.

It worked; he lives, and he is living well. What he thinks of me, I don't know. I was there to make sure the point of his sword entered the Dirak's nostril, and I followed him after his return. My promise keeps me from probing his mind. I'm not sure that it matters. He's alive! And he will have a good life, but a life that he structures himself, instead of an alcoholic's death in the gutter.

Does he remember now how I twice slipped and named him "son"? The load of eternal truthfulness sometimes settles on me unbearably.

Interchapter

I must shake this off! I made no promises not to interfere with the lives of others. The slum girl that Harmon met is indeed worth more than the setting in which she is forced to live. And she is Jarvis's heir; I owe him a debt. Now, in Upcruster Town, I have a former student, a pompous young man . . . Hmmm. This story should make for interesting reading, both as I write with the pen and with their lives. I find myself anxious to begin.

BOOK III

A Debutante in Barrow

DENALEE WAS DETERMINED: she would never go back. Where she was bound in the long run, she wasn't sure. Even death might be better than the Slews. Her family's drafty shack at the edge of the swamp had been the end of a long slide that had started sometime before Denalee had been born, in some better place on the other side of the Old Wat Bridge.

Along the way, Mother had picked up (and lost again) four husbands. She had also picked up fifteen children: some from each husband; some, like Denalee, from between husbands. Varied parentage was so generously distributed among Denalee's siblings that it had never been worth the bother to figure out whose was whose. Mother hadn't wanted to be a whore, but every time she had gotten two coppers ahead and set out to quit the business, she had come up pregnant. She had tried forms of larceny that were the conventional occupations of the slum, but there were too many hungry mouths at home to let her get settled. Another baby on the way always spoiled her touch before she could get really good at anything.

It was only luck that they had even found that last shack. It came open by default right after the latest baby was born. The shack's previous tenants had disappeared when the family was already on the move into the area. There was a story that something from the swamp had eaten the former owners, but the family had been at too low an ebb to be scared off. That hovel was as low as they had ever fallen, and that was saying a mouthful, but it was better than sleeping in the open.

Unfortunately, they hadn't outrun their problems. Food

was soon scarce again, and money was nonexistent. All the little ones had to occupy themselves was playing in the muddy ditches and whining. Everyone had been hungry and miserable before, but this was the worst. Other slum women commented that Mother had been lucky only to have lost three babies in her life. Few big families in the Slews were so intact. Now it looked as if the family's luck had changed permanently toward the black side.

Mother and the older boys went through the Swamp Gate every day into Slews proper, and sometimes clear across the bridge, to scratch for anything that could be eaten by the desperate or sold for food money. It was not an easy life for the gleaners. No one was surprised, then, when Snot-nose ran away. He had been griping for weeks and threatening to leave the "little kids" who had been cramping his style. He was about twelve.

Garny was the oldest, and the only one older than Denalee. He liked to swagger more than he deserved to and to sneer at everything with his pimply lips. He roundly cursed Snot-nose, even with Mother listening. He sprayed it from his face: damnation and good riddance to a deserter who couldn't take the hard times.

No one was surprised, again, when Chester disappeared. He was a year older than Snot-nose and was turned like him. Garny, who was anything but imaginative, played out the same wrathful-head-of-the-household nonsense, cursing Chester in almost the same words he had used on his other brother. Garny had begun to be a problem to Denalee in other ways.

Mother had always been careful not to bring "business" home, even if it had meant using a rag pile in an alley. She had seen what had happened to other girl-children when some rough and randy drunk tired of their prostitute mother. Mother tried, at least sometimes. Lately, Garny seemed to have hired or seduced some "business" for himself. After a few experiences, he had decided that he knew all there was to know about sex. And Garny came home *every* night, even when Mother didn't.

Thankfully, he was as superstitious as he was ignorant. He had been told by some other young hood that there was a kind of curse involved in taking a girl until she had been bleeding on schedule for a year. By hints and tawdry jokes he had shared both his belief and his intentions with his half-sister. Denalee had passed his "year" deadline over a year ago, keeping it a secret as best she could. Garny had been stupid enough to be fooled for a long time, but some months ago, he had caught her during her period. Considering the cramped way they lived, it had only been a matter of time. He had recently told her that next month his "year" deadline would be passed. He was careful not to let Mother hear, but he had made it plain: some night soon, when Mother was late getting home, he was going to drag Denalee out to the weed patch and "show her what loving was all about."

Denalee had no doubt that he would do it. He was both bigger and stronger than she was, and she was without adult allies. Mother had explained to Denalee as carefully as she could how a woman's body worked, but a professional woman who was a fifteen-time loser in the conception lottery was not the expert to end all experts. Mother would stop Garny—if she were there. The same thing had happened to her as a girl, and she was not broad-minded about incestuous rape.

However, Mother couldn't guard her forever. If Denalee successfully fought off Garny's first try, he would only come back later and beat her up first before taking what he wanted. He was not complex enough to have anything but a transparently sick and simple style.

Denalee wished that she were something besides skin and bones, topped with a mat of lank, blonde hair. Any looks she might ever have would develop later, depending on whether or not she got enough food to finish that development. Maybe she could have attracted some young man, like the ones she saw at the market sometimes. He might have defended her from Garny, even married her. One of Mother's axioms was, "Make 'em marry you before you pass it out for free." But it wasn't to be: the only one who even recognized her as an available female was her bully of a brother!

When little Norby had disappeared, the entire family knew that there was something wrong beyond the daily misery of life. He had always been the quiet one, a year younger than Snot-nose. He had been totally dependent on Mother, Denalee, and his older brothers. There was no one less likely to run away. The smaller children didn't talk about it, but Mother whispered her secret fears to Denalee. Maybe some *thing* did come out of the swamp and steal people away. Everyone slept indoors now, despite the heat: there was more room.

· 2 ·

Denalee had confirmed her worst suspicions within a few days. She did most of the cooking for the family now, and she was old enough to run errands away from the shack. Even the vermin of Slews-Inside-the-Walls probably wouldn't bother her in daylight: she was just too ragged and scrawny. By now, she could haggle in the market like a professional, stretching every copper. As Mother needed to be gone longer and longer, other chores away from the shack fell to Denalee. She had been heading for the Slews communal well for a bucket of the questionable water when it happened.

She had meant to pass by Gramper Jarvis's place on the way, knowing that she would find the old man out catching the morning sun. Though he was all whiskers and scar tissue, she really liked the old goat. When they had met for the first time, he had tried to talk her out of her ragged shift and into a quick roll in the hay. He was over sixty and half gristle, but she had been flattered. No one had ever noticed her before, except Garny. The tricky old devil had nearly succeeded, too! But when she had decided to slap his bony hands away a few times, he hadn't forced the matter, as so many men in the Slews would have.

He was everything that Garny wasn't, though they had both approached her for the same commodity. He was old, when it was nearly impossible to reach old age in the slums. He had been many places and done exciting things, before being forced by the wear and tear on his body to retire. He admitted to having acquired great amounts of gold in the past, and also to having spent every coin. He was witty and wise, or at least wise in her eyes. She had never had a father she could remember, or a grandfather. She probably loved old Jarvis, but love was not to be brought out in the open in the Slews: death was always too close by.

Whatever her feelings might have been, she would never get the chance to tell him. She was only a dozen steps from Jarvis's sagging front door when the monster took him. A thing like a giant, purple cabbage, as high as her shoulder and twice as wide, popped out of a drainage ditch and seized the old man in its huge bag of a mouth. She didn't even have time to cry out before it had bounced off into the swamp on stubby legs. The last she saw of Gramper Jarvis was a bare foot protruding from the top of the mouth slit of an obscene, toothed, lavender vegetable.

She stood crying next to her dropped bucket. She cried because she was terrified, not because a girl from the Slews would bemoan the injustice of the universe. She had just lost a friend, a friend who might have helped her escape the conditions among her family that were becoming intolerable. Though Gramper Jarvis had said that he had seen the Death Angel often enough to be unafraid of him, Denalee had only brushed against death indirectly in her fifteen summers. Though she was prepared for squalor and misery, she was unprepared for death. She sat and cried, too frightened to run.

She dried her eyes. Girls raised south of the Swamp Gate didn't cry long about anything. The hurt of her loss sank slowly into her heart, to join a short lifetime of other scars there. The spirits of women sunk in poverty would be struck and struck again until the scars on each soul shielded them from more hurt, but that barrier would also hold in the stolid despondency of life slowly guttering out.

She used her bucket to gather up all the portable food in Jarvis's hut. Her family's empty stomachs clamored louder than an injured heart. Gramper had always eaten well, even though he was too staved up to work anymore. Once a week, a delivery boy had shown up at his shack with a bundle of foodstuffs, from clear over in Upcruster Town. Gramper would chuckle over it through the stumps of his teeth. He knew, he said, a certain old man over in the Town who had a secret, that, for comfort's sake, he would rather have kept. Gramper had written down something about the secret, which explained to Denalee's practical mind why Gramper had not been done in long ago to keep him quiet. When she had mentioned it, Jarvis had given a cackling laugh at the notion of murder being used to stop his mouth. He had tried to explain something about an old teacher of his, from when he had been a boy long ago, but she hadn't understood the connection to the secret.

He proved that he had grown to like her, having no living kin of his own, by showing Denalee where his treasure was hidden. It was only a small scroll and a shiny pendant, wedged behind a loose knot in one of the posts of his shack. It had been part of his "secret" deal, he had said, to keep the pendant safe and never allow the inscription on the back to be read aloud, especially by a magician. Reading and writing were already close enough to magic for an illiterate slum girl. When Gramper mentioned how many decades he had been carrying and hiding the pendant, she was even more impressed by its mystery.

Any written secret was safe with her, but when she had seen the trust in the old man's face, she had decided not to wait much longer to take him up on his offer to move in with him, sexual strings and all. Maybe a gentle old man would be better for that first time than a careless young man. It was time for a girl of her age to be looking for a permanent attachment, before she became a skinny old maid, desired only by men wanting casual sex without worrying about the looks of the woman they victimized. She didn't want to be forced into the fetid form of prostitution that Mother had to practice.

She had only meant to delay a little while, until Garny pressed too close. Her half-brother would never have dared try to take her from Gramper. The tough, old man had been slowed by age but he had forgotten more about knife fighting than Garny would ever know.

Now that chance was gone forever.

She didn't even consider moving into Gramper's shack alone. A single girl in the Slews didn't rate a house to herself, unless she was in business. A week wouldn't have passed until a stronger man or family took over the shack, and possibly her as well. She would have to be satisfied to be the first to search undisturbed through Gramper's meager belongings. She was not surprised when she garnered only a few kitchen utensils and some ratty clothes that could be cut down to fit her younger brothers and sisters.

She took the scroll and pendant from their hiding place. They were hers alone, but as an inheritance rather than loot. She didn't consider selling them, but she did hide them far from the shack, under a stone that no one would accidently turn over.

At home, Denalee told Mother that Gramper had died in the swamp, omitting the detail of the monster. There was no use to frighten her family more: what could they have done? They were already huddling in the shack all night and staying near it during the day. None of them were fighters, and they couldn't possibly hire protection. There was no way for them to move, with no money and a housing crunch in the Slews, as older structures collapsed or burned down and were not replaced.

Mother asked no questions: in the Slews, a person didn't inquire after death. He called often enough without invitation. The food that Denalee had brought home eased their lives for many days.

· **3** ·

As during one of the slow-rising floods on the Wat, the cellars of Denalee's soul began to fill with a seepage of fear and desperation. A better-fed Garny renewed his leering promises. Another monster lurked beyond the edge of the swamp, a purple nightmare in the corner of her mind's eye for every second she was outside the shack.

On the morning that the stranger came by, Denalee had almost reached the point of propositioning him to take her with him. He would probably have wanted payment in the same coin that Garny was preparing to steal. The trouble was that he was such a *strange* stranger. She had never seen a young face so haggard, and a coating of flaking mud didn't add to his charm. Worse, he was headed *toward* the swamp.

The man did have a little money. He gave Mother a copper for water and food, though he could have gotten five times that amount to eat for the same coin in Slews-Inside-the-Walls. He must have been rich or mad or desperate to the point of being a fool—maybe a little of all three. Denalee's desperation was not yet so deep that she would hook herself onto one such as that. Besides, he had shown only one copper; perhaps it was his last.

The stranger went on toward the swamp, leaving the stage of the "now," where the poor played out their lives. He was forgotten within minutes. In minutes more, however, he returned, not for food this time, but for information. Secrets held by the poor, he soon found, were more dear than food. Strangers were supposed to see only a united front of blank, peasant faces and hear nothing but professed ignorance. Anyone alien to the slums might be the tax man or the law, some eye or ear of authority.

An exception had to be made at times, of course, in enlightened self-interest. Poor men's pride might not be for sale, but it could be rented under the right circumstances. For the sake of the family, this one alien stranger might be such an exception. This foreigner had money.

It made an odd tableau: a red-eyed young man wearing shades of gray mud, his hand gripping the hilt of his sword, surrounded by a circle of ragged natives. He had them mesmerized by the copper coin in his fingers. His arm rippled in the swaying motion of the snake charmer, to the rattling accompaniment of flakes of mud dropping off him. He fixed his edgy eyes on each family member in turn, holding the coin between himself and them like a talisman against evil.

He was only interested in one thing: What about the monster? Had they seen it? Denalee wanted to burst, to grab the coin when it passed in front of her and blurt out what she knew, but she was old enough to have the peasants' code fully ingrained in her. It was Mother's place to say whether they spoke or not. Denalee held her peace, though she was sure she knew more about the monster than the others did. None of them had so much as glimpsed it—so she thought.

One of the little ones, Ollie, burst Denalee's bubble by breaking over first in front of the stranger's coin. A whole pack of her siblings had *seen* the creature and said nothing, because it had *played* with them! Mother's stomach must have been tied in more knots than Denalee's was by the news, but the stranger had fixed on Ollie with his coin now. The story came out.

The most the little ones had seen had been the hands

of the creature, but her sister said that it had *eyes* in the palms. Little that that was, it was enough for Ollie to stake a claim on the coin. Mother would take the cash from such a small one, for food, but . . . what if the coin could be Denalee's alone? It was a decisive moment.

She pushed in front of the others and spoke her piece, calmly enough to convince the man that it was the truth and that it was her story alone. He listened in silence. Then, the coin was hers, in her hand! The stranger backed away. His face was a mix of feelings: fear, resignation, pride, determination, hurt, anger, and—out of time!

She should have been keeping her attention closer at hand. Garny was closing in.

"Give us the coin, then," he said, grinning a slimy grin.

"No! It's mine!" It *was* hers, in a world full of things that weren't, that were beyond her control. She might give it away, but, "You can't take it!" She closed her fist, curled her wrist, hugged it against her chest. She wrapped her whole, small body around the coin.

Her family, Garny in the lead, closed in on her, like a dog pack on a wounded doe. The bonds of loyalty that had held them together through the long slide into the Slews had been weakened by death, privation, selfishness, and, finally, by money. One copper coin had finished off what bad food and rotten bedding had not been able to break.

Garny seized her and shoved her down. He cruelly forced her back straight, but violence had always been his way. The shock to Denalee was the attack of the little ones, the ones she had tended and played with. They tackled her legs, punching and pummeling any part of her they could reach. They ripped at her ragged shift as if it were the curse that forced them down, ever down. Mother stood by, silent. A month ago, perhaps even a morning ago, she would have intervened.

With both hands, Denalee clutched at her coin. Garny had his weight on her stomach, but she still resisted his assault on her closed fingers. He was strong enough to break each finger, one by one, and he might have, if he hadn't chosen a lower way. Through the thin bodice of her shift, he pinched hard on a small breast.

Oh, it hurt! It hurt, hurt! It hurt so much that her

fingers moved by themselves to push his hand away. She broke her own hold on the coin, as he had planned. Both his hands attacked the fingers with the exposed copper and plucked it free. He wasn't finished.

Breathing hard, he forced his face near her ear in the din and whispered for her hearing only, "Feels like you've held out on me too long already, you little slut!" He roughly fondled the other breast, like a hog trying to root the last turnip out of a sack. "Tonight, then," he hissed, "when Mum's gone. Be ready!"

"No!" she yelled, trying to lift his weight off her chest.

With her legs pinned by small bodies, she couldn't dodge when he backhanded her across the upper face. Lightning exploded over her right eye, and she hit the ground like a bean bag. She lay there, moaning a little, as the group drifted back from her. The injured eye was already beginning to puff up.

Perhaps the others were ashamed now, deep down, away from Denalee's eyes. A tragedy had overtaken them so rapidly that they did not yet recognize it: the family no longer existed, despite the fact that they would live still together for a long time. Each, even the youngest, had placed personal greed above loyalty. They had destroyed one of their own for a copper's worth of food. They had taken the first step onto a longer slide that would take them, not to desperate life together as it had before, but to individual, lonely future death.

The little ones scattered and resumed playing. Mother turned away, to go inside to the baby. Garny walked away, toward the Swamp Gate. Perhaps their eyes held repentance, but their backs hid it. The coin that had destroyed the family might return to it as food, but it was just as likely to go to some street slattern for a brief, stinky sexual romp for Garny. The bonds that had once united the clan had been dissolved. From now on, each would be for his own. Denalee propped herself against the side of the shack, to let the sun dry her face and leech the pain out of it. There was no longer anywhere to go: no small ones to care for; no food to prepare this early; nothing.

"Nothing" opened its maw and beckoned for her to enter. What was left of life that would make it worth living? If it had not been such an effort to raise her bruised body from where it was, she would have wandered down to the Wat and thrown herself into its waters. The emptiness that overwhelmed her left all of existence in a dreamlike haze of tears, a brassy mist edging even the pain in gold. Even death was gold.

· 4 ·

Into her blurred tableau stepped a nightmare figure who meshed perfectly with the deadly nothingness that had swallowed her. He was a "something" of death instead of more nothing. His body was all mud and blood and ripped cloth. Across his shoulder was a bag that looked as if it had been dipped in purple wine after a roll in the swamp. Two sword hilts protruded from his sash, but one held no blade and the other retained only a jagged hand span of broken metal. When she raised her eyes to his face, she hardly knew the young man who had visited her family that morning.

When she looked into his eyes, the haze obscuring reality abruptly went away. It was like looking down an aimed thunderbolt into the eyes of a god. She flinched and began to move away, but stopped. In any direction lay more of nothing. This strange being had not done anything to make her afraid. She stared back at him.

She was brushing against something human, yet alien—altered since this morning. His gaze felt like a coupling of minds: the clean, spiritual aspect of mature physical coupling (but not the violence that Garny had in mind for her). As he touched her mind, she touched him. Somehow she knew that she was the first person he had encountered in a very long time, no matter how impossible that sounded. The strange, bright thing that had encountered her was becoming a man again. The human he had been, or had wanted to be, returned. He glanced away from her toward the city.

As an unimportant afterthought, he rummaged in his rags and brought out something, which he tossed to her. Although she caught it, she knew that *things* wouldn't matter again once he left her and the nothing returned. She glanced down at it.

It was a gold coin.

Indeed, gold was a "thing," but it was a "key" thing, a thing to open the door to escape. That one coin meant that she could leave behind a shack filled with strangers, leave a corner of the city so degraded that it had crept outside the walls and tried to drown itself in a swamp. With the skepticism of the Slews, she bit the coin. If the Prince himself had given it to her, she would have done the same. As she looked in wonder at the genuineness of the metal, the young man departed.

She could have run after him, following the trail of purple splatters that led toward the Swamp Gate, but he had left the feeling with her that their destinies lay apart. Instead, she hid away the coin and went wordlessly into the shack that used to be her home. She snatched a piece of the hard, black bread that was her share of the evening meal and dug her winter shift out from behind a wall brace. Mother rocked the baby and said nothing. The slow creep of the "nothing" of the Slews into her life had begun long ago for the older woman.

Denalee stripped off her torn shift, careless of her nakedness with Garny not at home. She pulled on her itchy winter shift, but kept the remnants of the other: her possessions were too few to throw away even the handful of rags that it had become. She stood still, then, staring at her mother, forming and unforming the images of the woman who had borne her—weighing. The swinging scales of judgment rested at last more on the side of the good. The epitaph that she was about to write for her mother's part of her life would read, "Sometimes, Mother tried." She bent down and awkwardly embraced the other woman's shoulders. One tear trickled from each woman's eyes: they were allowed that much, even in the Slews.

"Good-bye," Denalee said.

Their family, when it had still existed, had communicated best without words. Denalee was certain that Mother knew that her good-bye was forever.

Denalee had been inside the city's walls many times. She detoured only to retrieve her other treasures from under their stone and wrap them with the gold coin in her rag of a shift. Tucked under one arm, all her possessions made a package of no noteworthy size. A "johnny" at the city gate let her through without comment; he seemed distracted.

Poor johnny-straights: assigned to the armpit of the city, surrounded by moral decay and economic collapse, they still tried to do their jobs. Most of the watchmen were quickly swallowed by the spiritual sludge of the Slews. The smuggling gangs didn't take long to find out which newly assigned guards could be turned by a free bottle, a little extra copper, or a flash of thigh. The midnight commerce must continue to flow through the Swamp Gate.

Johnnies couldn't be turned, but as long as they weren't on duty when some important load came upriver through the bayous, it made no difference. Sooner or later, though, a johnny would be in the way of something big. When he called for help, he would find that his fellow watchmen were drunk or absent or in the bushes with their pants off. A johnny always fought hard, maybe even took a few with him, but he had to die. Poor johnny.

Denalee, able to see the west end of the city with the clear eyes of one leaving it forever, stopped and smiled at him. They exchanged a few words; he seemed genuinely sympathetic about her black eye. They parted friends, in a small way. Denalee hoped that the city would give him a nice funeral.

The boulevard leading to the west end of the Old Wat Bridge had once been a main thoroughfare, before the opening of the new bridge farther north. With that direct linking of Caravan Way to the west side of the river, the trains of goods bound in either direction no longer needed to swing through the south end of the city. Almost everything now went either to the warehouses along the wharves on the east side of the river or up the caravan road northwest toward Ichan. Nothing much stopped in the Slews anymore, not even produce wagons. The southwest of the city rotted, abandoned by commerce. Upcruster Town, in the city's southeast quadrant, had also dried up, but it had toughened and changed the tactics of trading in its bazaar. The Town lived on.

The avenue to the Slews end of the old bridge had never been built up. It remained wide enough for two wagons to pass abreast, though most of its meager traffic was now pedestrian. The run-down businesses that lined it were the best the Slews had to offer. Reeking warrens of alleys branched off it like brambles in a hedge, housing the city's most degenerate enterprises. To Denalee, it was a boulevard of dreams.

At its end lay the bridge, and across the bridge lay the Town. She had never been there as an adult. She did not aspire to the mansions north of Caravan Way, not with only one gold coin to her name. But the arch of the bridge was a rainbow that led to a place as high above the Slews as the mansions were above the Town. One gold coin, used properly, would go a long way in the south end of the city. She stepped out on her pilgrimage.

As a queen, she viewed a fishing boat passing under her feet, from the height of the bridge. A seagoing merchantman on its way to the docks at the upper end of the city was flying a streamer of bright signal flags, as if to salute her. She didn't notice the drying trail of purple drops that crossed the same bridge. As a girl once again, but still touched with magic, she descended the eastern end of the bridge into the promised land. It did require a magic in the eye to see much difference between the dilapidated buildings on the east side of the river and those of the Slews. There was no real alteration in the stone or wood at all. The superiority of Upcruster Town was soul or luck or emotion rather than material. There was a living something here that made even the dust of the street fluff differently. Denalee hurried to explore her domain, a bit of the queen still clinging to the skinny girl from the Slews.

• 5 •

Ibraim the money changer was fidgety and restless. Why, oh, why hadn't he left his curse alone? The terrible stomach pains he had formerly experienced seemed benign in his memory as he had to compare them daily to the cure. He had been desperate, or he wouldn't have gone to that Tellarani girl across the bazaar in the first place. Every herbalist in Barrow had given up on him, and the magicians had wanted gold before they would even do the research to attempt a cure.

She had laid out the cards by the ancient method of the People. She had peered and pouted over them, focusing and unfocusing as she hummed to herself. He had been impressed enough not to doubt the result, and the hard coin he had paid in advance lent the reading reliability. Finally she had stared directly at him.

"Ibraim zab-Norn, as your heart fights your head, your stomach mourns. You were taught by your mother"—she had tapped a card: the Queen of something—"always to be fair and honest. From the pressure to make a larger profit"—she had tapped a second card, the reversed Six of Pentacles—"you have not always been honest in your business dealings."

He had sweated and gulped, but he had known every word of it to be the truth.

She continued. "To heal your stomach, you must deal *exactly* in honesty for one month."

The sweat had popped from his face when he had heard the treatment. Why couldn't it have been something easy, such as cutting off a finger? "For (gulp!) only a month?" He had been momentarily hopeful.

"In a way, yes." The black-haired seeress had seemed almost smug. "But then you must choose one business day each week thereafter and deal honestly all that day as well. A month will heal your stomach; one day a week will keep it well." She held up a restraining hand. "If you cheat on either, your misery will return."

It had been a dismissal, from a girl who lacked three years to reach twenty, but he had taken it meekly and slipped out of the wagon. Now, with most of the month passed, the Tellarani girl had proven to be as right as if her prediction had come from her deceased mother, the seeress who had formerly used that wagon as both home and fortune-telling booth. However, the medicine had come with a curse of its own. Ibraim felt that if he had to smile once more as he passed over correct change for a coin, he would burst a blood vessel. Business had even increased, but it was *unnatural* business, based on scrupulously fair dealing that grated against his very grain. He had to keep smiling so that the customers would come back at some later date, when he could give them the skinning that they were begging for.

Typical of the way things were going, here came some slum girl, who had probably sold her virginity for a bit of silver. His muscular nephews, who were guarding his booth today, paid her no attention as she pushed aside

the door flap and let the setting sun hit Ibraim squarely
in the eyes. On a normal day, he could have fast-talked
her out of half the value of her coin, but now . . . He
steadied himself and smiled a fatherly smile at the skinny,
little thing, clenching his teeth behind closed lips.

"Sir?"

"Yes?"

"I heard in the bazaar that you are an honest dealer in
coins and metal."

"You heard correctly, my dear."

"I need a piece of money changed."

"Very well. Give me the silver, girl." He had resigned
himself.

"It's . . . It's a gold piece."

Ibraim sat stock still. Then, with a grimace, he raised
both hands skyward, as if to clench them in the skirts of
heaven. "Why me! Why me all the time?" His cry was
heard three stalls away.

The frightened girl turned to leave, but he was already
rummaging in his money box, muttering all the while.
She was very pleased with the handful of copper and
silver she received, never having suspected that a gold
coin was worth so much. Ibraim muttered some have-a-
nice-day blessing, but she probably didn't understand it,
with his teeth clenched as tightly as they were.

As the newly rich slum girl clinked merrily on her way,
Ibraim began another prayer for the month to end soon.
At least, he told the neighbors that he was praying when
they found him banging his head against the ground.

· **6** ·

Denalee slipped into an alley, away from the wonders of
the bazaar. It had been a glorious day, ending with her
richer than her wildest dreams, but the sun was going
down. After scouting to make sure that she had not been
followed, she brought out her coins and other small treasures and hid them all over her person: some inside the
rag of her old shift; some in the hem of her present
garment; three inside a braid she made in her straw-
colored hair. It was time to locate a lodging.

Tomorrow, she would look for a permanent niche somewhere. The stars in her eyes had not blinded her to certain ugly realities common to both sides of the river. The locks and bars on the businesses here made it clear that honesty was not always the policy in the Town. There were certainly Upcrusters who would molest and rob a girl alone in the streets after nightfall. Tonight she would luxuriate in a rented room in an *inn*. Surely, no queen could do better.

Her wandering feet brought her to a wider spot in the crooked lane that she had heard someone call Straight Street. She noticed the sign of what must surely be an inn. She had caught the name "Gryphon and Goblet" in a snatch of conversation in the bazaar earlier. The building's sign did have an ugly animal on it, painted holding a goblet in its outstretched claws. The sign, however, had been without a touch-up for a long time. The griffin appeared to have terminal leprosy, and the goblet had far too many holes in it to have actually held any beverage.

It took some pushing to open the front door, which appeared to have been knocked down a number of times and put back up carelessly. In fact, it was hard to tell whether it had originally been meant to swing inward or outward, since it was now fitted with floppy, leather hinges to swing both ways. She entered a common room, where the air was warm and stank of smoke, beer, and the other blended smells that adhere to any drinking establishment. Denalee, not long from sharing a hovel with a dozen odoriferous relatives, was not offended. She was able to pick out new odors among the rest—wines and spices.

She marched straight up to the bar. Behind it, a tall, fat young man in a dirty apron was trying to wipe a mug to look clean enough to use, without washing it. He was not gaining much, since the rag he was using was dirtier than the mug.

"A room and some food, if you please." She tried to make it brisk and businesslike, thankful that the baggy shift hid her quivering legs. This inn was as high in the big time as she had ever come.

The bartender looked up and appraised her: one skinny, almost-woman from west of the river, with a big, black shiner on her right eye; probably broke (they always were) and trying to cadge a couple of freebies.

"Let's see some money first, girlie." Barrelgut looked down on her with disdain from his position as an Upcruster merchant and from greater age, all of five years more than the girl's.

If it had come to a comparison of origins, the tavern keeper might have had to yield some of his superiority. He had gotten to be a "merchant" by default, when the previous owner had died heirless, of ptomaine poisoning after eating his own cooking. Barrelgut, who at that time had been the seventeen-year-old "day" man at the inn, had held a long discussion with Gorgio, the "night" man, a discussion involving fists and table legs. Gorgio had agreed to become the new day man and accept forty percent of the profits, before some gang of aggressive squatters grabbed the place out from under them. Barrelgut's partner had found the lighter load during daytimes easier to handle while his broken arm healed.

Facing the slum girl, the fat bartender began one of his famous sneers, but had to freeze it when she palmed three coppers onto the bar top and carefully walled them with her palm. Barrelgut eyed the coins, sniffing for monetary advantage.

"That gets you a meal, girlie. A room will be more."

"In a pig's eye, chubbo!" Denalee had been the only one that Mother had trusted besides herself to haggle for the family's food. Nobody but a rich fool ever took the first offer or treated it with anything more than contempt.

Negotiation in south Barrow was not a dainty thing. A round of sharp bargaining finally settled the three coppers as the price of dinner, breakfast, and a room until noon the next day. Barrelgut didn't press too hard when he discovered that she was a more experienced haggler than he had first estimated. He got secret satisfaction from the fact that he was going to palm off on her that scorched upstairs room, which was practically unrentable otherwise. It had needed a coat of paint for months, but paint cost money. The two settled their deal by spitting into the sawdust of the floor, with a "Done!" on either side.

Barrelgut pocketed two of the coppers in advance and sent the potboy back to the kitchen for a plate of "something." The Gryphon was too busy that night to waste any more time on one ragged girl, even one with top-notch bargaining ability. When that wounded crazy man, Harmon something-or-other, had arrived that afternoon, it had created a stir that had drawn a crowd to the tavern. A crowd meant many drinks to serve and a watchful eye needed against pilfering. It meant pickpockets to throw out and deadbeats to harass until they paid for their drinks.

Though a crowd meant more money, it also meant more work. Barrelgut had an aversion to any work not immediately connected to profit. He was also tired: Gorgio was sick, and Barrelgut had been working two shifts for several days. The mob in the taproom had thinned down somewhat, since the purple-stained mystery man who had drawn them had gone early and quietly to bed. There were still enough customers besides the regulars to keep Barrelgut moving at a spritely pace. That's when the call came from the bar.

"Hey, chunks, is this supposed to be food?"

He had forgotten the Slews girl. It had been a hard afternoon; he was in no mood to be condescending for three coppers' worth of business.

"What's it to you, girlie?" He stalked over to her. "My food's good enough for my other customers. Is Your Highness displeased with it? Would Your Worship prefer it on a gold plate?"

Barrelgut was incensed. Dirty Kevin, the inn's late owner, had taught him everything he had known about cooking. The fact that Kevin's "everything" could have been scratched on the back of one copper with a blunt nail was probably the reason that Kevin had departed for the Great Tavern in the Sky, or wherever.

The girl was not going to take that quietly. "Listen, chubbo, across the river we wouldn't use this stuff to drown cockroaches!"

In the Gryphon's kitchen, the dish before her had certainly been used for that purpose several times, but Barrelgut likewise had decided to stand his ground. "Across the river cockroaches don't live long enough without being smoked or eaten to drown, girlie!"

"Well, if it wasn't for the roaches, this . . . whatever-it-is wouldn't have any meat in it at all!" Denalee had eaten low and she had eaten skimpily, but she had decided that her first "boughten" meal was going to be

better than food whose only name was "something."
"And the name's Denalee, fatso!"

"You think you can do better, Dent-a-beet? And the
name's Barrelgut, to my friends. You can call me 'sir'!"

Denalee did think that she could do better. She had
been doing nearly all the family's cooking for a couple of
years. Even having to stretch every vegetable butt and
used-up bone, she had done better than the gray sludge
before her. Her spoon stood up in it like a dented flagpole.

"Would you care to put some coin where that big, fat
mouth is, Sir Barrelbutt?" If this pushy bartender had
anything at all in the pantry, she might be able to start
her sojourn in the Town with her fortune growing a little.
It would be another happy omen.

Barrelgut wasn't much interested; he knew he would
be pumping a dry well. "If you had anything on you
besides those three coppers, you bet I would! But you
already made arrangements to spend your entire family's
fortune, sweetie. Or did you roll some drunk west of the
river for his poke?"

He wasn't worried about hurting the feelings of Miss
Rags. If he ran the smartmouthed little broad off, it
would only cost him three coppers. Make that "one copper"; he already had two in his pocket. He wished that
she did indeed have some money to bet. He was certain
that this batch of "something" would stand up against
anything a Slews girl, who could never have been in a
real kitchen, might turn out. He had made this batch
fresh only a week ago. It was down to where it had
character.

Barrelgut didn't eat "something" very often himself.
Commensurate with his standing as a merchant, he usually patronized some other eating establishment near the
bazaar, or fixed himself an individual meal after closing
time. The tavern regulars would back him, though.

Clink! went his wish on the bar top, calling him with
his favorite music.

"Three coppers will do for now. I have more," she
said, with shrill royalty. "What are you putting up,
Squirrel-gut?"

The bartender's face deepened in color. "You can
have the room and meals for naught if you win. We had a
deal!"

"And I do the work for nothing?" She crossed her thin arms.

"With *my* ingredients, you mean?"

The haggling began in earnest. The tavern crowd was loving it all. Some wagering and old-fashioned bargaining, with name-calling on the side, helped revive an evening better than a knife fight. The group formed a respectful circle around the two combatants, just out of reach. A flailing arm thrown up during an emotional exchange might put a finger in the eye of an innocent Townsman.

There was a general agreement that the new girl had a slight edge at the end. She convinced Barrelgut to put up an additional copper piece, along with the meals and lodging. She had one hour after the water boiled in the kitchen's big kettle to come up with a better meal than his.

As the girl disappeared into the kitchen, the real betting began, along with a necessarily obscene discussion of the claimants. To his delight, Barrelgut discovered that the interruption had renewed everyone's thirst. He was not as happy to notice that the regulars, whose loyalty he had counted on, were backing the possibility that anyone, including a hypothetical retarded eunuch, could better Barrelgut's cooking. Perhaps he had been a little hasty with his bet. There was also the matter of who was to judge the contest.

"How about Hally for judge!" an anonymous voice called from the back of the room.

"The only thing Hally could judge is the shape of some trollop down at Wanda's!" another voice fired back.

Hally grinned back toothlessly. He was a good ol' boy, which translated as being essentially worthless, but well liked by his circle of friends, most of whom were also good ol' boys. His net worth would always hover near zero because of a weakness for spending most of his pay at Wanda's bordello.

"How about Orno?" someone called from another corner.

Orno was a Saikhandian cleric with a higher-than-accurate opinion of both his worth and position. In his limited circle, however, his pretentious manner and carefully groomed piousness had given him a reputation for gravity and soberness—soberness being a somewhat relative matter at the Gryphon. He was naturally elected to judge the quality of the challenger's cooking, by beer-soaked acclamation.

In the kitchen, Denalee lighted the candle that Barrelgut had reluctantly provided, to reveal an unspeakable mess. There were enough coals in the fireplace to easily relight the fire, but the pot she was supposed to cook in would have to be scraped and sanded without mercy to remove all the traces of burned-on "something." On the completion of that heroic task, she called for the potboy to bring a bucket of water that would be set to boiling.

There were vegetables in Barrelgut's kitchen. Many others had been peeled there over the years, as the mummified remains of their husks testified. While plowing off a counter top, she discovered a crock of grain as well. Both basic food ingredients were plentiful, compared to what she was used to. She ground some rock salt into the stew pot to follow the other ingredients. While blowing the dust from the block of salt, she discovered some small canisters of dried spices. Neither Kevin nor Barrelgut had known how to use them; they had been inherited from an even earlier owner. Denalee was also sparing with them: she had heard about spices, even smelled them in shops, but her family could never afford them.

In an upper corner, behind the cobwebs, she found an ancient rasher of bacon. It had been out of reach of the rats, but once forgotten, it also had been out of sight of the cheapskates who wouldn't light a candle in their own kitchen. The rind was so hard and salty that she had to hack it off by main strength, but she didn't throw it away. Throwing away anything that might someday figure in another meal was unthinkable to a Slews girl. Some finely diced, desiccated bacon went into the caldron, followed by a few pinches of spices and a couple of onions. It began to smell like food almost at once.

A crock in a lower corner had probably once held yeast, but it had dried and died long ago. The grease in the crock next to it was rancid enough to walk by itself; neither would be of any use to this meal. She was able to render some fat from the bacon rind over the fire. With it and some flour, and some beer she demanded from

Barrelgut, she mixed a batch of flat bread. There were just enough weevils in the flour to give it crunch. Pan-fried in a skillet, the bread smelled pretty good, but she was beginning to grow uneasy.

She had bet on her cooking, but the judge was to be one of the bartender's cronies. She must have been tired to have been so stupid: first to wager away a piece of her fortune and then to work like a dog to feed the people who were about to cheat her. Well, they weren't winning without a fight! They'd have to cheat to beat her, and the word would get out. Even across the river, she had heard about what the Townsmen thought about welshers.

When the stew was done, she scoured out a bowl with sand until it shone. No lingering trace of "something" was going to ruin her stew! Next time she would invest her time in something besides cooking. A woman could do anything a man could do; often better. She just happened to be good at cooking, but the whole world was before her now: she could learn to do *anything*. First, though, she had to face this humiliating defeat and spit in the eyes of the ones who had tricked her.

When she entered the common room with a platter of flat circles of beer bread and the bowl of stew, she was greeted by an ominous silence. All of the Gryphon's clientele were grouped in a loose line, just beyond the bar. Every eye was on her. One whiskery gent, whose name she later learned was Hally, hastily wiped a line of drool with a sleeve. Barrelgut was watching from the far end of the bar, looking sour.

A pudgy, tonsured priest sat at the center of the bar, his hands holding a dainty eating dagger and wooden spoon expectantly upright. She set the food before him. This little man was about to gut her tiny fortune. She hadn't figured out a way to replace it yet, without selling what she had run away from home to keep, but she would. It might still come to selling herself, but better a stranger than that slug Garny. She found herself trembling.

Denalee need not have worried: the "fix" was in. It had been in ever since the smells of a genuine meal began to drift out of the kitchen. "Something," when cooking, smelled as good as it looked. Above the rank odor of the room; over senses deadened by drink; beyond the camaraderie that the crowd felt toward Barrelgut;

past every prejudice against women, people from the Slews, and smartmouthed, skinny blondes, the aroma of the meal had reached out and twanged some primal chord, stretching back to boyhood. No man in Barrelgut's masculine domain, no matter how poor, had reached adulthood without at least once having savored the essence of a real meal wafting in the air.

Orno clutched vainly at his dignity before digging in. It was shocking to watch the supposedly fastidious cleric hacking off chunks of beer bread and slurping stew like a hog at the trough.

"Hey," the perennial voice from the back cried, "he's going to eat it all!"

There was an immediate chorus of demands for bowls all around. Denalee was almost overwhelmed by the rush. The question of her food being better than "something" was never brought up again. Her stew was dubbed "something else," a name the fates had destined for it. Two eager helpers toted the large kettle into the main room, obscenely trying to keep inadequate pot holders between their fingers and the hot stew pot. The crowd attacked the stew with mugs converted to makeshift bowls. The few spoons available lacked a lot toward cleanliness, but that didn't stop the hungry tavern regulars.

Barrelgut quietly paid off his bets, which turned out to be surprisingly few. He had spotted his mistake early and let the tavern crowd do the betting. He once again revealed a reservoir of good sense beneath his sloppy bulk. In fact, he was rather embarrassed that an emotional attachment to his own cooking had cost him the few coppers it had. He watched the mob of his friends lap up the stew, swipe out the stew pot, and look expectantly around for more. The innkeeper, however, was not going to invest in another free feed anytime soon.

"Hey, Barrelgut! If *she's* cooking here tomorrow, then I'm eating here instead of at Mama Threechin's!"

It was the faceless voice from the back again, but the comment warmed up a chorus of "yeah's" and "me-too's." Barrelgut didn't have a choice: he offered her a job on the spot. Crow wasn't his favorite meal, but he had just seen as good a meal come out of his kitchen as could be had in any establishment in the south end of the city. (And she had used cheap ingredients, too.) No sooner had the words left his mouth than he was certain that the decision would cause him trouble. This girl had disturbed him from the moment she had walked through the door. Next thing, she would be wanting a salary.

"What . . . what would the job pay?" Denalee asked.

For the last few hours, she had been living out of the top of her head: floating, exhausted, moving too fast to think. She didn't understand why Barrelgut threw up his hands in a mute appeal to heaven, but the gesture looked familiar.

This time the dickering was brief. Denalee was so worn out that she would have accepted a lot less than she finally got, but she had a roomful of new allies. They harassed Barrelgut for being a tightwad every time he tried to lower the ante. She finally agreed to a room and meals, and enough copper to have seemed like a princess's dowry—yesterday.

Barrelgut was tired himself after sixteen hard hours. He shooed the drinkers out; there would be no "sleepers" tonight for him to worry about. No one really objected: it had been a real whizzeroo of a day at the Gryphon. He showed the girl up to her room and even left her a candle to find her way to the privy that overhung the alley, feeling mildly guilty now about palming off the scorched room on her.

During a final sweep through the tavern, he woke up the potboy and let him out the back door to go home to his family. He had almost forgotten about the bizarre stranger from earlier in the day, until he almost stepped on the cudgel man that Harmon what's-his-name had hired to guard his door. The watchman was snoring on his stick, curled across his employer's threshold. In the commotion, the man with the purple stains had slipped Barrelgut's mind.

The young innkeeper paused to rest on the landing near the door of the room where the girl had spread the pallet that he had supplied. Tomorrow needed thinking about, but he was just too tired.

Denalee had tidied herself and settled onto the thick-seeming pad. The whole day rushed past her memory—the bad beginning and all the good that followed. And the future held more good still! She was rich, rich, rich! She had a roomful of new friends, though they needed some sorting out. She had a *place*, a job, and a room of her own, even if it did smell like an unswept chimney. She had a room—a great, wonderful, empty room, all to herself! It had shutters that could be opened and shut, a cracked pitcher and basin, and her own chamber pot—and a trunk! Never mind that the trunk was almost empty now: she had a place for her treasures. She stood again and spun to survey her kingdom.

Denalee lay down, hugging the folded end of her blanket to her. Never again would she be wedged into a box of a shack, stinking from too many packed bodies. Then, to her surprise, she began to cry. She cried because she could never hold her little brothers and sisters again. She cried because the meals that she would cook now would be for strangers. She would never see many of her family alive again, and she sobbed her heart out for the loss of that family. Her heart had known before her mind that her new birth was also the death of her old life.

The tears ran and sobs shook her because she was fifteen and had never slept alone before; never crossed a great river into a wondrous, strange city; never been rich, but never been so very alone. The night sorrows faded at last into an exhausted slumber.

Denalee didn't hear it when the big man who had hired her roused himself from his tired stance and listened at her door. He raised a hesitant hand to knock, but dropped it again. He began a second time, but sighed instead and trudged to his own bed downstairs. Once, not long since, he had spent his own first night alone in Barrow. None had seen his tears then, and he was not ready to open his own door to any other person that he would trust with that fact.

· 7 ·

The night finally went away, without enough real rest for either cook or employer. With the sun up an hour, Barrelgut opened the shutters on his barred windows. Though their light was far from the kitchen, enough filtered into the greasy, shadowed cubbyhole for her to inventory its assets. It was surprising that Barrelgut had only misplaced a rasher of bacon and a few spices. She demanded a lantern, and got it, but with a scowl. Barrelgut viewed artificial light sources that consumed fuel the same way he would have looked at devices that burned money directly.

Denalee's first major discovery was that last night's stew had virtually exhausted the inn's food supplies. Before her daytime debut as a cook, she would have to make a lengthy trip to the bazaar. The second major discovery was the kitchen door: there was one. Behind an abandoned barrel and a broken crate, glued to half a dozen defunct broom handles by a gooey mass of ancient cobwebs, was a perfectly good door.

Dirty Kevin hadn't been willing to pay kitchen help enough to keep any for long. Another unwatched back door had been a nuisance. Barrelgut had inherited a load of questionable traditions when he took over the Gryphon. For instance, the younger taverner had not realized that anyone but the owner should do the cooking, or that candles were allowable in the kitchen. Kevin had simplified the troublesome details of cleaning; he didn't clean at all. Barrelgut bested that only slightly. He had never lighted his cooking area, and he had added to the clutter in it. Outside, he had mistaken the long-unused door for another piece of wall. Barrelgut was as surprised as Denalee to find that the inn had an additional exit.

The bartender was up unnaturally early, and it had made him grumpy. He dearly hoped that Gorgio would get over the case of the trots that was keeping him away from work. That partner had better realize that he was collecting forty percent of nothing as long as he played slug-a-bed. Denalee removed the clutter from the inside of the door and drafted him to prise it open from the outside. He was surly and unsubtle about his complaints, but he went. He might have been ignorant about the presence of the door in his establishment, but so far, he hadn't had to admit it.

Once outside, he had to run off a mangy dog and knock down a wasp's nest before he could reach the door. Heaving on it produced creaking, but no movement. He dug out a couple of inches of accumulated soil from around the sill with a broken board.

"Are you getting it?" the girl's muffled voice called from the inside.

"Push on it yourself, you little . . . Never mind. Now, if you're ready, Miss Busy-butt, push!"

With the dirt gone, her simultaneous shove and his pull hurtled the old door open all too easily. Barrelgut flipped onto his back in the alley, and Denalee's momentum carried her through the opening to land on him, driving a "Whuff!" from his chest. She untangled from him with a red face, as quickly as if he had been a biting dog.

The big man rose in silent rage, patting around his backside to see what he had fallen in. What he found was just as distasteful as he had first suspected. Clenching his fists, he stalked wordlessly through the new kitchen opening. He restrained himself because he never wanted it reported that he had slugged some skinny girl because he had fallen down in what a dog had left in his alley.

Denalee found him later in the common room, sprinkling sawdust on the worst spills and scuffs on the floor and checking the furniture for breakage. She stood behind him and cleared her throat, noting that he had changed clothes.

"Well, what is it?" He made no attempt to be civil: he hadn't planned to change his garments for three days more.

"I . . . I need some money to buy food and supplies."

He had known that was coming, but he had planned not to be nice about it. He stalked to the bar. On a scrap of parchment, he drew a barrel with an initial on it. He then laboriously signed his name below the picture.

"Take this to my suppliers in the bazaar." He named off a half-dozen merchants. "When you show them this, they'll know where to deliver the stuff. Get what you *need*, and don't beggar me, girl! Make this mark on each bill." He drew a hook with a slash mark in the sawdust with his toe. "There'll be no cash put out until I see that, and until the wares are inside my doors. I don't do business any other way. Now, here are what I pay for staples . . ."

He lectured her as one would a dim-witted child, stringing together choppy syllables listing the prices of supplies. She took it meekly (this time). She still owed him for the alley. Besides, she was secretly impressed: she had never known anyone besides Gramper Jarvis who could write his name like that. As for the prices, though she noted some of them in passing, she quickly realized that she could best all the ones she had heard. When he had finished, she nodded and slipped out the door, unknowingly missing the excitement that buzzed around the tavern when the mysterious sleeping stranger rose from his rest late that morning.

Denalee had a lot of shopping ahead of her. It wouldn't be as easy as just pointing and ordering what she needed. Nothing should ever be purchased without proper dickering. As the cook, it was up to her to see that the Gryphon didn't become the target of highway robbery disguised as retail pricing. Barrelgut had already been getting mildly skinned on several items, probably because of his general ignorance of food preparation; that would stop. Denalee was very good at beating down prices, and she intended to put her talent to full use this morning.

The trouble was that the bazaar was enormous compared to the market in the Slews, and she had never purchased many of the items before. She was eyeing some unfamiliar foods and listening to others bargain for them when, for the second time that day, she bumped into a dark-haired girl not much older than herself. The girl, Brieze, was a Tellarani; she seemed immediately friendly and ready to talk, as if somehow she already knew Denalee. Brieze said something about her blood leading her to Denalee, but the Slews girl didn't understand it.

Their differences didn't detract from the friendliness. They were like two faces of the same coin, though Denalee admitted to herself that Brieze was much the prettier of the two. The Tellarani girl wasn't exactly a "girl," but a married woman, with three brothers and sisters and a more-or-less husband living with her in the wheelless wagon across the bazaar from Ibraim's booth. When it became obvious that both young women were headed for the same food shops, they combined forces.

The two, dark and light, shapely and thin, discovered a great deal of common ground as they chatted happily on their rounds. Together, they confounded merchant after merchant with a combination of bazaar experience and knife-sharp haggling. Denalee parted with reluctance from the first female friend her age she had ever had. Her family had always been crowded, but never seemed to have been near other big families. The pair promised to meet again soon, before Denalee hurried back toward the inn and the ton of work waiting for her there.

The food had been even less expensive than she had figured; better quality went for fewer coppers. One of the contradictions of Barrow was that in a city that exported food, there was regular starvation. Worse, because of a change in the pattern of traffic flow, the poorer sections of the city had the worst food supplies and the highest prices. Vegetable leavings that garnered top prices in the Slews weren't even offered east of the river: the competition was too stiff.

Barrelgut was still fuming when she returned; some of the deliveries had arrived. He was happy enough about the foodstuffs, but another *broom*? His face looked like a red balloon when the shovel arrived. By that time, Denalee was too rushed to be lectured. She sharply pointed out that the lower price she had gotten for potatoes in one month would pay for the broom, the shovel, and the apron she had ordered.

Apron! That set him off again, but Denalee, who had a total of one shift in her wardrobe, wanted the heavy canvas of the apron between her and spills as much as she wanted her new job. With fists on hips, she offered to let Barrelgut do his own sweeping, shoveling, *and* cooking. He was already facing a rough noon crowd, some of whom had wanted food that wasn't ready. Although she hadn't served a single regular meal, Barrelgut had already discovered an indispensable need for a cook. He also decided to discover some important business elsewhere than the kitchen. He left in a grumbling huff.

All through the afternoon his voice could be heard in the common room, berating spendthrifts and avowing that he was not made of money, especially when any other delivery arrived. Denalee, slaving in a strange kitchen that needed four hands to clean and three to cook, again missed the return and second departure of the mysterious adventurer who had crossed her path the day before. She would hear the story of his overnight rise to riches in bits and pieces of gossip over the next weeks, but that night she learned his name: Harmon Yorn.

Overall, Denalee's first day as a cook was a success. Her food, though plain, was received like delicacies from the tables of the gods, when compared to the former swill. Barrelgut made a little money, though food lacked the high markup of beverages. The fact that the inn had been connected to that Harmon Yorn who had the Town all abuzz kept the crowds high all day.

Two days ago, Yorn had been a wine bibber and ne'er-do-well, best known to bartenders and fellow drinkers. He had gone on the briefest of quests and returned, wounded, with knowledge of the location of an unusual treasure. When his hired team had fetched the treasure, he had sold it for enough coin to him take out of Upcruster Town forever.

The Gryphon and Goblet was a natural place to gather and gossip for those who had been trailing behind Harmon Yorn all day, hoping that some of his luck or money might rub off on them. Drink flowed freely, and Denalee stayed up late trying to keep up with food orders. The evening saw a sellout of everything she had cooked. Boss and employee went to bed happy, for different reasons.

· 8 ·

That first evening was a harbinger of the weeks that followed. Food profits might be small, but the volume was high. The presence of good food attracted more drinkers. The coppers that Barrelgut invested in Denalee's salary and in supplies swelled into a little silver. Denalee began to fill out as well, in places she hadn't expected, places she hadn't even *had* places before. She had never had three meals a day before, and now she had *meat* once a week! She had made enough coin to buy some sandals so that she no longer had to walk the bazaar barefoot, like some peasant girl come to town. She now owned *three* shifts and other small items. Life was good.

She had changed in another important way: The kitchen had become her kingdom. She had never minded dirt while she lived west of the river; grime had existed in neutrality with her family. Perhaps the change came from having to clean up the layers of sediment that two male allies of dirt had left in her work space by years of neglect. While shoveling out the kitchen over a period of a week, she had dug unexpectedly into a deep vein of compulsive cleanliness within herself. Never again would the surface she was trying to work on begin evolving toward independent life under layers of organic coatings. The counters shone! The oven was clean; the utensils almost glowed, hanging in neat rows. Everything had a place and it was *in* that place. Barrelgut only dared poke his head into the kitchen once in a while, and he was careful to keep his reaction to its new state to himself.

The kitchen wasn't the only thing at which he had been looking, but he kept his expression unreadable when she caught his eyes on her. He had grown into a better frame of mind about the food handling as time passed, only complaining now about the meat bill. Once he discovered how to pad that bill, using the private meat purchases of one eccentric tenant, even that complaint disappeared. Denalee had proved her worth as a cook. He had grown tolerant enough that sometimes they talked late, after the customers had gone. Most of the conversation was business of the inn, but bits of personal history began to slip in.

Barrelgut had been raised by a street-wise mother who had filled his head with good, common sense. She had died when he was sixteen, not long after she had helped Barrelgut get his job with Dirty Kevin. He didn't mention a father. Denalee secretly wondered what his mother had called him; she doubted that it was "Barrelgut."

He had hung on to his job, mostly because of his size, by his telling. Not much over a year later, he had become an accidental man of property. At first, he had sprinkled his hair with dust to age himself artificially, and talked deep, until the regulars accepted him. Barrelgut had a strong dose of good-ol'-boy blood in his own ancestry, and he had fit in with his customers. Remembering the bluff he had run on them made him smile. He wasn't a bad-looking man when he did. The tall bartender with an old man's pompous ways would be twenty-one on his next birthday.

Denalee told him about the good times and the hard times of her family, and a little about leaving home. She left out the part about the monster and the purple-stained adventurer, and Garny. Her life as a girl would have sounded too complicated to be believable, and some things weren't to be shared with just anyone. He seemed genuinely sympathetic about the bad times she had had, but she couldn't tell if it was bartender sympathy or the real thing. Still . . .

When Gorgio came back to work, she saw less of her large employer. He worked later now in the evenings and slept longer mornings. She was usually gone shopping when he rose, and then busy with the noon meal and the afternoon cooking. Gorgio proved to be no problem to be alone with. He was a sallow, greasy Maldavian who had been run out of that wine-growing peninsula over a scandal involving the theft of some vines of special vintage. He now was living with some Lowlander woman from Ichan near the river. His position as co-owner had been arrived at as accidently as Barrelgut's, but the Upcrusters considered the inn to belong to the big man alone. Having been beaten once, Gorgio was affable about it, as long as he continued to collect his forty percent.

Things were going well for Denalee—ominously well. She worked so hard that she had no time to be lonely. She was well paid. Why did an inner voice keep prodding her toward perfection, toward a fear that that job would soon be gone? Twice a week, she had to cook no midday meal. She visited her friend, Brieze, and her chubby "husband" in their wagon at the bazaar. Brieze's siblings made it crowded, but that made the wagon homey to Denalee.

The two women shopped together almost daily, and the regulars at the tavern treated Denalee as a friend, though she could rarely get out of the kitchen to mingle with them in the evenings. They made halfhearted passes at her and kept the obscene comments to a minimum in her presence. It was almost as if someone was warning them away from her, but she had no standard to judge their behavior by. She suspected that she had become a kind of mascot to them, since few other females ever seemed to frequent the Gryphon. Maybe Barrelgut had told them not to molest his prize cook. (Now, that thought certainly generated an odd mixture of feelings!)

· 9 ·

On a slow, mid-week day like any other, Denalee was in her kitchen assembling the evening meal with experienced efficiency. Barrelgut was at a table in the common room counting a couple of days' receipts. A single customer snoozed next to his small beer; it was too early for most business. Gorgio had gone home early, feeling poorly again. The open kitchen door let in the summer's air, and the flies, though Denalee had covers now on anything the buzzy little devils might try to drown themselves in. The voice that also came through the kitchen door was the last one Denalee had wanted to hear.

"Doin' all right for yourself, I see, sis." Garny slouched against the doorframe, grimy and red-eyed.

He stank of grabit weed; Denalee had almost forgotten the smell. The Upcrusters ran off anyone they caught selling it east of the river. Honest farmers pulled it out of their fence rows when they found it. A few not-so-honest farmers grew it and dried it. It sold well in the Slews to people who had died to genuine emotions. Grabit weed enhanced emotions—all emotions.

If you were mildly happy, grabit weed made you ecstatic. If you were momentarily unhappy, the weed brought on cathartic crying jags; sometimes suicide. Emotional shifts came on a user as sharply as the snapping of an overloaded spring. If the chewer jolted from, say, extreme anger to extreme thirst, he would likely be even further off the norm than before. He would chug down half a dozen liters of liquid before the next shift hit him. Other changes were considerably more dangerous.

"Let's have it, then. You must have turned plenty of coin working here."

Greed was evidently the primary desire driving him at the moment. Trying to turn him from it would be like commanding the tide to stand still, but if she gave him every bent copper she had, the drug would still not be satisfied.

"I've got nothing of yours. Hit the road!" The filth on him made her clean-happy skin crawl. The bad times were back, as if she had replaced a mouthful of clean food with grit.

"You *deserted* us, you little slut!" His pupils were like black pits, with only a thin ring of iris. "You cheated me. . . . Me! You owe us . . . me! Pay, pay me! I want . . . I want . . . I want . . ." The drugged machinery of his mind made the shift. "I want . . . you! You! You promised *me*, that night you left. . . . You promised me. . . ." He moved across the space between them like a striking snake, his unfocused eyes staring.

There was no time to cry out. Instantly, he had Denalee bent backward across a counter, his rank body jammed against hers and a grimy hand over her mouth. She tasted the grit, but it wasn't the first time. She tried to strike back, but he had the strength of the insane. His other hand clamped behind her waist, dragging her toward the door to the alley. His distorted mind was seeing the weed patch at the edge of the swamp, where he had first planned to force his half-sister. His mind was rampaging across memories and tripping through strange places where sanity could never walk.

Though Denalee was heavier and stronger than she had been, in a handful of seconds they were through the door. One of his hands ripped the bodice of her working shift to the waist. His lust-driven eyes widened with delight at what he saw. Like a rutting beast, he forced her down into the alley's slime, the green foam at the corner of his mouth splattering her bare stomach with vegetable residue. His left hand tore her shift the rest of the way down, exposing her gray undergarment, as his right hand entangled her flailing arms. One of her own arms was mashed up over her mouth, allowing only a growling moan to escape. If he smothered her by accident, he wouldn't discover it until he had climaxed his satisfaction.

Her struggling, sprawling fall had spread her legs. Garny wedged them further open with his hips. Now, he tugged at his crude fly, and—

A hand the size of a plate plucked him into the air, the way an owl might seize a mouse. He was lifted to dangle like a hanged man, his shirt bunched under his chin by two huge fists, eye to eye with Barrelgut.

A bear couldn't have growled the words any more gruesomely. "Something bad (shake!) is about to happen (shake!) to you (shake!) twerp! I'm going to get your blood (shake!) all over my nice (shake!) clean (shake!) hands!" (squeeze!)

Garny had gone through another emotional shift. He gibbered and flailed his arms; he wet himself. His entire being was now directed toward escape. His legs were running, even though he was only able to touch the tip of a toe to the ground every third try. He had saved himself from immediate dismemberment by devolving into something less than worth killing. In a few seconds more, even that wouldn't have saved him.

Denalee pulled herself up out of the alley's mire. "Don't kill him: he's my brother." She had paid off the last mite of debt to her family. She wouldn't have to run anymore.

Barrelgut glanced at her, with conflicting feelings twisting his face. He decided. The big man picked Garny up like a rag ball and threw him the length of the alley. Garny skipped once in a puddle at the alley mouth, bounced across Straight Street, and came to rest against the wall of the Gryphon's half-abandoned stable across the lane. He sprang up like a stressed bundle of wire and, still screaming, fled out of sight. His bleating faded into the distance.

His drug and his terrified spirit pursued him off the arch of the Old Wat Bridge into watery death, but he had already been erased from the existence of the two who remained in the alley from the moment that he left their sight. Barrelgut had made a half turn toward Denalee when she crossed the space between them as a nail would to a lodestone. She clung there, sobbing in relief.

His hands fluttered in midair like flying hams until they settled on her shoulders. By the Thousand Stars, they felt good there! The bulge around his waist that she had assumed was beer-soft stomach, turned out to be only an inch of fat layered over a slab of abdominal muscle. (Barrelgut had gotten his name because he always unloaded and stacked his own barrels in the spirits room. His was the rotund shape of the weight lifter.) Denalee's collision on her first day of work had been too brief for her to notice the difference.

On impulse, she suddenly threw her arms about his neck and kissed him, on tiptoe. He was surprised, but he returned the kiss with enthusiasm. She wanted to say something to him as he held her. She wanted to whisper his name, but "Barrelgut" lacked something as a romantic appellation.

He thought it must have been instinct that made him blush and say, "Denalee, my real name is Clarence-Kim. But don't tell anyone!"

She hugged him, with eyes wide. "I . . . I think I love you, Clarence-Kim!"

It was her turn to blush: what was this "love" talk? Something within her felt as if it had bloomed like a rose hidden in a vase in the cool dark of her kitchen. In the Slews, love was something you heard about, but like so many other things, you couldn't afford. It felt so *strange*.

The big man stood stiff and still, but after a lot of gulping, he said, "You know . . . I . . . think I love you, too!" He helped her hold her torn dress together by holding her very close to him.

Love, or whatever this was, didn't mind being played out against the backdrop of a grungy alley. It never had. After a long time, during which nothing was said but a great deal was felt, they moved toward the kitchen door together. As they were edging through the confines of the small room, the bartender's hip caught a pan of slops and flipped it onto the clean floor.

"Never mind," she said, and stopped to kiss him again.

He was enjoying the kiss when realization hit him. He broke off to stare from her to the mess on the floor that she was ignoring. She was further transformed in his eyes. "Say, you *do* love me!" Then *he* kissed her, and the exchange went on.

In the main room of the tavern, Cavin-the-Cutpurse had been dozing at his regular table when Barrelgut had gotten up and walked toward the kitchen. The big man's rushing exit from the room had roused Cavin fully. He looked up to see every larcenous daydream he had ever had come true. Several days' receipts for the inn lay neatly stacked on a table within a meter of him—unguarded. That was simply too much to resist. Although he was as loyal to Barrelgut as any of the Gryphon's regulars, the trove before him was more than any self-respecting thief could leave alone. He scooped the coins into his floppy hat and ran. He would have to drink west of the river for a few months and maybe grow a beard before he returned to the Town, but the take was worth it.

Cavin's dust had long settled by the time the mutually involved couple squeezed through the door behind the bar. She was the first to notice. "You were counting the—it's gone!" Only the flattened moneybag lay on the table.

Barrelgut became briefly grim as he looked over the situation. There was no difficulty in identifying the robber, and as little trouble calculating Cavin's head start. "Never mind," he said, and bent to kiss her again.

This time it was Denalee who broke it off. "Why . . . Why you do love me!" She was in his arms in a leap.

After many forgotten minutes, Denalee pushed him away. "Watch the hands, fella!"

"I'm trying to, but you keep pulling your dress together."

"Don't be too smart. We're not married yet!"

"Married? I didn't say anything—"

"Yeah, but *I* did. (Mother, you better have been right: I don't want to lose him!)"

Barrelgut, who was suddenly having cold feet to near midthigh, hadn't been thinking any further ahead than the large bed in his quarters. Being married was rather complicated; best not to think about it. . . .

His reluctance reached Denalee. "You weren't so slow thinking about things when your hand was inside my dress a minute ago."

That started him thinking about "things" again, as it was meant to. "Wait!" she said. She fairly scampered up the stairs to her room. She dug her coins out of every memorized hidey-hole and pulled the pendant and scroll from her trunk. In a few seconds more, she slipped into an unripped shift.

Barrelgut hadn't had time to puzzle the situation out before she was back in the taproom with her treasures in hand. "It isn't much of a dowry, but—"

"Never mind." He had glanced at the money in her hand, only to find that it was second in importance in his thoughts. That settled it: anything that took his mind off business the way the look in Denalee's eyes did had to receive priority. The "never mind" had been as much for himself to discontinue searching for ways to get this woman in bed without marrying her as it had been for her. It immediately got him another resounding kiss.

When they stopped for breath, Barrelgut poked at the pile of treasures she had dropped on a table. "You had *this* much?" He turned over the coins with an expert's eye, having obviously missed a chance to bargain her out of more of this wealth the first night they met. Had he done so, he wouldn't be sharing it now, as well as gaining something more valuable.

Idly, he unrolled the scroll and read it. " 'Take . . .

this . . . pendant . . . to . . . old . . . teacher . . . in . . . the Scoop.' Say, I know him! He taught me to read." He picked up the pendant and studied it. There was some squiggly foreign script on the back, but its metal was of no obvious worth.

Denalee stood quietly, impressed with the education of her man. Wow! What a jolting phrase: *her* man!

"Let's go see him now! The Old Man quits near sundown." He took her hand.

"But the inn—"

"Let it go. There's no one upstairs right now, and being closed for a while won't hurt it."

He could tell that he had impressed his woman again, putting business aside to do something together. (His woman. Wow!) They barred the main door and the back door off the common room and slipped out the kitchen door, pulling it shut behind them. The two hurried hand in hand, north up Straight Street until it collided with Pimpgut Way. The Scoop was a hundred paces beyond the intersection, a slightly wider spot on the Way. A small group of students was clustered around the teacher.

The white-haired man stopped his lecture and watched their approach. The Old Man's appraisal gave Barrelgut a strange "feeling" that only puzzled him, but Denalee had experienced something like it many weeks before. She shivered, without knowing why.

"Clarence! It's been a long time!" The Old Man's face beamed like the sun. He turned to the last few students of the day. "We're through for now, children. Come meet another student of mine."

A group of noisy children gathered around Denalee and the embarrassed Barrelgut. He seemed to have shrunk in the presence of his former teacher. He smiled nervously and nodded like a child being shown off by a proud parent, but the street urchins quickly lost interest and scampered off in all directions.

"Well, young people, what can I do to help you?"

Though the Old Man was beaming as any elder would in the presence of a couple in love, Denalee realized that he had manipulated the dismissal of the children so that he could talk to them alone. In fact, her gut kept telling her that the old teacher knew *exactly* what they wanted already. Her man obviously felt a relaxed security in the presence of the man, but Denalee felt a rising wave of shyness: something just wasn't right here. Still, she dug out her small treasure and held it out to the white-haired teacher. The Old Man turned it over gently and examined the inscription.

"Yes, this is the one. I knew my friend Jarvis had been killed, but I didn't know what had happened to this when he died. Would you mind selling this to me? I value it because it belonged briefly to my son, who died recently."

Barrelgut was already nodding agreement.

"How much . . . ?" Denalee began.

"Would ten gold pieces be enough?" The Old Man pulled a clinking pouch from a crevice in his garment that was far too small to have held it.

Denalee sputtered: was ten gold pieces *enough*? Jarvis's treasure had not been hers long enough to let its sentimental value exceed the fortune he was offering. She was still standing stunned when Barrelgut agreed to the deal. The enormity of it! First a king's ransom for a cheap-metal pendant and then her fiancé's nerve in selling *her* pendant: she was speechless.

"I wish you two happiness forever." The Old Man smiled and quickly passed over the gold. Tucking the pendant into a pocket in his robe, he excused himself and walked away.

Denalee and Barrelgut were halfway back to the Gryphon before she realized: if the pendant had been worth ten gold pieces on the first offer, then it had been worth *more*, and she hadn't even had a chance to bargain!

· **10** ·

Orno, the Saikhandian cleric, received the surprise of his life that night. He would have bet more coin on the likelihood of nuptials between a nanny goat and a bear than an impulse wedding between Barrelgut and his sharp-tongued cook. On the other hand, the blond girl had plumped out nicely over the past weeks. Orno figured that their choice of mates was none of his business (unless it interrupted the flow of superlative food from the Gryphon's kitchen). He performed the ceremony with due pomposity.

After some tearful well-wishing from the Tellarani girl who came to stand up with the bride and a great number of crude jokes for the groom, the Gryphon closed early. The newlyweds retired to Barrelgut's quarters to fight about money matters and then make up several times in a most delightful way.

Of course, they did not have happiness forever: no mere wish by the greatest of magicians could have carried that much power. Besides, occasional misery was to life what Denalee's spices were to her "something else." There were times when she would call her husband a blubbery tightwad. On a few occasions, she would throw a skillet at him and use some words that she had once picked up west of the river. She would never let him live down selling *her* pendant too cheaply, though they decided together how to spend the profit from it. Those who knew them would never be surprised whenever that lightweight woman occasionally threw her enormous husband out of her kitchen bodily.

For his part, he would, when angry, bring up her origins in the Slews or call her a clean-crazy broad. Though he tolerated no lip from rowdy customers, no matter their size, he would never raise a hand to her. When bullied out of the kitchen, he would counterattack by accusing her of being a wild-eyed spendthrift with the tastes of a queen, and on his diminutive income, too!

Then, they would always make up again, a joyful and imaginative pastime; so, perhaps they did have a kind of happiness forever. At least, she got him to repaint the sign.

Interchapter

Ah, young people in love: I had to do so little! On the other hand, without some creative nudges at the right moment, Barrelgut and Denalee might have taken weeks or months more to realize that what they wanted was each other. Still, it would have happened eventually, even if I hadn't put the right words in their mouths at the proper moment. Did they really need me?

Well that I was keeping a trace on Denalee's mind, or I would have allowed another woman whose life I had manipulated to be viciously raped. Garny wasn't part of my plan, nor was Cavin. Would Barrelgut have arrived outside in time without the "sense of danger" that I planted in his mind?

Frustration! I am reminded again of my lack of omniscience. I think I was right, but . . . It is comforting to know that I did help the upright young guardsman at the Slews gate that Denalee met. That girl has just enough magic in her blood to make her distrust me forever. She might have been trained—but not by me: she reminds me too much of another blond girl from Upcruster Town, from many years ago.

Now, about that guard, the one that Denalee called the "johnny-straight": when I realized what was about to happen, I happened to remember a young Mugambese who stops to listen to me "preach" whenever he can. With just the right touch . . .

BOOK IV

The Johnny-Straights

UKRUSU WANDERED THE CITY, his anger boiling within. With each step, he shook the rounded rattle with its colored streamers the same way he would have a war club. He wished with all his heart that it were a war club. The exotic attractions of the Upcruster Town bazaar called his attention constantly to his lack: he could not walk there as a warrior. The Townsmen respected his gold, but the rivers of Mugambu had been so full of that yellow metal that even an adolescent such as Ukrusu had several bits of it. Those foreign eyes saw him only as a young black man with money, not as the potential warrior that his age gave him the right to be.

He seldom ventured north of Caravan Way. The mansions and high temples there contrasted too much with the raw, unfinished state of the Mugambese quarter that Barrow's prince had ordered built just outside the city's southeast wall. Clan chiefs or warriors of note might be welcome among the great houses, but not boys who could not as qualify for Clan status. That reminder made him shake the rattle again on its hardwood stave. He slammed the carved handle into the dirt, as if into the skull of an enemy. The stout staff might make a good cudgel, if he were forced to use it for that, but it was neither a war club, with its iron knob, nor a half-man-high stabbing spear, nor a quiver of throwing spears, their barbs like little leaves of death. Only a warrior was allowed those.

Mother had told him to wait until next year, when things would be more settled. What did a woman, even Mother, know about the soul of a man? She had retained her household more or less intact, even if it had been jammed into the bottom of a war canoe for the long voyage to Barrow. She would be happy in any house as long as she could place her clay earth mothers on her shelves for all to see and hang the walls with the striped skins and other trophies of her husband. The coming year promised to bring her a large house in the new quarter—a house built to accommodate the colder Barrow weather, but hers to manage nonetheless.

Father was constantly busy, it seemed. As chief, he had to rule the diverse and emotional elements within his own Clan, without ruffling the touchy plumes of the subchiefs. Everyone had been heavily stressed by the forced migration; minor quarrels could easily become blood feuds. It was also his responsibility to be the interface between his Clan and the ruling house of the Mugambisa. He had risen to become her personal counselor in many important matters. Recognizing that, the native Barrowmen also often consulted him in Mugambese matters generally. There was no space in his life, it seemed, to notice his son's distress.

The locals were not hateful or vicious, and not even especially curious anymore about their new dark-skinned fellow citizens. The enormous mingling of peoples during the Prince's Big Party, at last year's winter solstice, had removed a great deal of the Mugambese novelty and broken down many barriers. Ukrusu felt that it had only stolen what uniqueness he had had left.

The wharves had been briefly interesting. Ships of the size the northerners used were something Ukrusu had seldom seen. The fishermen along the southern quays were so busy that one more boy hanging around was either underfoot or ignored. Ukrusu had no interest in fishing. He had no fond memories of the sea: the trip to Barrow in a double-hulled war canoe had left only remembrance of continual bailing and spitting out salt water in his sleep. He had been considered a boy then, too: old enough to bail dirty water but too small to be a paddler.

His wanderings had carried him north, among the merchantmen at the docks along the Wat River's eastern bank. Most were round grain carriers, bound for the Arpago River cities. A few were tougher, smaller ships, willing to risk the dangerous voyage around the end of the continent to Svernig for a cargo of that city's fabulous silk. He gave no real consideration to the scattered offers to sign on as a cabin boy or deckhand, but the talk helped seat him better in the new language. He had picked it up without difficulty, though it sickened him to think of parting with the language of home.

He found the naval craft moored below the citadel of the Prince's palace more interesting. He was disappointed to find that they were not actively recruiting seamen. Poorer young men from throughout the Empire kept the navy's ranks full, finding good pay and, presently, few seagoing battles to fight. The business of those ships was war, but an alien kind of war against smugglers and pirates. Ukrusu might have wheedled a place aboard one using Father's influence, but he wasn't ready to beg for the attention his parent should have been giving spontaneously.

Eventually, none of the city proper had been left for him to explore, seeking blindly for relief of inward tension. Only the Slews, that reeking sore on the city's west flank, had remained unvisited. He had avoided it because so many local forms of nasty death made their homes there. Now, with hope gone, where he went didn't matter.

At home in Mugambu, a boy could become a man on his own: a Clan member; a warrior allowed more weapons than a belt knife and a rattle on a stick. Though it was better to have a father or an uncle to guide him, a boy could still stalk, say, a water buffalo and make the kill that proclaimed him a man. The Water Buffalo Clan then would accept him by his proof tokens into their warrior membership, whatever the Clan of his birth.

Ukrusu had wanted desperately to become a member of his father's Leopard Clan. He had begun making plans on his own to make his manhood hunt as soon as his isolation in this city of thousands had begun to settle sourly into his blood. He had found out where weapons and wilderness supplies could be purchased before he had asked the most important question of the locals: where, in the forests or swamps or plains ruled by Barrow's prince, could a leopard be found? He would greet Father with the proofs in hand: the dried claws of the great cat he had killed alone. Father wore his own set of claws, and the scars he had taken to get them, with pride.

The answer had stunned him: there were no leopards this far north; not in the swamps or forests or in any other clime accessible from Barrow. Life might as well have ended then. He could never be a Leopard, a Water Buffalo, or a Python, nor any other Mugambu-pure Clan. He might have qualified for the low-status Crocodile Clan, but he was so depressed that that Clan seemed only a tiny step above the mud into which he was sunk. His last option was to find some new, dangerous game in this strange country and establish a new Clan line. Every other Clan had begun that way. The small Cobra Clan was the latest, only fifty years old, proud of the capes they wore, each of twenty cobra skins. Cobras were a rarity in Barrow, however.

There were dangerous animals in plenty within reach of the city, but there were few city men who hunted them. Predators that could threaten humans or farms had been pushed far back from human territory. Ukrusu was reluctant to admit that he feared to go south into the coastal swamps, but other than the smugglers near the river, Barrowmen also avoided them. The forests to the north held several kinds of great cats, but no one could tell him how to find one, much less kill it. He had no idea what a "bear" was, and a "wild boar" sounded something like a warthog, an animal unacceptable as a trophy, no matter how fierce. There were other beasts; it took little prodding to get some oldster to talking about the days when the Old Prince was alive and the wilderness was closer to Barrow. However, Ukrusu was amazed by the ignorance of the average Townsman: they no longer gave hunting the slightest attention. Everyone was too interested in money. They ate meat that someone else had raised, tame, and vegetables from farms they had never tilled.

Perhaps he would go northeast and seek the remnants of the wisent herds. A wisent bull was almost a water buffalo, he had been told, but no one much traveled that direction anymore, not since the Scallion Wars and the extinction of the Tellarani who had followed the herds. When he went, no matter the direction, the most likely thing that would happen would be getting lost and not returning—ever.

The songs of the Mugambu clans had been created as maps in music, leading the initiate warrior who had listened, safely through the trackless rain forests and across the mountains and savannahs; teaching him the ways of the search, the stalk, and the kill of each Clan. Only a fool or a foreigner could watch the Water Buffalo Dance and not see how thoroughly it instructed the neophyte in tracking the buffalo to its water hole and striking it from above. Over hundreds of years, that dance, like the dances of all the clans, had been modified and refined by consensus into a saga in body and song that was an encyclopedia of hunting.

After the traditional dancing and singing of each saga, the best of the living warriors would dance out his own hunt in symbols, crying out the names of the places his feet had touched. Their bodies painted a story on the air, detailing the creeping rush, the wounds, the strike, the blood, and the honor of the kill. A youth could see, as surely as with eyes that had been there, how Father had stalked his leopard up the spotted cat's own tree, or how Kanasku, the Water Buffalo chief, had lured his bull again and again beneath the killing tree with a dummy made of broken branches and his cape. Were they not all magnificent?

Ukrusu did not recognize that he was mourning the evolutionary death of an ancient culture. Similarly, since he was not yet a member of the emerging new culture, either of Barrow or of transplanted Mugambu in Barrow, all he felt was a leeching sickness in the guts. He saw little left to live for. Across the river in the Slews, death had a citadel for his own Clan. If it was rotten, dangerous, degenerate, or illegal, it could be found in the Slews.

Donning his best clothing, so that death would not find him in a state without honor, Ukrusu set out day after day to walk that final, forbidding part of Barrow, to turn out the last pocket of the city seeking his destiny. If it was not there, there were always the swamps. Death lived there as well.

• 2 •

Kinsworth Vomanger, chevron of the city guard, shifted from foot to foot in boredom. It was another quiet day at the Swamp Gate. Toothless old Hammertoe, about the only farmer anymore who bothered to swing down the muddy lane west of the city wall and deliver his produce directly to the Slews, had come through early with his half-witted farm hand, Norgan. Later, a slim, blond slum girl with a notable black eye had stopped and smiled at him. Fed a little better, she might have been pretty. He wished her well as they talked. She was bound for Upcruster Town and a new life, she said. Except for the wounded man with the purple-stained clothing, the rest of the day had been as forgettable as the stale mush for breakfast.

He could sympathize with the slum girl's "new life" dream. Father might be content to vegetate in their modest manse, to be the Honorable Norlok Vomanger, Knight of the River, but Kinsworth remembered that honorary knighthoods expired with the bearer. Either he would make his own name prominent, or he would someday be only the untitled Ian-Vomanger, inheriting money, mansion, and inertia. He was not yet twenty, but he could already feel the decay trying to creep into his bones.

The Empire's continual harping on making a profit was not for him, and he had not wanted to leave Barrow to seek fulfillment elsewhere. There was plenty of opportunity along the Empire's northwest frontier beyond Ichan. Wherever the caravan routes were accessible to the vicious Highlanders, there would be action and opportunity. Barrow itself had been peaceful for a long lifetime; the chances of extending the family's knighthood within it by some great deed were few. The title might have to be allowed to slide, but by that time Kinsworth hoped to be well on his way toward advancement in a career he could respect.

He had joined the city guard as just another "boot" hopeful of advancement. However, he had advanced the one step to chevron only by death or retirement higher in the ranks, not by his personal merit. Though there was a whiff in the wind of an upcoming shake-up in the guard because of corruption, opportunity to advance in it by exceptional service was conspicuously absent so far.

There was no doubt that corruption was present. Kinsworth should normally not have been on duty alone, even during the slack of the day shift. Bartholomew Bagman, an aging boot, was to have stood the watch with him, but Barto was helplessly drunk in the guard shack, as usual. Of the six watchmen for the Swamp Gate, two were lushes, two were on the take, and one spent time he was supposed to be on duty with a "lady friend." The guard corporal had the green stains around his chin of a grabit-weed chewer, though he had so far kept his vice outside duty hours. You didn't get sent over to the back end of the Slews, it seemed, unless you were a raw recruit or had washed out of every other post in the city. Kinsworth was in the "raw" category.

He had been on duty two days in the Slews when the first offer came: free drinks from a "friend." The flunky who had been sent as a go-between eventually hinted that the drinks were to ensure Kinsworth's looking the other way someday, when "something special" had to come through the gate on his shift. Kinsworth had threatened the "friend" with arrest for attempted bribery, and he had rapped the flunky's departing rear soundly with the butt of his halberd.

The next offer was more direct: money or drugs for favors. That time he had arrested the messenger, although he was only another small fish. That offender was now in the dungeon under the citadel across the river. The third approach recapitulated the crude subtlety of the first. A youngish woman, heavily made up and a little worn around the edges, began making more and more pointed promises about what she would do to him and for him in return for his cooperation. Some of the ideas were appealing, but he sent her away also. He didn't arrest her. The way her eyes had been running away from something inside her had told him that she was already a victim of the same people who wished to exploit him. He saw her again later, trying to hide a bruised face under too much rouge, paid off by her bosses for failing with him.

Today was no different from any other day; there just weren't any good days in the Slews. He paced his post alone.

• **3** •

Harry Hardback had become the leader of the most desperate band of smugglers in the Slews by default. "Desperate" referred to the near extinction of their capital rather than their danger to others. They were broke; Harry made that plain immediately when he called them together.

They were a mean lot. Most had cut a throat or two in their careers, but they weren't killers by profession. If Wheezer hadn't snagged the syndicate's cash and hightailed it across the swamp, they would have been moderately well off—even rich—this side of the river. Mention of Wheezer always called for a prolonged round of cursing, lacking in imagination, but fervent. Everything hinged, Harry told them, on the next load.

Though Wheezer had absconded with the operating capital, at least a third that much was tied up in the drugs that were soon to come upriver. It would all be Mugambu Black, the gummy resin that when mixed with pipe weed and smoked, produced ecstasy during certain sexual acts. It was worth more than its weight in gold, but supplies in Barrow had dried up over a year before when a coup in Mugambu had overthrown the ruling family. The new Mugambiso had finally negotiated his bribe for export rights with the syndicate's agent, and the first dearly bought load was on its way.

Unfortunately, the Mugambiso's blessing had only been rented instead of permanently purchased. He had agreed to let others ship out the black, sticky treasure also. The Big Onion Gang would soon have a load on the way. Unless the syndicate moved fast, their prices would be undercut by the bigger gang's volume. The Big Onion Gang were the movers and shakers in the Slews right now. They had been climbing for close to thirty years, led by a face-less felon who was the most ruthless headbreaker ever to grace the bloody-minded pocket of crime west of the river. He had no name other than the Big Onion, and even some of his lieutenants had never seen his face.

If the syndicate failed to sell and sell quickly, they would be flooded out by below-cost Mugambu Black. It was no secret about Wheezer's departure with their cash; too many loud and obscene words had been said about it by the members themselves within others' hearing. The Onion Gang had the contacts, runners, and reserves to sit out a drug price war, and they knew that the syndicate didn't. Later, with the competition out of business, the prices would go up and up again. There was no hope for Harry Hardback's troupe unless that load came through the Swamp Gate *today*. Grimly, the hard-core crew of the syndicate set out south.

Their package was being held downriver three kilometers. The ship it had arrived on had already docked innocently at a Barrow wharf. The run through the swamp had yet to be made. The plan was, as usual, to trickle out of town a few at a time, dropping off lookouts. Harry's crew were fingering weapons more often than usual. No one had better try to stop them: this was a matter of survival in a quarter that gave no prizes for second place except a grave in the swamps.

• 4 •

Kinsworth felt the beginnings of unease. This day might not be as ordinary as he had first thought. There had been an unnatural flow out the gate, all on the up-and-up, but still not quite right. What were a bunch of Slews toughs doing out in daylight, much less going south toward uninhabited wilderness? The thugs didn't usually stir before afternoon. Their nocturnal movements outside the walls were often to try to bring something illicit into the city. Maybe they were going to fetch a load instead!

He gave the area around the gate a once-over check and hurried to the guard shack. Shaking Bartholomew did no good. It looked as if someone had slipped him an extra bottle of hair-of-the-dog this morning, if the amount spilled around the shack was any indication. The corporal was not around. Even though not technically on duty, he was supposed to be available. Kinsworth had seen him meandering away from the gate area earlier, not long after old Hammertoe had come through, and he hadn't returned yet.

Kinsworth was stuck: he couldn't leave the gate unguarded to look for the corporal or another off-duty guard on the basis of suspicion only. Neither could he singly fight off a determined rush by a group, especially if all the thugs he had seen going out decided to stage a violent reentry. He checked his halberd: both ax blade and spear were sharp, and the handle was smooth and unsplit. His guardsman's dagger was long and serviceable, but if it came to knife fighting, it would be too late for him anyway. Maybe, just maybe, he had been wrong. Maybe the bad heads would run the gate on someone else's shift. Maybe they had been up to some other felony entirely. Maybe . . .

· 5 ·

Harry Hardback was sensitive about his job; he hadn't been leader for long. The pickup had gone well, and they had lost no men in the swamp. Others had been disappearing there over the last few weeks, and other gangs had lost a few loads. He had split up their own parcel initially, not gambling their future on a single carrier. The well-spaced bearers had had no trouble traversing the familiar marsh trails, but the gate would be another matter. A lot of little packages in different hands might work, but if one were caught, past experience showed that several would be caught in succession. Just within the border of the swamp, all the smaller packages were fitted inside a fake woodcutter's bundle that had been used on many runs.

Harry chose to carry it all himself. Most of the crew peeled off to enter the city by way of the Farm Gate, around the wall to the northwest. Everyone would meet down by the Wat in their safe house for cutting the drug and dividing it into salable packets. For his lead man, Harry passed over the grabit-chewing Garny; the weed made him unreliable in a pinch. Instead, he chose Ralfo, whose grizzled face had been at more knife fights than he had fingers and toes. Like his deceased brother, Ig-the-Shiv, Ralfo carried only a narrow-bladed knife in a sheath behind his neck, perfect for a hit on the spine from behind. Ralfo was technically unarmed, since daggers were as necessary as spoons at mealtime. He was carrying no drugs, and he would be let through the gate without trouble, well ahead of the main party.

Next would come Harry in his woodcutter's rags, with the precious bundle slung over his stooped back. He would be limited to a dagger, but his staff could become a cudgel as well. On his heels, watching his back, would be Mark-the-Stock Deaver. Mark was young, but he was a steady swordsman, and he would be unencumbered. If push came to shove, they would outnumber the two gate guards and could hit them from both sides. Better still, when they had gone south, only one guard had been on duty. Maybe that bottle, that Harry had had Garny slip to the other guard, had had the desired effect. The plan looked solid. The syndicate started through the pitiful outskirts of Slews-Outside-the-Walls.

• 6 •

Ukrusu found that he had made a mistake in exploring that last particular den in the Slews. The drug fumes inside the Bloody Boar had been so thick that the casual occupant became a user, whatever his intentions. The beer had been watery and bitter; obviously it was not the mainstay of the tavern's business. Ukrusu had also had to fend off the propositions of three ugly, painted white women. He had staggered to the daylight, weaving and light-headed, sorry he hadn't gone back to the Pig's Navel again today. That tavern was looking like the best the Slews had to offer.

The fresh air helped clear his head as he paced in the general direction of the Swamp Gate. His exploring trips had revealed how little there was to the miserable quarter west of the river. Today he would scout Slews-Outside-the-Walls, to see if there was anything there except more of the social misery he had seen so far. A few more days of poking around this quarter would show him everything important. After that . . . He didn't like to think about it.

Nearing the gate, he noticed a group of ragged slum dwellers in the gate area. There was also a city guard there, with his halberd angled in the "ready" position. One scruffy local was between Ukrusu and the gate, but he seemed to be turning back toward it, reaching for something at the back of his neck. The gate guard's weapon came down suddenly, blocking the path of the two still in the gate. Ukrusu heard a distant shout.

"Corporal of the guard! To arms! Murder!"

The man between him and the gate began running. To his surprise, Ukrusu found himself running as well.

• 7 •

Kinsworth had known that it would probably be hours before the toughs could travel to whatever illegal rendezvous they had in mind, and return. Those hours had gone by far too quickly, with still no sign of the guard corporal or any other member of the watch. Barto had not so much as poked his nose out of the shack. When Kinsworth had last stolen a moment to check, the older boot had been snoring like a hog in a puddle of his own vomit. When he had recognized the first of the returning thugs, Kinsworth knew he would face them unaided.

The first man was alone and gave Kinsworth no reason to do more than eye him suspiciously. He had no unusual bulges, and he almost seemed ready to dare Kinsworth to search him. He carried a shiv at the back of his neck, but there was no law in Barrow that forbade him carrying a knife anywhere that suited his fancy. Kinsworth was forced to let him through.

The two that followed him five minutes later had been part of the same southbound group that Kinsworth had noted that morning. However, there had been some notable changes: the man in the lead had different clothes and had muddied his face. He was bent under a load of sticks, partially hiding that face. If he had not been hypersensitive to the situation, Kinsworth would not have recognized him. Just behind was a younger man, shorter than Kinsworth, with a hand easy on his sword hilt. Kinsworth saw no choice.

"Stand, citizens, I'll have to search you."

The man with the bundle of sticks stiffened visibly. He froze with his hand on the bundle's strap and his innocent peasant's expression petrified into a snarl. He straightened, and his eyes lost their pretended look of resigned ignorance.

"You just don't want to do that, boy!"

The man's hand crawled toward his dagger. That cinched it, that and the professional way his companion slid out his sword. Kinsworth brought his halberd down from "ready" to "guard," and he began to shout for assistance. His guts might not have been knotting themselves if he had really expected the help he was yelling for to arrive.

· 8 ·

Mark-the-Stock had been in brawls before, and he thought he had probably killed one man, more or less by accident. He liked the drug-running trade, and he got on well with the fellows in the syndicate, but sharp things—like halberds—made him nervous. Harry had taken a step back when he straightened up, putting him right in Mark's way. An instant later, the guard had snapped down his halberd and started to yell. Mark resigned himself to a fight, at least a brief one, before more guards could show up.

He saw no need to gamble with his life. They needed only keep the guard distracted until Ralfo got him from behind. Mark moved automatically toward the butt end of the halberd, leaving the sharp end for Harry on his left. They had their opponent three to one, he and his leader tying up both ends of the pole weapon and Ralfo sneaking up to put his shiv in the guard's uncovered back. Even if the watchman spotted the danger behind, any one of the three would catch him off balance and finish the fight in seconds.

Ralfo was coming up fast and silently, pulling out his knife, with only a shadow behind him. Ralfo's left hand reached forward to cup the guard's throat. The shiv in his right would be in the spine before the guard could so much as twitch his pole arm. Then, something like a head on a stick whipped up behind Ralfo. Trailing colored streamers, it cracked down on Ralfo's skull and disintegrated. Bits of something, maybe Ralfo's brains, showered all over Mark and everyone else. Ralfo went down like a poleaxed steer, colliding with the guard.

The guard was startled and turned slightly by the impact, dropping the end of his weapon a fraction. Mark saw his chance: he swung up his sword for a slash and stepped in. The butt of the halberd snapped straight up at his face.

The shattering explosion in his mouth splattered bits and blood all down the front of Mark's jerkin. Most of it was fragments of his own teeth. Mark found himself two meters back, still on his feet, but out of the fight until he could spit out the bloody fragments of his dental apparatus. His sword wavered, forgotten, over his head. The hand holding it was trying to stanch his bleeding jaw.

• 9 •

Harry wasted no time, shifting the staff into his left hand for a club and pulling his dagger with his right. All he and Mark had to do was stall until Ralfo took the watchman down. And there was Ralfo, right on schedule.

Surprise! Ralfo went down in a shower of . . . beans? At least he had distracted the guard. Harry's cudgel whacked down across the halberd head, knocking the point toward the dirt. Harry's follow-through with the dagger couldn't reach the guard's torso, but it sank soundly into the forearm exposed when the halberd head dropped.

• 10 •

There was no time to think about why. Ukrusu's racing legs overtook the slower man in front of him. The rattle on its stave whipped through air on the run and smacked into the back of the man's head, just as he reached for the guard. The buzz of a solid hit ran up Ukrusu's arm. His target fell like a dropped stone. Beans and bits of the gourd rattle rained all over the group. He was in the fight now for sure! One of those erratic thoughts that appear in the midst of chaos reminded him how much Mother disliked his love for a good fight.

With his staff trailing a few streamers, he moved to the left to face the swordsman. At that moment, the halberd butt came up to smash that opponent's mouth into a gaping ruin. With the swordsman already retreating in pain, Ukrusu rushed him, swinging the stave at the man's head. The stranger gave ground under the rain of blows, too surprised by an injury so early in the fight to do more than dodge. Spitting teeth and blood, he didn't seem to realize that his sword was being faced down by a stick.

• 11 •

Kinsworth's hard hours of halberd drill paid off. He had made a green boot's mistake by letting himself be distracted by the bump of something against his left leg. Amid a shower of some kind of debris, his eyes had flicked to the left and back for just a moment. He corrected instantly, as his left-hand opponent raised his sword and stepped in for a cut. Kinsworth drove the hardwood shaft of the halberd into the man's face, exactly as he had in fifty dummy drills. The rap that drove the point of his weapon into the dirt on the right came as a surprise, along with the searing pain in his arm.

His pole arm dropped from his numbed right hand, and the weight of the shaft tugged it from his left. He hastily hopped back, tugging out his long dagger awkwardly with his left hand. Though the guard-issue dagger was almost a short sword, it wouldn't be effective in his off hand. He had made another idiot mistake, one that might cost him his life. Luckily, his opponent had also pulled back to shuck the bundle of sticks off his back.

A blur passed him on the left, and Kinsworth was startled to see the now-toothless swordsman being backed through the gate by a new ally. Where had that black man come from? There was no time to worry about it. His other antagonist was still intent on taking Kinsworth's life. Freed of his pack, the smuggler was circling, threatening with both the staff and the dagger. Only the longer guard knife was keeping him at bay.

• 12 •

The stave whirling at his head caught Mark painfully across the knuckles of his sword hand. That was the last straw. He turned and ran, streaming blood down his chin and across the leather neck piece that had given him his nickname. The black fury continued to pursue him, screaming insults in Mugambese. He flung something after Mark that hurt when it slammed him below the kidneys.

Mark's feet had found wings, and his heart had discovered a new purpose. He would circle through the outer shacks to the northwest and enter the city at the Farm Gate, quickly, before the alarm spread from the other gate. He could let his friends at the safe house know that their operation had collapsed. They'd give him no trouble for running once they saw his bloody gums. Maybe Harry would still win and arrive with the Black, but in Mark's defeated mind, Harry was already gone to sleep with the worms.

A career change was in order. Merchant ships were always looking for crewmen. They wouldn't care if he were toothless: lots of sailors had lost their teeth to scurvy anyway. Let Garny and the rest take up with the Big Onion or make another try to go it alone (or take a wild leap at the spinning moon, for all Mark cared). Mark was through with the drug-running business; his luck in it had deserted him. By the time he hauled back into Barrow, his mouth would have healed, and the watchmen would have stopped looking for a recently undentured smuggler. Ho, for the sea life and an obscene farewell to the Slews!

• 13 •

Ukrusu picked up his staff, the blood of battle still roaring in his ears. He stopped his pursuit because his defeated opponent had the legs on him and because the battle at the gate yet continued. Trotting back with his stick in hand, he realized immediately that the guard wasn't doing well. He was trying to face down a knife and a club with a knife only, and running blood from his right arm all the while. Ukrusu slunk as a crouching leopard might until he could swing at the back of the ragged enemy. He struck.

• 14 •

Harry had once had a shivery experience when he had witnessed the death flops of one of Ralfo's victims, dying from a blade in the back. He had sworn that when he went, it wouldn't be from a shiv in the spine. He had ordered the making of a special back protector of hardened leather, and worn it beneath his jerkin during all waking hours. The gang had coined his second name from his affected wearing of that body armor.

The black man with the staff got his attention when he whacked Harry across the back, but Harry wasn't hurt at all. His counter with his own stick caught his unprepared attacker across the temple and laid him out flat. He turned to finish off the wounded guard, and—surprise!

Harry had always hated surprises like that. As his vision darkened, he most regretted that he hadn't gotten to be leader nearly as long as he wanted.

• 15 •

Kinsworth was growing light-headed. He had to get that arm bound up, but the man before him wanted more blood, not less. He could only keep circling, waving the guard knife in what he hoped was an intimidating manner. Out of the corner of his eye he noted the return of his unknown ally. Kinsworth prepared himself to take advantage of anything that might develop.

The black man swung his stick at the smuggler's back with both hands. Unexpectedly, their enemy was only jarred. He stayed upright and lashed Kinsworth's ally across the head with his club. Within a second, the alliance had once again fallen to single-member status, but in that second, Kinsworth had taken his last remaining opportunity and lunged.

His long knife slipped through an opening left by the minute choreography of movement and inattention during battle. Even with the minimized force of a left-handed thrust, the blade went into the smuggler's heart. The ragged man folded downward into a twitching bundle from which life, as a feigned love will, faded as Kinsworth watched. Kinsworth dripped, his own sweat and blood mingling with that of the man he had killed . . . killed. Ebony circles were forming in the air before his eyes. Kinsworth dropped to his knees, turning away from the still-quivering body, and retched himself dry. Blackness folded over him.

• 16 •

The corporal of the guard ambled in, a few minutes later, and surveyed the mess as he wiped green smudges from around his mouth. The black boy had tied a sloppy but serviceable bandage around Vomanger's arm that had probably saved his life. He had also roughly trussed an ugly thug who was just beginning to stir. The corporal cinched up the tie job on the probable smuggler and improved the bandage on Vomanger. He also bound up an ugly welt on the head of the Mugambese. What a collection! He propped the two young men against each other to one side, leaving them to shiver as shock set in.

In the guard shack, he found a partially clean blanket for the heroes of the battle and wakened Barto with a few well-placed kicks. He sent Barto for a sergeant and a squad from the barracks across the river, after he let the drunk boot puke up his liquid breakfast behind the shack. The corporal was a veteran. Maybe he had a minor problem with grabit weed, but he could still tell that this day yet had a lot of business to be done, even if it would be predictable.

There was the matter of another body—bloody, mutilated, and dead—that would need some explaining. The whole gate area was scattered with blood and with what looked like bits of teeth and beans. This would make quite a guardroom story when all the loose ends were tied up. He sighed. It would take the same amount of time to play this out, no matter what he did; there was very little he could do to speed it up.

· 17 ·

Eventually, Ralfo and the bundle of drugs were hustled off. He would be questioned by some unpleasant people, in rooms beneath the Prince's citadel that had been built for just such a purpose. Kinsworth and Ukrusu were questioned by the corporal, the sergeant, an officer, and a scribe before they were finally released. Kinsworth was placed on two weeks full leave to let his arm heal; he would be on limited duty for a variable time after that. The wound showed little contamination, having flushed itself out, but he needed time to rest and build more blood. If one more person had questioned him, his leave would have begun early: he was one wavery step short of fainting on the spot.

Ukrusu had a long, welted knot across the right side of his head, and that head ached understandably. Because of Ukrusu's touchy diplomatic position, the guard officer had had a Mugambese delegate fetched from the Palace.

He and Ukrusu had fallen into a wrangling disputation in Mugambese, bureaucrat against hostile teenager. Ukrusu had demanded that his father not be told anything of the incident. The guards were relieved to hear that Ukrusu's part in the fight at the gate was not some kind of interracial attack: in the past, some of those had mushroomed into full-scale riots.

The Mugambese bureaucrat left in a huff, having called the Clan chief's son a series of names decrying his youth, arrogance, and smart mouth. In return, he had been heckled with titles that children weren't supposed to know, obscene names involving the way he had obtained his position.

The two young warriors almost parted without sharing names, but Kinsworth, almost as an afterthought, invited the chief's son to his home for a meal the next night. That meal went well, and the beginnings of a friendship sprouted. The fight had changed Ukrusu: he no longer thought about suicidal manhood journeys, and his new friend saw only an eager face of his own age. Within a week, they were meeting for comradely drinks and conversation at the Green Garter. Drinking still held some novelty for Ukrusu, and Kinsworth's favorite tavern was just far enough south of Caravan Way to be interesting and still respectable. The two wounded warriors had the resiliency of those to whom the age of twenty was still a large number.

With parallel ambitions, the two often talked far into the night. Sharing personal information helped tie the nonidentical pair to each other. Out of their union came a certainty: something had to be done about the drug traffic, and they were just the lads to do it.

• **18** •

"Father, it is time and past that I made my hunt of manhood." Ukrusu stood rod-straight before the Clan chief.

The graying elder was taken aback by his son's forthrightness. "I know, my son, but—"

"Father, you did not teach me. Nor have you taken me to hunt. Nor have you instructed my uncles or cousins or any other warrior to train me."

"That is true, my son, but in this new country—"

"Father, there are no leopards here. There are no water buffalo. There are too few cobras to hunt."

"I know, my son." Guilt was edging the older man's face.

"Father, I have decided to establish a new Clan. A Clan suited for this new land."

His father brightened. "What, then, have you decided to hunt one of those 'bear' creatures or some other northern beast?"

"No, and I already have my proofs." He patted the ceremonial belt pouch. He was dressed in the finest for this hour.

"Proofs from what, son?"

"I will hunt the most dangerous of game in this domain. I will make its people safe from their killers, for its people are now ours. Witness, then, O Chief, the founding of the Clan of the Manhunters."

From his pouch, he laid the proofs before his father. The chief gaped, but his mouth slowly closed into a huge grin. Tears sprang into his eyes as his son recited the formula for the foundation of a new Clan. He straightened to his full two meters, gray curls almost brushing the ceiling of their temporary quarters.

"My son," he said, "you would honor me to carry my war club as chief of your new Clan. I know it would then belong to a warrior of renown."

"Oh, yes, Father! Yes!"

The two hurried around the low table between them to embrace, the tears of fathers and sons and warriors streaming from their eyes. For the moment, they could ignore Harry Hardback's two dried ears, lying on the table, portents of the future.

Interchapter

I hardly touched the lives of the young warriors. A small nudge put Ukrusu in the right place to help Kinsworth, before both lost their worthy young selves to the evil forces of this Plane or to misdirected self-destruction. I fine-tuned, but I was not a major player in this pageant. Perhaps I am aggrandizing the necessity of my own role.

Meditation will be necessary, but I will add to that meditation the story of the Prince's Big Party. The Young Prince, Bartelo Bancartin, was able to resolve a dilemma that threatened his city, months before I decided to become a hidden force in its destiny. The tale begins with the meddling of one conniving human cleric. . . .

BOOK V

Every Dog

DILMARION RELLINOR, the Honorable Grand La-trak of Barrow, High Priest of Milbrant the Magnificent, Keeper of the Faith, etc., was irate. In fact, an irrational irritation seemed to have settled on him in perpetuity. Barrow, home of disrespect! Barrow, city of the ungovernable! Cursed-be-the-day-that-he-was-sent-here, Barrow! What had he ever done to deserve the place?

Had he offended some great one in Sai-khand, some principal of the temple who had kept a secret hate for Dilmarion until he could open this trap under his feet? The high priest had tossed many nights in this godforsaken hole, rolling that question like a marble rattling in a jug, his meaty body using time better spent sleeping, twisting from position to position on his noble bed. That bed was soft enough, just as his lofty post was supposed to be soft. Had it been his own ambitions, blind to the realities of this then-distant pest hole, that had trapped him here? A prestigious office, a mansion, a temple to rule, power— from Sai-khand they had seemed so desirable, so great, so many stepping-stones to still loftier things. Only after his recovery from the grueling caravan trek to Barrow had he wakened to the daily struggle just to hang on here.

Instead of relaxing in the glory of heading Barrow's Saikhandian temple, he had to dance, as a man might on the upper floor of a burning building, never knowing where the fire would next break out under his feet. And Sai-khand, cursed-with-nameless-curses Sai-khand! Had his own people tried to help him? No! They had been too busy playing at politics with the Emperor and the Council of Ten to worry about Barrow. Not that Dilmarion

wouldn't have happily played with them again, but he
was imprisoned here, in the armpit of the Empire, hundreds of kilometers from home. To make matters worse,
the home temple seemed to have planned for him to
carry the load of the local temple alone. The elevated
morons in Sai-khand didn't seem to realize that the mortality rate in Barrow ran double that of the capital. To
one used to Sai-khand's whited civilization, death seemed
to stalk the local streets in every form.

Because it sat next to the slow-moving Wat River and
its stagnant swamps, the city was a haven for every kind
of pestilence. In a region noted for its agriculture, within
the city walls diseased food was a likelihood.

Nevertheless, his Saikhandian superiors continued to
supply Dilmarion with replacements as if his priests had
become immune to Barrow's plagues or the daggers of its
footpads. He needed new men daily, but what did Sai-
khand send him? With every healthy, young acolyte he
got three overaged eunuchs. For every *honest* acolyte—
never mind. He doubted he had ever been sent an honest
acolyte. Every poor-box pilferer and coin shaver in the
home temple had been packed off to Barrow! Those
were altogether too comfortable in this den of greed.
Barrow might be distant from the capital, but the same
capitalistic drives had risen within it that had made Sai-
khand ruler of much of the known Plane. On the other
hand, the locals had missed out entirely on anything that
could be considered a higher spiritual nature.

Sai-khand, with its eternal worship of profit, had found
yet another way to save a copper. Every time they trimmed
their hierarchical tree, Barrow got the dead wood.
Dilmarion might have been able to subsist by recruiting
decent men locally, but his overseers weren't willing to
leave him in peace to do it, even the dubious peace of
this sludge pot of a city. Every load of useless ne'er-do-
wells and meatheads (that survived the migration) staggered in with a load of memos and sacred decrees that
would have killed a mule. Sai-khand knew nothing of
Barrow, took care to continue knowing nothing, but the
holy officers continued to behave as if they could run his
temple by indirect proclamation. He was to confirm his
every local decision by checking it against the pile of
bureaucratic horse droppings sent from the capital. He

was certain that somewhere in that wordy pyramid his superiors had issued orders on exactly how each category of his holy off-scourings was to break wind!

("Look! Just look at this!") he thought. He whacked the loosely rolled leather scroll against his desk. ("More nonsense!")

Some milk-eyed eunuch, stargazing on some temple roof in Sai-khand, had decided that the year—the year, mind!—had 365 days instead of the obvious 364. Any sensible man could multiply the twenty-eight-day cycle of the moon (or of women) by the thirteen natural months and get the right total. The old calendar had needed a day or two of adjustment once in a while when the moon had been hidden too long, but right was right. A little honest fudging was not the same as this imperious decree. They just didn't know how things were here!

Dilmarion had had to struggle against the back-stabbing local priesthoods from the first day of his arrival. No matter that they were part of the Empire, they had been excessively slow in catching on to who should be the big fish in Barrow's religious puddle. He had never let them celebrate their nonsensical 365th day without loud protest in the name of Sai-khand's civilized religion. Now the priests of Valnor, chief god of Barrow's mangy pantheon, would smirk at him behind their hand and again rush to celebrate Valnor's One Day at the winter solstice. Only the arrival of the Mugambese canoe fleet the previous fall had stopped them last year.

Well, we would see! We would just see! Among the castoffs that Sai-khand had pawned off on him was a stargazer of his very own. Perhaps it was an omen that an astronomer had been appointed to Barrow. After last winter's food riots, during which a rumor that the temple had been hoarding supplies had cost him many of his staff, he had requested replacements, but he had no more requested an astronomer than a pig farmer knowingly orders a milking stool. Perhaps there had been a slip in Sai-khand, and they had sent him someone he could use.

That usefulness was still doubtful. How Cleon Lacklander had risen to second-level acolyte remained a mystery. Cleon's promotion might have been a joking parting gift, the joke to be on Dilmarion when Cleon arrived. The man was unbelievably inept at anything that involved a second person. Dilmarion had assigned him initially to watch over the valuable statuary of the inner court. Almost at once, the temple had lost a handful of semiprecious stones, prised out by amateurs under Cleon's nose. Within five hours after he was assigned to the temple school, he had been mugged and rolled by two juvenile Upcrusters, one of them a crippled ten-year-old.

After he had been retrieved from behind the chapel and untied, Cleon had been barred from other students, for his own safety. He had lasted only a few days longer after being moved to the temple kitchen. Three fires and a series of blundering accidents had placed his life in danger: the cooks had vowed to kill him, holy person or not, unless he was removed immediately. Dilmarion had finally discovered that Cleon could sweep stone floors with minimal damage to himself and the buildings. Milbrant knew that the temple had plenty of stone floors! At night, he had become the temple's token sky watcher. Milbrant was a sky god in one of his forms. If no one stood watch on his temple heights, half of each day would have been surrendered to Barrow's local gods by default. Unthinkable! Through that symbolic watch keeping, Dilmarion had discovered Cleon's secret talent.

Making an irregular check of the roof post, Dilmarion had found Cleon busy with forked sticks, hourglass, numbered wheel, and record scrolls. Fierce questioning had jolted Cleon from his glazed stargazing, but it had revealed that his hidden hobby was harmless. Astronomy made Cleon sleep late and kept him from underfoot. The underpriest was guarding little of value, and the roof entrances were kept by other, more wakeful staff members. Dilmarion had gone away satisfied that Cleon had finally been filed in the correct niche.

The high priest was proud of his survival in Barrow, even as he hourly cursed the city. A stint in the Holy Knights had taught him that survival might depend on remembering where you had left a utensil, even if that tool had had no conceivable use at the time it had been laid down. Thus, when the new stargazer's calendar had arrived, Dilmarion had immediately summoned Cleon. The acolyte was to hie himself—wheel, scrolls, and all—to the high priest's office. If Cleon knew what was good for

him, he had better have the *right* answers. A tool could
be discarded permanently if it failed its use.

· 2 ·

At his summoning, Cleon was terrified, confused, and
jittery. The emotions were unsurprising: no day had yet
dawned on Cleon's life, in which he was to be near
another person, that he had not been terrified, confused,
and jittery. The coming interview represented one more
pinnacle of emotional discomfort, dotting his history like
ice floes in a polar sea. His latest encounter with the high
priest on the roof had been one more in the series of
piteous disasters that marked his every past meeting with
authority figures.

The world would have been a better place if Cleon had
chosen the life of a reclusive holy hermit instead of the
interpersonal contacts of a priest. If he had retired from
society early in life, then his middle age wouldn't have
congealed into the rigidly molded form of priesthood, but
no one had thought to tell him. His life mold was unstable and sometimes painful, but he lacked the social imagination to break out of it. Even his appearance worked
against him. His face was a sculptor's experiment that
had been saved from destruction only out of curiosity.
He was short and dumpy, with a wispy manner that
labeled him "loser." Brown freckles stood out on his
pasty scalp like a herd of ticks. He needed no effort to
maintain a monk's tonsure: except for a skimpy rime
over ears and collar, hair had long ago deserted Cleon in
disgust.

At the moment of summons, he had still been groggy
from his late hours the night before. Daylight made his
eyes water. Though he walked toward the appointment
with a built-in cringe, he had remembered to tie his
precious star wheel to his belt. If he dropped it, as he
dropped so many things, it might become misaligned and
be unrepairable by any craftsman closer than Sai-khand.
The wavering pile of record scrolls that he was also
supposed to deliver kept squirting units from his grasp.
Vagrant scrolls had to be chased down and scooped back
into the rebellious mass of others. He resembled a one-

armed thief trying to make off with a load of long, white loaves. His lurching progress toward the interview was a comic dance of catastrophe and pursuit.

Dilmarion had him ushered in immediately, but the teetering armload of parchments chose the moment he stopped before the high priest's desk to avalanche in his superior's face. Cleon was left wringing his hands, with only three scrolls snagged at odd spots against his person. Sweating like a man on the gallows, he gibbered apologies and pursued the offending records, only to have any one he returned to the left side of the desk bump three others off the right side. He would have certainly wet himself if he had not hurriedly visited the privy before departing for this inquisition. Not since an embarrassing incident before the headmaster of the temple school years before had he failed to empty his bladder before facing anyone even mildly intimidating.

• **3** •

Dilmarion quickly lost patience with the twittering sideshow the acolyte was performing on his desk.

"Leave the benighted things alone!" he roared, slamming down his hand.

Naturally, the recaptured scrolls that Cleon dropped scattered the rest off the desk in all directions. Dilmarion clenched his teeth, and his face turned the color of polished wood. A unique thought cooled his anger: this confrontation would now be off to an auspicious beginning—if he had been in need of a clown instead of an astronomer. He decided to cater to Cleon, hopeless scatterbrain that he was, and to save the berating for later. A craftsman didn't break a tool needlessly.

He limited himself to giving Cleon an icy stare, the scowling equivalent of the silence before a lightning stroke. That stare had made him the terror of the students in the Sai-khand temple school even as a young acolyte. He had used it later to good effect on warrior recruits in the Holy Knights. Properly applied to subordinates, it had been known to cause those of weaker constitution to faint in a heap. The high priest eased off only after Cleon had dropped palely to his knees. He substituted a broad,

sunny smile to melt the chilled underpriest. Dilmarion
was an accomplished social actor, capable of emotional
manipulation that could have had the inept acolyte slob-
bering on his sandals in relief, but there was no challenge
to it. Besides, there was work to be done.

"Cleon," he began in a fatherly tone, "I have need of
your expert help in a certain matter."

The underpriest bobbed in agreement. At that point,
he would have agreed to anything, including his own
dismemberment.

"Look this over." He handed Cleon the offending
scroll.

Cleon finally managed to read it, hopping from foot to
foot and tangling the simple parchment roll into irreme-
diable loops.

"Well?"

Dilmarion's patience was fraying, and he was longing
for his pleasant manse. His acidifying stomach had had
all of Cleon it could stand for one morning.

"Well, w-w-what, Your Eminence?" Cleon peeked over
the edge of the rumpled scroll as a traveler in the Waste
might peer over his veil.

"Don't be impertinent!"

Dilmarion snapped another withering look at Cleon,
who had not knowingly been impertinent since sometime
not long after weaning. The underpriest's knees began to
knock like harness buckles on a trotting horse.

"Are they right? Does the year have 365 days, or 364,
as Milbrant knows it should?" The high priest realized
that his question was as loaded as a honey wagon in the
Slews, but he was past caring. Let someone cater to him
for a change!

Poor Cleon stuttered several times, but he eventually
began an explanation. He was so painstakingly thorough
that the high priest's eyes glazed over under the barrage
of expertise. Twice, he angrily stopped the acolyte and
tried for a new tack, as if he hadn't been catching the
drift of the information. Unfortunately, Dilmarion's superior education had made the central points of Cleon's
garbled discourse altogether too plain. According to every one of the little astronomer's remembered sources,
the year *did* have 365 days!

The high priest commanded Cleon sternly to redo all

his calculations and not to return until he had precise confirmation of the year's length. He refused to let down in front of a subordinate, no matter how depressing the news. Dismissing the relieved underpriest and all his paraphernalia, Dilmarion mentally slammed a door on the acolyte's departing backside.

As the sound of dropped scrolls faded into distant hallways, he forced himself to relax and clear his mind. His commands had reconfirmed his authority and gotten the foggy-brained acolyte out of his hair, but he had been convinced by the testimony of his own expert. Though that expert was generally a nonfunctional fool, the chief priest of Milbrant was not. He must now act, as befitted his position in this backed-up sewer of a city. The flap-mouthed hangers-on who had arrived at the same time as the new calendar had undoubtedly already spilled its contents to all and sundry. Their idea of "secret" was to tell everything they knew only to anyone who offered them a loose copper or a free drink. By week's end, the local priests would be planning the Valnor's One Day festival, intending to taunt Dilmarion with his own sect's testimony.

They would, that is, if Dilmarion *waited* for week's end. Quickly positioning ink pot, sand, and blotter, he began the letter that would leave his clerical competition stunned and outflanked. This would teach them not to trifle with their betters and not to dismiss the congregation until the last hymn had been sung!

> Your Royal Highness, Val-trak of the Empire, Prince Bartello Bancartin, Keeper of the West; etc.:
> Concerning the celebration of Milbrant's One Day at the winter solstice this year . . .

• 3 •

"But, my black-eyed darling," said the unhappy Prince, trying to soothe the angry person of his lover, "surely you can't be upset over some priestly fuss about a holy holiday!"

He tried to slip an arm about her narrow waist, only to

have it whipped out of his hands as the Mugambisa sidestepped. Even in this very private room, that they never shared with others, her back spoke volumes of reproach, and her back was all that she would present to him. The green parrot on her shoulders, one of her symbols of office, sensitive to its mistress's emotions, poked its head back and hissed at Bartello. For the hundredth time, he wanted to throttle the little vermin until its eyes popped and its spurred legs flopped in the air. Wooing a commanding and highly emotional woman was trying enough without an unexpected spurring by her pet during some climactic moment.

"But, Malia, my love—"

"Don't 'but-my-love' me! *You* have let those quarreling priests ruin—ruin!—my surprise for you. I've tried! I've bundled up like a sheepherder for you and your friends!" She was almost sobbing. "And now you've ruined it!"

The Prince would have very much liked to hold the bare, brown shoulders and stroke the shapely bosom her "sheepherder's" dress enticingly enhanced, but she was not to be consoled. The guarding parrot was watching him with appetite-for-prince's-ear written on its stripy countenance. She didn't have to be reasonable or intimate.

"My bronze sweetheart, I know nothing about a surprise you'd planned for me. How could I—"

"That's only an excuse! You *are* the Prince. You're always bragging about your spy system. Surely you'd heard."

(Well, he *had* heard a few rumors, but at the time, the activity had seemed unimportant. He had decided to be "surprised.")

"I ordered every clan chief to prepare to celebrate with their *very, very* best on Mugambaba's Day at the winter solstice—our very first* in this new land. Last year . . . last year, things were too confused." She was quiet for a moment, remembering the flight from Mugambu and other, less pleasant things.

"You and I could have publicly cemented our bond and brought our peoples closer together. Now your prissy priests have spoiled it all, and *you* let them!" She threw up her chin and stalked regally from the room.

By the Thousand Stars, it was going to be a long, cold winter.

· 4 ·

Kilnore, the royal chamberlain, was annoyed at his prince for having to climb so many stairs at his age. If the boy must meditate, why couldn't he do it at ground level? Instead, he must perch like a sea gull on the high wall of the citadel, looking out over his city. The chief servant climbed to within sight of his ruler and paused for breath. Gesturing for the servant boy, Stilden, to wait at the top of the stairs, he advanced toward the Prince, his dignity restored by returned wind. The view *was* good today, with the clear fall air sweeping away the summer's stagnation, but not yet bringing the winter's chill storms. The old servitor cleared his throat.

"Harrum! Your Highness, several groups are seeking audience with you."

There was a long silence.

"Your Highness surely knows what they want."

"Yes, Kilnore, I'm more than aware of what they want."

"The delegation from the Saikhandian temple is here, including Dilmarion himself. The—"

"—delegation from Valnor's temple is here, headed by their high priest." The Prince went on in a shrill voice. "The Mugambese delegation is here, but they don't really want to talk to me: just keep an eye on the other two. If we had one, there'd be a delegation here from the Loyal Society to Preserve the Purple Flerp! Something about the winter solstice would have flushed them out of the brush. There is at least one representative from every minor temple, kennel, and fish-watching society in the entire region in my audience room, all to try to get me to do the same thing!

"I'm not about to declare the winter solstice *anybody's* day, today or anytime soon! Tell the whole crowd of them to take a wild leap at the spinning moon!

"Wait . . . Kilnore, hold off on that 'spinning moon' phrase. Yes, yes, I know you would have anyway, old friend. Make it sound official: 'No decision has been made at this time.' But tell each group privately that their claim is being given our full consideration."

Kilnore was sympathetic: he was in position to know that the life of a prince was not always happy or easy. Now, when the Old Prince had been alive . . .

"If you need anything further, Your Highness, I have left a boy at the top of the stair for messages."

"Very well, Kilnore. Do your best."

The Prince slumped back in the ornate chair that had been hauled up from some apartment below and fell into a depressed contemplation. Kilnore started his creaking knees back down the steps. Neither envied the other his duties.

It was difficult for the Prince to remain depressed, however, wrapped in the clear sky as the sun settled toward evening. Voices normally lost in the distance carried sharply to the young ruler in his aerie. He could hear even the details of ordinary, loud conversation. He watched a well-to-do woman, probably a merchant's wife, hurrying home along Caravan Way in the twilight, with a servant trotting ahead to clear her way. Her expensive shawl slipped from the back of her shoulders, but she continued, unaware of her loss. The Prince leaned forward, intent on the play his people were performing for him. The players were real and self-interested, ignorant of their audience of one. He did not use the citadel's heights for meditation, no matter what he told Kilnore. Vicariously entering the lives of his citizens made his own problems fade into the background. Sampling the reality of others eased the frustration he felt when his own destiny slipped out of control.

Three young Upcrusters, prowling the wide avenue in the gloom for whatever crossed their path, spotted the shawl and pounced. The garment would sell for a good handful of copper at half-a-dozen fences in the south end. Each of the three seized his own corner of the cloth simultaneously. Their shrill cries of dismay carried up to the Prince.

"Here, Ralphie, I saw it first!"

"Well, I grabbed it first. You and Pig-eye can just let go!"

Shifting and struggling, but not daring to tear their prize and reduce its value, the three rotated in the shadows of the street. They were as alike as any set of lower-class children, with no more than three years spanning their ages: brothers, certainly. The tug-of-war continued.

"I don't care if you're the oldest. Money's thicker'n blood. Gimme!"

"Lay off, or I'll tell the old lady!"

"G'wan! Then none of us'd see a copper. Now, leggo!"

The group was scuffling up a dust but still taking care of their find: half a shawl was worth less than half the price. None of them noticed a fourth player come on stage.

The Prince could hardly restrain an urge to cry out a warning, though it would have spoiled his play. The fourth boy topped the largest brother by a head and had ten kilos on the heaviest. Wasting no time, the stranger punched the first, shoved the second, and cuffed the hands of the third off the shawl. All three were half-down and surprised into speechlessness in a handful of seconds.

"Thanks for holding my shawl for me." The big newcomer sneered. He held up his capture for inspection, gloating.

The three on the ground made white eye contact with one another. The smallest of the brothers went for the interloper's leg and planted a hearty bite on the thigh. The middle brother butted their adversary in the stomach, cutting off his startled shriek with a "Whuff!" The oldest brother sailed in, fists flailing.

In less than a minute, the larger invader was forced to exit the scene empty-handed, stage left, dodging a shower of stones, offal, and high-pitched curses as he limped east. Sporting a cluster of bruises and at least one black eye, the trio trotted off in the other direction, slapping each other on the back and yelling mutual congratulations. Ralphie was carrying the shawl, and all were talking "thirds" as they left the Prince's street/stage, headed for the nearest fencing location.

As the curtain rang down on this act of his drama, the Prince's eyes went out of focus. He sat frozen on the battlements like some wingless gargoyle, canted forward with his face toward the sun's setting, seeing nothing. He remained motionless until there was not enough light to show his profile against the evening sky. The dozing servant boy almost fell backward down the stairs when the Prince shot from his chair with a yell.

"Yes!" And then, "Yes—yes—yes!" The young ruler spun and danced along the top of the wall, heedless of danger. "Yes! Indeed, yes! Wheee!"

The Prince had confirmed for the forgotten servant boy what every servant suspected: putting on nobility or a crown knocked the brakes right off a man's good sense. Instead of "Uneasy rests the head that wears the crown," they believed it should be "Unstable." If anyone backstairs had behaved in that fashion, they would have come for him with nets and chains. The boy hunkered down for safety. The Prince returned to awareness and sat down with a *plop!*

"Kilnore!"

The chamberlain was long gone, as any sane man would have known. His eyes fell on the cowering servant.

"Quick—quick, boy! Get Kilnore back up here!"

The boy Stilden had reached a stage of fright wherein he soon wouldn't have needed the Prince's permission to run. Run he did. Kilnore complained all the way up the stair and cuffed Stilden twice, threatening him with permanent injury if this were a wild-goose chase. The old servitor was greeted by his prince's smiling face.

"Kilnore," he said, clapping the chamberlain on both shoulders, "I'm going to make a speech!"

· 5 ·

Before the night was gone, the Prince had sent to the captain of the guard for his six "most honest" guardsmen. He gave each guard the same orders: go to the stables and saddle a horse without speaking to anyone; ride to the city gate (a different gate in each case); spend an hour watching that gate without being seen; report the exact behavior of the gate watch to the Prince personally.

When the puzzled guardsmen returned later that night, the Prince rewarded each with a Saikhandian gold crown piece. Candles burned late in the palace, not only to take reports from guardsmen.

The palace rumbled the next day with constant traffic,

as orders and invitations were dispatched. Clerks scribbled until their fingers were numb. On strictest orders, a copy of the Prince's announcement was to be posted in every tavern and temple and on every public notice board and message tree. A personal invitation under the Prince's own seal was to go to each high family in Barrow; to each clan chief of the Mugambese; to each high priest; and to all captains of the Imperial Navy now in port. No segment of the city's population was to be able to overlook the coming event. Criers shouted the announcement through the miserable streets of the Slews and in the bazaar of Upcruster Town, where literacy was as common as bathing.

Workmen scrambled like stirred bees to recondition the carnival grounds. Its boxes and platforms had been allowed to fall into disrepair for years, since right after the Prince's coronation. His one attempt to stage a public circus had been a disaster. It was sadly suggested that the Prince just didn't have the touch for mass entertainment that his father had had. Many felt that in a whole array of "touches," the Young Prince fell short of the late Old Prince.

The contractors at the carnival grounds would have preferred another arrangement than three days or no pay. There would be no time for properly fixing kickbacks or finding suppliers of second-quality materials who would bill at first-quality and split the difference. Their hurt was mollified by an unusually high fee.

The proclamation, whether a private message or public, was essentially the same everywhere. The Prince was about to make a speech that would settle the winter-solstice controversy once and for all. Invitations to especially interested parties strongly hinted that their special interests would be particularly served. Prince Bartello's messages were personal and intimate, but all were lacking one detail: no one was told exactly what he had decided to do.

At first, there was relative peace, with the embattled parties smirking at one another in premature victory. They gave up their noisy infestation of the palace receiving room. The Prince's first circus might have been a disaster, but his speech was shaping up into a circus of its

own. Every citizen who could walk or be carried vowed
not to miss the show at week's end.

Kilnore almost dithered himself to death under the
pressure of trying to seat the feuding groups without
giving obvious preference to any. At the same time, he
had to convince those sent to him for seating specifics
that theirs was the group given precedence. Seating of
ordinary, massive crowds was easy by comparison. Barrow was no quieter than an ant colony with boiling water
inching its way into the nest.

Prestige surged and ebbed as group after group claimed
to be the Prince's anointed, but were then able to show
no more evidence than any other party. Glory clung
briefly to the workmen and contractors at the carnival
grounds, until it was learned that they had no control
over seating and knew as little as everyone else. The city
exercised its hyperactive curiosity, as rats in a new cage
must nose out every corner. When those corners proved
to be empty, it was time again to begin nipping at the
tails of old enemies.

If there had been more than three days of waiting,
Barrow would have experienced a multicornered civil,
religious, and racial war that would have erased it from
among the member cities of the Empire. The weekend
deadline was a leaking dam holding back the city's seething factions. The worst fighting during the final hours of
the countdown, however, was not between those factions, but between those who would go to hear the Prince's
speech and those who had to stay away.

Information brokers had compiled a half week of selling rumors the like of which had never been seen before.
None of them, however, had pinned down the truth,
regardless of what they told their clients; the Prince was
the only one who knew for sure. Other business simply
ceased during the final evening. Wives, husbands, and
older children traded bribes and threats concerning who
would stay home to watch the little ones. Parents discovered that many of those "little" ones had decided that
they weren't so little and were demanding to go. Masters
discovered unsuspected rebellious natures among their
hirelings when those servants were expected to stay and
mind the master's property. Hardworking thieves, with a
night before them filled with poorly watched belongings,

still found reason to take the night off, even in the face of a flat purse. There was an increase in burglaries just after the wealthy departed for their prepared boxes at the carnival grounds, but the crime rate peaked early. Late in the evening, it fell to almost nothing as the burglars hurried to find seats on their own. Ships in the harbor left at most a skeleton watch, and taverns were closed. An invader would have found the city gates barred but almost unguarded. Smugglers, prostitutes, and confessional priests alike refused to make appointments for that night.

All of Barrow's reserve guardsmen were on duty to try to jam more people into the carnival grounds. Every pickpocket in the city was also present, being the only class of thieves who could do "business" and still watch the show. Mobile hawkers of consumables reaped a similar double advantage.

The arena's floor had been crowded with new benches; the Prince alone was to be the performer. The general population of Barrow now milled and shouted among those benches, placing wagers on the Prince's coming message. The sweating rainbow that filled the stands had become a circus in itself.

The evening was roaring toward a crescendo to climax the week. Only a few of the poorest Barrowmen, who had made the long walk from the Slews, failed to find seats. Those seated had their rumps as close as fingers in a fist, and tempers were beginning to fray. Factions were again fingering their daggers. The general roar took on a hostile undertone. Just before the riot would have erupted, the Prince stepped from his private entrance onto the dais. He raised both arms. The platform was empty except for the Prince and two guardsmen at the mouth of the tunnel through which he had entered. However, his podium was flanked on either side by two sets of three chairs.

The roar subsided in a flurry of fingers pointing out the Prince. The star of their extravaganza was on stage. The noise settled to a lower and lower mumble and finally to the susurrus of thousands trying to be quiet themselves and to quiet others around them.

The Prince stepped forward to speak. His podium had been built by craftsmen, specialists from Sai-khand who had been in the city repairing the "speaking" apparatus of some minor god. What seemed to be decorations was actually a well-concealed megaphone. The Prince's reedy voice lacked the bull-roar carrying power of his father's (another deficiency). However, the closemouthed craftsmen, who were now on their way home with a bonus, had done their work well. Only an unlucky few who had sat too near a crying baby or a boisterous drunk missed his words.

The Prince had left no place in his program for benedictions (lest he either have to honor one religion over the others or, worse, listen to a prayer from every priesthood in the city). Similarly, there was no traditional reading of his own titles and accomplishments (few enough, it was said). "People of Barrow! You know why I have called you together here."

He wanted the audience's attention. His opening remarks were no more a surprise than announcing the sun had set.

"There is much more to the situation in our city than most of you have heard about." He indeed had their attention now; everybody in Barrow loved a secret.

"Four days ago, I was visited by a delegation from Sai-khand itself. The news of our controversy has reached even to the capital."

The megaphone/podium was doing a fine job, echoing the Prince's speech across the whispering multitude. At his unexpected news, their humming rose a trifle higher, but his revelation was not exactly earthshaking. At the speed of a fast post messenger or picket boat, it was possible that Barrow's situation had been made known in the capital. However, the slower return time for travelers responding to Barrow's news made part of his statement logically impossible. On the other hand, crowds were never long on logic, and the Prince had no intention of giving them thinking time.

"The messengers claimed to be nobles of Sai-khand, but they spoke to me as no nobles have the right. They claimed to be spokesmen for our dear Emperor, but not one of them could show the mark of an Imperial seal, nor any document from the Council of Ten."

It was noted later that the Prince had done an amazing job of keeping a straight face while using "dear" and

"Emperor" in the same sentence. Voltair III was better known in Barrow by his nickname, Voltair the Tightfisted.

"I am embarrassed to tell you their message, since it stains the very idea of nobility and blackens the name of the Empire."

By now, the crowd was on the edge of their chairs, slavering to be told whatever the young ruler was oh-so-reluctant to reveal. The common opinion of nobility and the Empire was not nearly high enough to be dashed by hearing a little more dirt about either.

"They came, *they* said, to settle *our* dispute for us." The distaste in his voice was plain; local rule within the Empire was supposed to be *local*. "They referred to our city as 'a feuding backwater that needs a stern hand.' They *ordered* us to have *no festival at all at the winter solstice*! In the name of some pack of bloated capital nobles, *they* ordered *us*!"

He punctuated his last words with slams of his small fist on the podium. The megaphone gave the blows a gavel-on-bench quality. An unhappy hum entered the crowd noises as his words sank in.

"They referred to our fine Saikhandian temple as 'provincial hovel unfit for Milbrant' and to the Grand La-trak of Barrow as 'an overaged degenerate shipped to the back country to rot.' I was to *order* him, *they* said, to celebrate *no* day in Milbrant's name or any other. Saikhandians, *they* said, are above such peasant nonsense!"

In his stadium box, Dilmarion's face turned a slow brick red, and he clenched his fingers into the arms of his seat. What the young Prince said sounded entirely too much like Sai-khand's attitude toward the Barrow temple. The priests with him rose to cry indignant protests, but the Prince had hardly finished.

"Of the honored gods of the people of Barrow, *they* said 'inferior idols in mud-and-dabble temples.' Of Valnor, loved by so many, they only laughed—*laughed*! I was to forbid you all celebration and set a curfew on you instead!" He named a ridiculously early hour of the evening.

The metallic, mineral sound of grinding teeth and daggers being loosened was added to the hostile crowd undertone. The mob was an ugly thing to hear when rising toward anger.

"Of our friends from Mugambu, *they* said 'black-skinned

antelope herders that should have been thrown back into the sea' and 'ignorant savages without proper gods.' I was to *segregate* them from other citizens and forbid them the streets at night, *they* said."

For decency's sake, it was just as well so few understood Mugambese. A ripple of translation spread through their boxes, followed by a wave of tossed ostrich plumes, raised voices, and shaken spears. No translation was needed when two-meter black men began to stamp, roll their eyes, and hammer their spear butts against their shields. Teeth gnashing on lion-claw necklaces became part of the angry crowd's sound. They were on their feet now, but still at the yelling stage, without a unified target on which to vent their wrath.

"Wait, my friends, you did not hear my answer to them!"

His upraised arms on the central podium and the boom of the megaphone momentarily headed off the building riot. This time, the hush that fell was a before-the-storm stillness.

"One of my loyal guardsmen escorted those noble charlatans from the Barrow the very night they arrived. I did not hand-fast them as guests or give them a soft bed. For the Empire's sake, I did give them a head start on your just vengeance. You see the rest of the answer before you." For the first time, he gestured at the half-dozen chairs on the dais. "I gave them a choice. They could sit their saddles the same night, or three days later, tonight, their heads alone would sit beside me and their bodies would float down the River Wat for the crocodiles!" He folded his arms.

It began low and spotty; it trickled and spread, but it grew. It swelled and grew until the cheer that rose from the carnival grounds flushed the birds from the swamp on the far side of the Slews. Every person that had missed the gathering found himself suddenly wide-awake and hurried into the street to locate the cause of the disturbance. Friends and strangers, of every color and every temple, seized each other and yelled, flung hats into the air that would never be recovered, screamed themselves hoarse, hammered the benches until they roared. "Long life to the Prince!" was shouted in many languages. The shouting went on and on: the people of Barrow loved a secret or a quality riot, but they loved heroic celebration even more, especially when they, through their prince, were the heroes. The Prince finally quieted them after they had run down a little.

"Hear my decree, people of Barrow!" the megaphone boomed. "We are going to have a festival: a party, the likes of which this city has never seen!"

They cheered him again, almost as long as before.

"Let the news be spread: The winter solstice belongs to *this* city! Let it be called 'Barrow's Day'!"

Naturally, they cheered him again, but he was not finished.

"Since we have all received insult together, then that is what we shall be—together!" (Scattered cheers.) "We will not have a procession. No, we will have *four* parades: one for the temple of Milbrant; one for Valnor's temple; one for all the smaller temples in the city; and one for our brothers of Mugambu!"

The crowd found breath for more cheering.

"I will personally give the greatest ball and fete ever known in this city, and there will be celebrations in every quarter! Instead of a curfew, I command you: Every healthy citizen of Barrow must remain awake all the night through! We will welcome the new year at its dawn! We will honor the Empire, but together we will thumb our noses at the bloated snakes who try to slide by night to undo its good!"

There was some hysterical cheering, but they were winded.

"Wait, my friends. There's more! We must undo the insult to every portion of our city or leave all of it smeared. No one is to come to my celebrations as themselves, but as members of other brotherhoods. If you were born in Barrow, you shall not attend my fete unless you are dressed as a citizen of Sai-khand or of Mugambu! Our Mugambese friends must don the costume of this city or the dress of Sai-khand. Saikhandians must be arrayed as Mugambese or Barrowmen. Every guest, of whatever nation, must dress in another people's costume!

"What a party to end all parties it shall be!"

Somewhere they found the breath. They cheered until the walls shook; they demolished the benches and boxes, exhausting themselves in righteous frenzy. It was already

the beginning of the party to end all parties! They finally
did wear themselves down to the point that they would
allow equally wrung-out guardsmen to herd them through
the exits. They would need all their energy tomorrow to
plan the celebration. There would be no time to worry
about calendars or politics—only food, drink, and decoration. The celebration—THE celebration—was only a
month away!

· 6 ·

When the day arrived, it was surprising how well it went.
There was the usual amount of mayhem, but between
individuals rather than factions. There was, for example,
a huge rise in the number of seductions. There would be
an echo of the new year in a surge of births late next
summer. Many would choose marriage after the effects
of the winter "came home" to them. There were even a
few babies born that strongly resembled tall, dark fathers
or who did not entirely resemble their brown, willow
mothers. There were some public interracial marriages
later that, considering the season, did not raise eyebrows
greatly. Barrow moved a few steps closer to becoming a
true cultural melting pot. Everyone had not been translated into perfection overnight, nor did everyone enter
the new year with equal happiness.

The mass of the citizenry were very happy. They loved
a party to which they had been invited, no matter who
was giving it. As the Prince's ball swept into full flower at
the palace, their own festivals blossomed in the winter
night. The Slews experienced the first celebration ever to
include them. The Prince himself sent three wagons of
food and two of beer, and a band. The food was cheap,
the beer was flat, and the band was mediocre. All were
packed into a muddy field outside the city wall. No gold
could have bought the joy they generated.

Children ate until they were full, many for the first
time in their lives. Adults didn't have to beg for another
round or cringe before the servers when they asked for
seconds. Ragged people who had forgotten how to dance
greeted the dawn on their feet, shouting with the music.
Smugglers and harlots would continue to rule the Slews,

and the most common profession would be some variety of felony. Two-thirds of the babies born there would never see their fifth year: the gray folk there would have gone on enduring without a tremor. But let a stranger speak too loudly there against the Prince ever again, and he would find his weazand slit and his body sunk in the swamps.

Upcruster Town lighted the bazaar and roared the night away. They were only a little above the Slews, but they knew what the "good stuff" was. The beer and food were better. The music was folksy, but excellent; several bands played themselves into exhaustion. Since the most skilled robbers were found among the Townsmen instead of among the chicken thieves across the river, the city's crime rate fell to an all-time low. Every tavern boomed. Even Barrelgut at the Gryphon and Goblet bought a round for the house once an hour.

North of Caravan Way, the great merchants' manses competed to see which could swirl the most gaily with dancers and wine. The palace burned a month's supply of candles in a single night. The Prince delivered on his promise of the greatest ball in the city's history. To their surprise, the nobility found that the costume switch ordered by their ruler was just the ice breaker needed to make a *big* party into a *good* party. They had almost as much fun as the Upcrusters, the ordinary Mugambese citizens, or the farmers who had come into town for the festival.

The merchants were mostly happy. The supplies of food, drink, party favors, drink, hired bands, drink, building materials, and drink had come from them. Demand was so high that it made up for the "one time" tax the Prince had laid on them to pay for his fete (and for the damage to the carnival grounds). Some of the tax money had gone to feed poor people across the river, folk who would go to bed hungry every other night. The merchants could not claim credit for the good deed, because they were ignorant of its financing. Likewise, they could not be blamed that the practice was not continued.

Thieves were happy. Some people couldn't afford party decorations at retail price. Fences considered themselves almost a public service, providing goodies for the festivals at affordable prices. With the help of certain less-than-honest associates, they could sometimes steal and resell the same items three times.

The smaller temples were happy. They had a parade without the snooty priesthoods of either Milbrant or Valnor horning in, and each group could name the procession in the honor of their own deity. Nevertheless, Valnor's priests were also happy, displaying their we-told-you-so attitude for all to see. The celebration harkened back to some of the unrestricted ones that they had had when the Old Prince had been alive. All agreed, however, that this year's was the best of all time.

The Saikhandians and their clergy were happy. The honor of the Empire had been upheld. Besides, it had been fun! Many of them had been misfits at home in the capital—third sons of lesser nobility, etc. Their hearts were closer to Barrow, even though their official loyalty must be to the distant, money-grubbing capital.

Information brokers were *not* happy. Many customers had demanded refunds on bad predictions. Every gossip monger had been caught looking like a bald-faced fool by the Prince's announcement. They grilled their best sources, but no one had seen the delegation from Sai-khand come or go. They must have slipped in incognito, with some caravan. Several possible ones had departed down the northwest trade route before the right questions could be asked. The brokers would find, however, that asking the right questions later would leave them still mystified. The guardsmen the Prince had summoned told the same (obviously prepared) story of spending an hour watching a city gate. Some of them had been paid off in gold, so there was no way to identify with certainty the guardsman of whom the Prince had spoken. Unlike his slippery father, the Prince himself was too much of a guileless do-gooder to have fabricated the story.

Six guardsmen found themselves happily on the receiving end of an odd situation. Not only did each have a bit of gold, but everyone in the city seemed eager to set them up for drinks. Strangers gave them gifts, and women propositioned them, and all anyone wanted in return was to hear about how they had been sent to watch the gates. Each had also been promoted, replacing some gate guards who now either found themselves unemployed or walking patrol in the worst quarters of the city. Several smuggling rings would have to start from scratch to suborn the johnny-straights who now guarded the gates, or the flow of untaxed goods would never get back to normal.

Kilnore, the royal chamberlain, claimed to be unhappy, having worked off ten kilos in a month. He threatened to retire, but never seemed to get around to it. He and his new assistant were the vital cogs on which the machinery of the Prince's government actually turned, and he knew it. His complaints about bad knees and gray hair were a fog to hide from the rest of the city what a kick he got out of his job.

The former servant boy, Stilden, who had witnessed the Prince's inspiration and the events that followed, was happy. Given a choice of returning home with his mouth closed by enough money to buy a farm, or remaining, he had instantly chosen the latter. As one of the few able to understand the Prince's actions after the fact, he planned to work for the rest of his life for the eccentric, ingenious young ruler. In another move to keep him quiet, he had been promoted upstairs and had worked his tail off for a month as the assistant to gruff old Kilnore. That childless servitor was grooming the boy to be his replacement . . . someday.

Cleon Lacklander had not become very happy so far, but Cleon was rather confused about the nature of happiness or of any other emotion. He was one of the few to have missed the celebrations, and he had never heard about the Prince's speech. He had spent those nights watching the stars. The wonder and regularity of the Thousand Stars in their courses made him feel vaguely pleasant, which was as close to happiness as could be expected, considering the shaky base on which it had to be built.

The Mugambese were happy. They were at last part of the city of their exile, even if it had meant having their ostrich plumes and exotic clothing pilfered for weeks to make other people's costumes. When they were happy, the Mugambisa was happy. When the Mugambisa was happy, Prince Bartello Bancartin was very, very happy. He had dented his treasury, gambled with the fate of his city, and bluffed thousands of people to their faces. He felt wonderful. Father would have been proud of him.

One green Mugambese parrot was unhappy. Now it

spent a couple of nights each week alone in a wicker cage, far from its mistress's shoulder. You couldn't please everyone.

• **7** •

Dilmarion was again irate. His careful, logical mind had eventually figured out that he had been bilked, but too late. Why, he had felt a sustained burst of loyalty for this cesspool of a city! He had organized his temple's parade, he had dressed up like a Tellarani shaman for the Prince's ball, and he had . . . had enjoyed himself doing it! He was not fooled anymore by the "guileless" Prince, but try as he would, he hadn't been able to squeeze all the goodwill back out of himself. Intrigue just didn't have the tang it used to have. Nothing had come along to stir him since the winter solstice. He seemed to do nothing but sit at his desk and grind through unimportant routine. Why, he had even caught himself mentally planning next year's Barrow's Day procession!

A scratching at his door, no louder than a mouse clearing its throat, recalled him from staring into space. He looked up to see part of Cleon's face peeking around the frame.

"Yes?"

"Y-y-your Eminence, I . . . I have what you asked for."

"What I asked for? I don't rem—oh. Well. Yes, bring it in." It had been so many months that he had forgotten the complete calendar report that he had told Cleon to prepare.

The underpriest advanced timorously to his superior's desk and laid down a largish scroll. This time he had sensibly brought no others.

"Just give me the summary. I'll look over the complete report later (as when cows fly). It *is* 365 days, then?" The confirmation would do nothing to change his own gullible actions during the new year's celebrations or erase Barrow's Day from the city's permanent calendar.

"Well . . . Well, Your Eminence, it's not exactly . . . Well . . . It's not *exactly* 365 days. You see . . ." He launched into paragraphs of arcane information that did not enlighten the high priest whatsoever.

"How many blessed days is it then?"

Dilmarion hoped his question was precise enough for the intellectualized acolyte. Otherwise, he would have to face another avalanche of verbiage.

"I can't be truly precise, Your Eminence. In the future, we may develop better tools that—"

"Never mind that! How many blasted days? All right! All right! How many, *as best as you can calculate now*?"

"Three hundred sixty-five and . . . and . . ."

"And *what*?"

"And . . . and one quarter!" Cleon shrank away from the desk.

"So? What's a quarter of a day? How could that be important enough to change anything?"

"To be correct, sir, we'd have change all the calendars again. We'd have to add an extra day every four years."

"Add . . . ? Every four years . . . ?" The high priest's eyes went out of focus. "Add . . . Every four years . . ."

A wonderful new possibility opened before him. With a little creative politicking, Milbrant might have his own day after all. Let's see: in a month or so, he could invite Valnor's chief priest to dinner. He would fill the old goat with beef and fine wine, and then casually mention, "What if there were *another* day available on the calendar?" In an expansive mood and the spirit of brotherhood, as a conciliatory gesture to good-loser Dilmarion, Valnor would cede the theoretical day to Milbrant. Over a year's time, the Mugambese and the others could be plied the same way. It was as if the dawn had come up for Dilmarion. He rose dreamily and moved around the desk.

Cleon cowered, sure that he was about to be struck, but the high priest not only lifted him to his feet, he embraced him! The fact that Cleon knew too much was no problem for Dilmarion's freed consciousness. Cleon didn't *know* that he knew too much.

"Cleon, my son, you are to have your own observatory on the temple roof, your own apartments built there, your own secretary and servant (who would be incredibly closemouthed)."

If Cleon had ever qualified for a dream, that was it. In that moment, he discovered what happiness was really like. Even so, except for Cleon and the Prince, Dilmarion was the happiest man in Barrow.

Interchapter

Writing it down has reminded me how little I am actually needed. As long as Barrow has her Prince, or as long as mortals of his caliber continue to lead humanity, my services are of only questionable value. If I were not here, the city's problem would have been solved by others.

Will they always be? Will a Prince Bartello always rise at the time needed? Tell it to the Dragons. Tell it to the Elves. By all reckonings, they are gone from this Plane. Did no leader appear among them in the hour of their confrontation with extinction? I remain unconvinced either of my need to cease interfering or of my need to interfere on a larger scale.

It is soon to be the time of test for this city. I feel it, but I cannot grasp it, Master though I claim to be. It may be that some godling, perhaps even the assembler of this Plane, or some other Master, is blocking my probes. I, like all Barrowmen, must wait and see. But I alone know that I *am* waiting for whatever dreadful set of events has been set in motion. Let the mortals here live in the sunshine for a little longer.

I have held back from my meddling for two years now. I believe that I will visit a certain young man who, when last he crossed the path of Kinsworth and Ukrusu, lacked an honest vocation. He had potential, however. I will observe his life: has he made anything of that potential, without the push of a "higher" being, or does it still molder on the vine, buried by the felonious habits? I will eavesdrop. . . .

BOOK VI

Mark's Teeth

THE OLD GRAIN CARRIER *Bandag's Belly* came leaking its
way into port, up the broad River Wat. Her crew tied her
up to a pier on the west side of the Wat just as the tide
turned, allowing backed-up scum and sewage to be swept
toward the sea again. Many felt that the *Belly* should also
have been counted as floating offal. Indeed, if beauty
had been the prime function of ships, it would have been
more merciful to have let her wash quietly down to the
ocean and settle into worm fodder.

The *Belly* never failed to make port without the clatter of
her pumps being heard five hundred meters away, but
she had always made port, sometimes when other, better-
fitted ships had been lost. That said a lot for her crew,
but the credit of her success generally went to her captain, Dak-the-Claw Bandag. The old *Belly* had hauled
wheat between the Wat and the Arpago River cities for
years, until her seams had opened a little too much from
the swelling of dampened grain. Dak, a parsimonious
Barrowman in his later years, had picked her up cheaply.
He hadn't thought of a new name for his ship, formerly
the *Tulip*, before his crew had christened her in his
honor, more or less. The "floating barrel" shape of master and ship were so similar that the comparison was
unavoidable.

Dak had taken the naming well, banging his metal-
clawed arm against a table at the Jumping Salmon and
roaring with laughter when he heard it. He always treated
his crew to a dinner at the Salmon when they made port
in Barrow. The lot of them ate well on the Barrow-to-
Saikhand leg of their shipping run: their usual cargo now
was barreled salted meat and pickled vegetables. The crew

saw to it that there was the usual amount of "spoilage." Dak and the merchants he carried for ignored the pilferage: pickles meant no scurvy and a healthier outbound crew.

Coming back from Sai-khand, loaded with whatever came to hand, wasn't as easy. A ship could be becalmed or blown off course by the unpredictable storms that lurked outside Arpago Bay. Many a seafaring man now had to enjoy his dinner in softened form because scurvy had left his teeth as souvenirs for the fish. As a counterweight of good luck against that dietary danger, the *Belly* seemed almost charmed against encounters with the pirates that laired in the rough islands off the Maldavian Peninsula.

Perhaps the seagoing robbers steered clear of her because she carried little concentrated wealth, but that hadn't kept them off other, less lucky ships. It was rumored that the captain knew more about the pirates' methods and recognition signals than any entirely honest man should. Hailing originally from Svernig, clear around the end of the Dragonsback Mountains to the northwest, he had entered these southern seas as a cabin boy aboard a Svernigian galley, blown off course in the Sea of Storms. His activities and whereabouts for the years that had followed that were only vaguely established. Exactly where he had obtained the money to purchase his ship and how he had lost his left arm were among the few subjects that Dak would never discuss.

• 2 •

Mark-the-Stock Deaver did not stand out from the rest of the crew in appearance. Scurvy had thinned his sandy hair only a little in the two years that he had been aboard, and few now remembered that he had had no front teeth when he had first signed on. He was a strong young man of average height, an able seaman now, good with a sword in case of trouble. There had never been trouble aboard the ship at sea, but Sai-khand's dock was no place to leave an unguarded cargo. Barrow's was worse. Some unsavory types also liked to hide longboats in the Wat bayous and surprise the tired crews of inbound ships. There had never been a connection between Dak and those chicken-thief river pirates, and the returning ship was more likely to be carrying the kind of general merchandise that could easily disappear into Barrow's black market. Mark had stood a few nervous watches with his weapon in hand, but he only made token use of his sword in a couple of tavern brawls.

Although life aboard the ship had been good to him, Mark was signing off the *Belly* at the end of this voyage. Dak had asked him to stay on, but he hadn't begged: there were plenty of seamen wanting a berth. The heat was off Mark now: two years before, he had been a wanted man because of his part in a bungled drug-smuggling incident. Two years was a long time in fast-moving Barrow, and its watchmen had better things to do than to look for one runaway punk. There had been a virtual drug war in Barrow after Mark's escape: the gangs against each other and against the Prince's personally reorganized city watch. That was over now. Exotic drugs were again scarce, expensive, and generally unpopular in Barrow.

Mark had no desire to go back into the drug business: his connections were all dead now or on the run. Besides, he had matured enough not to want to dirty himself with that line again. He had run away to save his skin, but during his several voyages, flight had turned to ambition. Jenny had had a lot to do with his transformation.

Jenny and her sister Nadia were barmaids at the Jumping Salmon. Their tavern-keeping father, Fishin' Jed, had retired from the sea. He had salvaged a valuable cargo with his fishing boat, but he had badly broken his leg in a fall on the same trip. The injury had put him ashore with enough cash to buy the Salmon. His wife was a seldom-seen homebody who did most of the cooking for the tavern. His daughters worked hard, moving food and ale to the customers.

The girls were in little danger of being abused by the patrons, though most were sailors. Jed kept a sawn-off spar behind the bar for those with roaming hands or too-specific suggestions. There was clear difference between friendly passes and uninvited grabs, and between suggestive banter and propositions that involved extra services for money. The two, under their father's eye, were not likely to be enticed into an older profession practiced by some other barmaids. Jenny and Nadia were not living the lives of cloistered virgins, not while serving drinks to seamen in a dockside tavern: they were just a couple of Barrow girls boosting a family business.

The regular patrons helped weed out any newcomers who didn't respect the father/daughters relationship of barman and barmaids. Many of the regulars were solidly married fishermen, but a number of others were young, and not so young, crewmen from the fishing fleet or from merchant ships on the Wat. Mark was not the only sailor for whom Jenny was the chief reason for patronizing the Salmon.

She was as warm and round as a bun fresh from the oven. Her slightly plump arms and calves flashed in and out of her sleeves and skirt as she moved. Her tanned bosom was a joy to behold, and there was always the hope that she would forgetfully bend too low in her loose bodice at your particular table. Her following of suitors, in every stage from puppy love to serious, formed much of the Salmon's clientele.

Jed had cleared a space outside the tavern's swinging doors into which he was regularly obliged to throw young men who disagreed in his taproom over Jenny's favors. He discouraged indoor duels; the second time that you endangered his furniture, you weren't invited back, no matter the color of your money or your yearning for his daughter. He almost encouraged outdoor contests, since the Salmon provided no professional entertainment. Many a copper had exchanged hands while gambling on the fighting prowess of various suitors.

Jenny herself settled no fights by bestowing particular favor: encouraging one might keep the others away. She enjoyed being the center of attention. Though she was a treat to the eye, her personality was rounded out by fickleness and vanity. Although she had the ability to rise above petty airheadedness, she had no need. It would have been as difficult to change her successful shortcomings as it would have been to convince a man born rich to learn a manual trade. Jenny had been born with the riches of an amplified figure, as if she had received her sister's share as well as her own.

Nadia seemed positively skinny in her sister's presence, and because of their mutual occupation, she spent far too much time in situations where the siblings could be compared. Nadia was cast from a different mold. Quiet and serious, she had developed her intelligence and circumspection purposely, in counterpoint to her sister's obvious, though superficial, qualities. The fact that Nadia's positive features had so far been overlooked by the young men that patronized the Salmon was a strong indication of how shallow that gender could be. Nadia was pretty, but she lacked the eye-catching intensity of her sister's looks. Suitors fairly swarmed around Jenny.

Jed had solved the problem of how the excessively popular Jenny could be courted in her off time from the tavern in a way that only compounded the girls' differences. There wasn't that much daytime business at the Salmon, and girls would be girls. Jed had ruled that Jenny could be about the Town with a single suitor only if Nadia accompanied the couple. In fairness, Nadia could be accompanied by a beau of her own if she wished. Naturally, it hadn't worked out that way. The twice only that a young man had asked to tour the bazaar with Nadia, the foursome had collapsed as soon as the sisters were out of sight of the tavern. Jenny had acquired two escorts, and Nadia none.

In Nadia's opinion, twice could be no accident. Her only hope was that her flighty tease of a sister would marry and move far, far away. Meanwhile, she was forced to trail behind Jenny and some paramour, seldom the same one more than twice, and listen to the beau's desperate banter. The teasing, the hand-holding, the kissing games, and her sister's mobile wrestling matches were beginning to turn her stomach. A seafood diet had given her good teeth, but gritting them constantly couldn't be good for the jaw.

• **3** •

The Salmon was humming with activity. The fishing fleet was in that evening, with a good catch, and several merchantmen were in port whose crews considered the Salmon their Barrow home. The talk was fish-fish-fish and sea-sea-sea: the ocean was so large compared to mere men that it forever drew the minds of those that sailed it. It was a prime evening for both business and pleasure.

Jenny threaded her way among the tables, plying her charms universally (and selling an amazing number of drinks for her father as a consequence). She sold them in the sense that she took the orders and delivered a few drinks personally to the tables of her momentary favorites. She was much more interested in chatting than in carrying trays. It was Nadia who packed the heavy loads of pitchers and mugs to tables filled with thirsty fishermen. Jenny's face had a faint sheen of perspiration that highlighted her superior features in the lamplight. The sweat that plastered Nadia's blouse to her only made it easier to make an unfavorable comparison of her figure to Jenny's.

Dak's crew was grouped at a large table, drinking heavily and plowing through platters of roast beef and fresh vegetables; no fish for them, thanks. Their making-port celebration was also a going-away party for Mark. The sandy-haired sailor drank with his friends and laughed at their jokes, but his eyes followed Jenny. He was a strong contender for her affections that night, competing mostly with oldsters, ugly seamen, and married men. Mark was single and good-looking, His missing teeth gave his flattened grin a little-boy air of gravity.

Nadia, weaving under two trays of food, and Jenny, hand-delivering two mugs of ale, arrived at the *Belly*'s crew table at the same instant. Covered by the clatter of dishes, Mark was able to grab Jenny's hand and look into her eyes. She didn't pull away. (She now had a good reason to stop clearing away dirty dishes: Jenny hated dirty dishes.)

"Jenny, I'm back."

"Yes, you are . . . uh, Mark."

"I know you can't talk right now, but remember what we talked about before my last run to Sai-khand?"

"Yes . . . Sure." Jenny's mental files were in a sad state of disarray—too many suitors; too many promises. Still, Mark was one of her nicest beaux. She didn't want to discourage him.

Certainly, she had flirted heavily with Mark the last

time the *Belly* was in Barrow, and several times before, but for the Thousand Stars she couldn't remember if she had promised him anything, or what that might have been. Out of the corner of her eye, she caught the fact that Nadia had the table almost cleared. Jenny hastily grabbed three empty mugs, before Father got on her back again about not doing her share of the work. Abandoning intellectual subtlety, since there was no time to learn something new, Jenny spoke to Mark in her best voice—body language. With a wiggle that caused a ripple to run the length of her torso, she bent down and brushed her unspeakably magnificent chest against his shoulder.

"I'm off tomorrow. Come by, and we'll talk. We can go to the bazaar." She swayed away from him with a melting look and swished toward the kitchen.

Had the rush of hormones that hit Mark's system been any heavier, his circulation would have stopped entirely. The taproom fairly vibrated with the increase in heart rate among its male patrons—young and old; single or married—even in its farthest corner. Those in the near-miss area were stimulated; Mark, at the center of her sensual blast, was stunned into glazed-eyed mental disfunction. If, instead of a trip to the bazaar, Jenny had suggested that she carve out Mark's liver with a dull knife, he would have bobbed his head in an equally foolish series of nods and continued to drool on himself. Nadia, watching the entire scene, would have thrown up her hands in disgust if she hadn't been so heavily loaded. Men!

The rest of the evening proceeded to anticlimax. Mark ate and drank heartily at his farewell dinner, tasting none of it, his eyes perpetually homing in on Jenny. The few times he showed signs of returning to consciousness, Jenny would fire him a wink or a sultry look that returned him to oblivion. He departed late, intoxicated by much more than alcohol, supported on each side by understanding fellow crewmen. He would sleep one last time aboard the *Belly*.

• 4 •

Morning came late, with a high, lifting fog. Mark, with no watch to keep, slept late and awoke with a chemical and emotional hangover. This morning he had to make his mark in the big logbook for the second mate and sign off the ship for good. Dak had risen early and shaken off the night's excesses. Today, he would make the rounds of the merchants who were expecting his deliveries and of others who might be interested in the speculative goods he had brought to harbor.

Mark stirred slowly, despite Jenny's warming promise for later in the morning. No one would be up yet at the Jumping Salmon. The present tides sent the fishing fleet out before dawn, with the fishermen leaving their homes to go directly to the boats. The tavern's hours were being kept late, instead of being tacked onto the morning, as they would be during other seasons of tide and storm.

The galley fire was out in the *Belly*, and a breakfast of cold salt beef did not entice a man just in from the sea. Carefully packing his sea bag with the small parting presents of his friends, Mark remained no less decided about leaving the life of a sailor. He felt the mild sorrow of being uprooted from a familiar and homey place, but he was bound for something better.

The *Belly* was docked at a sturdy pier on the river's west side, just below the Old Wat Bridge. Dak could have found better on the east side, but "for old time's sake," he always brought the ship back to the spot where he had bought her. The Slews had been less of a reeking slum at that time. Not many years ago, prosperity had been more equitably distributed, east and west, north and south, in Barrow.

It was only a short walk up the bank and across the high arch of the bridge to the Town. At the bridge's eastern end, a turn to the right down River Street would lead south into the fishing district. The Jumping Salmon was tucked away in the center of that quarter. Mark chose instead to take the broad boulevard running east toward the bazaar.

It was a brisk ten-minute march to the Town's center. Businesses functioning in the trade along the Wat gradually gave way to a polyglot of small shops of every conceivable class. The slow thud of the heart of the disintegrating Slews yielded first to the smooth beat of the river commerce, and then shifted to the bird-quick beat of Upcruster Town. The Upcrusters were forever hungry, not for food but to scratch their way up or to get off the slide down. "Up" was north, toward the mansions of the powerful; "down" was west, into the Slews.

Mark's feet carried him across the wakened bazaar to Mama Threechin's eatery. Mama herself was there, badgering her cooks. Dozens of loaves of bread and caldrons of stew were rolling out of the half-open kitchen. Early-rising customers had already gone to their business; Mark was able to have a small, messy table to himself. A heavyset waitress with long blond hair served him a bowl of steaming stew, a wedge of sharp cheese, a handful of onions, and a chunk of Mama's brown bread. The only other item on the menu was small beer.

Mark was satisfied with the simple, filling fare. The food at the Gryphon and Goblet farther north was both better and more varied, but Barrelgut's wife and cook didn't serve a regular meal until noon. To have asked that burly taverner or his partner Gorgio to cook breakfast was said to be a guaranteed trip to indigestion. Once he had discovered the beauty of the Jumping Salmon, Mark had stopped looking for other places to eat.

The stew warmed the chill of the Wat fog out of him and blotted up the last of his hangover. The tang of the onions brought him fully awake. Their odoriferous presence reminded him that he was to see Jenny soon. Romance might be crippled by the stink of onions! He dropped the last few bites of them back in the stew bowl and hurried out. Mama Threechins gave him a cheery wave (which he didn't see) and went back to harassing the cooks. It was said that she shut her mouth only when asleep.

Mark found a herbalist's stall sandwiched between a silversmith's shop and the wagon of a Tellarani fortune-teller. The robed and whiskered Upcruster sold Mark some minty leaves to chew and grinned at his departing back. Young folks in love might as well have carried a sign around announcing it.

Mark brushed down his hair at least a dozen times and repeatedly rearranged his clothes on the long walk to the Salmon. The fishing district was built around crowded lanes, interspersed with sheds that ran fifty meters or more, used for smoking fish. If you hadn't grown up in its alleys, you had to stick to the twisty main streets.

Mark had been raised in Slews-Inside-the-Walls. In his home neighborhoods, he could have cut the time to travel the distance by half. Still, he needed that extra time to squirm in his new landsman's clothes and to adjust his legs to footing that didn't roll like the deck of a ship.

The Salmon had three entrances: front, for the customers; side, for deliveries; and rear, for the family. Mark counted himself one of the privileged few to be invited to the family entrance, happier in his ignorance of how substantial a number that "few" was. His knock was answered by Nadia, whom he perpetually thought of as "Jenny's sister," though he knew her name perfectly well. Nadia told him that Jenny would be a few minutes, and she invited him to sit on their weathered back porch. She decided to wait outside with him. Though Mark had a sinking feeling that her presence meant that she would be included as an unwanted chaperon later, he was polite when she struck up a conversation.

Jenny was making herself beautiful, though her admirers would have insisted that such an activity was as pointless as coating an orchid with paint. She never went into action half-armed, nor gave any available male less than a full-bore blast of beauty: That was a matter of policy. Perhaps she felt the unfaceable premonition that someday curves would sag and voluptuous youth would give way to pudgy middle age. Though willfully ignorant of cooking and cleaning and learning generally, Jenny was among the most knowledgeable women in Barrow on how to touch up with rouge or how to make a blouse hang for best effect. Her enhanced appearance would stretch her youth by a decade, keeping her the envy of many women her age. However, that enhanced charm took time to put on.

Mark had set his sea bag on the porch and was beginning to enjoy his visit with Nadia. She was alert and intelligent, and without Jenny to throw her looks into relative squalor, she was quite pretty. Mark was a healthy young man, just back from a long voyage, with nothing amorous to sustain him so far except the promise of a chaperoned liaison later. The presence of an attractive young woman had brought his glands to a simmer, and his brain hadn't noticed yet that it should be feeling guilty for his endocrine unfaithfulness. Had the same experience happened to him in far Sai-khand (or if Jenny hadn't made a timely, devastating appearance), who knows where such a communication might have led.

When Jenny swung onto the porch like a duchess descending a staircase, Nadia became invisible. Mark rose and drifted toward her like an unmoored kite in a warm breeze. Jenny greeted him, and he responded with unremembered salutation, followed by an enthusiastic compliment on her appearance. She feigned modest acceptance and filed away another mental trophy. Gathering the strings of her puppet more firmly, she gave him a verbal tug toward the bazaar. The threesome departed for the center of the Town with Nadia trailing behind like a ship in darkness. Mark could not later have described a centimeter of their journey; in fact, he was not certain they walked at all. Your feet have to touch the ground to do that.

Jenny and her beaux were regulars in the bazaar; the shopkeepers needed no hint as to how to react to them. She would admire; he would offer to buy. She would mildly protest the expense; he would, naturally, be twice as eager to show off his purse. The shopkeeper and the suitor would haggle. The suitor, always too eager to be rewelded to Jenny's side, would make a poor bargain. She would depart happy; the beau would depart dazzled, to chide himself later. The shopkeeper would pocket a profit and wait eagerly for Jenny's next visit. The situation seemed celestially ordained to work that way.

Jenny and Mark (and their shadow) had worked their way around the bazaar by late morning. The everchanging marketplace was fascinating even to those with little money to spend. Though Mark was a little out of touch, Jenny and Nadia were long accustomed to it. The three strolled and chatted among its wonders, although their conversation would have been considered shouting in any quieter quarter.

There was food in every form: grain, vegetables, and meat that was sold to every home east of the river and to every eatery. If your tastes ran to the unusual, such as wisent meat or some rare spice required by your religion, it was to be found somewhere in the bazaar. If you were thirsty, you could purchase anything from a hogshead of cheap wine to tiny, ancient bottles of Maldavian White, worth more than gold. If you lacked cloth, you could clothe yourself in Slews burlap or Svernigian silk, with half a dozen tailor shops eager to sew to your specifications, no matter how bizarre.

There were goldsmiths who doubled as bankers and silversmiths who made loans at usurious rates. There were blacksmiths who were weapons makers and herbalists who doubled as healers. Everyone had his fingers in at least two pies and wanted to shout loudly about both. It seemed as if every tradesman were an agent for somebody else. The swords maker would be glad to send you (and your clinking purse) to a friend up on Caravan Way, who just happened to have the filagreed dagger you were seeking. If you weren't satisfied by the small, but excellent, string of mounts the dealer in animals had with him, he knew of a "better" horse in the yards near the West Gate—just mention his name. Ask a hedge wizard, trying to maintain his mystique while crouched beneath a hot awning, for a spell he couldn't handle, and he was bound to know a higher-level adept who could perform it. He would be put in contact, for the right "finder's fee," of course.

Small animals abounded: goats, pigs, birds, and even a few scraggly chickens. There were always a few strings of horses and camels present. Farmers brought oxen to pull their cart and to sell. Stray dogs seemed to be everywhere, while the nighttime bazaar belonged to feral cats and enormous rats. The by-products of that zoo made walking an adventure in itself. Experienced strollers had a high-stepping gait peculiar to the bazaar, as if they had developed second sight in the tips of their toes. Naturally, there were at least two crews of Upcrusters working to shovel up the droppings, which would become fertilizer for some rich man's garden or dried fuel for some poor man's fire. If anything held profit, a Townsman would find it.

Many of the bazaar's businesses were without tangible merchandise, though they prospered nevertheless. There were three of the brightly painted wagons of the nomadic Tellarani, fortune-tellers of the best. (The best was said to be Brieze Wagonhawk, a young matron of the People, who lived in a wheelless wagon with a bevy of brothers and sisters and a native "husband.") Women of another "profession" discreetly peddled their wares, waiting for the night to bring out male foolishness.

Information brokers of every stripe sold what you wanted to know. Some were semiprofessional gossips, others were advisers in investment futures, and some were agents of unnamed men in power, whose contacts reached every major enterprise in the city. Barbers trimmed hair and applied leeches to black eyes.

Watchmen patrolled everywhere, accepted as acquaintances during daylight hours. They broke up fights and caught pilferers. The miscreants received quick trial at the bazaar magistrate's booth at the north end. It was their job to keep beggars constantly on the move: no one wanted them near their stall, but most felt too guilty to persecute them directly. Who knew if you might be begging yourself next month?

Everyone shouted. Every seller had the best, the brightest, the most unique. He had to cry it above the shouts of other sellers, customers, and hagglers. Each seller was also a potential buyer, whose attention must be caught. Hawkers had to unload consumables while they were still fresh. Professional criers called the crowd to their show, their inn, their forming caravan, their enrollment of soldiers to win glory beyond Ichan, their master's hiring of seamen, their information booth (hinting at the top of their lungs with juicy bits of half news). The open market square roared like a never-ending surf.

Strangers were likely to be stunned by the pounding sights and sounds. Children who hadn't grown up there stuck close to parents: lost in the bazaar was lost indeed. However, though it was an enormous commercial success, the bazaar's nature made verbal intimacy difficult, when protestations of love or delicately turned phrases had to be delivered in a yell.

Mark had not been behaving quite as predicted. He hadn't rushed to buy every bauble that Jenny had admired. Instead, he had dropped occasional remarks about how they "would need the money later." Jenny had not objected too strenuously: a big present later in the day would make up for missing a few small ones early. Eventually, Mark tired of shouting his intimacies and suggested that they buy a lunch and carry it out of the bazaar, to Pocket Park. The girls agreed, or Jenny agreed, which was all that counted. Mark purchased pastry-and-meat rolls for all three and mugs of cooled root beer, paying the deposit on the mugs from a purse still well filled. They exited the noisy marketplace down a narrow side street on the northeast corner.

A decade before, during the Town's height of prosperity, a wealthy, heirless Upcruster had willed his mansion and grounds to the Town as a park. The mansion had burned down not long after the executor (Mama Threechins, of all people) had sold it in order to have a park operating fund. Economic collapse had followed by only a couple of years, with shops and houses crowding into the mansion's former location, but the small park survived. It had gotten its name from a disparaging remark by a Saikhandian visitor: "I could fit the whole thing in my pocket!"

Still, there were grass and trees there, maintained weakly by Mama Threechins' fund. Once in a while, a rabbit or pigeon would camp out there, until some Upcruster got lucky with a rock. Many found the spot of green that the Town hadn't overgrown a relief from the smelly riverfront or the congestion south of Caravan Way.

Mark and Jenny were not the first to stroll into the park hand in hand. (Mark had missed a lot of "firsts" with Jenny, but she wasn't planning to bring them up.) The twosome and baggage sat down in the shade on an oddly shaped bench: some wagon had come to Barrow in the past and had broken down too badly to get home. They munched and let the bazaar fade out of their ears.

"Jenny," Mark said finally, taking both her hands, "do you remember our promise?"

Actually, she didn't, but talented girl that she was, her smile kept him talking.

"I know you've had lots of offers, but I'm not as poor as I used to be." An unbelievable run of luck shooting dice with some drunks in Sai-khand had given Mark a relatively huge stake. He hadn't frittered it away in port, as most sailors would have.

"I have enough to buy a good house, this side of the river, and I can get a job as a warehouseman. Dak showed me some easy book work."

Dak's "book work" was a set of personal hieroglyphics and simple numbers; the old pirate was otherwise illiterate. Mark was also no reader, but he had learned the simplicity of Dak's substitute system. Thus, he was considerably more literate than the average Barrowman.

Jenny was impressed, but hardly overwhelmed. Mark was talking about marriage, in comfort perhaps, but not in wealth. At the moment she was having too much fun with a field of admirers to dump them all for a single suitor. Still, there was no need to chase off this well-to-do beau, even if marriage was out of the question. Mark evidently thought she had promised herself to him. He was vague about the details, and Jenny remembered no such promise. What she needed now was a way to string her fish without hooking herself. Looking at his anxious, smiling face, she was inspired.

"Mark," she began, "I like you, and I *could* marry you. We'd be happy, but for one *small* thing. I wouldn't want to begin marriage with even one thing working against us. Since you'll be in Barrow, perhaps in a couple of years more I could become used to it, but right now . . ." Jenny planned to ease him down, but not out. A couple of years of nibbling away at the price of a house could mean many lovely trips to the bazaar. Mark was already looking ready to be gaffed; she didn't wait for him to ask.

"Mark, it's your teeth. You're still young, but all those teeth missing in front make you look older—ready for gray hair. You need to give me some time."

Mark was crushed; his entire body wilted. However, Jenny was surprised by his reaction when he looked up.

"Teeth, is it? Well, I'll get teeth for you! I'll find a way! They won't stand between us!" He leaped to his feet. "I'll start now—this minute!" He swung Jenny to her feet and gave her a resounding kiss. "Don't look for anyone else. They're as good as in my mouth!

"Girls, I know you can find your way home. I don't want to waste a second! By this time tomorrow, I'll be at the Salmon to tell you how I'll do it." He waved jauntily and almost bolted toward the park's entrance.

Though lacking dental work, Mark had been lying through his teeth. Jenny's (qualified) rejection had hit him like a kick in the pit of the stomach. The jauntiness was faked, to allow him to get far enough from the girls' sight to drop down behind a tree trunk in misery. He rolled the scene over and over in his mind. If she really loved him, teeth shouldn't have made any difference. For a moment, his idol tottered on her pedestal, until he remembered that she had promised to be his. All he had to do was get some teeth. He slumped again in woe. How, by the Thousand Stars, did anybody get more teeth?

Jenny was surprised and a little disappointed by Mark's sudden departure. He was supposed to have stayed and been soothed out of his hurt and into spending some more cash on her. On the other hand, though her hastily concocted plan had taken an initial setback, it should work anyway in the long run. Teeth weren't for sale in some shop in the bazaar. When Mark found that out, he'd be coming around again, to spend money on her while she "got used to" his toothlessness. Somehow, she was certain that the money would give out before she gave in. Satisfied, she stirred her silent sister and began to stroll back toward the bazaar. No use to waste the day; maybe they would run into another of her beaus.

Nadia, unexpectedly, had something to say. "Why did you do that to him? Those missing teeth only make him cute, and you know it. He'll never find a way to get any more!"

"None of your business, Beanpole." Jenny used a pet name from their childhood that Nadia especially detested, and it shut her sister up, as intended.

Mark, behind his tree, had heard the outburst. It so confused him that he let the girls walk on without interruption. Nadia seemed to like him and be worried about his welfare. She was no "beanpole," either. Before he could pursue that thought further, her words reminded him of his impossible quest. His worry was so deep that he didn't notice that that was the first time he hadn't thought of the girl as "Jenny's sister."

• 5 •

His depressed reverie was broken by a hand on his shoulder.

"Hey, how's the mighty seaman?"

Mark's eyes flew open, and he looked up into a plump face with a blond mustache.

"Cavin! Hey, pal, how goes it?" He jumped up and gave the smaller man a brotherly slam on the shoulder. "What brings you east of the river? I asked about you every time I was in port, but we haven't got together in two years!"

Cavin-the-Cutpurse was an old drinking buddy from the Slews. Cavin had bought many a round for his friend, and Mark had returned the favor often, especially since Cavin had a weakness for getting himself rolled by some woman anytime he got a decent stash together. Mark's hasty departure had ended their running around together, though it was common knowledge in the Slews where he had taken off to.

Of course, they lied grandly about how well the other one looked. Though Cavin was essentially unchanged, Mark was leaner and browner. The missing teeth had also changed the profile of his face. They headed toward the bazaar and Bargo's Beer Stand, to talk over old times.

Bargo's was unique, in a square jammed with rarities. Out in the open, it sold only one product—beer. Its only furniture was a bar forming three sides of a square and a worn bench paralleling that. The fourth side was formed of two enormous hogsheads of beer, and the roof was a canvas awning. Bargo's never closed in warm weather. At any hour, Bargo or his son, Bargo-the-Little, would either be serving or sleeping between the taps, rolled up in an ancient wisent hide.

The place had never been unwatched long enough for anyone ever to cadge a free drink. The taps had been fitted with clever finger locks that only the Bargos knew how to work. Either operator could remove them or slip them on in seconds, in case the on-duty Bargo had to run a quick errand. The bartenders had never been gone long enough at a stretch for a mug to run dry or for some clever rogue to figure out their locks. A lush of a Saikhandian locksmith had traded the locks for lifetime drinking rights at the stand. They had proven more lasting than his liver; he had long been beer-soaked worm fodder.

Bargo's never ran out of beer, though the barrels hadn't been moved in years. The brewery daily sent lesser barrels of beer to be hauled to the top and dumped into the hogsheads. The antique tanks gave the brew an earthy flavor that could be found nowhere else. It was so good that freeloaders who might have secretly drilled holes to obtain a private supply were afraid to disturb the beer's quality. Manhandling beer barrels had given the Bargos arms like oak beams. Bargo-the-Little was also one of the largest men in Barrow and the arm-wrestling champion of the Town—all the more reason to dismiss thoughts of trying to defraud them.

Mark and Cavin traded exaggerated descriptions of their successes as they emptied a tankard each. By unspoken agreement, each settled at last to a version nearer the truth. Cavin wasn't broke at the moment, but he was feeling the pinch. A few weeks after Mark had departed the city, Cavin had come into a nice take of silver that he had snitched east of the river, but that had made it necessary to keep to the Slews for quite a while. Bad luck and a fast-talking woman had separated him from his cash all too soon, and he had had to take up dipping purses from drug runners. Those midnight pharmacists were always long on cash, but they would have used Cavin for target practice if he had been detected. The Prince's crackdown on the drug trade had ended that game for Cavin, though he had made a last score by turning in a couple of pushers for the reward. (Naturally, he didn't share that information with Mark; a snitch was not well looked upon, no matter the circumstances.) He had moved east into the Town again and resumed glad-handing small, valuable items and cutting purses.

Mark's tale covered as much past time, but he dragged slowly through the later incidents of his life. He was as embarrassed by his love sickness and wish to settle down as Cavin had been about peaching on a pusher. Mark knew that Cavin had no great respect for women, having had his backside burned more than once by foolish skirt chasing.

Sure enough, Cavin needled Mark roughly about his love life, but he backed off once he was sure his friend was serious. Cavin had some good, humane qualities, even though they were well laid over with larceny. After Mark described the latest incident and his impossible quest, Cavin did have some more unkind things to say. No woman should put a man through the wringer over nothing: lots of folks had no teeth. Still, Cavin was able to supply Mark's first ray of hope.

"Mark, lad, you can probably get those teeth *magicked* back in, if you know the right mummer. Ain't much they can't do—for a price."

It was true that magic could accomplish almost anything, even to the point of creating an entirely new Plane. Fabulous feats had been attributed to great magicians, simply to fulfill some personal whim. For all other folk, magic had a price tag.

"Do you think I could get old Hugor over there to grow me some new teeth?" He gestured at a gray-bearded shaman crouched in his booth, wearing a threadbare robe sewn with magical symbols.

"Nah. He might be up to unspoiling some milk or frightening off a flock of crows, but he's not that much of a wizard. He might make you a love locket, but the charm would wear off in a week—like it does with most women anyway. Who you want is someone bigger."

"Yeah, but maybe he knows someone—"

"You can bet he does! And he'll charge you for sending you on to that next charmer. Now, I think I know just the wizard you need, and I won't hit you for a fee for finding him."

"Really? Where would a magician like that be found?" Hope was rising in Mark.

"He hangs out at the Gryphon and Goblet."

"Is it Brandelvar? I've heard of him."

"Nah. Brandelvar's somewhere up north working for some old pervert of a baron. This one's named Threebortin. He ought to be able to do the job, and he won't charge you as much as the rest. He's good, but he's also hit hard times, I hear."

"Well, c'mon! Let's look this guy up!" Mark was already rising from the bar.

"Nah, not me. I'm not going anywhere near Barrelgut. That big stash I told you I got right after you left was some of his cash. I hear that he never griped about it much; maybe he wasn't sure who done it. But I'm not lettin' him get those big hands on me. A couple of squeezes, and I'd admit to anything. You'll have to take it from here without me."

Even though it meant losing touch with his friend

again, Mark *had* to go. He wrung Cavin's hand warmly and promised to get together soon and reestablish the good old days. Cavin, having once been in love himself, doubted that they would ever regain much from former times. He resumed drinking his beer, hoping that Bargo would do something with his tap locks so that Cavin could begin figuring them out. Mark hurried out of the bazaar, north along Straight Street.

· 6 ·

Threebortin always felt miserable these days. For the thousandth time, he wished that he had had the sense not to challenge another major wizard. It was no excuse that he had been drunk at the time. Inebriation among poor, nonmagical folk might be overlooked on occasion, to ease their dreary, limited existence. A mage, however, should have known better than to dull his mind and cripple his gestures. Somebody else had been buying, but that alibi for lack of control was as thin as an everyday cloak in the Slews.

Brandelvar was a high-level adept, but Threebortin was no slouch himself. A third of the lesser wizards in Barrow had funneled business beyond their ability to him. With a few glasses of Maldavian Red in him, it had looked like a good matchup to Threebortin. He was tired of hearing about what a hot item Brandelvar was among the "scientific" magicians.

Threebortin's plan had been to challenge Brandelvar, but the contest was supposed to have come out a draw, as such usually did when the sorcerers involved weren't out for blood. Threebortin had intended to walk away with his reputation enhanced by his audacity, and Brandelvar's diminished. Instead, Brandelvar, who had never openly discussed how high his magic extended, had evidently been doing some private research. The new trick he laid on Threebortin knocked down the challenger's defenses after only the briefest struggle.

To the observers at the Gryphon, Threebortin had called Brandelvar some unpronounceable name; the two had glared at each other and made a series of gestures. From behind the inn's furniture where they had hastily taken shelter, the tavern regulars had seen Threebortin flip physically through the air and land at Brandelvar's feet. The cold sweat that had popped out on Threebortin's face had been a real soaker.

The nomadic Brandelvar was held to be a black mage who had dealt with demons on occasions. He had Threebortin caught like a cockroach under a boot: just a small pressure and *crack!* Continued existence as anything more complex than a field mouse had been looking doubtful. Brandelvar, however, had been in a good mood. He had been about to make a big score with his friend Mungo. (So he thought. Looking back, Threebortin realized that if his encounter with Brandelvar had happened later, after Brandelvar had been forced to slink out of town following the Ba-La-Nar Temple debacle, he would probably have turned Threebortin into a pollywog immediately and pitched him into the Wat to dodge hungry fish.) As it was, Brandelvar had been feeling creative. His words still echoed in Threebortin's head.

"So . . . I have you like a plucked chicken. . . . Yes, a chicken!"

Threebortin had tensed. With Brandelvar thinking "chicken," Threebortin could almost feel the pin feathers sprouting.

Brandlevar frowned. "Are you ready to admit that I'm the better mage and the better man?" He paused. "I thought not."

Threebortin had decided that if he had to end as a chicken or a pollywog, he would exit silently—a *proud* pollywog.

"Well, hearing you admit my worth means more to me than feeding you to the fish or listening to you cluck. 'Chicken' it shall be until you're ready to eat crow. You shall desire the white meat of the bird as an addict desires Mugambu White and the dark meat as he craves the Black. You shall *eat* chicken every day until you're ready to crawl before me and eat crow—a whole crow, feathers and all." His hands had flown through some complex gestures as he mouthed the certifying words of the curse. He had been laughing heartily as he seized the paralyzed Threebortin and tossed him out the Gryphon's door into the night.

The defeated wizard had lain warmly conscious, but

unable to move all night. Only after Brandelvar had departed for that business at the Ba-La-Nar Temple the next day had Threebortin been able to kick off the street dog that had been using him as a bed and return to a normal life. He had been inconvenienced, but he judged the curse on him to be mild and ineffectual, something one wizard would do to another who, though beaten, might someday turn the tables. Threebortin had not been poor; he could easily afford one chicken a day, though the meat was relatively expensive. Farmers couldn't seem to raise the fowl in any numbers without disease wiping out their flock.

At first, it had been inconvenient to send a servant to the bazaar daily to buy a bird. Similarly, he could no more cook a chicken than he could alter Brandelvar's curse. Smoke and searing flesh invariably brought out the urge in any "scientific" sorcerer to do esoteric study—a holdover from early training. By the time their concentration returned to the moment, any meal was ruined. A bubbling caldron or a sizzling griddle had meanings to a mage that ordinary folk didn't appreciate.

His one-dimensional dining had soon become intellectually boring. Every day, he had to face chicken boiled or broiled or fried or stewed or—ugh! Threebortin, the former gourmand, began to hate chicken in every form, though he was cursed to love it. The subtle, sadistic magnificence of that curse began to dawn on him. He had tried to overcome his urges by willpower, but he always broke after a few sweaty hours. His skin had felt ready to crawl from his body, and his bones had been trying to split themselves from internal pressure. It *had* to be chicken! In fact, it had to be a whole bird daily.

The first spring and summer hadn't been too bad. His servants had taken care of obtaining and cooking his avian dishes. As fall waned, chickens became scarce in the bazaar, and the price rose correspondingly. After an aborted attempt to raise the birds on his own, Threebortin was forced to dismiss one servant and use the savings to make the daily purchases himself. His account with Ibraim the money changer began to diminish.

There were a few frightening times when winter closed the roads and the farmers didn't come to town at all. Couriers, who wanted beggaring fees at that time of year, fought their way to the farms west of Barrow and fetched Threebortin's feathered medicine. He quickly bought up all the few birds within the city proper. The meat was more than food to him now, and those whose services he needed took little time to realize it and to begin to squeeze him.

He had still performed magic, but his studies in the art flagged and finally failed entirely. He dared not try to force any other being into fetching the birds for him, because of some interesting "fine print" that Brandelvar had built into his curse. Some subphrase prevented Threebortin from using sorcery directly on the problem as well. Thus, the fees he gathered as he used up complex spells disappeared into chicken flesh, messenger's fees, and the purses of those who cooked for him.

The leeching of Threebortin's life didn't happen in a month or even a year. Brandelvar's curse gnawed away below his surface with untiring staying power. A food, uncommon but hardly unknown, was eating away his soul. Though his innate wizardly strength was as great as ever, he was continuously distracted by his unnatural hunger and by the pain hovering only a few hours in the future. The most his mind would contain now was one major spell. If that last strength failed him, he would slide downward to become one more mumbling shaman.

Later, when even minor spells might fail him, there would be the Slews across the river, where the residents weren't as choosy about quality, magical or otherwise. Beyond that lay the life of hunted pain of a farmer whose livestock were literally his blood and bone. He might die in pain from a missed day of his clucking drug, or he might die a failed chicken-farming peasant, or he might break and humble himself to Brandelvar. On the other hand, he was still living in the season when the prowling beasts of his curse, hungering for his bones, could yet be kept beyond the firelight. He would not crawl until he *had* to crawl, though every night now he dreamed of white, fluffy fowl and rose squawking from his nightmares.

Threebortin had sold his own property and had moved into an upstairs room at the Gryphon and Goblet. Barrelgut's blond wife now cooked his meals: the days in which he could afford personal servants was past. Business, what remained of it, could be found as easily in the

Gryphon's common room as in private quarters. He was still considered a moderately strong magician. Though he wasn't among the best anymore, he would work fast and cheaply. When Mark Deaver found him, he was leaning against the tavern's bar pondering the vagaries of life.

• 7 •

"Teeth, is it? That doesn't sound impossible. Hmmm." The challenge of a new spell had momentarily pushed the thought of lunch from Threebortin's mind. It would be baked chicken today.

The magician's mind inventoried his magical stock, stored in a stable shed across from the Gryphon. Barrelgut had seen destructive magic worked inside his inn often enough not to invite its practitioners to employ it freely within his walls. Turning the abandoned shed into a makeshift laboratory had been a compromise that both innkeeper and mage could live with. Not enough patrons of the Gryphon owned horses these days to make maintenance of a stable worthwhile, but the building would have become a fire hazard and a magnet for squatters, without attention.

Threebortin had never grown teeth for a customer before, but the task was within a theoretical matrix that he understood well. He would require some tooth chips from his skull candle, some blood-and-sulfur powder, and the proper incantation. The whole required nothing that he did not already have on hand. When he refocussed his eyes on Mark, he was ready to deal.

"You know that my magic won't come cheaply. (Oh, for the days when something as tawdry as haggling over the price of a spell was beneath me!)"

"Yes," Mark agreed, reminding himself of Cavin's assessment of the magician's financial status. He wouldn't even consider the mage's first offer as legitimate.

The pair girded their economic loins for a showdown. Mark wanted to conserve his premarital nest egg, but Threebortin desperately needed more cash in his account. Winter would come again soon enough, with its frightening scarcity of chickens. The contest would be settled in the form of combat favored most in Barrow: haggling. A few noontime regulars gathered near the two, betting on the outcome in whispers. Haggling in private was considered unacceptable social behavior, on the same order as a bare-knuckles fighter refusing to allow spectators at his matches. Next week, any member of the audience might find himself having to barter with one of the contenders; thus, everyone wanted haggling styles to be a matter of public record.

Threebortin named a ridiculously high price. Mark, almost beating his breast over the tragedy of his own poverty, made an equally ridiculous counter offer. The wizard brushed away the bottom offer by expounding on the unique nature of his services, but he also lowered his price to merely beggaring. Mark, pleading respectful ignorance of sorcery but regrettable insolvency, raised his bid into the mildly insulting range. The main themes were established: poverty versus professional quality. The two could now maneuver within that territory, edging toward some central price that they could both live with. The winner would be the one able to tug-o'-war the other onto his side of that expected center at the close.

Threebortin seemed headed toward a marginal victory, having detected and exploited an undertone of desperation in Mark, until Denalee, Barrelgut's wife and cook, took the lid off the baking chicken back in the kitchen. Even the trickle of odor that slithered into the taproom was enough almost to overwhelm the mage. Barely hiding his drooling, he lowered his price one more notch, and the match ended in a draw. The magician and his new patron spat into the sawdust of the floor to bind their agreement. Threebortin had no trouble finding the necessary saliva.

The sorcerous dental work was to be done in Threebortin's laboratory in two days' time. The wizard needed a reasonable amount of time to work out and memorize the forty syllables of the incantation, though he had tried to claim that the delay was to gather rare and costly ingredients for the spell. This magic, like all magic, would be a product of the wizard's mind. A scientific magician such as Threebortin, however, used gestures and chanted phrases to move his mind from step to step of the operation.

Magical ingredients were props to "trick" nature into doing what the magician wanted, using them as a template. The plan of attack that Threebortin had in mind was to place chips of the correct teeth, from the skull he already owned, on Mark's gums in the positions where they would normally grow. Uttering the forty syllables in a single breath, Threebortin's mind would introduce Mark's body to the strange teeth, grow those teeth to proper proportions and lock them in place, and begin the flow of Mark's lifeblood into them. No aspect called for Threebortin to summon fantastic familiars from other Planes or do anything that another sorcerer would have found spectacular. Mark's body could have almost handled the job unassisted.

Threebortin rubbed his hands together in anticipation. He was about to collect a solid fee, for a reputable piece of magic, thus extending both his financial life and his self-esteem. And he was about to have lunch. Mmmmmm! Chicken! Once again he was appalled by the orgasmic surge of expectation as another fowl meal approached, but he simply couldn't help it. He would consume his bird one more time, hating it and himself, and loving it passionately. Once again, he reminded himself that he had sworn off both alcohol and wizardly challenges forever.

• 8 •

A handful of errands caused it to be well past noon before Mark could travel south toward the Jumping Salmon. He would have to hurry to retrieve his sea bag from the back porch of that tavern and still have time to get back to the room he had rented from Barrelgut for the night. That burly bartender was boastful about his inn having six or eight rentable rooms, whereas the Salmon was merely a taproom and eatery. Unconcerned with intra-Town snobbery, Mark had only been wanting a place to sleep that night. At the moment, he most·wanted to see Jenny.

Both Jenny and Nadia were on duty in the dining room, and the supper rush of fishermen was keeping them too busy to talk. Mark was only able to snatch a few words with Jenny. He held off telling her the big news in such a crowd, but his hopeful face had probably tipped her off. Nadia stopped near the couple and expressed an interest in hearing more immediately, but Jed sharply called both girls back to work. Jenny seemed relieved somehow to be resuming tasks she usually found odious, but Mark had trouble reading emotions from her back as she turned toward the bar to pick up more trays.

"How about tomorrow?" he called.

"I can't," she cried, pooching out her perfect lip, "I have to clean house tomorrow!" She phrased her excuse in the tones anyone else would have used to say, "I have to disembowel a skunk tomorrow!"

Mark was clearly not going to get a chance to speak to Jenny alone that evening; Jed was very strict about after-hours callers. Instead, he went around to the back of the building to repossess his bag. Jed's wife was sweeping the back porch. Each shyly measured the other: a polite, young seaman meeting a graying, but still pretty house-wife, who might someday be his mother-in-law. Mark hoped that Jenny would favor this happy homebody as he and his inamorata grew old together, but truthfully, Jenny's mother—Delvina—reminded him more of Nadia. His emotions became confused as the conversation continued.

Delvina's voice still retained the spritely remains of a Maldavian accent. "Jed's boat rescued me off the wreck of the *Arpago Princess*," she explained. "And I never let him get away." She blushed.

Nadia had told Delvina about Jenny's sensible beau, the one who had the price of a home and prospects of a steady job before he proposed. The young man's flattened smile was as piquant as her own levelheaded daughter had described. Mark reminded her of a younger Jed, tanned and lean from the sea.

Mark would have tarried longer in her pleasant company, except for the need to be across town by dark. Once twilight was past, your presence in the streets marked you as predator and/or prey. The entire city was in on the game: the absent watchmen, the muggers, and the few armed, wary pedestrians. Mark had grown up in Slews-Inside-the-Walls, where No Man's Time differed only in that it began with the first hint of twilight and could extend into daylight hours without notice. If you walked

Barrow's nighttime streets, you needed both a sword and an inclination to use it.

He reached the Gryphon without incident, to find his sea chest had been delivered, as the second mate had promised. The streets had been nearly empty. Farmers especially had farther to travel and little love of the city at night. The departure of both them and their livestock left the bazaar largely empty until daylight once again called the traders and opened the shops. Only certain marginally honest businesses or those catering to magical needs kept their doors open in the square.

There was little for a jittery Mark to do that night. He drank sparingly, caught up on recent Town gossip, and bedded early. His sleep was fitful. Near dawn, a nightmare came calling that involved both of Jed's daughters, but it eluded conscious memory. The peeled remnants of the vision left memory only of having dreamed. They were without substance, but the reality of his nightmare had jolted him awake for the day.

Downstairs, he got to watch his hired wizard bolt down a breakfast of cold chicken like a starving wolf. Such base behavior from a professional was puzzling, but who could second-guess a mummer? Threebortin soon left for his laboratory, making no attempt at conversation. His was the only breakfast served by Barrelgut's sleepy partner, Gorgio. Mark was sent off to Mama Threechin's when he expressed an interest in food.

Dawdling over a bowl of hot barley, Mark watched the weekday bazaar come to life. Every seventh day, the square was relatively quiet, by mutual consent. Although conflicting calendar systems placed the day of rest at the end of some calendar's weeks and at the beginning for others, Barrow generally followed the 365-day, thirteen-month Saikhandian system. There were enough holdouts of every stripe to produce an argument with religious overtones anytime the exact date was brought up. Worse, there were rumors of another shake-up of the official calendar to take place at the next winter solstice.

Early in the day, Mark dropped by the booth of Ibraim the money changer to withdraw from his account the amount he had agreed to pay Threebortin. After Ibraim's fee, the amount remaining was no longer enough for a large, east-side house, but it was still the price of a

wharfside cottage. Ibraim questioned him in the Upcrusters'
information-digging manner about the destination of his
cash. With no particular hurry to be anywhere else, Mark
told him about his prospective magical teeth. It must
have been one of Ibraim's "good" days, by his friendly
laugh. The money changer was an affable gentleman one
varying day each week, and a penny-pinching crab for
the other six.

"I wish I had known what you are telling me yesterday
when you deposited the money. My cousin, may-the-gods-
protect-him, just arrived from Sai-khand. He makes teeth
of metal and ivory that fit a man's mouth like the origi-
nals, and not by sorcerous foolery. I could have gotten
you such a deal!"

Mark flushed with disappointment. He would have preferred a simple, mechanical arrangement to solve his
problem, but it was too late now. In Barrow, raping your
grandmother on her deathbed would have been more
socially acceptable than going back on a finalized deal.
Mark parted cordially from the banker, reminded of something else he wanted to do while in the bazaar.

He walked across the square to the wagon of old Fawn
Wisentwagon, a Tellarani seeress. He would have preferred the services of the more reputable Wagonhawk
woman, but her fee would have been higher. He ought to
be hoarding his coppers now, but the previous night's lost
dream had left him curious enough to want a professional
reading of the future.

That reading was as confusing as it was impressive.
The old woman had laid out the cards in a special pattern. She was most interested in two that depicted
women—the Queen of Cups and the High Priestess, she
had called them. The seeress hinted at upcoming love and
marriage, but with an unfathomable duality of influences
affecting them. The only other card that stood out from
the rest was the sixth to be turned.

"This is before him," the brightly dressed nomad had
intoned, seated cross-legged before the cards on the tail-
gate of her wagon.

The reversed Five of Wands had meant nothing to
Mark, until he had heard its negative explanation. The
fortune-teller informed him that the card meant compli-
cations and contradictions in the matter of some contract.

That started him worrying about Threebortin and his new teeth and caused him to be too distracted to appreciate the numerological and prognosticatory tricks that the seeress tried to lay on him. He paid her and left, bemused.

Fawn Wisentwagon was unhappy, having defeated her own chance at profit by giving a customer a disturbing prophecy too early in the reading. However, she had had to remain true to her cards and her blood, leaving her no choice. The offending card had glowed in her mind with genuine meaning.

Mark wandered the bazaar for the rest of the day, sampling and dickering in a desultory fashion, but not really buying anything. He saw Threebortin once, haggling with some farmers over a crate of chickens, but he made nothing of it. Their appointment wasn't until tomorrow; what the wizard did with the rest of his time was his business. Cavin would have been a welcome sight, but he heard that the short pickpocket was somewhere in the city's north end, probably working some newly arrived caravan.

Night began to creep in, but it seemed to throw a mental obscurity over Mark. Depressed, he couldn't find the energy to make the walk to the Salmon. Back at his lodgings, he diced with the Gryphon regulars, trying not to think about why he hadn't rushed south to see Jenny tonight. He won a little more than he lost, but he couldn't rise to the point of caring. The evening waned, and Barrelgut began to put the pressure on his customers to either hit the road or hit the sack so that he could do the same. Mark could have gone down to the bazaar, and as a healthy youth with a sword, he would probably have found no trouble unless he went seeking it. Because he didn't, he missed seeing Bargo-the-Little beat the whey out of a pair of foolish footpads who had tried to get money and free beer out of him at knifepoint.

Instead, he went to bed, with that feeling that there was a dream waiting that he hadn't finished. The dreams came early, well enough. He found himself pursued by a giant chicken with gold teeth and Ibraim's voice. He diced with Dak and Cavin on the back of a monster crocodile in the Wat; the loser was to be eaten by the reptile, who had the eyes of Harry Hardback, Mark's deceased drug-running boss of years before. Toward morn-

ing, his dream legs began running, chasing some prize
that dipped and dodged and laughed at him. A firm hand
turned him away from the frustrating pursuit, and a familiar voice offered him something greater, when—he
woke up.

· 9 ·

The greasy dawn light coming through the cracks in the
inn's shutters, washed away the dream's memory in seconds. He felt cheated, sure that if he examined the dream
more closely it would spill the secrets that only teased his
wakened mind. He roused, already exhausted, and descended to the dim common room.

A yawning Gorgio was just unbarring the taproom
shutters, planning to snooze until business presented itself. He had completed his few opening tasks, including
setting out a bowl of cold stew, thick with chunks of
light-colored meat. Within a few minutes, a jumpy
Threebortin had come down and was gobbling the stew.
He visibly relaxed as he ate. Propped up in a dark booth,
Mark watched the wizard lick the bowl clean in five
minutes.

The sorcerer turned from the bar. "Are you ready?" he
had been aware of Mark the whole time. His question
was as direct as a prod in the chest.

"Yeah. I guess I am." More than the morning chill
made Mark shiver. Mark's stomach had been feeding
mostly on stress and beer for the last two days, and it was
slippery about settling down to the task ahead. Everything was going perfectly. (Wasn't it?) Mark couldn't
understand why he had lost the anticipation that he should
have felt as his quest neared completion.

The mage interrupted his thoughts. "Well, *I'm* not
ready! I don't care how early you got up; magic doesn't
turn on and off like a beer tap. Meet me across the street
in an hour." Threebortin stalked sourly out of the tavern.

A crestfallen Mark took his agitated stomach for a
walk, pacing up and down in the common room and
taking an occasional turn a few paces in either direction
on Straight Street. Gorgio napped, once he was sure that
Mark wasn't in a drinking mood. Denalee emerged from

the rooms she shared with Barrelgut in the back and prodded the kitchen fire back to life. Although she ignored Mark, he noticed that she looked a trifle nauseated and that her trim waist was bulging slightly. Mark was acquainted with the facts of life well enough to suspect that Barrelgut was going to be a "papa" in the next few months.

Mark smiled at her; he wondered if Barrelgut had noticed yet. The big bartender was just obtuse enough not to be aware of the impending event. The pretty, small girl that he had married didn't weigh half what the taverner did, but she could lead the big man around like a stunned ox when she wanted to. Barrelgut thought that his friends were ignorant of the mushy core of sentiment that he carried inside. Mark hoped that he and . . . Jenny would be as happy. Now, why, today of all days, did her name snag for a second in his mind before coming loose?

When the hour was up, he sauntered across the lane to the little-used stable. Most horses were stabled closer to Caravan Way these days, but the stable had been built sturdily enough so that it remained mostly waterproof. The roof of the side room that Threebortin used for his laboratory was sound; it had been the perfect compromise. Barrelgut appreciated a customer who rented by the month, but he wanted nothing to do with magic: he had the scars to prove it.

Threebortin's study door was open, and he impatiently gestured Mark into the room. The edgy magician directed his customer to a cluttered chair. Mark had been expecting some sorcerous gesturing; he had tensed himself for it. Instead, the wizard made a much more familiar gesture—hand out; palm up.

"Oh. Yeah." Mark reddened and tugged a small bag of silver out of a deep pocket.

Though Ibraim was banker to both men, that made the old tightwad no more honest. Threebortin counted carefully and checked each coin for shaving. All the silver was good, and the amount was correct. Mark was not impressed by the spell caster, a man supposedly in touch with the higher realities, who bit each coin like a bazaar peddler. This had better work!

Threebortin fussed over Mark, positioning him just so in the chair, head back and mouth open wide. The magi-

cian warned him to expect some pain each time a sharp
tooth chip was embedded in his gums. It did sting; each
sharp sliver was meant to draw blood. Mark, on a quest
for his true love, would have been a little disappointed if
the process hadn't hurt at all. The blood-and-sulfur powder spread across the tooth sites was as appetizing as it
sounded, but Mark was being tough. Knight errants really killed the dragon for themselves, no matter what
they told the fair lady.

Threebortin stepped back and raised his arms, signaling that things were about to become more intense. Only
the mage's strained face and dancing hands were visible
to Mark's down-rolled eyes, but they were frightening
enough. He had never been close to high-level magic
before. Sorcerous events that were about to happen inside his own mouth were *close*!

Blue ghosts of light formed around the wizard's hands
and face. The auras fluttered, then flowed across the
room into Mark's mouth. The magician uttered a syllabated
incantation, all in a single breath. Pink-tinged, yellow
smoke rolled from Mark's mouth to mingle with the
elongated auras. The whole space stank. With the forti-
eth syllable, the sorcerer snapped his lips closed, took a
deep breath, and slumped. The power to accomplish
what he had, had been drawn from his own mental reserves. The smoke began to clear.

Mark's mouth tasted like scorched fur, but he was not
in pain. Gingerly, he raised his lower jaw, to let the new
teeth meet gradually. Two years had been a long time to
develop habits associated with toothlessness. Threebortin
had warned him perfunctorily to ease into the teeth's first
use, though he had said it at a time when he had been
coarsely manhandling Mark's jaw into the position he
had wanted. The jaw eased up, and eased up and . . .
nothing! Mark darted his tongue forward: no teeth! His
gums were lumpy and tender, but even the tooth chips
the mage had put on them had disappeared.

"Hey! Where are my teeth?"

"What?"

Mark's upset tone had alerted the relaxed wizard. He
rushed forward, shoving his larger customer back into the
chair. He prised open Mark's mouth as if he were buying

a doubtful horse. There were only pink puckers where new teeth should have been.

"What? I . . . I can't understand this." The mage was genuinely puzzled.

"Well, I can, you faker! Get out of my lap! I want my money back!" It had felt like magic and looked like magic. It had even smelled like magic, but it hadn't worked. A Barrowman didn't buy theories; he wanted tangible results. Mark shoved Threebortin back and rose threateningly. The wizard retreated, holding up his palms to restrain his patron.

"Wait! Let me check! There must be something—"

"No, there's *nothing*! It's *my* mouth. Now, give me back my silver!" Mark continued to advance.

Threebortin was thinking fast. He desperately needed the money: the market for another major spell might not open up again before winter. If his angry client would just hold still and let him examine his mouth, but . . . no. In another ten seconds, the sailor's hands would be closing around Threebortin's throat. It was time for a bluff.

The mage stopped retreating and raised his hands. He stared intently at Mark, and a shining aura formed around his fingers. "Hold it there, sport, unless you want to spend the rest of your life as a dung beetle!"

The threat of an alien attack using magic stopped Mark. Threebortin backed carefully into the larger space inside the old stable. Though Mark followed, his aggression had been replaced by fear.

"Now, get going or face the consequences! Don't come back until you're ready to let me check that spell out thoroughly, without demands!" The auras around the magician's face and hands flared into brilliance.

The sorcerer's eyes seemed to burn with murderous intent (or dung-beetle-polymorphing intent, to be precise). Mark, who had entered the deal already nervous about magic, turned and ran. With the mortal's fear of those who played with etheric forces, he sped down the twisty length of Straight Street the way green grass goes through a goose. The crowds of the bazaar forced him to slow. He mooched through the hubbub of the square, totally dejected, robbed and humiliated. Impotent in his own eyes, how could he ever face Jenny?

He plunked himself listlessly on the bench at Bargo's

and got a beer, only because you couldn't sit on Bargo's benches and not order. His head was whirling in misery. Not only was he still toothless, he had also lost a huge bite out of the stake he needed. He drank the beer, untasted, and had another; in fact, he had several others. His chin was resting sorrowfully on Bargo's bar when Cavin popped up at his elbow.

His friend spotted Mark's depression immediately. His tongue already loosened by drink, Mark let the tale pour out of him. He finished lamely, almost crying.

". . . and if I try to get my coin back, he'll kill me—turn me into a beetle or blast me with lightning or—"

"Whoa!" Cavin interrupted. "I should have told you more before I sent you up there. That mummer can't kill you! Old Threebortin can still do plenty of minor stuff on demand, but he can only manage one major spell at a time anymore. He might have made you itch temporarily or made your nose glow, but he couldn't have done you any real harm with magic."

"He . . . he couldn't? He was bluffing? Why, I'll . . ."

That particular news should have been delivered more gradually to an agitated young man with a bellyful of beer. Mark was stalking north out of the bazaar before Cavin could even rise. The thief started to restrain his friend, but stopped and shrugged instead. He ordered a beer from Bargo. If life got rough in Barrow, it got rough.

• **10** •

The tense sweat that he had worked up earlier in the morning had dried on Threebortin. He felt better now: the customer who had threatened him would be forced to take time to think it over, restrained by his fear of Threebortin's nonexistent defensive spells. The first thing an apprentice magician learned to do was to create a personal glowing aura; Threebortin's remaining bag of minor spells was equally useless in any battle. Despite that, in a few days, his client would be back, cautiously requesting analysis of the misapplied magic, certain that Threebortin had a thunderbolt up each sleeve.

Threebortin planned to have plenty of time for thorough research, and when Mark returned, the spell gone wrong would be corrected in short order. The mage settled down to enjoy the cool breeze blowing in the Gryphon's front door. Lunch was—ahhh!—fried chicken. Deep in the addictive enjoyment of his meal, he failed to notice when a shadow momentarily blocked the light from the door. The first inkling that things were amiss came when a pair of strong, seaman's hands closed about his neck and began to shake him.

"Give me back—" (Shake!)

"Gack!"

"—my silver—" (Shake!)

"Erk!"

"—you faker!" (Shake! Shake! Shake!)

"Glack! Glorg! Urk!"

Threebortin's conjuring hand waving in the air was as effective as his speech. His aura wouldn't even sputter, and even a minor offensive spell, such as itching, was beyond him. Even before the physical assault, he had been under the attack of his blood-and-bone-habituated diet. His other hand pawed uselessly at the pair around his throat. Sparkling lights were beginning to swirl before his eyes before he was able to grope for the offending pouch of coin out of his vest and drop it on the floor.

Mark gave him one last shake and shoved him off the bar stool, to skid for several meters in the sawdust of the floor. The toothless seaman grabbed up his coins, before spitting directly into Threebortin's face. He stalked out, ignoring anything the magician might have left in him to do. Mark was not usually that nasty a sort, but he was partially drunk and emotionally battered from his off-again-on-again love life and the doubtful prospect of regaining his teeth. He had burned off most of the beer and the anger before he again reached the bazaar. His hands continued to shake as he leaned on Bargo's counter. Cavin had gone somewhere again, so Mark couldn't talk out his problem. Within thirty minutes, he had decided: right or wrong, he was still going for the teeth, but no more magic!

Ibraim was pleased to see Mark again, pleased that Mark had business for his teeth-making cousin after all, pleased that Mark could pay cash—just pleased all around. The reason for his pleasure soon became obvious: his

cousin had authorized Ibraim to negotiate the price of
the teeth for him. Mark was not so pleased at that. It was
as if he had been planning to arm-wrestle some moderately strong stranger, only to have him replaced at the
last second by Bargo-the-Little. Ibraim might be a wiz-
ened old man in lumpy robes, but he was a champion-
class haggler, and this was *not* one of his "good" days.

As expected, he skinned Mark royally. The younger
man had taken both chemical and emotional blows to the
chin that day; he was a pushover before the experienced
bargainer. Mark would need the bag of silver that he
redeposited, and more, to pay for the teeth. The deal
lacked only finalization, with Mark and Ibraim's cousin
meeting face-to-face for a mutual spitting-in-the-dirt.

A weary Mark trudged southward, toward the Jumping
Salmon. Only the hope of seeing Jenny buoyed the spent
sailor. Changes in the tide were bringing in the fishing
fleet a few minutes later now; so that neither Jenny nor
Nadia should yet be required to be on duty. Unknown to
Mark, however, the *Silent Swan* was just in from Sai-
khand, bearing a handsome bosun named Skeve, with a
pocketful of spendable cash. He had just initiated an
evening's flirtation with Jenny when Mark walked in.
Intellectually, Mark knew that he would have to get used
to other men reacting to Jenny's attractiveness, but at the
moment she was doing too much "reacting" of her own
to suit Mark.

He stopped near her. "Jenny, I need to talk to you.
Out back. Before the crowd gets here." He wondered if
his voice sounded both as hard and as pleading to others
as it did to himself.

Skeve, rising predictably to the spur of his hormones,
eased over to "protect" Jenny, planning to throw Mark
out bodily, if necessary. Jenny used a plump, white hand
to hold him back.

To Mark she said, "Yes, I'll come with you now." But
a flip of the eyelids and a brush with her hip told Skeve
that she would be right back.

The pair walked silently out the front entrance and
around to the private side of the building. Though she
knew it wasn't right to eavesdrop, Nadia had observed
the meeting. She shortcutted through the family quarters
to a position near the back door. She didn't try to exam-

ine the jumble of feelings that prompted her action. She heard Mark speaking first.

"Jenny, the magician I hired to replace my teeth, failed."

("I knew it when he showed up still without his teeth. Now maybe we can get back to a normal relationship.")

"But, darling, I've found another way," he went on.

("Uh-oh!") "Oh?"

"A craftsman from Sai-khand will make me a new, beautiful set of teeth, but . . ."

"Go on. (Yes, *do* go on!)"

"They're expensive."

"How expensive?"

He named the price, and then told her how much of their nest egg would remain.

"Mark, that's not enough for a house. That's not even enough for a cottage on the east bank!"

"Yes, but it'll buy us a cottage on the west bank, and I'll have work—"

"I can't live on the west side!"

"If you loved me, a cottage there—"

"I *won't* live on the west side."

"Just a second: I was born on the west side. It's not all bad, especially since the Prince cleaned up the drug trade. It's—"

"I won't do it!"

"If you loved me, you would."

"When you have enough money for a house on the east bank, then maybe . . . A girl has to have security." She was suddenly coy, inviting, teasing. She had almost bungled away Mark's still-substantial bankroll. In her heart of hearts, she was sure that she could spend money faster than Mark would be able to save it.

He sat down on the edge of the porch, his head hung down. She slipped over to sit beside him and began to fire up her physical charms. This time, however, they had no time to reach full flame.

A strong, feminine hand yanked her off the porch. "You're not going to do it to him again, sister!"

"Do what, Beanpole?" Jenny was trying to tug loose the handful of blouse that was in her sister's grasp.

"You're not going to keep on stringing him along! You know you'll never marry him!" Nadia was not letting go.

"So what? Stay out of this!"

"He's too good for you!"

"Yeah, well, his money spends like anyone else's."
Jenny had never learned to school her mouth where her
sister was concerned. With her limited supply of intellect
taken up by struggling and arguing, she had forgotten for
a moment that Mark was present.

"Spend this!" A small, brown fist, backed by an arm
that had done its share of carrying (and Jenny's, too),
sailed through the air and closed one of Jenny's blue
eyes. Jenny lurched backward and skidded her perfect
buttocks through the gravel in front of the porch.

"Ooh!" she cried. Her hands flew to her face; the eye
was already beginning to puff to the touch. "Ooh! Ooh!
Ooh!" Up the porch steps she raced, through the door,
and toward the nearest mirror.

Mark was huddled, unmoving. The tracks of two tears
trailed down his dusty face. His heart was shattered: she
didn't love him; she wouldn't marry him; all she had
wanted was his money and a good time. A great hole had
opened in the cosmos to swallow him.

A pair of arms went around him. "Don't cry," said a
voice, whose owner sounded as if she were crying herself.
"You don't need her! You're fine like you are, teeth or
no teeth. You don't need a big house or a lot of money—
you're just fine. Don't cry!"

The shattered pieces of his heart reassembled themselves and jumped off into Nadia's hand, where they fit
perfectly. Mark discovered that he had a lot to say to
Nadia, and it was better said with his arms around her.
Nadia discovered that she had still more to say to Mark,
and that the words came out of her usually silent lips
more easily if she kissed him regularly. Jed came to the
back door to berate his younger daughter, having seen
Jenny's eye. He would have, too, if Delvina hadn't taken
him by the ear and made him listen to the two young
people first. The edge of the porch where they were
sitting was so tenuously moored to reality that it would
have taken force to rejoin it to the Plane.

Jenny received attention and spoiling in plenty from
Skeve and her other admirers. In fact, if it hadn't been so
painful, a black eye would have been a wonderful ploy to
add to her flirtatious collection. On the other hand, the
tricks that she already knew worked so well that she

eventually married a minor Saikhandian aristocrat and moved to the distant capital. Jed had to hire a second serving girl anyway: Nadia would no longer be living or working at home. Until her departure, Jenny remained the business-attracting pony she had always been, but not the draft horse needed to actually do the tavern's work.

Mark and Nadia were quite happy in their large house on the east side, until the upset of the war changed things. (But that is another story.) Though Nadia loved him enough to live in the reawakening Slews-Inside-the-Walls west of the river, that was not required. The deal with Ibraim's cousin was never finalized. The young couple was doubly happy when the white buds of new teeth broke through Mark's gums. (Threebortin had simply inverted two time-controlling syllables, when the thought of lunch had crossed his mind during the spell casting.) Mark felt badly about his treatment of the mage and tried to find him to apologize and repay him. He had no luck in locating the sorcerer, however.

The last anyone had seen of Threebortin, the wizard had been headed north out of Barrow, with a crate of chickens on his back, looking for an easy crow to catch.

Interchapter

Not a jiggle, not a jot! I left Mark and Nadia alone, though I traveled about in the minds of all concerned without their permission. They didn't need me! On the other hand, one raindrop does not make a cloudburst.

I will revisit my son, Harmon. Though my promise still holds not to interfere in his life, it does not take in those whom he encounters. I shall concentrate on some worthy soul among them, perhaps pruning his life; perhaps not. Can such a randomly sampled human struggle to success? We shall see.

BOOK VII

Barrow White

WILVAN ERGINSON was ungodly tired of being a servant. The Green Garter was as good an inn as could be found in Barrow, and Natho-the-Cook was as good an employer as a man could ask for. But he *was* an employer—a boss. Wilvan was a free man, but he lacked that ultimate freedom: He wanted to be captain instead of crew. He wanted to *be* the boss, not have a boss.

He wasn't starving, as some folk were, in the dregs of poverty across the river. He wasn't pinched to the point of stealing for three meals a day. A hundred good Townsmen would have gladly taken his place, not that Natho would have fired him without cause. Wilvan's discontent came instead from the rich men, the ones who came to the Garter for a friendly drink or a good meal. If he had been working at the Gryphon and Goblet or Charlie's Beer Garden, he would have been among Upcrusters who talked only of the Town. Their homey gossip would have cured his soul the way the salty wind blowing up the Wat in winter cured a gutted fish. He could have settled into that life, maybe found a good woman to marry, and could have served stew and hard bread to his friends forever, instead of marinated beef to wealthy merchants.

The bloody rich folk didn't talk about the Town; they talked money and trade and gold and property. They talked about deals that involved coffers of silver, not handfuls of copper. They were, by their lights, on top of every developing situation, maneuvering like fighting ships with each change in the winds of commerce.

Wilvan was supposed to be invisible among them, not so much a man as a pair of legs to carry food from the kitchen, hands to pour and serve, and lips to inquire after customers' satisfaction. The merchants who frequented the Garter were not rude to him: they didn't even see him. Wilvan had heard that in far Sai-khand, foreigners were actually allowed to *own* men. The Prince, now, didn't allow such nonsense in Barrow, but as an invisible servitor, Wilvan doubted that there could be much difference between an unseen freeman and human property. He was shackled to his station in life by a rule that he knew by heart: It takes money to make money.

Not all the power traders were equally unobservant. That Harmon Yorn, for instance, didn't miss anything. The man couldn't be twenty-five, but let him lock eyes with you, and you'd be sure he was 125. No wonder he made the other grain merchants seem like lapdogs. Wilvan had heard that Master Yorn had once kicked around the Town for a couple of years himself, not doing anything well. Then—splash! He had shown up in his father's grain business and began cutting deals that skinned competitors out of their robes. Master Yorn had gone, it was said, from a penniless drunk to a man with a fortune, in a single day. Wilvan had adopted him, or gossip's version of him, at least, as a model to emulate.

Harmon Yorn didn't smile much, not that he frowned either, and he looked even servants in the eye. That put him another jump up on the others, in Wilvan's book. He didn't talk much either, but the other merchants more than made up for his silence. They talked trade-trade-trade and deal-deal-deal, noons and evenings both, as if the best talker could somehow *speak* money into his pocket. Wilvan was not impressed. He had grown up near the fishing district, and he knew that the only fish bigger than the one that got away was the one the storyteller was going to catch next week. Wilvan's near-silent profession allowed him to observe how many of his competitors' secrets Harmon Yorn harvested for free, simply by keeping quiet.

It was his observation of Master Yorn's strength in silence that decided Wilvan. He chose a day when Harmon Yorn had tarried behind the others, sitting at his table, swirling a glass of mineral water. That water was all that Yorn ever drank in the Garter; Natho kept a keg of it for him, from some famous spring. Suspecting magic in it, Wilvan had secretly tried some. It proved to be

bitter and . . . watery. Perhaps it warded off the gout and
kept Master Yorn's eye clear, but it was not for Wilvan.
He hoped that the help he planned to solicit would be
more palatable.

Wilvan approached the silent trader's table, ready to
clear it. "Master Yorn?"

"Yes?"

"If it wouldn't be inconvenient, sir, I'd like to talk to
you."

"Very well. Sit down."

"Oh, sir, Natho wouldn't like—"

"If you're going to talk to me, sit down. You're not
making yourself any more humble by forcing me to crane
my neck to look at you."

Wilvan glanced around. The Garter's main room was
empty except for the two of them, and he was already
well along with his cleanup duties. Nervously, he sat.

"Well?"

"Well, sir, Master Yorn, sir—"

"Well, *what*?"

"Master Yorn, how could a man go about making a lot
of money, quickly, the way you did?"

"You *don't* want to make it the way I did, I can assure
you! Hmmm. For most of those I meet in this place, I'd
say, 'Invest wisely.' You have very little to invest, do
you, Wilvan?"

"No, sir."

"That makes it tougher, all right. You'll have to watch
for something breaking—something that no one else has
thought of before—and get on at the very, very first. A
man with a brain and an eye can always make it in
Barrow. Wilvan, have you heard of the Vernig Company?"

"Yes."

"You probably heard it in here. Because you did hear,
it's wrong for you. Sure, somebody has had a smart idea
to rebuild old Vernig Village, east along the caravan
route. It's time the city started opening up to the east
again; the Scallion Wars were over thirty years ago.
Anyway, they'll eventually turn a lot of silver, once the
fields are recleared. In five years, they'll be sitting pretty,
hawking vegetables and inn space to the caravans who
crawl in off the Waste tired and hungry. There's even a
Holy Knight outpost not too far away. The call for in-

vestors is already circulating by word of mouth. Am I right?"

Wilvan nodded.

"Too late. You're no major investor. You'll have to find some idea for which *you* will be calling for investors: an idea that will make money by its very nature; an idea that is worth money that you don't have."

"Oh," Wilvan said.

It had to have been something hard. He had known it all the time. Well, he wasn't stupid and he would keep his eye peeled, but every Upcruster was already doing that.

"Thank you, Master Yorn."

"Indeed, Wilvan. My pleasure. I meet few enough unsubtle men in the north end. Keep an eye out for that idea. If you find a peaking wave, come and see me: I like to ride 'em, too."

• 2 •

Wilvan returned to his work, girding himself for a long haul. Time passed. The itch to join the rich and famous, regardless of Harmon Yorn's advice, became too strong. He wasn't able to wait for a nebulous opportunity that might or might not come. He had almost enough coin saved to manage it alone; the rest had come from a "loan" from Michael-the-Fence. Wilvan bought five shares in the Vernig Company.

The shares had been inflating well, certain to double in short order . . . until the bad news came. A flash fire had wiped out half of reopened Vernig Village, leveling most of the buildings and all of the crops. The project would still make money, but it would be next year. The investors with a hundred shares could swear at their bad fortune, shrug, and wait. Wilvan, with his tiny holdings, could not wait that year, not at Michael's killing interest rates.

Wilvan gritted his teeth and sold his five shares at a rate so low that he got little more than the amount he had borrowed from Michael. With his principal in his pocket, he hiked down to the sundries store that was the front for Michael's actual businesses. After checking to make sure there weren't any customs men around, Michael's counterman waved Wilvan through, into the fence's cluttered office.

Michael wasn't much to look at: tall and gangly. He might once have been an athlete, but he had deteriorated, as if a mean internal life had spread to his body. He had watery eyes, a big nose, and a smile that was as genuine as his official occupation. Michael was a rat, crawled over from the Slews and now nesting east of the river, but still a rat. His whiskered nose was always out for anything that stank of profit, mostly unclean profit. He loaned money at bloodsucking rates, he fenced anything stolen, and he was suspected of running Mugambu Black into the Slews. If he had ever been caught hawking drugs east of the river, the Townsmen would have carved out his gizzard, but he was slippery. Slimy things often were.

"What can I do for you, Wilvan-me-boy?" Michael was as gracious as a Monk's Hill merchant.

"I've come to pay off the money I owe you."

"Ah, always good!" He rubbed his hands together in anticipation. "And the interest?"

"Yes. A month's worth."

"Tsk! Tsk! You weren't listening really close, I guess, when old Barndoogle rattled off our guarantee spell?"

"Huh?"

"Oh, you probably heard the part about how either of us would break out in boils if he tried to cheat, but my clients lots of times forget to listen to the part about . . . Let's see. 'A year must come and go.' Not familiar? Too bad. You owe me a year's interest, not a month's."

"But I'm paying you off, you leech!"

"Close. You're paying the balance and part of the interest. You owe the rest of a year's interest."

"You weasel! And if I don't pay?"

"I tell Barndoogle, and you break out in boils. Remember Arnie—Arnie-the-Shoemaker?"

"Yeah. Say, didn't he—"

"Threw himself off the Old Wat Bridge when the boils got too bad."

Wilvan swore at Michael for a few minutes, without effect. He tried politely requesting a break, and eventually he lowered himself to begging. Michael pared his

black nails with a small dagger and said no regularly.
Wilvan finally raised his fists to beat Michael into Wilvan's
way of thinking.

Wilvan was sure that he could have taken the lank loan
shark, one-on-one, but Michael tinkled a small, silver
bell he kept on his desk. His massive counterman, Luggo,
was behind Wilvan in a split instant, with his sausage-
sized fingers digging into Wilvan's shoulder.

"Come back when you have the coin," Michael said.
He flicked Wilvan's presence away like brushing a fly
from his food.

Luggo frog-marched Wilvan to the front door and threw
him out.

"Look out, clod!" a voice snapped in his ear.

He had collided with a solid, long-haired young woman
who had been entering Michael's establishment. She
stormed past him, ignoring his existence. Luggo made no
move to stop her from marching directly into Michael's
inner sanctum. Though he couldn't make out the words,
Wilvan could hear her muffled, hostile voice through the
door—another dissatisfied customer. Wilvan turned toward
the bazaar, disgusted.

By the time he had threaded his way to Bargo's in the
center of the bazaar, his anger had eroded to hurt despondency. Michael might be a weasel, but he had caught
Wilvan beyond a doubt. It would only be a matter of
time until Michael sent his strong-arm man around to
squeeze out next month's interest. If that didn't work,
Michael would notify his tame wizard, and Wilvan would
be in the same shape as Arnie-the-Shoemaker. He flopped
down at Bargo's counter and rested his chin on his
knuckles.

"Beer, Wilvan?"

"Nah. Nothing."

"You know the rules." Bargo's counter was for drinkers.

"A small beer, then."

The gnarled, bald bartender brought the drink. "Woman
trouble, Wilvan?"

"Nah."

"Then it must be money." One predicament or the
other formed ninety percent of a Townsman's troubles.

"You're too right, Bargo." Wilvan explained in detail
about his magically guaranteed contract with Michael.

"Mmmph," Bargo snorted. "You should have asked me first. You're not the first one Michael has nailed with old Barndoogle's surety spell. And the word is that he uses Claudio-the-Candle to sort of . . . create the right conditions for some of his customers to be pinched for money."

"Claudio? The arsonist?"

"Aye, but he's never been caught, and few folks know what he looks like, including me." The barman sucked at a gap between his teeth.

"Do you think . . . Vernig Village?"

"Aye. It sure would stink that way to me."

"May Michael and his pet torch man rot in the deepest pit! Aww, never mind. Who am I trying to fool? He's got me. I'll be in the hole to him for a year, and when I pay him off, I'll have to start out broke again! How am I ever going up, if all I have to look forward to is that hunk of beef that works for him coming around to squeeze me for my pay?"

"You mean Luggo?"

"Yeah." Wilvan massaged the finger marks the strong-arm man had left in his shoulder. "Set me up another one, Bargo. I might as well use my last few coppers as a freeman on something friendly."

· 3 ·

Bargo's beer proved to be good, despite the fact that it wasn't expensive. On the other hand, Wilvan, who was more used to serving drinks than consuming them, found that he had to walk very carefully after downing four large tankards of the brew. He was not staggering, but his head tended to float. However, alcohol's first tendency was to knock out a man's good judgment, long before it reached the legs.

On the way back to his lodging, Wilvan really should have ignored the raised voices in the alley he was passing. In curiosity, he nosed around the first turning of the alley. A sober or sensible Upcruster would have continued on his way, once he saw what was happening.

The girl who had rammed him in Michael's doorway had been backed against a wall by a ragged thug with a large knife. The beer whispered to Wilvan that any enemy of Michael's was a friend of Wilvan's. He started forward, shouting, "Hey!"

The knife man turned toward Wilvan. "Butt out, dip!" He waved the knife efficiently toward Wilvan, with a gutting motion.

Wilvan's adrenaline told the beer to shut up and instantly ordered his legs to begin backing away. The mugger turned back to the girl.

"All right, girlie. Either I collect from your old man, or I can collect a 'piece' of the price from you. I—"

She kicked him firmly in the crotch. Her assailant was a man who liked to gesture as he talked; he had let the knife wander. She followed with a roundhouse left that decked the man. Though he was bigger than she was, he had been surprised. The knife, its sharpened, white edge flashing, skittered from his grasp as he had to use his hands to break his fall.

"Why, you . . ." The mugger lunged after his weapon. He was hardly out of the fight.

The knife had skimmed along the littered alley floor and landed between Wilvan's feet. Wilvan picked it up experimentally. The thug stopped, crouched over in pain. He had gone from an armed, overwhelming aggressor to an unarmed, outnumbered casualty in two seconds. Snarling curses, he made a limping run for the alley mouth, clutching his bruised gonads. Neither victor tried to stop him.

Wilvan moved toward the girl. "Are you all right?"

"Yeah. Thanks," she said, "unless you're going to use that knife on me."

"Huh?" He noticed the blade dangling from his fingers and dropped it like a slithering viper. "You want it; you take it!"

"Thanks. I can probably use it at work." She scooped up the weapon.

"Where's that?"

"Mama Threechins'. I cook and wait tables."

She stood and brushed herself off. Though she was thirty centimeters shorter than Wilvan, her skin had the tight tone that spoke of health. Her hair was long, the dark blond of droughted grass. She was buxom and strong, with the alertness of a she-bear.

"Got an eyeful yet, clod?"

"Oh. Sorry. But . . . you are quite an eyeful."

Wilvan blushed. What kind of fool talk was this sneaking past his lips? By the Thousand Stars, he had to learn to go easier on Bargo's beer!

"Thanks, clo—say, what's your name, anyway? I might as well know it if I'm going to let you save my life."

"Save your life? I didn't really . . ." He blushed again, feeling like a clod indeed. "You're the one who drove him off. And it's Wilvan."

"I'm Mickie. Are you headed toward Mama Threechins'? I have to get to work."

"I . . . It's right on my way." There went more of that fool talk!

Somehow during the weeks that followed, Wilvan, though he could eat for free at the Green Garter, found more and more reason to dine at Mama Threechins'. No matter how they stacked up reasonably, things began to feel not so bad after all.

He saved up another month's interest, scraping the meat of his cash reserves down to the bone. When he delivered the payment to the counter in front of Luggo, he spat on it and demanded that Michael count it in person. Michael disappointed him by doing just that, with oily satisfaction. Next month's payment, Wilvan knew, would be a different story. Poverty was licking its lips, waiting for another recruit to fall over the edge of the pit.

He toiled away at the Green Garter, but the joy was gone from his occupation: every coin he earned would go into the pocket of a slug named Michael. Wilvan waited tables, scraped pots, and took care of the dozen minor jobs between potboy and chef, but a cloud hung over all his life. Only the occasional mornings off that he could spend with Mickie were brighter.

She might have first crashed into his life, but since then, she had crept into his heart. He was amazed at the unlikeliness of it: he viewed himself as entirely ordinary, and her as remarkable and lovely. To his surprise and delight, she seemed to see in him something far more special than he actually was. Some very intense moments they had spent behind a tree in Pocket Park had confirmed those feelings, as far as Wilvan was concerned.

However, she was reluctant to move deeper into com-

mitment, and she wouldn't talk about it. Women! Wilvan
was jittery all the time now, his adrenal system reacting
to the constant stress of the end-of-the-month payment
deadline and his reproductive system pumping still more
hormones into his blood. He was hardly able to sleep; he
went through the motions of his job in a daze.

· **4** ·

It took all his faculties even to be up on a ladder, washing the Green Garter's prized colored-glass windows.
The small panes circled the entire crown of the building,
and Natho was inordinately proud of them. In the kitchen,
Wilvan had to work above a tightly lidded pot of boiling
wine in which the cook was marinating a piece of tough
beef. Wilvan had to be careful to drop neither himself
nor his dirty rag into the pot. When Natho lifted the lid,
a puff of steam rolled upward toward Wilvan. The building was tightly shut against the late-fall chill; so, the
vapor instantly condensed into large droplets on the clean
glass, right in front of Wilvan's nose.

As a particularly large drop began its sinuous run down
the angled glass, Wilvan reached out a curious finger and
dabbed it up. He tasted the liquid, taste being one of the
first ways a child learned to analyze his environment. The
tingle on his tongue was a surprise. The fluid was color-
less, but it warmed his mouth like a potent wine. The
closest thing to it in strength that he had ever tasted was
the dregs of some of the expensive Maldavian White a
customer had once left in a glass.

Wilvan didn't know why, but what had just happened
was important. However, before he could dissect the
reason, his rag slipped from tired fingers and splatted on
the edge of the vessel below: half in, half out. Wilvan
quickly slid down the ladder, but Natho simply pulled the
wipe out of the wine himself and pitched it aside.

"Be more careful, Wilvan." The innkeeper didn't seem
particularly upset. He was making no move to discard the
meat.

"Sorry," Wilvan said. "Say, isn't that stuff ruined?"

"No, I'm about to dump it anyway. I just use that

Canary Red to soften up the meat before I cook it properly in real wine."

"*That* was Canary Red?" Wilvan asked, remembering the taste of the drop on the window. "Canary Red wouldn't get a cockroach drunk if he drowned in it."

"Don't I know it. Cheapest swill that comes out of Maldavia, but I can always tell the customers that I marinate their beef only in Maldavian wines." Natho smiled at his deception.

"Could you rebottle it and sell it after you've boiled it?" Lack of real worth did not mean that something couldn't be sold in the bazaar, and some drinkers would down anything alcoholic, no matter its previous use.

"No. If you think it has no kick when it's fresh, taste some of it after it's had the steam let out of it—nothing but bad-tasting, red water. Whatever it is that gives wine its zing, all escapes as soon as I take the lid off. Now, wake up and help me get this pot outside. Watch the meat: *that* I keep."

Somewhere inside Wilvan's mind, wheels began to turn. Far into the darkness of that night, those near his single room were startled by cheers and shouts of triumph from within. However, none thought more about it. If a few nocturnal yells had been the strangest thing that happened in the city by the Wat, the Thousand Stars would have started turning backward.

• 5 •

Wilvan watched carefully over the next few days for a chance to speak to Harmon Yorn again. At last, he found the trader alone.

"Master Yorn?"

"Yes."

"Remember how you asked me to keep my eye out for something hot, something just opening up?"

"Yes. I take it that you think you have just such a thing?"

"I do. Or I think I do. What if I knew a way to make the cheapest wine into a high-powered drink, as strong as Maldavian White? What if I could concentrate, say, Canary Red into something potent enough to sting your tongue?"

"Wilvan, you ought to know better than to mess around with amateur magic—"

"Magic? No, nothing like that! I . . . I . . . Look, I wasn't joking. I know a way, but I don't have the cash to set it up and work out the snags."

"I thought you had some savings. Have you gotten yourself into money problems, or is this just too much coin for you to handle?"

"No—yes!"

Harmon Yorn was a man who simply couldn't be lied to when he turned his eyes on you. Wilvan blurted out the truth about his situation with Michael-the-Fence.

"Boils, huh?" Yorn commented when Wilvan had finished. "You do know how foolish you were, don't you?"

"I do now."

"Good." He paused. "Wilvan, are you willing to trust me completely?"

Of all the men in Barrow, Harmon Yorn was probably the only person Wilvan felt that way about. He nodded.

"Then tell me what you know," the young merchant said. "Convince me."

Wilvan swallowed. "Master Yorn, if you bring wine to a boil, the strength of it goes out into the air with the steam. Then . . ." It took him a half hour. "And, you see, if we trap the cooled liquid, the strength is in it."

"How do you propose to do it, to trap that concentrate?"

"Glass. Cold glass. Just look at Natho's windows any-time it's wet inside or out."

"Hmmm. Yes, I believe you have something. What's more, I know just the man for you to see: my father-in-law, Aragon, the wine merchant."

"Master Aragon? I wouldn't dare—"

"None of that, now, Wilvan! You're a Man with an Idea. Start acting like it. You will have to sell this to him on your own. Aragon is an honest man, but . . ."

"But?"

"But he's had some business reverses lately, and he's a little edgy. A ship in which he had heavily invested is overdue from Maldavia. It probably won't be coming in. I suspect that the brigands on the Pirate Isles are enjoying his cargo right now."

"What will that mean for me?"

"He won't be easily sold, and if he is, he won't be able

to come up with a limitless supply of gold. You weren't the only one with shares in Vernig Village. Compared to you, he's still a rich man, but he'll get no richer investing in something too chancy. It will be up to you to convince him."

Wilvan had the backbone of a Barrowman. "Lead me to him!"

· 6 ·

Within a few days, Harmon Yorn had set up the meeting at the wine merchant's mansion. Harmon personally escorted Wilvan, but took a place in the corner of the room. Both Wilvan and Aragon were a little above average in height, with an unspectacular body build, but Aragon had a few deep lines etched around his mouth and between his eyes. His hair was a scraggly brown, and thinning, where Wilvan's was thicker and darker brown. Years of decision making (and having a shrewish wife at home) had cured Aragon into a tough, middle-aged businessman. He listened attentively as Wilvan outlined his plan. Aragon had promised confidentiality, and his word was good. He pondered the proposal.

"You have the beginnings of a workable plan, young man. How do you plan to keep the steam from escaping? Could you use something besides Canary Red? Won't the amount of the product be very small? What kind of condenser do you have in mind? Describe the shape of it. How will the liquor be marketed? What sized bottle? What price?"

Wilvan's mouth dropped open.

"Do you see now, Wilvan, why Aragon is the man for you?" Harmon Yorn rose from his corner. "I'll leave you two at it." He showed himself out.

Wilvan stammered for a few seconds, but he had been doing very little for two days but thinking about this project. "We'll need a boiler with a fitted lid, probably made out of copper or brass, with a pipe coming out of the top."

"What about boil-over going up the pipe?"

"We can make the top tall and gradually narrowing. This ought to work even on Swamp River wines—"

"Ugh!" Aragon's good taste was offended.

"—or maybe even beer. There *will* be a lot less product than starter." He remembered the kettle that he had helped Natho dump. "But that makes sense. We *want* a concentrated product.

"The condenser needs to be glass," Wilvan continued. "Maybe something else smooth, that we can get cold, would work, but iron would rust. You can't see through copper or brass to tell if it's working. I don't know yet, because I can't afford to buy copper or glass. I need a partner to help me survive financially while I work out the minor problems of the process."

"Wilvan, my boy, I think we can talk a deal. Seventy-thirty?" On the "seventy," Aragon had tapped his own chest.

"I had more in mind fifty-fifty," Wilvan countered.

It was said that in Barrow, unweaned babies learned to haggle with their mother about how long they could stay at the breast. After ten intense minutes, the pair settled happily on sixty-forty, with Aragon's "sixty" justified by his cash outlay. The great venture had been launched.

· 7 ·

In the days that followed, other problems faded from Wilvan's mind. Aragon negotiated for the boiler, but no reasonable amount of cash could hurry the time it would take the metal smith to craft it. The glazier had the panes of glass on hand for the condenser, but the cost made Aragon wince. Barrow had a few glass makers who could produce crude bottles, but flat panes of the size needed came only from Sai-khand. The partners chose an empty building just east of the Wat for the experimental equipment. They might have found more privacy west of the river, but the Slewsdwellers would have pilfered anything even nailed down (and then have stolen the nails).

As it was, Wilvan reluctantly had to quit his job and move into the large, single-roomed shed. Despite the weather, he wasn't too cold, since the shed had a good fireplace and wood was one of the first items delivered. He wasn't there for comfort: nosy Upcrusters were also known to be free with others' unwatched property. He spent the days impatiently, stuffing every drafty crack with mud before it could become a spyhole into the building. The partners had agreed that the essence of the new process was so simple that its secret could easily be stolen, especially once they had worked out the quirks of the equipment.

At the same time as the delivery of the huge bronze cooker, Aragon sent Delft, a hard-faced foreman from his warehouse, and a muscular workman to assist Wilvan. The reasons behind Aragon's choices soon became obvious: Delft had a mouth that threatened to ossify from lack of use, and the worker, Hombert, was just bright enough to dress himself and follow orders. He wouldn't be able to remember a secret, much less repeat it.

Wilvan was glad to see them: it would give him the time to take a break from guarding the shop and find Mickie. He was anxious to tell her the good news. That wasn't to be, however. With both crew and equipment arriving together, Wilvan had no choice but to begin. Problems began to crop up at once. He had to send Delft and Hombert back to the wine merchant's warehouse for a barrel hoist. Wilvan could envision having to dump a couple of hundred liters of hot wine dregs by hand. While they were gone, he dug a drainage trench under one wall, down to a ditch to the Wat. Just as he was dusting his hands of the first problem, the second arrived.

The cooker obviously wouldn't fit inside the shack's fireplace. When his assistants returned, he put them to installing the hoist in the center of the room while he hurried to a supplier of building materials for brick and mortar for a new fire pit and timbers to reinforce the rafter the boiler would hang from. He had to keep the curious wagon drivers outside when they delivered the materials, though it meant many hand loads for the crew of three. Word would be getting around now that something was stirring in the building by the Wat. Wilvan began wishing for a strong fence and a biting watchdog. By the time they had the cooker swung from the strengthened rafter, the first day was gone.

The second day was eaten up by the three amateur masons trying to cobble together a raised fire pit in the center of the room. The result was ugly, but sturdy enough for the exhausted bricklayers to go to sleep satisfied. The barnlike building was even less comfortable, with a cold snap moving into the region.

On the third day, they tried out the fire pit, to see if the mortar would hold. The warped cylinder held together well enough, but they discovered that where there's fire, there's smoke. The choking fumes refused to creep horizontally and exit conveniently up the fireplace chimney. The coughing experimenters had to fetch water from the Wat to douse the fire, and then spend more hours waiting in the cold as the room's air fell to the merely irritating point. The absolutely essential hoist prevented their installing any kind of chimney above the pit. A cursing Wilvan finally climbed on the roof and chopped a hole for the last wisps of smoke to escape. The threesome spent their third night trying to huddle near the room's original fireplace and avoid the icy draft from the ceiling.

On day four, the boiler, fire pit, and hoist abandoned their perverse ways and worked perfectly. The crew all had colds now and went about their tasks sniffing, with their eyes watering from the badly vented fumes. With the greatest of care, they constructed the long box that would hold the panes of glass to condense the steam. Only then did they send for the glass. The wine merchant himself brought it, in his private carriage.

"It goes well, Wilvan?" he asked.

Wilvan's haggard face was answer enough.

"That bad, eh? Can what we're trying still work?"

"Oh, that. Yes, it should. It's just been a lot tougher to set up than I thought it would be."

" 'It should.' Can you offer me no better?"

"Not yet. Maybe soon. Do you have time to watch the first try?"

"I'll make time." Aragon took charge. "Delft, go with my driver to the warehouse and bring back a barrel of Canary Red. Hombert, start the fire. We want it to be finished with the worst of its smoking before we have to work right over it. Wilvan, let's see if we can't tar this bloody, gold-sucking glass in place by the time Delft gets back." The wine merchant hadn't gotten where he was by being indecisive.

With Aragon's new spirit driving them, the participants began operating together as a team. The project seemed to move faster. By the time the two owners had the glass in place, careful not to get tar on the inside to flavor the product, Delft was ready to lower the cooker onto glowing coals.

Never had liquid come to a boil so slowly. Finally, steam began to seep from crevices in the boiler. Wilvan and Aragon had been waiting the entire time on tiptoes, watching the glass rectangles for signs of condensation. Wilvan spotted them first.

"There! See the drops on the glass!"

Aragon saw.

"Taste!"

Aragon stirred a cluster of droplets together with a fingertip and tasted.

"It's . . . It's awful!" He glanced at Wilvan's paled face. "Ho, don't be down, lad. It's awful *as wine*. I'll find a way to flavor it up, right enough. But the kick—it is just as you said!

"Say," he continued, "why is the steam coming out? I thought the glass was supposed to catch it all." Indeed, white vapor was now pouring from the open end and following the smoke of the fire pit toward the ceiling.

"I don't know. I'll—oww!" Wilvan had burned his hand on the hot glass. "Something's not right. Hombert, no more wood, and shut the draft on the fire. Delft, winch it up—carefully! We have to cool the boiler until we figure out what's wrong."

"What's the matter?" Aragon's face was red and his eyes were watering in the smoky atmosphere.

"I'm not sure. The only time I saw this done, the glass was right over the steam, and the glass was a lot cooler. One face of it was to the weather outside. Maybe we need more pipe, enough to reach the glass if we move it outside."

"Why not keep it here and just knock down a wall to make it colder?"

"Because we're already freezing our butts off! The best way is to build an extension that can be covered against nosy neighbors, but which will still stay cold."

"Right. And that means more coin from me for materials, right? Blast it all, I am not made of money, Wilvan!"

"We'll have to take out a wall anyway, looks like. We'll need a cover that keeps it cold but hidden."

"More coin! Blast!" Aragon's facial lines flexed, show-

ing how they had attained their depth. Buildings and
boiler and wood and a hundred minor items had been
draining his purse, with nothing to show for it but a few
drops of stinging, bad-tasting wine. "Get the problems
with this settled! I'll order more pipe. Delays!" Aragon
departed under a cloud of depression.

At a momentary dead end on the project, Wilvan
decided to take a break and visit Mickie.

• 8 •

Wilvan had been humming through Town on his way to
Mama Threechins' when a pair of huge, hairy arms dragged
him into an alley. He was completely surprised: he was
not rich enough in appearance to make robbery likely,
and it was daylight besides.

"You missed your payment," Luggo said in his ear.

"But—" The sinister memory of his dangling debt had
been suppressed by days of activity.

"Do you have it now?" Luggo's single-mindedness was
understandable. His brain would have made a chipmunk
blush. On the other hand, his hands would have been
adequate for a gorilla.

"No, but—"

"Get it before I find you again." Luggo's idea of
punctuation was a fist the size of a bucket.

Wilvan struggled uselessly in his grip and took three
jarring blows before Luggo dropped him and left the
alley. One of Wilvan's eyes had been closed, and his
abdomen felt like he had been run over by a wagon. The
world of monetary success that had been sustaining him
crumbled. He staggered on, his sight whirling. His feet
took him to Mama Threechins'.

"Wilvan!" Mickie rushed to him as soon as he entered.
There was no mistaking the affection and concern in her
face. "Oh, Wilvan, you're hurt!" She hugged him.

He winced.

"Mama!" Mickie yelled. "I need to take a few minutes
off."

The hefty owner of the restaurant stuck her head around
the kitchen doorframe. Mama, who had more romance in

her soul than anyone had ever given her credit for, sized up the situation.

"Take off a half hour, but no more, mind."

Mickie hastened to bring a damp rag from the work area. She led Wilvan to a warm, dark corner of the eatery. "What happened?" She gently sponged his face.

"Luggo. I forgot a payment."

"Luggo! You still owe Michael money?"

"Yes." He explained the situation.

"Great." She was suddenly not so solicitous.

"What's wrong?"

She was silent.

"Look, I know that's bad, but I have good news." He explained his financial arrangement, without detailing the creative idea behind it or the technical problems. "I can borrow enough money from Aragon to pay Michael each month," he finished.

"And Aragon is going to agree to that?"

The question stopped Wilvan. Maybe Aragon would help him; maybe not. The wine merchant was already unhappy about too many cash leaks. Perhaps he would just let Wilvan go under and abandon the project. Similarly, if Luggo killed Wilvan or ran him out of town, Aragon would be left sole owner of a valuable idea. Mickie noticed his pause.

"Will he give you the money—for sure?"

"Probably."

"Only probably?"

"Yes, but—"

"Forget it. As long as you owe my father money, I don't think I'd better see you anymore."

"Your father?"

"Of course. Don't you know that Michael-the-Fence is my father?"

• 9 •

Wilvan hadn't known. He had never mentioned their first unpleasant meeting. Money matters had seemed unimportant when he and Mickie had been nestled together in the bushes next to Pocket Park. He fired question after question at her.

"He killed my mother," she concluded. "Some slimeball who owed *him* money took it out on her! Michael," she spat, "wouldn't even talk about a ransom. The guy in the alley—you remember—was going to try the same thing with me."

"But sweetheart, what does that have to do with you and me?"

"I swore. I swore by all the gods. I promised myself, and I won't go back! I can't have anything to do with anyone tied to my father by money. I've always been afraid that someone would try to sweet-talk me to get at him.

"Oh, Wilvan, I know *you* wouldn't!" She leaned forward and kissed him.

He returned the kiss with enthusiasm, his hopes renewed.

"Now, no more of that!" She disentangled herself from his hands. "It isn't going to be easy for me, either, but come back when you've paid him off. If it takes the rest of the year, don't let me see your face until you're done with my father." She kissed him again, a kiss to last a year.

It was a fantastic kiss, and it was over too soon. She rose, wet-eyed, and headed blindly toward the kitchen. He sat, gasping like a banked trout, and watched her go. His legs again proved to be smarter than his brain. He was up and running after her within seconds. "Wait!"

Mama Threechins appeared in the kitchen entrance, fists on hips. The door could not have been more effectively blocked if you had backed a beer wagon across it. "I don't want to catch you giving one of my girls trouble!" She frowned at Wilvan.

He gulped, and all the fight went out of him. A sow bear could have no more effective shelter for her cubs than Mama was for one of her "girls." He slunk from the eatery with tears blurring his one good eye.

There was no use to go to Bargo's for a beer. The price of one drink was now a significant part of his fortune. Instead, he made the long walk across town to beg the payment from Aragon.

The merchant was not at his warehouse, having gone home early. Naturally, the servants at his mansion sent Wilvan around to the tradesman's entrance, and with his luck continuing in the same depressing rut, he first had to be raked over by Gargina, Aragon's biting mare of a wife, before his insistence got him an interview with the wine merchant himself. Gargina exited from their meeting only after chewing her husband out about this and that, leaving Aragon in anything but a receptive mood.

He heard Wilvan's complete story before commenting. "So he's a fence, eh? Why, I can have the Prince close him down!"

"No, don't. He'd just get away and reopen west of the river. Then he'd hunt me down anyway. I'd be just as hurt or dead as if he'd never moved. And no one in the Town would speak to me because I was an informer."

"It has to be more money, does it?"

"Yes."

"Curse you and your schemes, Erginson! By the Thousand Stars, I have a good mind to let him have you!"

Harmon Yorn's father-in-law, however, was the honest man that he had been advertised to be. He stamped from the room and returned in a few minutes with a small moneybag. Harmon could hear Gargina sniping at him from another room.

"Erginson, by next month your scheme either pays off, or I'm out. This is one month's interest; you take care of your own debts from now on. I'm banking on this coming out of your share someday—if there *are* any shares for it to come out of! Now, get out!" He almost threw the bag of coin at Wilvan.

Considering the circumstances, Wilvan's reception by his partner was as kindly as he could have expected. He marched straight back across town to Michael's sundries shop. He flung the coin in Michael's face. After getting a receipt, he made an obscene gesture at Michael, and another at Luggo (now that he was free to run) before stalking out.

"Luggo, lad," Michael said thoughtfully, "didn't it seem that our friend Wilvan came up with the cash awfully quick? Have him followed. And I want to speak to Claudio."

Luggo grunted and moved to make the arrangements.

• 10 •

By the time that the extension for the copper exhaust pipe had arrived, the boiler crew had knocked out a wall and built a drafty, hide-draped annex. The pipe was lashed into place, looking like a lateral chimney. The glass condenser box was tarred into place at the end. Aragon refused to witness anything but a success; the boiler crew were on their own.

The cooker had been refilled and eventually had begun to boil. The pipe nearest the boiler heated rapidly, but the cooled glass did condense a trickle of tongue-tingling liquid—for five minutes. Then the glass heated as well, and steam began drifting upward from the open end.

"By the Life Giver, why won't this thing work?" Wilvan was ready to pull out his hair.

"Boss, this wood is a lot of trouble," Delft offered. "Maybe we could control the heat better with charcoal."

Wilvan was taken aback: that statement had been the longest he had ever heard pass the foreman's lips. "Charcoal? Yeah, I see what you mean. And if the steam is still too hot by the time it reaches the glass, maybe we can cool it some.

"Hombert, take that empty wine keg down to the Wat and bring it back full of cold water.

"Delft, trot down to the ragpicker at the end of Sow's Purse and bring back an armload. Hombert and me will tie the rags around the pipe and wet 'em down. If you know of a charcoal burner, stop there after you bring us the rags and order a small load for tomorrow, if we can get it. Get as good a price as you can, or Aragon will be on my back again.

"I'll check the pipe angle, too. If some starts to condense in the pipe, we want it to run to the collector instead of back into the cooker. By the time you get back from ordering the charcoal, we should be ready again."

"Right, boss."

Wilvan was too distracted to notice that his innermost wish had been granted: he was somebody's boss.

• 11 •

Another day of alternate sweating and freezing was under way. The boiler with its tantalizing contents was ready again. After an eternity of inactivity, it came to a boil.

"Wet the rags down good, Hombert.

"Watch it! The river water is going to run down and drip into the collecting bucket. Hold on." Wilvan scooped up a handful of thick pitch and made a ring around the pipe so that the trickle of none-too-clean river water fell short of the collector.

"All right, Hombert, more water. Soak 'em good. Watch out for the hot—"

Ting!

"—glass."

A few splatters had landed on the glass that had already begun to heat from the steaming kettle. Two panes cracked completely across. Wilvan sat down on the floor and put his head in his hands. It wasn't worth the trouble even to swear at Hombert. If it hadn't been the glass, it would have been something else. If it hadn't been this time, it would have been the next. The best solution to his problems seemed to be to walk down to the Wat and jump in.

"What now, boss?"

"Oh, take the glass box off, I guess. Careful: it's hot, and there may be sharp edges. By the Thousand Stars, don't break it any worse!"

Wilvan himself remained slumped on the floor, the weight of the Plane on his shoulders. Delft and Hombert worked the tar seal loose from the pipe and swung the glass free. Wilvan had made sure the box had been braced above and below, but he had not thought to protect it from hot/cold shattering. Woe! Woe! Woe!

"Boss, what should we do with this stuff that's running out of the pipe?"

Wilvan looked up. A trickle of clear liquid was running off the glob of pitch at the end of the disconnected pipe. He crawled toward it, as a man lost in the desert might crawl toward the last water hole. He stretched his arm out, as a primal man would have reached for the first fire. A crystal drop oozed down his index finger and across the base of his thumb. He lapped at it animalistically.

Except for a tarry undertaste, it was the same as the drop he had tasted from the window of the Green Garter! (By the Thousand Stars, they were going to need a name for this stuff.)

"It's going to work!" He leaped up and twirled. "Even without the glass, it's going to work!" He seized Hombert by the arms and began a jig. "It's gonna work! It's gonna work!"

Work it did, though it took cleaning away the excess tar and making a dozen adjustments. It took several batches to decide when the product had become too diluted to make the wine not worth more cooking. It took days to reach a consistent yield, but this time as Aragon watched, he was as pleased as a new father. Some of the gullies in his face almost disappeared.

Aragon convinced Wilvan that they needed more financial backing. He also began to buy up empty Maldavian White bottles secretly. The snooty Maldavians refused to refill any bottle that had held their top vintages. Hundreds of the small White bottles were drifting around Barrow, dusty, empty, or filled with cheaper liquors or medicines. Glass was too expensive to be discarded by the prudent, but Maldavian White bottles were too tiny for most uses. They were not too small for the clear concentrate that was rolling out of Wilvan's cooker. The product had a name now: Barrow White.

The shed hummed with activity; Wilvan seldom left it. There were problems always waiting: supplies; experiments with the kind of base to be used. Aragon himself spent days filtering the product and looking for ways to disguise some of Barrow White's more obnoxious flavors. Storing the clear liquid in a charcoal-lined vat for a week with some crushed mint leaves elevated it to an acceptable quality. Trial and error showed that anything alcoholic could be used as a base, though beer tended to froth too much in the pipe. The best choices for starters were some incredibly bad wines grown west of Barrow. They were cheap, but they worked.

The problems tying Wilvan to the cooker shed gradually dropped from major to minor. Aragon had found the right backer: Arthello Bancartin, a third cousin of the Prince himself. Arthello was willing to invest in guarded wagons and other expenses needed to debut super-powered

Barrow White in far Sai-khand on the same day as it would be released in Barrow. The second day of Browngrass, the next summer, was chosen because it was the date the Emperor was to open a new wing of his palace in Sai-khand. There would be extensive celebrating: the ideal time to introduce a new beverage. Aragon and Arthello planned to steal a march on the arrogant Maldavians, gutting the market for the more potent Maldavian vintages before the secret of Barrow White's manufacture leaked out.

Part of Arthello's twenty percent would be the cost of building a new headquarters of stone, laid out from the first with the right winches, fire pits, and chimneys, made to house an even larger cooker. The new boiler would have a joint specially made for the horizontal cooling pipe, replacing the make-do apparatus now being used. When the first boiler came down, it would be similarly fitted and loaded on a wagon for the caravan to the capital. Though all three partners were planning to take the first load to Sai-khand in person, Arthello was to stay there to set up a second production plant.

Wilvan was itching in his soul to see Mickie. Arthello seemed to have enough money to be slightly careless with it. He was giving Wilvan an allowance just large enough to make payments to Michael for ten more months— horribly long, painful months that he must pass in loneliness. It no more occurred to him that he could end his celibacy by finding another woman than it would have to cut off his hand, hoping to find a good artificial replacement.

Even if he couldn't see the woman he loved, he could still visit other friends. Not only was he well acquainted in the Town, but now he was beginning to meet new contacts north of Caravan Way. With a break between batches, he decided to walk to the bazaar.

Swinging down the street that he usually took and passing a familiar alley, he was intercepted by the same set of hairy arms.

"Luggo? Hey, watch it! My payment isn't due for a week."

"No, no, clod. You watch it. The boss says your payment is due then, but you pay two times. Twice as much."

"What? He can't—"

"The boss says that you got somethin' goin'. He says, you pay or there will be a fire: a funny fire, like the one at Vernig Village. The fire might be in that shed down by the river or in the new stone house you boys was talkin' about.

"An' next month, it doubles again, and in six months, doubles again. It ain't a loan, he says: it's insurance. He told me to be sure you remembered."

"Hey, you're not going to—ungh!"

He was. Luggo just liked to beat people up.

• 12 •

Wilvan staggered into Bargo's doubled over. Luggo had cracked a rib for him. Bargo vaulted the counter and helped him to a seat. After making sure no one was watching, he also brought him a small beer, on the house. Bargo had known Wilvan for years, and his parents before him. They could not help Wilvan: his mother was dead, and his father had returned to Ichan. Bargo was sympathetic as Wilvan babbled out the latest chapter in his renewed troubles.

"What I can't understand," Wilvan moaned, "is how Michael is getting away with cheating on my loan. Old Barndoogle's guarantee was supposed to keep him from jacking up the interest, no matter what he calls it, just like it was supposed to keep my purse bleeding for a year."

"Haven't you heard?" Bargo asked. "Old Barndoogle tottered out in front of a grain wagon two days ago. He's dead."

Wilvan was jolted. In common thinking, magicians, even minor ones, were supposed to be able to live forever. He needed a place to lie down and rest his aching side while he thought over the news. Thanking Bargo for his kindness, he began the long trek to his bachelor room. Passing the same alley—no! It couldn't be!—a pair of hairy arms dragged him in.

"Luggo, you—oh, it's you."

"I've been looking for you, little man," said Mama Threechins. "I told you not to mess with one of my girls."

"What! I haven't seen Mickie in a month!"

"Don't I know it! She hasn't eaten or slept right since. You've made her near useless to me as a cook."

"She told me not to see her for a year."

"And you *listened*? Men! Get this business settled and soon, or you'll have me to deal with." She let him go and rolled out of the alley.

What next? Maybe he would be run down by a grain wagon himself. Or maybe the Prince would mistakenly issue orders to have him hung for murder. Murder . . . Murder . . . Perhaps that was the answer. A dead Michael couldn't extort money from anyone.

It wouldn't be easy. Wilvan would have to bluff his way past Luggo. The act would take more nerve than he presently had. Foolishly, as so many had done before and so many will do hence, he decided to have a few stiff drinks to work up his courage.

· 13 ·

A waiter, even a waiter full of beer, was not a warrior or an assassin. Wilvan was filled with the raw, emotional anger of an abused person at last able to take revenge; he had a sharp knife and the urge to kill; he had quavery legs that would carry him as far as Michael's. It remained to be seen whether he could use that knife on another person. The waterfront loomed ahead in a winter fog that had drifted in off the Wat in the chill of the evening.

The dregs of the sunset seemed unusually bright to Wilvan; in fact, it was growing lighter instead of darker. The fact that something unusual was happening finally penetrated Wilvan's beer-soaked brain. He hurried. Michael's sundries store was a roaring pyre. The flames had not yet reached Luggo's body, lying across the doorway with its throat cut. Barrowmen were scrambling from all directions to try to douse the blaze before it spread.

It had never occurred to Wilvan, wrapped up in his own disconcerting miseries, that he was not Michael's only enemy. He had never questioned, for instance, why a top professional like Claudio-the-Candle would be working for a lower life-form such as Michael. Old Barndoogle's death had removed the guarantees from a number of loans, including one to a certain vengeful arsonist.

• 14 •

The couple sat at a back table in Mama Threechins'
restaurant.

"He's dead, then?" Mickie asked.

"Dead."

"You didn't—"

"No, but I would have. With him gone we can get
married."

"Hey, I never said—"

"I know you didn't, but you didn't have to."

"I . . . I don't have a dowry or a bridal dress."

"It doesn't matter about the dress. A half hour after
the cleric finishes the ceremony, I plan to have you out of
it anyway. No waiting a year for that." He loved the way
the strong girl blushed. "Besides, you do have a dowry."

"What?"

"You're Michael's only heir."

"But the business burned, and no creditor will pay me
off now!"

"I know one who will. I'll just have to marry you to
keep my money in the family!"

When she came into his arms, he didn't realize that he
would no longer be the sole boss of his life, but half his
dream did come true: he was the richest man in Barrow.

Interchapter

I would swear in frustration, except for the danger involved when any mage does so. I was poised to assist Wilvan with his love life. I was prepared to tip the battle with Michael in his favor. He did it himself! Frustration! Another inconclusive experiment!

My one satisfaction is that my son Harmon showed himself to be less than deific. He believes strongly in not drinking anything alcoholic; yet he assisted his father-in-law and a friend in loosing on the populace a new way to make alcohol much more concentrated. That may damage society on this Plane more than any war. Time will tell.

I will try once more, going back almost to the beginning of my tales to find a branch to explore. This time I will follow Brieze's brother (and his Highlander friend). If they have no need of my meddling, I will retire, but I have an entirely different feeling about this set of happenings. This time I will observe first and write later. He lives now, I believe, in Slews-Inside-the-Walls. . . .

BOOK VIII

A Secret
Not Sought After

FLEETFOX WAGONHAWK was depressed, and for no reason
he could think of. He still had money to spend from the
reward the Prince had given him and his companions for
their part in breaking the Big Onion Gang in the Slews.
Over the last two years, Fleetfox had seen action almost
daily: sometimes fighting;, sometimes slinking about for
more information. Maybe he was feeling the letdown of
the war being over.

The drug war had heated up for a year after he had left
home, and then exploded. Home . . . home had been
impossible. Mother had been killed, and Brieze's man
Krovik had moved into the wagon. There had been no
place for another man in the crowded space. Krovik was
all right, and he had taken good care of Fleetfox's little
brothers and sisters, but Fleetfox had not been "little"
anymore. The chance to become the apprentice of old
Horserunner-the-Loremaster had come like a boon from
the Life Giver. It had meant moving to the Slews, to
share a crowded apartment with the old man, but all of
that had been more than worth it.

Horserunner had been the oldest living Tellarani, the
last full shaman of the People. He had been able to
remember the Scallion Wars and the extermination of
the People by the invaders from over the mountains.
Only the fact that he had been in Barrow trying to
negotiate an alliance with the Old Prince had kept
Horserunner from being present at the Tellaranis' final
battle. He had fought the Scallions beside the Barrowmen,
but that had not brought back the People-of-the-Grass or
healed the curse on the Grasslands.

It was his memory of the Scallions that had brought Horserunner's death. He had seen the faces of some of their officers, and he knew the marks that they used on their bodies, especially the sword-through-onion tattoo on the right breast. Not many alive still did; not many of those lived in the Slews; few of those had had more than the barest acquaintance with individuals among the invaders.

Barrowmen believed that the Scallions had been exterminated thirty years before. In fact, at least one had survived. An officer of the raiders had chosen to hide among the outcasts of the Slews. Over the decades, he had organized the Big Onion Gang—terrorists, murderers, and drug runners without equals. Though his gang had grown to the point that it had become a real power, not just in the Slews, but in all of Barrow, the outlaw had taken care that only a few trusted lieutenants had ever seen his face. No one knew him—no one, save possibly one old Tellarani shaman. The Big Onion had ordered Horserunner's execution.

Horserunner had taught Fleetfox what few of the younger Tellarani knew about the lore of the People-of-the-Grass: their songs, stories, and legends. Those had been lost to the rising generation of the People by dilution with the cultures of well-meaning strangers. Fleetfox had learned the Tellarani cards and their reading, as he once might have from his mother. Horserunner had no deck of the expensive cards for Fleetfox; yet the Loremaster had promised him a set in the near future. Fleetfox suspected that the shaman had had a glimpse of his own death.

Like a spark, it suddenly came to Fleetfox in his remembrances: today was two years to the day that Horserunner had died. It was no surprise that Fleetfox had been feeling depressed; his blood had remembered even if he had not. The proper thing to do, then, was to lift that gloom by honoring the old man the way a Tellarani loremaster should be honored—by the lore that he himself had left behind. Fleetfox rolled from the non-Tellarani bed where he had been lying and fell into the effortless crouch of the wagon people, in the center of the room that he had shared with the shaman. In meditation that reached even to his blood, Fleetfox remembered Horserunner.

Chanting subvocally, as he had been taught, Fleetfox was able to bring to mind every word the shaman had ever said to him. The old seer had chosen him, Fleetfox, instead of some other Tellarani lad, probably mystically, through the same blood music that he had taught the younger man to hear. Perhaps a reading of the cards had led him; he had never shared his reason with Fleetfox.

The hours fell away in visions, remembrances of his lessons; memories of the readings with the cards by the People's method, that the old man had let him witness. At last, he relived the Loremaster's death.

Two assassins had rushed on them without warning, in the half dark of the evening. At close quarters, Fleetfox's sling had been useless. He had been slammed aside before he could even draw his eating dagger. Horserunner had swung the stick, that he used to steady his ancient frame, as if it were the legendary Saber of Sarri. He had stretched out one of the attackers, but the other had gotten through, striking with a dagger below Horserunner's ribs.

Fleetfox had rebounded quickly, but he had faced both the successful assassin and his bruised partner with just a stick and a small knife. His own life had continued only because of the three shouting men who had rushed out of the Pig's Navel to his rescue. The attackers had done for Horserunner; they had retreated as Kinsworth Vomanger, Ukrusu the Manhunter, and Delgen McTarn came up.

As Fleetfox had knelt, sobbing, beside his mentor's body, the Loremaster had opened his eyes.

"Weep not, Fleet," he had said, in the language of the People. "It was for this I chose you. You will carry on for me and accomplish what the blood power would not allow me to attempt. Help cleanse the city of the last of the vermin who slew our folk, but, ho, more!" He had coughed and a trickle of blood had run from the corner of his mouth. "You must find the lost ones of the People. Look for the *wrong* card! It is the foundation of the matter. Look *beneath him!*" His hands had clutched at Fleetfox's arms with the strength that befitted a Tellarani shaman and warrior. Then they had relaxed into rest forever.

Fleetfox, an older Fleetfox now, sang again the death chant for the shaman in the emptiness of his room. He had done as he had promised the dying man. He carried a long stabbing knife now, and he had used it well. The bones of the last of the Scallions now swayed on a gibbet erected on the Old Wat Bridge, in part because of Fleetfox's efforts. The worst of the remaining drug dealers were either dead or in the Prince's dungeons. The little fish in the operations were either lying low or had fled Barrow to any refuge they could think of. The drug war was over.

Fleetfox had buried Horserunner west of Barrow and seen to it that grass covered his unmarked grave. He would have taken the body east to the Grasslands where the Loremaster had been born, but the Grasslands were no more. Only the Waste lay where they had been. As a Tellarani, Fleetfox felt bitter about the Waste, because it had been both the doing and the doom of the People.

The final battle, in which the last of the Tellarani warriors had met their deaths, had ended with a curse by the Loremasters on the Grasslands themselves: no grass could grow there until the last of the Scallions were dead and the People returned. On the other hand, the scattered survivors had been unable to return because the grass, which had supported the wisent herds that were their livelihood, no longer grew. A few small wisent herds had survived by grazing half the time inside the forests, but the social pattern of the Tellarani had been broken.

The remnant of the People agreed that the "return" mentioned in the curse did not refer to them, but to the missing body of Tellarini women and children that the Scallions had never been able to find and enslave. Unfortunately, though the Scallions were gone, no one else had been able to locate the missing People either. Horserunner, by his final words, must have meant for Fleetfox to continue that impossible search as well. The old man must have been delirious: what had he meant by "the wrong card"?

No! Fleetfox's blood shouted it. No Tellarani shaman, even in death, uttered a meaningless oracle. Fleetfox chided himself for slipping into the thinking of a Town man. He must treat what Horserunner had said as vital. The only "cards" that he knew of were the Loremaster's cards of seeing, still in the dusty trunk against the wall after two years. Fleetfox had left it undisturbed, but now his blood cried for it to be opened.

Fleetfox had seen the trunk's contents, long before. Moths had done for the cloaks and furs the shaman had left. All that remained undamaged was a small sack of coin and the hardwood box in which the old man had kept his cards and reading cloth. Pocketing the coin bag, Fleetfox took out the box. The cloth and cards within were unblemished. Though he was sure that Horserunner had meant for him to have them, Fleetfox had been too busy being a vengeful warrior and a spy over the last months to attempt a reading with the cards.

He gathered up the loose deck, deciding to refamiliarize himself with the nature of the cards. They tingled in his hands, as if itching to have the blood power of a Tellarani seer pouring through them once again. He laid out the entire set on the black cloth and counted them off: thirteen cards each of Swords, Cups, Wands, and Pentacles; twenty-two major cards besides. No, there were twenty-three! One by one, he ticked them off: the Sun, the Moon, the High Priestess, the Magician, the Fool, the Star, Death, the Magician, the Hierophant, the Tower, the Wheel of Fortune, and the rest.

A card remained, a card that didn't belong. It was the *wrong card*! Though the pattern on the back was the same as the others, the face of the odd card was a rainbow of swirling colors and moving figures. No part of it would remain in focus long enough to be seen clearly. Fleetfox felt a cold sweat pop from every pore. Such a thing could not be, but it was. He must *read* it—now!

· 2 ·

He mixed the deck rapidly, knowing that the hands were more knowledgeable than the eyes in beginning a reading. He lay the mystery card down as the Significator, and immediately realized that it was completely wrong in that position. Fleetfox himself was the Significator. The unusual card belonged *beneath him*, as Horserunner's oracle had indicated.

Fleetfox's hands were shaking as he laid out the cards by the pattern that all Tellarani used. He selected the card most like himself: the Knight of Pentacles. He was the Lord of the Wild and Fertile Lands; his dark eyes looked patiently on the tasks he had to perform. He might almost be dull to some, but on his comings and goings rested the fate of the lost lands of the Tellarani.

"This covers me," Fleetfox intoned. He had to be deadly serious; he had never made a solo reading, much less one of this much mystery. He laid down the Ace of Pentacles on the Knight's face.

It spoke of a beginning, a good beginning. In his spirit, he stood before a featureless plain on which he would journey. The reading would be his map.

"This crosses me." He stared at the Moon card, the signature of those who would oppose him.

His blood stirred. The face in the pictured moon changed to an impossibly old male countenance, evil only because of its indifference to mortality. The baying dogs became rough-clad men on ponies, their faces as hard as broken bones. The background became rolling hills of unhealthy green with the sun burning down on them. Fleetfox was frightened; he knew he would be frightened again when he met those enemies.

It was time for the mystery card. He laid it between the central pile of cards and his own heart. "This is beneath me." It was the foundation of the matter; the wordless question that had called him to this seeing.

The colors swirled again, but this time they spun into a clear picture. It was as if he were looking through a window toward where a tunnel led into the ground. Figures were entering the hole, women and children of the People. Occasionally, a woman would stop to embrace some Tellarani warrior, and then, weeping, march on into the underground. A stranger, knowing the legend of the lost People, might also have realized what he was seeing, but none but a seer of the People-of-the-Grass could have revealed the scene. He found himself weeping at each parting, because he knew what waited for the men.

Finally the last of the women climbed into the tunnel as Fleetfox watched. The men filled the mouth immediately with earth and stones and rolled a huge boulder over the entrance. The ground was still scarred and muddy from digging. A shaman of the People stepped into view.

He was older even than Horserunner had been; dignity rode his shoulders like a cloak. He raised his arms and chanted to the skies.

Fleetfox witnessed one of the great magics of the People. The earth healed itself: scarred soil smoothed its folds; grass shot from the ground. Within minutes, the boulder was surrounded by waving grass stalks that any nonwitness would have sworn had taken months to grow. Then the Tellarani left the view of the card.

There was a swirl as time passed. The picture steadied again to show some rough men with whips, driving slaves, some of them captured Tellarani, among the dead grass stalks. The slave masters could have been brothers of the men he had seen on the Moon card. They were rolling other boulders into position, to erect some kind of structure or monument. The view shot into the air, looking down and back on the scene below. Great stones had been moved into a circle, with a single rock set at the top. The whole resembled the outline of an onion, the symbol of the hated Scallions. With a final flash, the scene disappeared.

Fleetfox rocked back and forth, sobbing, unable to go on. At last he dried his tears; the reading called him. The card had shown him what had been: the vision that the other cards would pour out would show him what he was to do now. The card of the lost People was blank when he looked at it. On its face lay a bit of crystal that he had once heard called Dragon crystal, fabled among magicians for use in "seeing" spells. None living knew all its secrets. He offered another prayer to the Life Giver, in sorrow for the mighty knowledge that his scattered folk had lost.

He brushed a wet strand of black hair out of his eyes and picked up the remaining cards to complete the reading. "This is behind me." His voice croaked as he turned the card of past influences: the Hermit.

There was no mistaking the silent council of Horserunner in the hooded figure. The old eyes said to Fleetfox, "I will be with you in the blood spirit of the People, though I am gone across the great gulf to meet the Life Giver." A tear dripped from Fleetfox's nose onto the card, shimmering the old man's face into a wry smile.

Fleetfox sniffed. No matter that he was the only witness, he was not happy with his weeping self-image as a warrior and seer. He turned the card called the Crown card. It was the Nine of Wands. This was indeed a true seeing; the man pictured on the counter immediately took on the face of his friend Delgen McTarn.

There would be fighting, and a probable victory, but Fleetfox would not have to fare alone against the problems ahead. He could think of no one he would rather have defending his back, as the man on the card was defending the gap in the wall of wands, than the wisecracking Highlander.

"This is before me." Unlike the merely possible future shown by the Crown, this card showed a future that *would* come to pass. It was the Tower, lightning-struck and crumbling. Before he could pinpoint the destructive change that would come in his own future, the Tower blurred and metamorphosed into a sharp, rocky spire standing above the same sickly green open country that had shown on the Moon card.

That rock Tower could be only one place on this Plane: the Pinnacle, the abandoned fortress of the Scallions that no man alive had ever entered and escaped. Shuddering, he quickly turned another card.

"My fears." The Wheel of Fortune lay near his right hand, reversed. He would need courage against the setbacks it promised. Again, the painted features of the card shifted into other forms.

The bird at the top grew a killing beak, a long tail, and four killing claws. The ox at the bottom lost its wings and became the bleeding body of a horse. The sphinx raised the sword she was holding to point it straight toward the top of the card: north, or into the air where an eagle would be. The vision was too strange for Fleetfox to fear now, though he knew he would fear, and deeply, when this part of the vision came to pass.

"My family." The Ten of Cups showed an arch in the sky formed of cups, above a happy family. The arch moved to curl into a circle of cups, with the top one standing slightly above the others. It was the same onion shape he had seen on the crystal card. The family below no longer had a father, and the mother and children were now dressed as Tellarani. They were his family for this reading. The cup third from the right glowed with a green fire, and the women and children pointed toward it. There, in the circle of stones, must lie the hidden entrance.

"My hopes." The reversed Five of Pentacles showed a window with two poor folk before it. As he watched, the window became an ornate door, and the beggars altered into two warriors carrying a lantern, with their backs toward Fleetfox. He knew, as surely as his blood was red, that some of his hopes lay beyond that door. Where *it* lay, however, was not revealed. Perhaps inside the Pinnacle . . .

He sighed as he played the Capstone—the card of ultimate outcome. The Five of Cups, reversed, was not the card he had wanted to see, because its message was ambiguous. Three of the cups shown had spilled their wine, and it was as red as blood. Though some of it had not spilled, he felt that some of it which had would be his own blood. Two cups remained untouched, and undecipherable. And who was the square-shouldered figure among the cups, with his face turned away?

Fleetfox crouched where he was, drained. The reading was finished.

• **3** •

Like a song sung by a distant bard, Fleetfox had understood the messages that the cards had shown him—almost. He *must* go; that was beyond doubt. Whether anyone went with him, he *would* go, but the cards had spoken of at least one companion on his journey. Fleetfox knew who to seek as fellow travelers: the three sturdy men who had acted with him against the drug dealers, even before the Prince had brought the war into the open.

Buckling on the belt that held his stabber, Fleetfox left his quarters at full stride. The first friend he would look for would be Delgen McTarn, since he lived closest and the cards had shown him particularly. The young Highlander should still be staying at the Pig's Navel, only a few minutes' walk away, even in the dark. Fleetfox had left the sunlight behind during his long day of continual visions.

He had to blink away the outside dark on entering the tavern's common room. It was well lighted and almost free of the fumes that choked most dives in the Slews. Delgen spotted him from across the room and gave a cheery hallo. Fleetfox hurried to his table, his urgency burning like a coal in his pocket. He had hardly sat down before he began.

"Delgen, I'm going on a journey: a dangerous journey. I want you to go with me."

"Out wi' it! Never mind the how-are-ye-Delgen's or hello's! Don't hold back so, Fleet!" Delgen had a belly laugh at his friend's expense. "Oh, do go on, Fleet! It must be somethin' great to shake up a stone face like you."

Fleetfox frowned at his friend. Delgen had changed in several ways over the last two years, since he had come to Barrow seeking a lost brother. He still had the same shock of black hair, but his Highlander's face was now rounder and ruddier. He had been investing the Prince's reward money in rich food and drink, the kinds not available in the mountains. For him, the war was over indeed: Barrow was not his home; little held him there now that hard Highland vengeance had been applied to his brother's killers. Through every action of the past two years, even the bloodiest, he had never stopped clowning.

"Delgen, everything on this Plane is not food or drink or a joke." Fleetfox needed a serious collaborator.

"Aye, ye left out women!"

Fleetfox growled and started to rise. Perhaps it would be better to do what he had to alone.

"Nah! Nah! Don't take it so. Sit! Sit! Tell me what earth shaker had rooted ye from that gloomy room of yours."

Fleetfox sat. It would do no good to berate his friend for his joviality. Delgen would have teased an executioner; it was his way. One of the anchors of their friendship had always been the way his sobriety and Delgen's mirth complemented each other. He launched into the tale of the strange card and his visions that day. Delgen listened to the whole, but he was more skeptical than a Barrowman would have been: the Tellarani did not live among the mountain folk.

"Ye mean, ye're takin' off because some *cards* said to? 'Tis a bit thin for me."

"You don't understand, Del."

Fleetfox tried for many minutes to explain the triple wedding of the Tellarani, their hereditary "seeking" power, and the cards. Though Delgen did not understand a fraction of what he heard, he did understand the sincerity in his friend's face.

"So ye'll be goin' out to that Grassland or Waste or whatever, to find out where your folk be gone?"

"Yes."

"An' ye'll be goin' wi'out Delgen McTarn, if I turn ye down?"

"Yes."

"Ye'll no such! We've covered each other's back more'n once, an' I'll not see ye goin' alone. Sounds dangerous."

"It probably will be."

"Aye, thought so. Ah, well, I'm sick o' the city anyway. Too bad there's no gold to be had for this, like there was for doin' in the Onion Gang."

"Maybe there will be. I have to go to the Pinnacle, the old Scallions' hideout. Everybody knows where it is, but no one's ever been in it. That is, nobody's ever been in it and come out alive to tell about it."

"Ye're not encouraging me, Fleet."

"The Pinnacle has to still be packed full of the stuff that the Scallions stole. After they finished off my people, they wiped out a dozen villages and no telling how many caravans. There's probably gold in every room."

"Ye're encouraging me again!"

"And me, as well," a deep voice said from behind Fleetfox.

"Huh?"

Fleetfox had been so eager to tell his plans to Delgen that he had ignored the rest of the tavern's clientele. A tall, muscular man seated at the next table had been taking in every word.

"Don't be offended, gentlemen. My name is Aldamar Ivandi, late of the Holy Knights, looking for an honorable fight or quest to join. This is my sword, Avenger."

"(What kind of moonstruck fool introduces his sword as if it were a person?) Sir, this was somewhat of a private conversation." Fleetfox began glancing around to find a table further from eavesdroppers.

"My apologies. I came to Barrow to enter the war against the vermin who were poisoning your people, but the fighting was over before I could join in. I have been patting my foot in this dump, looking for any chance at a man's work, and finding none. I don't want to join your watchmen. (I could always reenlist in the Knights.) Your city has been too peaceful for a man like me to find a cause worth backing. I had hoped—"

"I don't think so. I have plans for other companions."

"Very well. But could I at least listen? I haven't found anyone east of the river who even talks about anything but making money."

"Aye, why not, Fleet?" Delgen added. " 'Tis not as if he hasn't heard everything ye've had to say already."

"Umm. All right, but you're to listen and maybe offer advice as a fighting man. Don't try to worm your way into our traveling company."

"Done." He dragged his chair over to their table and propped his meter-and-a-half-long sword next to his right hand. "Now, how many days are you going to be out? Best think about food and water. What is the route like that you'll be taking? What kind of mounts? Will you need a packhorse?"

Aldamar proved to be a mine of information about life on the road. It was the profession of the Holy Knights to patrol the routes of the Empire and care for travelers. He would have made a good companion to have along, but Fleetfox had soured on him the second he had found the Knight listening in where he hadn't been invited. A second problem also surfaced. Fleetfox had been planning for Delgen and himself to cross the Waste on hardy, surefooted steppe ponies. He noticed the square shape of Aldamar's shoulders.

"You're used to wearing heavy armor, aren't you?"

"Yes. What of it?"

"And I suppose you have a horse to match that armor and that chopper of a sword? One of those skinny plow horses that the Knights favor?"

"I guess you could describe my mount that way."

"I thought as much. A horse like that probably wouldn't live to cross the Waste the way we're going. There's water, but no grass. The ponies we'll be riding are smart enough not to eat any of the poison weeds that grow there now, and they can go for days on minimum fodder. If we had agreed to take you along, you would have been on foot before we were halfway across the Waste."

It was Aldamar's turn to look sour, but he grudgingly agreed that perhaps this particular trek wasn't for him. As a Knight, he was strictly a straight dealer; he stayed up with them well into the night, refining a plan that he would be no part of. When he retired at last, Delgen spoke up.

"Fleet, I would ha' spoke up ere this, but ye seemed dead set against the big man. Ye have it in your mind that Kinsworth is going with us. He's a big man in the city guard now. The Prince listens to his advice. He's got used to the watchmen calling him 'sir' and 'Captain Vomanger'. Kinsworth isn't likely to be anxious to come with us.

"And Ukrusu is now Ukrusu the Manhunter. He's got three or four of those Mugambese lasses buzzing around him, eager to be the first mother of their new Manhunter Clan. He will be as big a man among the Mugambese as his father is now, and you know how him and Kinsworth are—thick as thieves, like you and me, for all that they're our friends, too."

"There is already a top manhunter in Barrow—Galen McTarn. Ukrusu will have plenty of competition," Fleetfox added. "Say, I never noticed before that that Galen McTarn has the same last name as yours. Is he—"

"No! No kin of mine!"

"Ooh, that's the way it is, eh? Never mind. You're right: neither of our friends is going to want to go with us. But I still don't want Beefy Bill along. I won't make the excuse that I feel it in my blood or that I saw it in the cards; I just don't want him with us."

" 'Tis your quest, Fleet. What say we tell Kinsworth and Ukrusu where we're goin' anyway. That way we can gloat when we come in with the gold."

"Let's also cover ourselves as far as we can by signing on with a caravan until we reach the edge of the Waste."

"Where are we gettin' the coin for this jaunt, moneybags? I'm not broke yet, but I'm a tad short."

"Horserunner left me some cash that I found only today. Now, where could we get a couple of steppe ponies . . . ?"

• 4 •

They had been five days on the road with the caravan of Manthin of Allaway. The time had passed without any incident of note; in fact, the two young men were getting bored. They could have ridden the distance in much less time, but the well-armed caravan was safer against the robbers who haunted the forests east of Barrow. A pair of riders, even though armed and alert, might have made too good a target for the predatory bands that the Holy Knights had driven down out of the mountains decades before. No one lived along the caravan route for the three hundred kilometers between Barrow and the Mad King Mountains—no one that a traveler wanted to meet, that is. The one exception was the Holy Knight outpost that the caravan had left behind two mornings before.

The forest was gradually failing as they trekked eastward into the continent's center, away from the rains along the coasts. Kilometers ahead, through the thinning trees, the different green of the Waste was coming into view. It lacked the honest green-brown color of summer grassland. Its ground cover was weeds and bushes, junk growth that had replaced the grass. Even at a distance, brown scars showed where the grasses' successors had not successfully held the soil against erosion. The whole was a maze of gullies and irregular growth, like the back of some great, green dog with a bad case of mange.

Fleetfox was again glad that he had not allowed the Knight and his heavier steed to accompany them. The land ahead looked like a prime place to break a horse's leg, and every bite of grazing for their mounts would be suspect. Weeds sometimes protected themselves from being eaten by being toxic; grass thrived on grazing because its body was largely underground. Ponies, whose origins had been in the Grazelands north of the Dragonsback Mountains, could eat almost anything a goat could, were seldom fooled by an inedible plant, and could use their shorter legs to negotiate the gullies of the Waste. The Knight's charger, used to both good fodder and flat ground, wouldn't have lasted a week.

The pair of adventurers talked the situation over. They had already decided to break away from the train of the caravan when there was a disturbance at the rear of the column. Manthin's son came riding along the file of wagons and riders, calling for armed men to investigate some strangers approaching the rear of the caravan. Fleetfox and Delgen hitched their packhorse to the rear of the nearest wagon and rode west with the group the caravan master's son had gathered.

Under Manthin's direction, they formed a crescent of riders that blocked the strangers from the train and half surrounded them. All the stir was for nothing, however, as the four newcomers simply wanted to join the caravan. Their leader gave his name as Galen Mountainson; the four were carrying the census of the province of Barrow to the capital, the caravan's ultimate destination.

The protective collection of horsemen from the train broke up and returned to their positions. Only then did Fleetfox notice the rigidity of his friend's features.

"What ails you, Delgen?"

" 'Tis time and for sure that we left this band of fools!"

"I agree, but what has you acting like this?"

"Just ride. I'll tell you when we're well away." Delgen's pony grunted as he spurred it.

Fleetfox gathered up the reins of the packhorse and followed more leisurely. He had told the caravan master already that they were leaving the train that day. When they reached a hillock north of the column, Delgen reined in. He spat decisively toward the distant line.

"What is eating you, Delgen?"

"That man, the one who called himself Galen Mountainson, was Galen McTarn!"

"So? I thought you said—"

"Never mind what I said. The man is the son of a renegade, a traitor to his own folk. I can't help it if he's of my blood! I'd be honor bound to fight him if we met face-to-face. I have no personal quarrel with him, and you and me have business to the north." He swung his pony away from the train and trotted away.

Fleetfox mulled over the information for a moment. He would never embarrass his friend by saying so, but from what he had heard, Galen McTarn was a noted professional fighter and man catcher. Delgen would probably have had his guts spilled in a fair fight. Highlander beliefs could be silly at times, Fleetfox thought as he turned to ride toward a deadly stronghold from which no explorer had ever returned, on the basis of a vision he had seen through a colored card.

• 5 •

Not only was it farther north to the Pinnacle than it had been to the eastern mountains, there was no well-scouted caravan road to follow. Any animal trail they chose, played out quickly. Game had come back to the Waste, but it was as sparse as the green growth. There were rodents and insects, and the predators that hunted them, but they were all wary. Fleetfox knocked down a ground squirrel with his sling. At the end of the first day, they had no difficulty finding a gully below the rolling surface of the land, in which to build a tiny fire. Fuel to cook the squirrel was the dried twigs of bushes that had not survived the periodic droughts. The nomadic Tellarani had built their fires of dried wisent dung, but the great herds had gone with the grass.

There was no reason at all to fear the Waste (that they knew of). The larger predators should have disappeared with the larger game, and the Waste had no known human inhabitants. Yet both Fleetfox and Delgen had had the feeling of traveling in enemy country almost from the time they left the caravan. Neither slept much after the fire guttered out.

The second day saw them started early. The ponies plodded stolidly in the midsummer heat, grabbing a mouthful of leaves to chew from any edible bush that their riders allowed them to pause near. At midmorning, Delgen spotted a distant herd of antelope. The presence of their bounding vitality encouraged both travelers, until Fleetfox pointed out that where there were antelope, there were things that pursued antelope. Any such would be likely to find horseflesh to their liking as well. They ended another dusty day early, in time to gather enough fuel for a fire that would last the night. However, the only eyes that came near their blaze were small enough to have belonged to nothing larger than a fox or a mouse-hunting cat.

If the haze had been thinner, they might occasionally have caught a glimpse of snowcapped mountains to the east. As it was, they might well have been traveling on a moth-eaten carpet of some giant, thrown carelessly on the earth and left in a green, wrinkled mess since time began. No forest or mountain broke the humid horizon as they crawled endlessly on.

In midafternoon, Fleetfox suddenly dismounted to examine something on the ground.

"By the Thousand Stars, those are wisent droppings! They're not all gone, then."

Delgen wiped the sweat from his red face. "Aye, you would be the one to make a fuss over dung. We haven't any kind of a bow to bring down something big, nor the time to cure the meat. Why not take some chips home for your collection?"

To Delgen's surprise, Fleetfox did exactly that. They rode on in silence for much of the afternoon; the Waste was a killer of conversation. Again, they gathered sticks, this time adding dried wisent chips, plentiful in the area they had entered. In the twilight, suddenly there was a chilling shriek from the darkening sky. High above them, the last of the sunlight reflected from something massively winged.

It was huge without a doubt, but the failing light and lack of perspective prevented the gaping duet of travelers from being able to tell just how large. Whatever it was, it glided off to the east and was gone.

"By the Rocks of the Thunderer, what was that thing?" Delgen was as pale as a fish's belly.

"I don't know for sure, but I'm afraid I have a good idea. I think it was a griffin."

"Eh? Wasn't that some kind of magical bird that died out a long time ago?"

"Not exactly. Horserunner told me about them; they used to be common on the Grasslands, but they didn't bother humans much. And they're not a bird. They had a hooked beak like a vulture, because they ate mostly dead wisent carcasses. They were plenty fierce enough to hunt live game, but they usually just followed the big herds and ate the ones that dropped of disease or old age. No one's heard of them in Barrow since the curse on the Grasslands. They nested back in the mountains and came out to the open to hunt."

"Then you know how big that thing was?"

"I know how big they *used* to be. Who knows what size

they are now? They had a wing span of eight meters or more. They've got four clawed legs underneath; the stories said that they could carry off a wisent yearling if they were hungry. A man, if he were gutsy enough, could have ridden on their back."

"Naahhh! Don't try to feed me that! I've seen the eagles among the peaks. They're mighty pretty when they're gliding, but let them try to take off from the ground, and they're as slow as Grandmama on a cold morning. The biggest eagle anybody ever heard of might stretch three meters across, wing tip to wing tip, and you're telling me about a flyer with wings three times the size that can take off from these opens. Naahhh!"

"It was true! They were born with a funny kind of organ under the wings that works by magic instead of natural law. Nobody knows why. Maybe the Life Giver wanted something on this Plane that could *really* fly, and to make such a thing, he had to cheat a little. When they took off, they *fell* straight upward a hundred meters or so, until they could get wing room. Anything they were holding (or a man on their back) fell with them. Once those wings got going, they could carry away about anything alive. Once in a while, when the People would find one dead, they would sell the flying organs to magicians in Barrow. A mage could make other things fly with the juice from them."

"I've no truck wi' magic. No wonder. And now, my fine Tellarani loremaster, what do *we* do to keep from becomin' the breakfast o' your griffin? And how is it that ye know so much? Anybody near one such would ha' been a meal before he could bring back the tale."

"Like I said, they didn't seem to bother humans much. Maybe it was because we walked on two legs, instead of four like their regular meals. Horserunner sang me the story of Wolf the Thief, a Tellarani who sneaked up on a griffin and ran up its tail. (They have long tails to balance against their necks.) Wolf rode a griffin—kept banging it on the head every time it turned to try to bite him. He did it more than once; he even learned to guide a griffin."

"I hate to ask, but what happened to this Wolf?"

"He tamed a huge male griffin to be his steed, but he mistakenly flew him into another male's territory. Wolf fell off while the two were fighting."

"Ugh. I'll wager he didn't have the guts to do *that* twice! Ye're still no closer to telling me what we should do."

"I don't know for sure. They may not bother us. If they do, what they'll want is the horses. Let's divide up most of the load on the packhorse between our two animals. If a griffin does go for us, we can loose the packhorse to draw him off. And let's start making camp where the sides of a ravine form an overhang. If those things still nest in the mountains, they leave early and stay late over the opens. I don't want to be either an early breakfast or a late snack."

"What—what? Ye're not goin' to try to ride one, like Wolf-the-Thief?"

"Not likely, Delgen. Now, start gathering what brush you can find. We'll try to make a lean-to tonight to hide us and the horses."

It was that same night that they heard the baying of the hunting dogs of the Waste. Listening to the distant howling gave them something to do to pass the time while not sleeping.

• 6 •

The bags under Fleetfox's eyes were deep enough to have caught rainfall, had there been any during the month of Firstharvest on the Waste. The heat baked the ground and the men on it. Water supply began to be on the minds of both travelers. They need not have worried: the game trail they were following widened and deepened, and the spoor of wisent and antelope became common. Within an hour, they sighted the water hole.

Fleetfox wanted to hold back, fearing an ambush by some meat-eater, but the eagerness of the ponies convinced him. Their senses would be better at spotting a hidden menace than those of the humans.

The mounts drank their fill, and the men topped off the water bags that would supply them later. Saving the cleanest remaining water for their own drinking, the pair of adventurers moved on, confident that by watching their horses they would be able to tell if predators were near. Unfortunately, horses were no more able to smell a griffin cruising in the thermals several hundred meters up in the sky than the humans were able to see the beast diving on them out of the sun.

There was a rush and a shriek, and the lightly loaded packhorse screamed as four sets of claws tore into its back. The momentum of the predator's strike had broken its spine as well. Fleetfox and Delgen did not have to encourage their horses to run: they were lucky to be able to pull them up half a kilometer down the game trail.

Turning their winded mounts down a steep-sided draw, the duo dismounted.

"Del, I think I had better go back—on foot. There is still too much of our stuff on the packhorse to give it up. Stay with the horses."

" 'Stay with the horses!' is it? Why, I'll—never mind. Ye're right. But 'tis your turn next time!"

A man on foot could keep a much lower profile than a mounted man. Fleetfox, sling in one hand and stabber in the other, was able to sneak to within a stone's toss of the griffin. It sat astride the downed horse, tearing huge goblets of meat out of the haunch with a beak the size of a shovel. The hairless tail stretched out two horse lengths behind it. Like a man, it hunted by sight, only with sight many times keener than a human's. The beast was aware of Fleetfox as soon as he raised his head.

Ice crept along the Tellarani's veins as he met the eyes of the great carnivore. He would make only a few bites for the griffin, if it decided to attack. Instead, it stared back with an intelligence that recognized his kind, and dismissed him. The pack strap had broken, but one end of it still lay under the horse. Fleetfox gulped. It was either wait for the griffin to finish, in which case it might change its mind about him as a meal, or walk boldly out to the horse and take the pack, in which case it might change its mind just the same.

He stood to full height and put his stabber back in its sheath. Calling on the spirits of his ancestors, whose bones lay beneath this land, he walked forward. Had Wolf-the-Thief felt the same tension in the gut when he approached the griffin he was about to mount? The question was theoretical; the griffin, blood dripping from its beak, was real. It mouthed a chunk of meat thoughtfully as it watched the Tellarani approach.

He needed two tugs to free the pack. The predator

gave him no more than passing curiosity. He backed away, slowly, for a hundred meters before he ducked and ran.

The horse proved to be the only toll they had to pay to cross the treeless expanse. Though they made camp with superlative care and watched every square centimeter of sky and land for trouble all that day and the next, they saw not so much as a hostile field mouse. By late afternoon of the following day, the spire of the Pinnacle rose out of the Waste.

It was an old volcanic spike, an outrider from the formation of the distant Mad King range. Magma had forced its way through a subsurface crack for twenty or more kilometers before it had exploded into a single cone isolated from the rest of the peaks. In later, quieter tectonic ages, the cone's surface had eroded, leaving a spire honeycombed with passages where the harder core of lava had been. A great rift had opened up one side, and later filled with soil, forming a natural entrance bay.

With two hours of sun remaining, the explorers rode once around the entire prominence, before turning into the bay.

"Did you see the three great doors that the Scallions built, Delgen?"

"Aye, and I don't see why we couldn't try one of them as well as this one on the east."

"I did a lot of asking around before we left. Fergo, the owner of the Pig's Navel, was a soldier here. He said he and some others helped loot the Scallion camp that was just south of the peak. (All trace of that is gone now. I looked.) But when the Barrow lads tried the doors, lightning came out of the very rocks and blasted them. The same thing happened on every door. The doors killed the second man who tried them just as dead as they had killed the first. Only the east door stood open. (I see that it still does.)

"Fergo said to beware of that door even more: he wasn't with the men who explored that side himself, but the survivors he talked to later said that the east way was so full of traps that they had to give up there, too. Nobody since then has been inside this place and lived to come home to brag about it. *We're* going to.

"To make sure we do, we're going to get a good night's rest here. There's more brush than usual along the base of this rock; fire will be no problem. I don't think a griffin can see us unless he flies right over and looks down this chimney."

"Aye, but the longer we're here, the more likely it is that some of the wee doggies off the Waste will smell out these horses."

"Don't I know it! We have to get finished here fast. We'll get done the quicker if we're fresh tomorrow."

"Aye."

• 7 •

The morning sun lighted the east bay of the Pinnacle. The great east door, a mate to the three facing the other cardinal directions, stood invitingly open, as it had for thirty years. Brush had grown up in the dust that had piled around its jamb. Litter, including some bones, was strewn about the entrance. A featureless hall led straight into the heart of the Pinnacle.

The tall, northeastern face of the bay had been carved with a huge outline of the sword-and-onion symbol of the Scallions. It had been marred by time with several cracks, and weeds were growing in places where loess had collected, but it was still impressive. The shadows of the previous evening had not highlighted it as the new day did.

Delgen was up, walking about and craning his neck like a tourist. The sun was at optimum angle to shine down the entry corridor. Dim, bulky shapes of furniture in some large room could just be made out at the opposite end. The floor and walls of the entry passage were clean, as if expecting visitors.

"Do we go in or what, Fleet?"

"Not so fast. Remember what Fergo said. Have you noticed how clean the floor is down that hall, though there's dirt everywhere else?"

"Aye, I take your meaning. 'Tisn't quite right. And if ye look just so, ye can see three lumpy things, that I can't make out, up on a shelf near the ceiling. Any time but morning, we would ha' missed 'em. What say we test this bloody shaft, before we step off down it?"

"Agreed. Remember the lightning: don't touch that door for any reason, even if it is standing open."

"Aye, and aye again! Let's step back a bit and chuck a rock down its throat."

"Good idea."

The stones they threw, however, had no effect. They simply bounded out of sight into the dark space at the far end.

"I'm still not happy, Del. It can't be that easy to get in, or someone would already have looted it. Look, the traps (which *have* to be there) were made for men, not thrown rocks. Even though it means going closer, let's heave a man-weight rock down the hall." Boulders of all sizes were plentiful.

Grunting, the pair of explorers tossed a fifty-kilogram stone a couple of meters into the tunnel. The first three meters of the floor obligingly collapsed before their eyes, splitting seamlessly down the center, dropping the boulder among rusty, meter-long spikes in the pit revealed below. A skull, bereft of all flesh, stared up at them from among the spears, its mandible dislocated in a silent scream of agony. There were at least two other sets of remains there as well; all the bones showed heavy gnawing, possibly by rats.

"So *that's* the trap Fergo was talkin' about! Looks like several good men tried to walk in here wi'out an invitation."

"Fergo said 'traps,' not 'trap.' That pit isn't that wide. Do you think you could jump it?"

"Sure. Easy." Delgen started forward, but Fleetfox grabbed his arm.

"The men down there were just as 'sure' when they took their last step. Dying may not have been so 'easy.' Let's try another rock."

When they launched a second, somewhat smaller boulder across the gap, its weight caused a set of hidden bars to drop behind the stone, blocking the entrance.

"Do you think you could jump across now, Del, and maybe hammer those bars apart?"

"Aye, I might. I might, but I don't think I will! And don't look so smug, Fleet. We're not five meters down that hall yet, and either one of us could have been killed twice! Makes ye wonder what jolly contraptions the Scallions (may they rot in the Nether Pits) fixed up for the rest o' the passage." He wiped the sweat from his face, not all of it from lifting rocks in the heat.

Delgen stepped away from the mouth of the entrance and leaned on the wall below the Scallions' carved symbol. "We could always dig through this rock. Or you could use one of your magics and make us a door by saying 'Open, Bloody Onion!' Whaaaa . . . !" There was a *thump*! as he fell through the door that had suddenly appeared behind him.

The entire face of rock had slid to the right, revealing a large, dusty room.

"By the Thousand Stars, Delgen, this is how the Scallions must have gotten in and out! They'd never want to take the time or chance a mistake turning off the traps on the east door. This must have been for their top men. The ordinary Scallions could no more get in the other great doors than we could. Fergo said they were stripped and tortured, looking for anything that might be a key."

"Do I have Your Lordship's leave to get up now, or would ye rather make another speech?"

"Sorry, Delgen." He helped his friend up. "And aren't those horse bones in that stall? Say, this isn't just dust in here: there's a lot of straw and dried manure."

"What—what? More for your dung collection?"

Fleetfox ignored the gibe. "This was their stable. But it's not big enough for many horses. It must have been for officers and maybe elite troopers. The wizards who led them might have used this door!"

"What wizards?"

"The Scallions were led by three black wizards. Those traps we sprung wouldn't have stayed so neatly set for thirty years without magical assistance."

"You're not encouraging me again, Fleet."

"Quit worrying! We're inside. I'll bet nobody else ever managed that!"

"Nobody that lived," Delgen added in a low voice.

"Let's get the horses inside and shut the door." Fleetfox was too excited to squelch.

"Now who's the one ready to jump the pit? Let's look around this room first," Delgen said.

Fleetfox grumbled, but agreed. There was a narrow hardwood stair on the right of the door. They had to light their lantern to check it out. The still-sturdy steps led only to a room filled with rotted fodder and harness, with a closed door on the far side. Across from the main entrance, a door led to a bunkroom with a dozen and a half sagging beds, each with its own rusty chest.

"Elite troops, like I said. Who else would rate a barracks this good?"

"Aye. Let's search the place. Maybe there's a bit o' silver in some o' those chests."

"Not so fast. You're the one that diverted me from bringing in the horses right away. We finish this room first."

Left of the door, a group of three stalls was partitioned from the rest. In the corner of one of them, the explorers found something unexpected—mud.

" 'Tis dried mud, all right," Delgen said. "An' there's some kind o' tracks in the dust here. Can ye make 'em out?"

"No, but look: they came out of the wall—no, here's the outline of a hidden door here. Want to—"

"No! Let's leave it be. That mud is old. Someone or somethin' came out there, looked around a bit, an' went back in. We shouldn't bother the wee whatever-it-is. I don't suppose ye have another of those bone-chillin' stories about the beast that made these tracks, like the one ye told me about the griffins?"

"No. I don't know any more than you do. But that had to be a 'someone': *things* don't close doors behind them. Let's check out those chests now."

The bunk room had been partially looted, and at least three men had died there. Fergo had mentioned a rumor that the Scallions inside the Pinnacle at the last had turned on each other. The crumbled bones seemed to tell the same tale; none of the bodies had even been dressed for battle when they died. Delgen, sneezing regularly in the dust he stirred up, found a dagger that he fancied and a handful of coins, but he wet on himself when he turned up a rat fully seventy centimeters long in one of the trunks. It nipped at him, before running squeaking out the door with Delgen hacking at it with his ax.

He was back quickly. "Garn! Lost it outside in the bushes. I thought first I was snake-bit when them beady, little eyes come up at me. Then, it kept comin', all covered wi' fur. No wonder all the bones we've seen have been gnawed!"

The room's real treasure was the spring that trickled into a basin in the northeast corner. The water was cool and sweet. The barracks had only one more door, which they left undisturbed for the moment.

"Let's bring the horses in here now, Del, and block the outer door. We can feed them some grain, and they'll have all the water they want. No hunting dogs will get in here. We can go on deeper inside without having to worry about them."

"Sounds like a good plan, but why doesn't it make me feel better? Do ye want to try to close the big door again? Two coppers will get ye one that all we have to say is 'Close, Bloody Onion!' "

"I don't feel like gambling right now. We need to leave it open, in case we have to leave in a hurry."

"Keep talkin'. Ye're still not makin' my insides stop flutterin' about like butterflies."

Within five minutes, they had their gear and mounts inside. "Good. Now for that other door," Fleetfox said, wishing that it weren't so plain a door. He was remembering the vision of the Five of Pentacles.

The barrier creaked, but opened fairly easily. The lantern light showed another set of bones beyond the door, half-covered by the layer of dust on the floor. Unlike the dust coating of the barracks room, the hallway dust had been tracked and stirred at some time more recently than the fall of the Scallions. Only when they had checked to be certain that any spoor was at least weeks old did the adventurers emerge, closing the exit behind them to keep the horses in. A door to the right stood partly open, showing the inner surface of a much larger portal not far beyond.

"That must be the inside of the great door on the north side of the Pinnacle. We've circled around to where it would be."

"Aye, and let's steer clear of it for now. There's another way off to the left, and it has two doors, if ye've a mind to look for a way that won't as likely be magic-trapped."

"Yes, we'll—" As Fleetfox lifted the lantern to expose the panel closing the first portal to the left, he froze.

"Fleet, what is it?" Delgen hissed.

"The door . . ."

"Aye, 'tis a door. I've seen one or two in the big city, ye know. What about it?" Delgen hefted his ax nervously.

Fleetfox leaped to stand in front of it with the light. "It's the door I saw in my vision! Something we have been seeking is behind it!"

"Aye, like a monster's den or a—*kahunk!*" Delgen sneezed loudly. "Ye've started me again. Shuffle your feet a little less. Go on, now: open it up."

Fleetfox rattled the handle. "It's locked. We're not the first to try to get in here: there are nicks all around the lock, like somebody tried to get in with a dagger. There's a couple of ax marks, too. It must be a heavy door: they haven't even made a real dent in it. Whoever tried gave up too soon, because the one who lived here must have been important. Hold the light."

Fleetfox rummaged in his belt pouches until he found a bent metal tool. "I knew it would pay off someday to have a brother-in-law who was a thief. Krovik gave me this and taught me how to use it, back when Mother was still alive. She'd have skinned us both if she'd found it." He worked the angled probe into the lock. "The lock is full of dust and rust, but this keyhole is so big I could spit through it. I think—there!" Something clanked inside the lock.

Fleetfox tried the handle. After wrenching it a few times, the handle groaned and moved downward. He took the lantern from Delgen and shouldered the reluctant door partly open, brushing up another flurry of dust as he entered.

Delgen peered over his shoulder. "I—*kahunk!*"

The spasm of the sneeze caused him to bend over—just enough so that the spiked club that had been aimed at his head took off his cap and some hair, and smashed into the doorframe instead of braining him.

"By Grandmama's Girdle, look out!" He dived through the doorway, pushing Fleetfox ahead of him.

The Tellarani had been cautious enough to enter the room with his stabber in hand, but the collision with Delgen knocked it from his grasp, to skitter somewhere into the dust under the room's bed. He dived after it, groping.

Delgen had not lost his ax. He turned to face a scaled monstrosity, like a walking crocodile. It was hampered from swinging its club again by the half-open door. Delgen had the room to maneuver; he rushed forward and brought his ax over in a vertical slash that knocked splinters from the monster's club, but did it no other harm. Suddenly the creature kicked at Delgen.

The Highlander felt a searing pain all along the inner

surface of his right leg. The thing had hooked him with a clawed foot! His leg buckled as he tried to flop backward out of reach. "Take him, Fleet! I'm down!"

Fleetfox was not prepared to "take" anyone. He couldn't find his knife! The lantern had landed left of the bed, propped at an angle in the thick dust. Thankfully, it had not gone out, but its light would only show him dying if all he could defend himself with was a ten-centimeter eating knife. The creature was in the room now.

Leaned in a corner beside the bed, a slim sword caught the light. It might be rusty enough to break on the first lunge, but Fleetfox had nothing to lose. He seized it, just as the beast closed, its club raised high to smash him.

Shouting a prayer to the Life Giver, he drove the point of his doubtful weapon into the brute's chest. It went in deeply, like a hot knife into cheese. The monster shuddered, half a dozen vital organs pierced, and collapsed in a heap, unable to complete its swing. Fleetfox had to stay out of the reach of the convulsing legs, with their claws, and the gnashing teeth.

He skirted the twitching body and hurried to Delgen. The Highlander was on his rump with his right leg straight out before him. He had both hands clamped on it above the knee, and his face was a gray. A red puddle showed beneath him.

"By the Thousand Stars, Fleet, shut the door! There may be more o' 'em!" he gritted.

Fleetfox gave the hall a cursory glance each way before complying. "It seems clear," he said as he crouched beside Delgen.

A deep gash ran from above the knee almost the length of the calf of his friend's leg. It was bleeding freely, but showed none of the squirting of a severed artery.

"Fleet, get my buryin' cloak out o' my pack."

"What? You're not dead by a long shot!"

"Who said I was, ninny? 'Tis the cleanest cloth about right now. Tear my good cloak into strips and stand me up. Grandmama would have a fit if she saw you do it!

"Now, bind it tight. Unnghh! That's it. Arraggh! That's—" He fainted.

Fleetfox caught him in time to lay him gently down, wishing for a cleaner place, but finding none. He agonized over his friend until Delgen's eyelids fluttered a few minutes later. He asked the same idiot question that friends always asked.

"Are you all right?"

"No, I'm not all right! I had my leg ripped open by a—what is that thing?"

"I don't know."

"Haven't you checked it over? What have ye been doing—walking the floor like some simp of a nobleman's daughter? Get this place searched so we can get out of here! I'll look over yon monster."

Fleetfox, startled, began a tentative search of the room's closet and bed. There was nothing of note in either. Delgen kept up a running commentary on the dead beast.

"This thing is somethin' like one o' them Dragons Grandmama used to tell me stories about. Could it be one, that lived on past its time? Nah! Look at its clothes—naught but a rawhide belt and a flint knife, and one stone strung on a cord round its neck." Delgen cut that free and put it in his pocket for later.

"Look over there, Fleet. There's a desk or dresser or some such, in yon corner. By the Thunderer, this thing may have little for a brain, but what claws and teeth! Do ye reckon that there's more of 'em about?" Delgen pulled himself fully upright using the end of the rotting bed as a prop.

Fleetfox was trying a drawer in the upright chest in the corner. "Maybe there are more, but we're not going to stay to find out. We've got to get you out of here. But . . ."

"But find what the cards told ye to find first. They don't raise many fools in the Highlands. We didn't travel all this way and near get ourselves killed to go home empty-handed, on account o' one bad scratch."

Fleetfox jerked at the front of the drawer, and it came off in his hand. "More rotten clothes!" He probed among the rags gingerly, not wishing to find a poisonous spider or a scorpion in the recesses. "Here's something." His hand had encountered two harder objects. He raked them out onto the floor. "If that bed'll hold you, check this one out." He tossed a small bag toward Delgen.

The Highlander winced with the sudden movement needed to catch the poke. His face lit up when he dumped its contents in his palm. "Now, this is more like it! Silver, a few gold pieces, and a couple of gems. I can rest like a king in my private chambers while this leg heals, and still have some left!"

"Best scale the fish after you catch it, Del. We're not in Barrow yet."

"Aye. What have ye found there?"

"Some kind of tube. It's not wood, or it would have rotted."

"Mayhap 'tis ivory. They make such in Mugambu to hold maps or important papers."

"No one in Barrow had heard of Mugambu thirty years ago, but you could be right. Ivory might come from other places than there. Yeah, I see where it can be opened. Unnngh! There!" Fleetfox tipped the cylinder toward the light. "There *is* something inside!" He shook and pried at the tube until a roll of parchment came free.

Fleetfox moved closer to both Delgen and the lantern as he unrolled the cracking scroll. "It's some kind of map! Can you read the writing on it?"

"Nah, I thought *you* could read."

"I can . . . some, but not this language." He continued to try to smooth out the curling sheet. "It covers the whole region. See, here's the Wat River, and here's the Mad Kings and the Dragonsbacks. This pointy thing must be the Pinnacle; it has a sword-and-onion beside it. There's a couple of more like that up near the Dragonsbacks, probably where they had the passes blocked to demand tribute from my people. They must have had a camp near the Great Forest, too.

"These squiggles on the Waste must be water holes, and . . . and . . . Delgen, what would you take the meaning of two crossed swords to be on a map?"

"Hmmm. Now, I'm not good at such readin'-and-writin' things, but I'd guess that to be where they fought a battle."

"And this mark?"

"Looks like a little wagon, like the ones your people travel about in. Like the ones—say, Fleet, that must have been where they battled your people!"

"That's it! This map is where the cards said my hopes would lie!" Fleetfox shifted the parchment several times in the light to get the best view. "As best as I can tell, the battle site was south-southeast of the Pinnacle, about a day and a half out." He clapped Delgen on the back.

"Ungh! If ye jar my leg again like that, ye'll be the only man in Barrow who can sit on his own shoulders! Now, pick up that sword ye found, and let's be out o' this cavern like the wind out o' the bowels of the earth!"

"I want to check the rest of the drawers and get my knife back."

"Well enough. 'Tis probably still daylight outside, but don't dawdle. I'll need a bit o' help gettin' back to the horses, and I'm goin' t' make a lot of faces while we ride. Once in a while I may mention things a right-talkin' man ought not, but ride we will!"

• 8 •

The great stone door of the Pinnacle had slid shut behind them on the same kind of "Close . . ." command that had opened it. Ride they did, though slowly, scouting the terrain and the sky. Delgen's prophecy about his behavior held true. As the wounded leg stiffened, he also became slightly feverish. He was insistent on not receiving special treatment, but he didn't complain too loudly when they made camp early. Fleetfox gathered enough brush for a lasting campfire. He staked the horses out under an overhanging clay bank, behind both the men and the fire.

Delgen got as much special pleasure out of counting the treasure they had found as Fleetfox did in poring over his map. The cash from the pouch would pay for the journey costs, and more. Delgen was talking about going back to the Highlands a rich man, though his past inclination had been to spend whatever came into his pocket. He was still ill and pale, but Fleetfox had found some herbs among the Waste weeds that eased the pain of his injury and drew out infection, thanks to the eidetic memories of Tellarani lore that Horserunner had instilled in him.

The concentration of the seer helped Fleetfox puzzle out the map, though he tried no card reading. Neither had he examined the sword that he had taken from the Pinnacle. It was simply thrust through the pack behind him in the scabbard that he had found under the bed when retrieving his stabber.

He was sure he had identified Barrow, Holy Knight

Pass, and the caravan road that ran between them on the Scallions' map. The pair of travelers were on the right path to discover the monument that the raiders had built to commemorate their victory over the Tellarani. Later, the same route would intersect the caravan road.

The second day was much like the first. Delgen's leg had swollen, even with a new dressing and herb treatment, but his fever was low and intermittent. Still, he looked drained. By day's end, after trying to watch every direction, including up, Fleetfox was in little better shape. Delgen helped more with camp chores, limping as he gathered fuel, but both were exhausted when night fell.

Fleetfox's last words before falling asleep were, "It has to be close ahead."

· 9 ·

It had been a true prophecy. A quiet night, followed by an hour's journey, brought the ring of boulders into view on the travelers' left. From a distance, they were just another rock outcropping thrust up through the Waste. Closer, Fleetfox identified them from the vision of the crystal card. He rode around the circle while Delgen rested on his grazing pony. From the stone representing the top of the onion, he counted three stones west. Waving to Delgen to come up, he dismounted and circled the boulder.

As Delgen reined in, Fleetfox found that a badger had excavated where no Scallion had thought to. The burrow it had dug a decade before must have pierced the hidden tunnel below. Runoff water had scoured the shaft until it was almost as wide as a man's body. Fleetfox went down on his hands and knees, scraping away loose soil and debris. Delgen fetched him the lantern, but did not offer to dig: this was the end point of the Tellarani's quest. Even a friend would have been in the way.

Delgen leaned on the boulder and stared out across the treeless expanse. His comrade hacked and heaved at the opening, making it constantly wider. Fleetfox was too intent to notice the dirt that his sweat was plastering to his body. After an hour of digging, only his legs showed as he crept in further and further, with the lantern ahead. He was retreating once again when trouble appeared.

"Fleet! Fleet!" Delgen hissed. "We have company!"

The stained adventurer pulled himself to his feet in time to see three riders pop out of a draw not three hundred meters away. They weren't moving fast initially. "Quick! We have to get the ponies under cover. They can't see where I was digging!"

"Too late, lad. They've spotted us. Let's move toward the outside of the circle of rocks. Maybe we can bluff them into staying on that side."

The riders, however, were not to be bluffed. One pulled a bow, and the other two drew sabers. They spurred their horses, with aggressive intentions clear. Fleetfox recognized them as the baying dogs he had seen on the Moon card.

"Those are enemies, Delgen. Fight like you never have before!" Following his own advice, Fleetfox pulled his stabber with his right and tugged his sling from his belt with his left.

"Aye, ye have the right of it, Fleet. They're not ridin' up to parley. A bit closer and I'm going to show yon bowman that he shouldn't ride too close to a Highlander for an easy shot. There!" Delgen sent his ax spinning through the air, snapping the top off the charging rider's bow and taking him full in the face.

The roughly clad bowman went backward off his mount like a sack of grain and lay still. Since he had been the rearmost, fumbling to nock an arrow, the others didn't notice his fall. Delgen had overbalanced himself by his throw and fallen forward, so that the attacker bearing down on him missed the slice he aimed at the Highlander and was carried past by his momentum. Trying to rein in, he spun his pony too close to the boulder behind Delgen. His normally surefooted mount stepped on a loose stone in the grass and stumbled. The wild-eyed aggressor flipped from the saddle into the standing stone, with a sickening crunch. He, too, lay still.

Fleetfox had no time to worry about Delgen's fate. The leading horseman swung his saber down at the Tellarani's head. Fleetfox blocked with his stabber. Sparks flew, and the young explorer felt the shock all the way up his arm. The rider pivoted his mount, for another slash, but held off when he realized that he was now one against two. Spurring so hard that his pony screamed, he shot back the way the trio had come.

"Stop him, Fleet!" Delgen called, flinging a stone after their retreating enemy. "He'll call down more on us!"

As his friend's throw fell short, Fleetfox fitted the lead ball that he had palmed into his sling's pocket. It sang around his head: one, two, three times. Throw! Like a bumblebee humming a death song, the lead ball buzzed through the air. The horseman lurched and dropped his saber, but rode on.

"By the Thousand Stars, he's got away! We've trouble now!"

"No, look!"

The distant rider had slumped when hit. He now sagged from the saddle. His loose limbs caught in the stirrup briefly, and his horse dragged him for a few meters before stopping. The pony snorted a few times before putting its nose into a tuft of weeds to graze.

"Del . . . Del, we just killed three men."

"Aye, it don't make the stomach easy. But they would have killed us. Come to that, let's make sure they're dead."

• 10 •

Indeed, the three had passed their spirits beyond Elsewhen. The bowman would have died from the hit with the ax eventually, but he had broken his neck in the fall from his horse. The neck and some of the ribs had also given way in the man who had collided with the boulder. The most distant enemy had been hit high between the shoulder blades by the missile from the sling. A couple of vertebrae were probably smashed, stopping his heart. He was otherwise unmarked.

Their war ponies had been well trained enough to stop a few steps after the reins had been dropped. The three men might well have been brothers, so alike were they. Blond and stocky, with tanned faces and slightly slanted eyes, all had been dressed in leather, furs, and heavy cloth jerkins and trousers. The riders had been sweating heavily in the Waste's summer heat, and now they stank of ancient perspiration and loosened bowels. They yielded no treasure to Delgen's searching fingers. The pony of the last rider to fall carried maps and mapping gear, in addition to trail rations and a water skin.

The maps showed the Pinnacle and the large water hole to the west, where the griffin had attacked Delgen and Fleetfox. There were only sketchy details marked in north of the Pinnacle, and south of their position was blank. "This was meant to become part of a bigger map," Fleetfox calculated aloud. "These were scouts."

"Makes sense, but who were they scouting for? And who's got the bigger map? 'Tis not on these lads. And what do we do wi' 'em? My leg is paining me again, but best to figure this out right the first time. I fear there's more where these came from, and with just as bad manners!"

"Del, if you were scouting the Waste from the north for the first time, you'd send good trackers. Right? We have to get rid of these bodies in such a way that anyone who misses them will have trouble connecting them to our trail. I'd bury them, but no grave that we'd have time to dig would fool a good tracker for long. I do want to try to hide the hole under the boulder, though, before we run."

"What did ye find down there?"

"I got in far enough to hold the lantern into the main tunnel. It's big enough to walk down easily, as far as I could see down it. We can't got that way now. The ponies wouldn't fit."

"Ye mean *I* can't go that way, not wi' this leg, an' ye won't leave me, no matter your heart yearns to go down that tunnel. I'll remember that, Fleet, when we come back to snitch the rest o' the gold from the Pinnacle. Ye'll not go down your tunnel alone, not while Delgen McTarn draws breath!"

Fleetfox silently embraced his friend, glad he still had the sharp-tongued Highlander beside him. "Now, we have some bodies to get rid of and a hole to fill. They came from the west; let's drape 'em across their ponies and shoo 'em off to the east."

"Aye. But I believe I'll sit for a bit and fill in your hole." He staggered around the boulder, his face pale. "I got a fairly good sword off the one that hit the rock," his muffled voice called. "See if it's better than the one ye packed out o' the Pinnacle. The metal on the other two was too old and badly nicked to be worth takin' to

Barrow, though I want one for a spare, in case I have to throw my ax again."

When he had finished heaving the last body onto a skittish pony, Fleetfox made sure the reins weren't dragging before he used the flat of the captured saber to chase the mounts off in three generally easterly directions. It seemed to be a pretty good blade, as Delgen had said. He pulled the saber looted from the Pinnacle from the pack behind his pony's saddle. He held the two light swords next to each other for comparison.

Fleetfox's eyes widened. The dead man's saber fell from his hand unnoticed as he gave the plundered blade his full attention. He walked slowly toward where Delgen was working. "Del," he said, "Del, look at this!"

"Eh?" Delgen looked up from shoveling a double handful of dirt down the enlarged badger hole.

"This is no Scallion sword, Del. See the markings on the blade."

"Thought you couldn't read Scallion markings."

"I said, this is no Scallion blade. These are Tellarani markings! Del, I think that this is the Saber of Sarri!"

"What's a 'sorry'?"

"Not 'sorry'—Sarri! The most famous Tellarani warrior who ever lived! He killed monsters and fought off bands of raiders single-handed with his magic sword. The symbols are old, but not too different from what Horse-runner taught me, and it hasn't rusted at all. I thought I hit a soft spot when I stabbed the monster in the Pinnacle, but it was the sword all the time! I never looked at it until now."

"What's a Tellarani sword doing in the Pinnacle?"

"It must have been captured in the final battle and gone to the Scallion whose room we looted. I said that he had to be an important man. The sword should have gone to Sarri's grandson, whose name I never heard, instead of to his son."

"Why was that?"

"Wolf-the-Thief was Sarri's only son."

"Oh."

"Beware, Scallions," Fleetfox shouted, swinging the saber around his head, "a warrior of the People has returned!"

"It's a little late for them to hear ye, don't ye think?"

"Don't ask me how I know, Del, but the men we killed were Scallions in every way but the name. Now, I'll get some brush to cover the hole. We've got to hit it for the south." He walked away, fondling his new find.

• 11 •

Less than half the day remained. They struck southwest, looking for large game trails in which to lose their spoor. Night came on too quickly, with the feeling of still being in enemy country. Until they left the Waste behind, that feeling would persist. Squeezing an extra half hour out of their mounts and themselves, they finally turned up a narrow draw off a larger ravine. After rounding a couple of bends, Fleetfox dismounted and went back to brush out their trail. Camp was a dugout in the bank of the draw, without a fire.

The precautions were immediately necessary. At full dark, Delgen spotted the glow of what must be a large campfire—in the main ravine they had just exited. Crawling along the top of the bank, Fleetfox crept back along their trail. In the broad floor of the ravine, at least fifteen hard-faced horsemen had set up camp, right across from the draw holding the explorers. Another kilometer away, the fire's glow would have been invisible. He retreated to confer with Delgen.

"Are we trapped in here?" the Highlander asked in a low voice.

"No. These ponies can scramble out of here easily further up, and that's just what we should do!"

"Wait a bit, Fleet. Did they have a guard at the mouth of this draw?"

"No. As best as I could tell, they only had one watcher out, on the top of the opposite bank. They seem confident that they won't run into any more fools out in the Waste. Nobody lives in this country."

"Now, might'n they not be talkin' about the three that won't be comin' back? Maybe we can overhear which way they're going and go the other way. There's no moon tonight. We could sneak down to the end of the draw and listen in."

"Hmmm. Are you up to it?"

"Aye. Ye were planning to have me ride a pony out of here in the dark. 'Tis a little late to worry about my state of health. Let's go."

It was slow going, but fairly easy. Where the draw ended, there were several crevices to hide in. One of the foreign scouts, probably the leader, was lecturing the others loudly.

"I can't understand his language," Fleetfox whispered.

" 'Tis a bit like the old Highlander dialect. Hush, now, or I won't be able to figure it out either." Delgen listened raptly for a few minutes.

"He's right upset about the three who didn't show up. Promises them some painful punishments for being lax. He's wavin' a map about; must be that bigger map ye guessed about. Now he's lecturin' them about their duty." Delgen paused to listen again.

"Some lad called the Mad King will be right unhappy, he says, if they come back with less than a full map of the Waste. When the army comes this way next spring, they're goin' to want to know where every water hole and trail is. Now, wouldn't Bartello Bancartin and the Barrowmen be interested to hear that? Shhh! One of them is coming this way!"

One of the scouts meandered over to the draw and relieved himself against the bank, not two meters from the crack that held Delgen and Fleetfox. Blinded by the fire's glow, he walked slowly back, stretching.

"Whoo! I didn't know a man could hold his breath that long. An' get your knee out of my back. Fleet, we've heard enough. Let's get out of here before another one gets the urge."

"Yes, indeed!"

Delgen was limping worse, but they were unable to check the leg in the dark. Fleetfox led both ponies out of the top of the draw before helping Delgen up. With the horses linked and the Highlander riding, Fleetfox led them through the black Waste. The stars were bright, but not really enough for human vision. Using the fire's glow as a negative beacon, they blundered along for over a kilometer until they could no longer see it. Only the ponies shying away kept Fleetfox from stepping off into a deep ravine. The weary adventurers stole what sleep they could, thankful that no hungry predators discovered the horses, until false dawn paled the sky enough to travel.

Delgen was haggard, but uncomplaining. The wound in his leg had stabilized into a swollen, reddened seam that leaked pus in only a few places. It would heal, given time, but they had none to give.

"As I figure it, Del, those men are the scouts for an army that is coming down on Barrow next spring, the way the Scallions did over thirty years ago. They are *not* good folk; we have to warn the Prince. I don't know how he'll take it: the Mad King is a children's story in Barrow, something that a mother would use to scare a naughty kid. We're going to have to convince him that this is for real.

"I'll bet the three that jumped us had orders to kill anyone they came across, if there were few, or alert the main body if there were many. There may be three or four bunches working between the mountains and the forest; any riders we see, we run from!"

"Agreed." Delgen was silent more of the time now, with his teeth gritted against pain.

"Let's cut southwest toward the forests. They're not safe places to travel either, but we *know* things aren't safe out here. We'll put a fresh dressing on that leg tonight."

• **12** •

For two days they pushed hard, without difficulty, though Delgen looked like death-on-horseback. Fleetfox wore himself out watching, not just for ambush by meat-eaters, but also for his friend to pass the point of maximum endurance. He also scanned the horizon for any suspicious cloud of dust. Twice they dodged what were probably small wisent herds. Near noon of the day they should have cut through a corner of the forest toward the caravan road, danger appeared.

A stray shower had wet down the area they were crossing. No dust gave away the cluster of ten riders who surged up from behind a roll in the Waste, west of Delgen and Fleetfox. Half a kilometer away, they pointed out the duo immediately, and they were between the fugitives and the forest. South, toward the caravan road, was the only option open, though it meant staying within sight of the enemy.

The fugitives gained at first; the scouts had probably not been expecting such an immediate flight. The pursuers knew their business, however. Instead of angling toward the fleeing pair, they turned at a shallower angle to keep between the sheltering forest and their prey. Both sets of horses were similar and had been ridden for many days. Relative distance separating the hunters and the quarry changed little at first, but then it began to diminish slowly. Delgen's mount was flagging, and he was unable to get more from it. In fact, he was holding himself in the saddle with difficulty.

It was a long ride to overhaul the Barrowmen. An hour before sundown, Fleetfox and Delgen galloped out onto the rutted caravan route and turned west. Their enemies closed fast, able to cut directly across to the track. They poured onto the road only a bowshot behind the fugitives. One or two arrows whistled overhead, but the speed of the chase was too rapid to aim a bow properly. Still, the gap closed.

"Fleet! Fleet! Look for a place to make a stand. I can't go on!" Delgen yelled.

There was no use to argue with the truth. "That cluster of rocks: two hundred meters more, and we turn and fight. Look out!"

An enormous horse at full charge had rocketed between them from the other direction. They caught only a flash of armor from the man riding it, and the arc of a great sword swinging up to the ready. At that second an arrow sank into Fleetfox's mount just behind the saddle. It screamed and bucked; he was only just able to jump free as it went down, bawling, with the front legs pawing but the rear legs paralyzed.

Fleetfox jerked the Saber of Sarri from its scabbard before the horse could roll over and snap it. As his hand closed on the hilt, there was a series of sounds behind him that a butcher's wagon might have made crashing into a hog pen: meaty thuds, screaming animal bleats, and the clash of metal.

Fleetfox looked down the road to see the armored stranger pull up, having carved his way through the pack of lighter riders. Two ponies were down and kicking, though their riders were on their feet with weapons drawn. Two others of the pursuers lay still on the roadway.

"Fleet! Wake up! Help me off this bloody pony! There are still eight of 'em wantin' our hides."

Fleetfox ran to comply. He and Delgen moved into the rocks, looking for a corner to put their backs against. Their unknown ally came pounding up, but his mount was limping from a sword cut on its shoulder. The square-shouldered rider swung down and swatted his steed with the flat of his great sword. As it trotted away, he raised the grilled visor that had protected his face.

"Where are you, friends?"

"By the Thousand Stars, Fleet, 'tis Beefy Bill! Up here, Knight! Look out; they'll be on ye in a second."

The big man climbed quickly to their hastily chosen fort among the boulders. He was puffing. "I got two of their bowmen going through, and a swordsman coming back, but they've lamed Lightning. We'll have to hold them off here."

"Well met, Aldamar," Fleetfox said, frowning. "You're the man of war: what chance have we?"

"Well met, Fleetfox. Delgen. We have some chance, for they'll have to dismount to come at us. On the other hand, there are more of them than us. I didn't get every man with a bow either." As if on cue, an arrow ricocheted off the rock above them. "Well, that tells that. If we stick our heads up too much, we get a bolt through the eye. Meanwhile, the rest close in until they can rush us."

Fleetfox tried two abortive casts with his sling at the loose group of attackers who were organizing below, but both times an arrow flew so close that his aim was spoiled. A couple of the enemy peeled off to try to flank the defenders' position. It seemed to be secure from either side, but a determined attacker might scramble over the top of the boulder behind them.

The rush came. Five men in furs and leather swarmed up the small slope and around the rocks. Because of the cramped corner, only three could come against the defense at once. Delgen's ax blocked the first slash by the snarling man in front of him, and the Highlander rapped him across the side of the head with the ax handle on the counterstroke. He looked pleased—until an arrow took him through the biceps of his right arm. He dropped the ax and fell back.

Fleetfox was fighting saber on saber against a second enemy, but Sarri's sword made him the swordsman he had never been before. He swept the blade in a complex loop that ended in his opponent's throat. He never saw the rock that took him in the back of the head, putting out his lights for the rest of the fight.

The lighter swords of the scouts had never been meant to go up directly against a sword like Avenger, with a strong, well-trained man behind it. Aldamar smashed through the first blade and took out the man swinging it. Out of the corner of his eye, he saw Delgen hit, and then Fleetfox. He stepped back against the boulder's face and stabbed straight up over his head, with both arms extended as far as they would reach.

The scout, whose stone had knocked Fleetfox down, screamed as the blade went into his crotch. He flopped forward, falling on the group in front of Aldamar. His fall deflected the blade that had been aimed at the Knight's throat, though it still tore into Aldamar's thigh. The saber's owner shrieked as Delgen hamstrung him with his plundered saber. The two wounded men began wrestling feebly on the ground. Aldamar was dragging his leg as he was beset by the three remaining scouts, like a bear circled by hounds, when the most beautiful music on the Plane reached his ears.

· 13 ·

"Why didn't ye tell us, ye great lout, that ye had sent for help from the Holy Knight outpost?" Delgen propped his bandaged leg up on a cushion and tried to ease the sling on his right arm into a more comfortable position. "That trumpet call was a surprise to everybody."

"It never came up. Besides, you might not have fought hard enough to save any of us if you depended on help that might or might not come. I've been living at the outpost for a few days, ever since the civil war in Barrow."

"What civil war? Ooooh!" Fleetfox had moved his broken head a little too quickly.

"Two days after you left, the Prince is supposed to have gotten proof that some of the old nobles were set to overthrow him. He squashed many of them, but enough got word in time that they put up a pretty good fight. Several bunches got away to the west or fled north to the forests. I had my choice: either join the loyal army of Barrow, or sell myself as a mercenary to one of the nobles—or get out of town. I figured that the Knights would keep order in the region until it's settled who's to be on the throne; so, I came out here.''

"Ye're going to join the Knights again, then?" Delgen asked.

"No. I don't think so. I like being *with* the Knights, but not *in* the Knights, if you take my meaning. They let me take out some of their green cavalry on road patrol: the officers were glad for the help, and I was uneasy about you two. I don't know why. I had two lads with me, with no more whiskers between them than there are feathers in a turtle's nest, when I got this . . . urge to come after you. I sent the lads back for help, and they did their job, the Life Giver be praised!'' He eased his bandaged thigh to the right using his large hands. "The fighting did me good; it's been too peaceful around Barrow for too long.''

"Aldamar, my friend, let's enjoy our stay in this out-post while we can.'' Delgen smirked. "When the Prince hears what we have to tell him and sees the papers we took off those scouts, he'll stop chasin' nobles soon enough. And you, my lad, will be wishin' peace was back, come next spring!''

Fleetfox groaned as he nodded. His quest to find the lost ones of the People would be delayed by a war against the brothers of the Scallions. He was depressed again, but this time he knew why.

Interchapter

I am myself depressed. The peace of this city has been shattered, and will be disrupted again when Fleetfox arrives with his news. That alone would not bother me: the Barrowmen are tougher than they appear. They would win a defensive war, given equal numbers, but not against the Mad King himself.

The Mad King—a tale to frighten children: it has certainly frightened me! He is a Master of the same grade as myself. With him at the fore, Barrow's army would be so much chaff. I may have to fight him face-to-face. Would it be a draw, as my battle with Fraximon almost was? I don't know.

What I do know is his Secret, which is no secret at all among the Masters of the Mysteries: the Mad King *cannot* die. He was cursed by another Master, whom he overcame in a struggle for powers that humans may not have business possessing. Though I am strong in the Mysteries, perhaps the strongest now, I can die. He cannot, and it has driven him mad.

It has been a long, long time since he has meddled in the affairs of mortals, except for the kingdom of berserkers that he rules beyond the mountains. They are nearly as insane as he is, though they are hardened warriors without peer. Perhaps he is reaching out to control all this Plane, to make all men in it as mad as himself.

How pious of me to condemn him! Have I not also used humans as puppets? Aldamar felt "uneasy" because I sent him that feeling. His "urge" to rush to Fleetfox and Delgen's aid was not his, but mine. From my meddling, Barrow will fight a long war instead of experiencing a quick conquest, but they would have been ruled by a madman of unchallengeable power had I not interfered.

Have I learned anything? I hope so. I will use my powers from this day as a father does for children who are at the borderline of being adults. Let them step out

on their own. Let them misstep and stumble; I will slap
my own hands away and let them get up alone. How will
they grow else? But when they are about to fall into the
fire, my hand will steady them. They must think that they
saved themselves.

I end this work now. I am not sure that next summer
will see me living to write any more. I will make several
copies and hide them various places about the Planes.
One, I will launch across Elsewhen. Perhaps others can
learn from the lives I have described, and from my own
blundering about in them.

Because of that possibility, I will attach one more
section of appendices. Those who read may not be as
familiar with Barrow as I am. May the true Life Giver
bless the reader. I close.

                                        The Old Man

Appendices

FIRST APPENDIX

Barrow's Calendar System

Month's name	Corresponds to . . .
Earlywinter	Dec. 22–Jan. 17
The Cold	Jan. 18–Feb. 14
The Breaking (of the Cold)	Feb. 15–Mar. 14
The Winds (of Change)	Mar. 15–Apr. 11
The Planting	Apr. 12–May 9
The Greening	May 10–June 6
Firstharvest or	
(The First Month of Heat)	June 7–July 4
The (Second Month of) Heat	July 5–Aug. 3
Browngrass	Aug. 4–Aug. 31
The Dry	Sept. 1–Sept. 28
The (Month of) Rains	Sept. 29–Oct. 26
Frost	Oct. 27–Nov. 23
Yearend	Nov. 24–Dec. 20
Barrow's Day	Dec. 21

SECOND APPENDIX

Timetable of Events

Event	Year by Saikhandian calendar
Founding of Saikhandian Empire	1
Opening of Holy Knight Pass	380
Bancartin family comes to power in Barrow	391
Bancartins make Barrow part of Saikhandian Empire	392
Mugambu enters Saikhandian Empire	398
The Scallion Wars	402–04
Ichan established as garrison for trade outpost	411
The Old Prince (Garro Bancartin) dies	428
Coup in Mugambu; Mugambese refugees arrive in Barrow (fall; the Dry)	429
The events of "Secrets of the Teaching Master" (fall; the Rains)	430
The events of "Every Dog" at the winter solstice	430–31
The telling of the tale "Secrets of the Teaching Master" by Jessup (late spring; the Greening)	431
The events of "Loose Ends" (late spring; the Greening)	431
The events of "A Debutante in Barrow" (spring and summer)	431
The events of "The Johnny-Straights" (late spring; the Greening)	431
The Barrow Drug War	431–32
The events of "Barrow White" (early spring; the Planting)	432
The events of "Mark's Teeth" (midsummer; Firstharvest)	432
The events of "A Secret Not Sought After" (midsummer; Firstharvest)	432

THIRD APPENDIX

Geography of the Barrow Region

Barrow is the only major city in the southwest corner of a
large continent, on a planet that is the central feature of
the Thousand Stars Plane. The continent is nameless
because of the general ignorance of the existence of more
than one such landmass. It lies at the first intersection of
the Wat River. Above it, the Wat and the Little Wat are
swift and difficult to ford. The river formed along a rift
where the continental rocks had risen to the east and
subsided to the west. Much of the east bank is bluffs;
much of the west bank is low-lying and swampy. Although rainfall is plentiful, there are no other important
rivers in this quadrant of the continent. West of Barrow,
streams flowing toward the ocean sink into a band of
porous rock and form the swamps that border the entire
southwest corner of the continent.

East of Barrow, rainfall diminishes, and deciduous forest gives way to grassland. Only the higher reaches of the
Mad King Mountains, that cut Barrow off from the east
portion of the continent, are as well watered. Precipita-
tion there is in the form of heavy snows that support
coniferous forest. Much of the grassland in that eastern
region has been blighted by human magical action to
form a ruined area called the Waste.

Northeast of Barrow are large areas of forest wilderness, once occupied, but now overgrown. Farther in that
direction, lie mountains that are effectively impassable,
where the Dragonsback and Mad King ranges merge. In
the Waste short of the mountains, a single volcanic spire,
the Pinnacle, figures prominently in Barrow's history.
North of the city lies heavy forest all the way to the
Dragonsback Mountains. Many passes through the Dragonsbacks lead to the grassy Grazelands to the north.
Only fragments of the Grasslands south of the mountains
escaped the curse of the Waste.

Northwest, the Dragonsbacks extend to the sea. On

their far side lies the city of Svernig, in another major
river valley. Not far from Svernig, there is another continent, unknown in Barrow. On the southern side of the
mountains is Ichan, the only other city of consequence in
this part of the continent, an Imperial outpost on the
trade route to Svernig. Ichan is the end point of the
Imperial Caravan Route from far Sai-khand.

West of Barrow, the country is flat and well suited for
agriculture, with only a slight roll to the land. All its
streams are small. All the western and southwestern shores
of the continent are too swampy to form harbors. The
west coast is a dangerous lee shore, and the ocean beyond
(the Sea of Storms) is poorly explored and subject to
unpredictable weather.

The city of Barrow itself straddles the Wat River. The
northeast quarter is separated from the rest by the broad
avenue of Caravan Way, the original trade route to the
Wat fords. Once mostly hills and bluffs, the north area
has been filled with the dwellings of the rich—merchants,
high priests, and officers. The East Gate into this quarter
is the entrance of the Great East Road that becomes
Caravan Way. The North Gate opens onto the alternate
route along the river bluffs that runs north eighty kilometers before crossing the Wat Valley and rejoining the
Caravan Route.

Along Caravan Way are businesses of quality and major temples. At the riverbank on its north side is the
palace and citadel of the ruler of Barrow. On the south
side are the docks of the Imperial Navy and the better
warehouses. The avenue continues west across the New
Wat Bridge to a built-up area of animal pens and warehouses where the northwest Caravan Route resumes at
the bridgehead. That quarter has been too recently added
to contain a diversity of businesses. Its egress is called the
Farm Gate.

The southwest of the city, west of the river, overlaps the
wall and borders on the swamps. It was once prosperous,
after the opening of the Old Wat Bridge, but with the debut
of the newer bridge upstream, traffic no longer had to divert
through the south end of the city. The inflated economy
west of the old bridge collapsed, and the area decayed into
one of the worst slums anywhere, the Slews. Slews-Outside-the-Walls is reached by way of the Swamp Gate.

The Old Wat Bridge is in good repair; it was sturdily built, for caravan traffic. It is high enough for seagoing vessels to sail under, since no other harbor of note exists along the coast for five-hundred kilometers in either direction. Its eastern end is in Upcruster Town. The Town makes up most of Barrow's south side. Some past, high-browed visitor from Sai-khand named it by a chance remark: "This must be the upper crust of your slums." It was a title designed to stick.

Instead of collapsing economically and spiritually as the Slews did, the Town tightened its belt and made do. In its bazaar can be found any merchandise for sale anywhere on the Plane, except pleasure drugs; those are kept prudishly west of the river. Its residents are tough and free-wheeling: always on the way up; always a step away from the slide down.

A new quarter is being added to the southeast of the city to house the substantial Mugambese minority, only recently arrived in Barrow. The wall for that quarter is still under construction. All the city is walled. Laws require three wagon widths clear on the inside and a long bowshot cleared on the outside. Enforcement is lax; there hasn't been a war in Barrow in over thirty years.

Creative and geological forces shaped the lands around Barrow. People, circumstance, and economy placed the city there. The latter are much more likely to change than the former.

FOURTH APPENDIX

Social and Economic History of Barrow

Light-skinned human invaders first occupied the Barrow area centuries ago. Entering the region unopposed, probably from the other side of the Dragonsback Mountains, they found only vague traces of the Dragons and the Elves, both of whom had undoubtedly occupied the region in the far past. The area was so well suited for farming and the invaders were of such a nonbelligerent nature that prosperous, seldom-interrupted peace has been the general condition from the beginning of its human history. Heavy deciduous forest extended from the western coast to the Grasslands, near the spur of Mad King Mountains that forms the region's natural eastern boundary, a distance of many hundreds of kilometers. Once the trees were removed, almost any plot of the rich, well-watered land would grow food.

There was some jockeying among ku-traks (earls) who controlled various farming communities, that still continues. However, the earls and their peoples have long settled into traditional relationships, bonded and bound by the Codes, a poetic set of civil laws that has grown up over the centuries. Four generations ago, a new, rich market for the region's potential agricultural surplus opened up when regular trade was established by sea with the Saikhandian Empire, in the Arpago Basin, several hundred kilometers around the coastline to the east. There was some vicious in-fighting as various families in the region grabbed for supremacy. Most of the ku-traks remained neutral, as long as their personal fiefdoms were not threatened. One class of nobles, the val-nor-loks (barons) was decimated and another, the val-traks (dukes) was completely exterminated from the region. Only the victorious Bancartin family retained their status. They have ruled since, taking the title Kal-trak (grand duke) of Barrow. Those wars of succession are now generally forgotten except by certain of the nonvictorious noble families.

Barrow, already established as a prosperous town where the caravan route crossed the Wat River, became the region's capital, since it was also the seaport through which even more wealth flowed into the region. The bustling prosperity of the city was diverted only once in recent history. A small, heterogeneous army, from somewhere on the other (unknown) side of the Mad King Mountains, appeared without warning over two hundred kilometers northeast of the town. They set up shop in an isolated volcanic spire called the Pinnacle that stood well out in the Grasslands. At first, Barrow itself was not particularly troubled. The raiders contented themselves with attacks on the Tellarani, the nomadic People-of-the-Grass who followed the wisent herds on the Grasslands.

The Tellarani, a brown-skinned, hawk-nosed people with black hair and eyes, had followed the same routes for centuries. They wintered near Barrow and traded there when the herds came south of the Dragonsbacks for the season. The raiders, who called themselves the Bloody Scallions, closed the passes through the Dragonsbacks and demanded tribute for passage. Any clan who objected too strongly was exterminated. The disorganized People were unable to unite until too late, and the Scallions didn't hesitate at genocide. In a final major battle, the last of the united clans was wiped out to the last warrior and shaman. (It is rumored that the women and children of the clans somehow escaped.) With their deaths, however, the Tellarani shamans cursed the Grasslands: no grass will grow there until the Tellarani return as a people and redeem themselves. With most of the People dead and the rest missing for decades, the remnants of the People have generally given up the idea. They are dispersed throughout the Plane, but most chose to remain in Barrow.

With their primary prey gone and their food supply dying before their eyes, the Scallions turned their attention toward Barrow. Their flag, with a sword piercing a bleeding onion, appeared over village after village east of Barrow. It was their plan eventually to circle the town with destruction and capture it intact. Their leaders, some of whom were particularly evil magicians, were no fools. They looted caravans on the newly opened route to Sai-khand and began squeezing the city.

The Barrowmen, unaccustomed to war, fell back at first. They rallied under the leadership of their kal-trak, his brother (La-nor-lok Throngon), and other founding fathers. They surprised and utterly defeated the Scallions in several small, bloody battles. No member of the raiding army was thought to have survived, though the Barrow militia left behind many widows of their own. The city was once again on track to prosperity; war has not entered the region for thirty years.

The grandfather of the present ruler ceded a certain amount of local autonomy to the Saikhandian Empire not long after the Scallion Wars, but the act did little to change the makeup of the local population. A number of merchant families from Sai-khand and members of the military contingents, sent by the Empire as trade-protecting forces, became part of the city. Their presence warranted the building of a large Saikhandian temple in Barrow. Their economic influence is felt throughout the city, but their social influence is generally ignored by the locals. Those remain virtual barbarians in Saikhandian eyes.

Rule of the city is theoretically autocratic, as exemplified by the previous kal-trak, the Old Prince, Garro Bancartin. He was a wily robber baron of the old school. His son, the Young Prince, though now ruler, is considered a wimp by comparison. The Barrowmen are too much social mavericks to be ruled imperially by anyone for long. Military aspirations of the city have always been low, with no other city near enough to consider conquering or to have to defend against. As is, the city's de facto rule extends over its entire section of the continent. Energy that might normally be spent on aggression has been transferred into causing the wealth of others to move into one's own pocket, legally or illegally.

Barrow is now a large city, with all the advantages and all the problems of a large city. Any industry available in any major city is available there, at least to a degree. Agricultural and maritime ventures dominate, with many of the older lines of nobles long since moved to the city, leaving one branch in farming and another in shipping. With few of the villages east of Barrow repopulated, most of that area is again unbroken forest. Timbering is important business, but the heart of the forest is rumored to be such an inhospitable place for humans that few venture there.

The Bancartin family has kept the economic health of the region high by keeping hands off the farms that support the city, and by making sure that others do the same. No noble higher than a ku-trak is allowed to acquire more land in the regions west of the city, and a ku-trak is limited to acquisitions only within his traditional domain. An important part of the Barrow economy, however, is unconcerned with laws of acquisition or with who makes those laws. There is a huge thief class in Barrow, ranging from the chicken thieves and riffraff of the Slews to wholehearted professionals, whose exact dwelling in the city is known to few. Smugglers have always existed to bring in untaxed goods; their profession has grown both in size and quality since Barrow's attachment to Sai-khand. (The Saikhandian Empire finances itself by collecting duties and tariffs.)

Other than a token peacekeeping contingent, Sai-khand has no army in Barrow, though it does maintain a substantial naval force to protect shipping. The closest thing to an army, other than private guards for some noble, is the city watch. The entire city is patrolled by day, but at night the streets west of the river and south of Caravan Way are ceded to the minority of less honest citizens. Guard posts at every city gate and both river bridges are always manned, but by unspoken agreement, a person in the streets of Upcruster Town or the Slews after sunset is on his own. An exception is made for fires. No matter how professionally uninvolved Barrowmen may pride themselves in being, fires are everybody's business in a wooden city.

Too many years without real challenges have softened the city's patrolmen. The closest thing to an invasion occurred with the recent arrival of the Mugambese canoe fleet. In Mugambu, the Empire's southernmost province, the Mugambisa was overthrown by her uncle. Instead of waiting for certain extermination for herself and her followers, that resourceful young woman gathered a fleet of double-hulled war canoes and led her people into permanent exile in Barrow. At the end of their nearly impossible voyage, the Mugambese simply rowed up the Wat River and unloaded. The Saikhandian garrison couldn't attack peaceful citizens of the Empire, and the black immigrants outnumbered the city watch several times over.

No one is sure if it has made the situation better or worse, but Barrow's prince and the striking black princess have developed a strong mutual attraction. Though the Mugambese are adding their own new quarter to southeast Barrow, the situation remains touchy, and the two rulers have not formally bonded with one another. Only time will tell.

As a place for a business venture, Barrow has great promise, but expect competition. To a Barrowman, all is fair in business, as well as in love and war. Only trying to weasel out of a finalized deal is considered morally repugnant. Genuinely free enterprise is the norm. Even magicians, of whom there are many minor ones and a few great ones in the city by the Wat, belong to no guild. They act for good or evil or for whatever strikes their sorcerous fancies at the moment. On the other hand, Barrow would not make the most ideal vacation site, unless you are of devious or adventurous spirit yourself or are prepared to clutch at your purse with one hand and your life with the other.

FIFTH APPENDIX

Sai-Khand

The city of Sai-khand stands at the first major river junction above the mouth of the Arpago River. There are a number of smaller cities in the extensive Arpago watershed, but all have been absorbed into the Saikhandian Empire, so that the name of the city is synonymous with the name of the region. The river valley is bordered on the north and west by the Mad King Mountains. A long southern spur of that range forms the Maldavian Peninsula, the western boundary of Arpago Bay. Normal west-east atmospheric movement would have left the Arpago Basin in the rain shadow of the mountains; however, a major ocean current of both warm water and air flows up the eastern side of Arpago Bay, bringing rain to the entire basin, except for a few arid areas close to the western mountains. The coast extends almost directly south from Arpago Bay for over a thousand kilometers, without significant break until it reaches the enormous, tropical Mugambu River.

East of the basin, the land rises into unexplored wilderness. An oddity of the mentality of the people of the basin is found in the fact that they never consciously consider what might lie to their east on the continent. There is evidence that their ancestors entered the area from that direction, but modern Saikhandians give the direction no thought at all. The matter is simply shrugged off, though the Saikhandians are noted for their aggressive expansion elsewhere.

Historically, the basin was populated by agricultural peoples, gradually rising to a group of small city-states. Sai-khand was the largest, but otherwise unremarkable when compared to the rest. Its dominance began with the capture of the city by a pirate fleet led by Krebfeld Knucklebreaker. Succeeding generations have more than once attempted a rewrite of history to blur Krebfeld I's profession and the fact that he originally took the city out of undiluted rapaciousness. (No shame should be associ-

ated with those credentials, however, considering the
origins of many other dynasties.)

The success of the Saikhandian Empire did not come
from either a large population or military might. Instead,
Krebfeld I proved to be more than a piratical aggressor
with a love for looting. With his political genius, backed
by a bloody-minded fleet during the first generation of
conquest, he established some simple principles of empire that allowed his descendants to absorb city after city,
without storming any of them militarily.

Behind almost every Saikhandian success is trade. Cities
can be conquered by trade alone: first, the outposts; then the
caravans; then the warehouses, all established with full permission of the local rulers. No need to send in the army: Before the locals know it, the lifeblood of their commerce is
being pumped through vessels whose heart is in Sai-khand.

Cities can be punished by trade. If Saikhandian assets
are seized, overtaxed, or suppressed, bring the traders
home and close the border: nothing in; nothing out. By
the time there are enough Saikhandian goods for a local
ruler to covet them, Saikhandian trade is vital to his own
nation's economy. Open the borders only when full repa-
rations have been paid. The one set of laws that must be
rigidly enforced is that of commerce. In capitalistic Sai-
khand, murders and rapists are treated (relatively) kindly
compared to embezzlers, smugglers, or tax evaders.

Do not kill commerce's golden goose with taxation. Tax it
at rates carefully calculated to stimulate growth. Nurture it
with tax incentives for expansion or opening new markets.
Squeeze inherited wealth so that each generation of new
capitalists is hungry, but encouraged to feed and grow.

The job of armies and navies is to protect trade, not to
guard private real estate or prop up inefficient local gov-
ernments. When a city becomes part of the Empire, its
economic health becomes important. Taxes from outlying
parts of the Empire are primarily to finance a navy to put
down piracy and smuggling and to help Imperial merchants in distress. Army garrisons are not occupying troops,
but are there to keep down bandits, to secure the Empire's borders, and to keep the trade routes open. The
well-paid protective forces, financed by provincial taxes,
can form a nucleus of experienced personnel in case of a
foreign war. Though their net cost to Sai-khand is negli-

gible, they have never been tested in an empire-against-empire war. All potential competitors have been absorbed. Military war has been made only against less civilized peoples testing the Empire's borders. War within the Empire has been replaced by economic competition that generates a healthy cash flow.

Local government must remain local. There is no such thing as an Imperial governor sent from the capital. If Barrow is ruled by its kal-trak or Maldavia by a council of winegrowers, it is their business. For example, when the Mugambisa of the Empire's latest added tropical province was overthrown in a bloody coup by her uncle, the Imperial troops fought hard—to protect the warehouses and docks and the citizens from Sai-khand in the trade zone. If Mugambese slaughtered Mugambese over who would govern them, it was their own affair. Had Mugambu been invaded by their eastern neighbors, the Zucrasa, Imperial forces would have fought as hard beside the Mugambese.

Krebfeld I also established rules of succession that guaranteed that his descendants would rule for many generations to follow in healthy intelligence. Peace, with enough tang to keep it interesting, was to be the order of the day, but other peaceful empires had collapsed when they had become *too* peaceful. Inbred, moronic descendants of capable founders had frittered their empires away.

An Emperor is to have many children, and there is to be no nonsense about "firstborn" automatic inheritance. The royal line is encouraged to become as hybridized as possible. Genetic impurity, by way of marrying rich daughters of merchants in the provinces, is the premier choice over linking with the thoroughbred daughters of Saikhandian nobility.

No prince (lan-trak) is to reside in the capital between the ages of eighteen and thirty, but they are expected to visit it regularly. That is only the first of the restrictions placed on a prince who wishes to become Do-lan-trak (crown prince). He may not marry before age twenty-two. He is expected to have many children, but a multitude of wives is frowned on. He may be dropped from consideration for flaunting any of the rules, or he may voluntarily drop out. The future Emperor is expected to keep mind and body sharp by traveling, to bring the vigor of the provinces, but to keep his loyalties at home. He is to guarantee a plentiful supply of lan-traks for the next succession, but not sour the capital with harem intrigues. Any prince who emerges from such a gauntlet of rules deserves to be Emperor.

The Emperor must designate a successor acceptable to the Council of Ten before he reaches age fifty. The Council is made up of the ten richest men in Sai-khand. Its makeup changes regularly, with the rise and fall of fortunes. Since inherited wealth is heavily taxed, few sons follow their father onto the Council. Unless their father gifts them great wealth before his death, the members will always be men of high personal ability and drive. The Council has the power to appoint an Emperor-designate in case of a ruler's unexpected death. They can rule the Empire without an Emperor for five years, if needed, though it has never been done. Ideally, the Crown Prince goes through five to ten years of gradual takeover of power. The Council can keep him "in training" for five years without releasing full power to him.

Emperors have a mandatory retirement age of sixty. Once Krebfeld I had set the machinery of succession in motion, he kept it on track himself until the city had adjusted to his ideas of empire. Then he set a good example by retiring on a generous stipend and frolicking through his last years. He lived to be eighty-three. Time and again, ambitious men in later generations tried to alter his system to favor their own interests, but within a generation the old system had been reestablished. It has too much public support to be replaced by any other. Inevitably, however, Krebfeld's system will be challenged by other power-hungry minorities who wish to replace the government, not with a better one, but with one that gives them more personal power and wealth.

The present Emperor, Voltair III (called Voltair the Tightfisted in some quarters), is one more example of the ridiculously rich, genetically sound, intelligent "royal accountants" who have held the throne for generations. As with the Emperor, so with the Empire: both show every sign of being around for some time yet. Only the intervention of as-yet-unknown forces could threaten either.

SIXTH APPENDIX

Structure of Common Titles

I. *Prefixes and Suffixes*
(1) Do- = supreme
(2) Kal- = grand
(3) Lan- = heir
(4) Val- = province
(5) Nor- = war chief
(6) Ku- = small
(7) La- = holy
(8) -trak = ruler
(9) -nok = fighting man
(10) -an = retired

II. *Titles*
(1) Do-kal-trak = emperor
(2) Do-lan-trak = crown prince; emperor designate
(3) Lan-trak = prince; a son of the emperor
(4) Kal-trak = grand duke; sometimes "prince"
(5) Lan-kal-trak = heir to grand dukedom
(6) Val-trak = duke
(7) Lan-val-trak = heir to dukedom
(8) Val-nor-lok = baron
(9) Lan-val-nor-lok = heir to barony
(10) Ku-trak = earl
(11) Lan-ku-trak = heir to earldom
(12) Nor-lok = knight
(13) Lan-nor-lok = heir to knighthood
(14) La-nor-lok = Holy Knight
(15) Do-la-nor-lok = chief Holy Knight
(16) La-trak = high-priest or bishop

III. *Special Notes*
Both the Prince of Barrow and the Mugambiso hold the title "Kal-trak of the Empire." Within his own province, the Prince of Barrow prefers to use the title "val-trak," because of the city's political history. Malia Mboto,

the Mugambisa in exile, is designated "Kal-trak-an of Mugambu."

The Barrow region officially has no other nobles of val-trak status. The holders of those titles were exterminated three generations before in the wars of succession that brought the Bancartins to power. Various heirs of the "old nobility," however, still cling unofficially to those titles, hinting that they still have the right to "move up" to the throne of Barrow, given the chance.

There are many ku-traks holding the farming area west of Barrow. There are also many ku-traks in the city itself who have left the land, but kept the title, with wealth from other sources. There are many nor-loks, but most knighthoods are not hereditary; thus, there are few lan-nor-loks. Anyone of val-trak status or above can create a new nor-lok. Only an office of kal-trak or above can create a hereditary knighthood.

La-nor-loks make up the order of Holy Knights. La-traks are associated with many religions; a few claim the title of "kal-la-trak," but only an exceptional cleric can sustain such a title, and it cannot be inherited. The concept of clerical celibacy is rare throughout the known Plane, but few temples allow a son to succeed his father (a lan-la-trak).